The Bad Boy

EMILIA ROSE

Trigger Warning

This book includes bullying, blackmail, dubcon, mention of sexual exploitation, and other potentially triggering topics. If you don't feel comfortable with the topics listed above, place the book down now.

To all the good girls who have wanted the angsty punk skateboarding bad boy <3

Chapter One

VERA

After buckling the play collar snug around my neck, Aiden clasped a leather leash around the silver D-ring. Freshly shaved with his graying brown hair parted to the side, Aiden smirked down at me. "What would your father think of you if he knew you were at a sex club with his boss?"

"Vera!" Maddie, my best friend, said, shutting her locker and staring down at me. "Come on. We're gonna be late for our next class!" She tugged on my wrist to pull me up from Redwood's dirty tiled floor. "You can write your little smut story later."

After scribbling a couple more words inside my loose-leaf notebook and pushing all the ripped-out pages into it, I grabbed all my textbooks from my locker beside Maddie's and hurried down the hall toward World History. God, I couldn't wait until I saved up enough money to actually get a freaking laptop because these cheap notebooks weren't cutting it anymore.

The second bell echoed through the empty halls. I moved my short legs faster, not caring how stupid I looked to Redwood's gang,

Poison, who still lingered in the hallway, smoking blunts and harassing one of the nerdy kids like me, Akio.

"Rodriguez!" João, Poison's leader, called to me.

"Fuck," I whispered under my breath, stopping for a brief moment to look back at him.

"Watch my sister tonight. I'll pay you."

After agreeing quickly because I needed the money and we needed to get to class as soon as possible, I waved him off and continued down the hall.

"Jeez," Maddie said, her ginger hair flying back. "You're so fast."

"We're late!"

I hated being late and especially loathed all the stares from the students when we walked into the room, as if they didn't even remember that I was in their class or something. We only had less than a year left at Redwood, and I wanted to get through them, unnoticed. That was how it had been since kindergarten.

"Well, that's not my fault, now is it, Miss I-Love-to-Write-Smut?"

After playfully smacking her shoulder and telling her to shut it, I opened the door and slipped into World History with Mrs. Greenwich—or The Grinch, as everyone called her behind her back. Through her green cat-eye glasses, she narrowed her eyes at us.

I hugged my books to my chest, stared down at the red-tiled floor, and pushed my glasses up my nose until I found my assigned seat in the back. God, I didn't know what the big deal was and why everyone had to stare. We were only a couple minutes late. Nothing huge.

It wasn't like I'd strolled in halfway through class, like the infamous Blaise Harleen did every day. Nobody said a damn word to that kid though. No, if they even looked in his direction, he'd kick their asses under the bleachers after school.

I pulled out my textbook and highlighter, ready to push through another boring history lesson about some kingdom that had taken over another kingdom after some war—the driest material The Grinch could muster.

After side-eyeing me, she tucked some gray hair that had fallen out of her tight bun behind her ear and turned to the board. "As I was saying, next class, we'll be starting a project on kingdoms and crusades. You'll be partnered up."

Maddie looked over her shoulder at me and smiled, scrunching her freckled nose, as if to say that I would be her partner and that I didn't have a choice in the matter.

"Don't get excited," The Grinch said. "I already have you partnered."

A collective sigh from the students echoed through the room. I slumped my shoulders forward and blew out a long breath. She was notorious for assigning students like Maddie and me to the most annoying, least hardworking people in the room.

And I hated it.

As she began listing off partners, I scanned the room to see who was left and who she could possibly pair me with. If it was one of the cheerleaders, I would literally stab my own eyes out. I hated them more than anyone—except Blaise Harleen, of course.

I didn't think I could hate anyone more than that entitled asshole.

"Vera Rodriguez," The Grinch said, glancing up from her clipboard at me, "and Blaise Harleen."

Closing my eyes, I cursed under my breath and curled my hands into tight fists under the table. There I'd gone, freaking jinxing things. Of course she'd had to pair me with the one guy who couldn't even make it to class within the first thirty minutes.

Skylar Walker glared at me, moving her red manicured fingers around a silver necklace that hung between her cleavage. I averted my gaze and turned back to my textbook, hoping people would stop staring at me for once today.

When The Grinch went back to teaching today's material, I went back to hating my life.

Midway through class, the door opened, and Blaise Harleen sauntered into World History, refusing to even look in Mrs. Greenwich's direction and instead heading ... this way? I sucked in a breath and stared down at my textbook, heat crawling up my neck. Why the hell was he coming this way? His usual seat was on the other side of the room, next to Skylar, not ... in my row!

Blaise grabbed an empty chair from the back and dragged it— literally dragged the metal legs on the tiled floor—toward me. He placed the metal chair in the middle of the aisle, not caring that he wasn't even sitting at a desk. I gulped and dared to peek over at him.

Sculpted jaw, dark—almost black—eyes, and a body so defined that all the girls swooned over him.

He looked over and fucking smirked at me. I turned back to my textbook and wiped my sweaty palms on my jeans.

Heat crawled up my neck, my throat drying. Why was he looking at me like that? He never looked at me, even when we had been paired up for projects in other classes. I was a plain nobody in this school, and I liked it that way. I desperately wanted to keep it that way. But for some reason, the world wanted to fuck me over today.

Once he finally turned away from me, I let out a deep breath and finally forced myself to breathe again. What the hell was I going to do? He didn't even know we were partners, and he had just been ... *gawking* at me.

Maddie looked over her shoulder and furrowed her brows at me, as if to ask what had happened. I sank lower in my seat and shrugged, unsure of it myself.

When the bell rang to signal the end of class, I quickly gathered up all my materials and stuffed them into my backpack, on a mission to put as much space between Blaise and me as I could. I didn't care that we were partners. The project didn't start until the next class.

Before I could walk away from him, Blaise grabbed my wrist in his rough, callous hand and pulled me back. Everyone in class— including The Grinch herself—stared over at us. My cheeks were burning up, my heart pounding.

"After school. Parking lot. Don't be late."

Then, Blaise released me and walked out of the classroom without glancing back. My eyes widened at the door, fear running through my veins.

What the fuck did Blaise Harleen want with me? Did he really think that I would meet him in the parking lot this afternoon? No, fuck that. I had to skip—skip class, skip town maybe ...

Because Blaise Harleen wasn't known to play nice. And I, Vera Rodriguez, didn't know what the hell I had done to catch the eye of the most ruthless boy in town.

Chapter Two

BLAISE

After picking up my skateboard from the dirty tiled floor, I held it by my side and sauntered into Redwood's main building for lunch period. I walked alone in the chilly fall air because I didn't give a fuck about the fakers in this town.

Nobody cared about anyone else. And nobody gave a fuck about me.

Except Vera now.

Vera had barely spared me two glances over the past four years, but the way she had looked at me today when I dragged a chair over to her desk and told her to meet me later was the best fucking thing I had seen all week.

With her brown eyes wide as fuck, her staring up at me like she actually gave a fuck about what I needed to talk to her about, as if she really, truly feared me, fuck, it had done something to me. People in Redwood only cared about themselves, but Vera ... well, she now cared about what *I* had to say to her.

It was comical, laughable almost.

And it brought me joy in this miserable place that everyone called

Redwood, so I wasn't going to just scare Vera off. Tonight, I wanted to see what she had to say for herself for the sex-filled story she had written in her notebook.

Vera had rushed down the hallway so fast before World History that she didn't notice the pages that had slipped out of her notebook. Thankfully, I had. And tonight, I wanted to steal her entire notebook from her, so I could read more.

"Mr. Harleen," Principal Vaughn said right before I slipped into the cafeteria. He stood in front of the doors and crossed his arms over his long and scrawny chest. "What did I tell you about skateboards at this school? They're prohibited."

A low chuckle escaped my throat. "And what did I tell you before, Steve?"

He gritted his teeth. "It's Principal Vaughn to you."

"I believe I said, 'Go fuck yourself, Stevie.' So, leave me the hell alone."

Deciding that I really wanted to get on his nerves today, I tossed my skateboard onto the ground right in front of him, hopped on it, and slid right through the open doors and into the cafeteria. He grabbed my shoulder as I passed him, but I kept my balance and shoved him away.

"Remember who pays your fucking bills, Vaughn," I snapped.

That was the only thing Mom and Dad were good for. Threatening teachers.

Principal Vaughn clenched his jaw and stormed down the hallway, back to his office, where that fucking creep belonged. I wouldn't see him for the rest of the day until I finally pissed him off enough to where he called my parents. Even then, they wouldn't give a fuck.

"Blaise!" Skylar shouted from our usual lunch table.

I stopped the skateboard and picked it up off the ground again, sighing through my nose. I didn't want to deal with her right now. I didn't want to deal with fucking anyone anymore. None of my fucking teachers seemed to give a shit what I did in their classes. They ignored it and me.

But Vera …

That look of fear in her eyes earlier… God, I fucking loved it. She cared about what I did, who I told, how I talked to her in front of the rest of the students and teachers. Vera Rodriguez didn't want me telling anyone anything.

As I scanned the cafeteria for her, Skylar pranced over to me in a white spaghetti-strap tank top, which did nothing to hide her breasts, and a short little skirt.

"What time do you want me to come over tonight?" Skylar asked, clutching my bicep

"Later."

"Nine? Ten?"

"I don't care," I said, spotting Vera sitting with one of her friends in the cafeteria.

She glanced up at me, her cheeks flushing bright red, then quickly turned away, gulping. Fear was written all over that pretty face of hers.

"Just come over."

"Fine," Skylar said, releasing my arm and walking away. "I'll be there whenever."

I followed Skylar's departing figure with my gaze and clenched my jaw. We were never nice to each other. We only fooled around. And I didn't like her, but … fuck, I didn't know. She wanted to have a good time. She didn't give a fuck who it was with.

After stealing an apple from some kid named Akio, I sat on the lunch table with my feet on the seat. Some of my *friends*—if I could even fucking call them that—nodded to me but continued on with their own conversation. I only hung out with them because they skateboarded too. Otherwise, I would sit by myself or be stuck with Skylar or whatever other girl wanted to throw herself at me.

Once I opened my backpack, I pulled out two sheets of paper that I'd found on the ground earlier in front of Vera Rodriguez's locker. The pages were completely filled in, from top to bottom and written on both sides.

And it was filled with nothing but pure, filthy sex.

My eyes scanned the sheet for the second time today, my dick twitching in my pants.

Vera might not have given me a second glance *ever* in her life, but after tonight, she would.

Vera Rodriguez was about to care about every single thing that I did to her. I would make sure of it.

Chapter Three

VERA

To say that I didn't want to be here would be an understatement. I really wished that I had the confidence to fucking leave Redwood without doing as Blaise had *politely* asked in World History—note the sarcasm. But I didn't.

So, I stupidly stood beside Blaise Harleen's blue Ferrari F8 in the parking lot that afternoon.

Why hadn't I left yet? Because Blaise scared the fuck right out of me. If I ran, he would track me down and do who knew what with me. It was better to get this over with now and not suffer the consequences later. And besides, I had been writing a super-sexy smut scene before History class this morning that I desperately wanted to get back to before I had to babysit tonight.

A crisp fall breeze chilled my skin. I zipped up my thin jacket that had a hole in the sleeve and rocked back and forth to keep myself warm. After glancing down at my phone, I debated on leaving. It was already half an hour after our meeting time.

Was he really coming? Or was he going to watch me from afar

with Skylar and laugh at how stupid I looked, standing here in the cold, scared shitless about whatever he wanted to talk to me about?

"Didn't think you'd actually show up," Blaise said from behind me.

Startled, I jumped and held my books to my chest. "Is there something you need?" I asked, glancing at all the other students who were able to leave on time and didn't have to worry about being picked apart by Blaise.

With a devilish smirk, he shoved one hand into his pocket and placed the other on his car, strands of his dark brown hair blowing onto his forehead. "You're geeky, right? Probably read a lot?"

"Um ..." I shifted nervously. "I guess so."

"I wanted some book recommendations."

"You like reading?" I asked, stifling a giggle.

He raised a sharp brow. "Is that funny to you?"

"No, no." *Yes.* "You just don't seem like a reader."

"I read a lot," he said, though by the way he showed me his pearly-white teeth, I could tell that was a lie. He leaned further against the car, shoulder slumping against it. "Actually, I recently read this really good excerpt from a story that I found lying in the hallway by your locker." He swung his backpack over his shoulder and pulled out pages that must've fallen out of that stupid loose-leaf notebook I carried around everywhere. "Let me read you some of the writing."

My heart dropped, my stomach twisting. *Oh my fucking God.*

I reached for the papers, but he held them high in the air away from me and started reading.

"After climbing on top of him, I sat facing him. He placed a lingering kiss on my lips. 'Turn around, Sweetheart. I get to see your face as you come every night. Don't you think your father's coworkers deserve to see it too. I don't want to be selfish with you.'"

"Give it back!" I shouted, lunging at him and jumping in the air, hoping to reach the papers.

He kicked himself off his car, folded the papers, and pushed them into his front pants pocket, right by his crotch. "I didn't know a good girl like you could write something like that," he said, turning toward me and trapping me between him and the car.

Sucking in a breath, I leaned against it as far as I could and stared up into his dark brown eyes. Pressing his body against mine, he shoved the bulge in his pants against my stomach, making me clench. I pushed the glasses up on my nose, my cheeks in flames.

"Now, Vera, you might not think I'm smart or that I pay attention in any of those stupid classes I attend with you, but I know a desperate, horny virgin when I see one," he murmured in my ear, his words making me shiver.

I pressed my thighs together and ignored the heat pooling between them.

"How long have you been waiting for someone's cock to slide all the way up into this pussy?" he asked, drawing a finger up my leggings and cupping my pussy in his large, tattooed hand. He pressed his fingers against my core through the thin material and chuckled against me, rubbing me even harder and faster. "A long time, it seems."

He slid his other hand up the side of my body, wrapped it around my throat, and pulled me closer, trailing his nose up the side of my neck and biting down softly on my jaw. My breath hitched, and my nipples hardened.

Desperately, I licked my lips to moisten them. I tried to rack my brain for any type of response, for anything to get out of this. Kids still lingered in the student parking lot, and I didn't want any rumors about this flying around Redwood.

Blaise grabbed a fistful of my dark hair and pulled it back, forcing me to look up at him. I squealed at the sudden movement as he continued to rub my pussy roughly, his hand slipping into my pants and claiming what no man ever had before.

"Is this what you need?"

I knitted my brows together and bit my lip, a soft moan escaping. He twirled us around, so he stood by the car, opened the passenger seat, slid into it, then pulled me on top of him, shutting the door behind us. After tugging the books from my arms, he placed them onto the center console, then tossed our backpacks by our feet.

With one hand around my waist to hold me still, he slipped his other into my panties again and into my sopping pussy. Fingers thrusting in and out of me, he stared up at my face with those piercing eyes and didn't stop torturing me with his fingers until my legs trembled.

The pressure built up higher and higher inside me, my pussy clenching his fingers tighter by the second. I took a shaky breath and closed my eyes, needing to find a way out of this situation soon.

But I couldn't seem to think straight anymore. Ever since I'd started writing that sex scene this morning, I ... I had been so freaking horny. I had been aching to get home to finish writing, to slide my hand into my panties and touch my clit myself.

"Are you going to come already?" he asked me, curling his fingers into me.

Gripping his shoulders, I threw my head back and let an earth-shattering orgasm rip through my body. I slapped a hand over my mouth to quiet my moans, so no student would hear, but he quickly pulled both my hands behind my back.

"Enjoy the orgasm. It's the first one anyone has probably ever given you." He continued to curl his fingers into me, making sure not to stop until I finished. "I wanna hear you scream for me."

My thighs quivered around him, waves of pleasure rushing through me. I moaned and rode his fingers, loving the feeling of something other than my small fingers inside of me. God, I was needy and so desperate to be touched.

When I finally came down from the high, he pulled his fingers out of me, grasped my hips, and forced me to sit on his bulge. I moaned again, heat pooling between my legs at the feel of his cock against me. He ground it up, the friction leaving my virgin pussy aching to be filled.

Over and over and over, he drove his hips up and against me.

"Fuck, Vera. I can already feel your pussy quivering through your leggings." He grasped my chin and held me still. "I'm going to fuck you here and now."

He shoved his bulge against me one last time, and I tipped over the edge, whimpering, unable to control myself.

"Please," I whispered, brows furrowed. Part of me couldn't believe that this was real. Part of me thought that this was all some sort of sick, wet dream. "Please, fuck me."

After tossing me into the driver's seat, he swiftly pulled my leggings down to my ankles and then pulled me back on top of him as he fumbled with his button and zipper on his jeans. Veiny, thick, and bigger than I'd imagined, his cock sprang out of his pants. He wrapped his hand around the base and guided it to the entrance of my sopping cunt.

I hated Blaise Harleen. I had hated him for so long and with so much passion.

Now, I was letting him use me for no other reason than because I was a horny virgin girl.

"I won't be gentle," he said before shoving himself into me.

I screamed out as he continued pushing himself deeper inside of me, the pain almost unbearable. I had never had something so huge inside me and had never made such a senseless decision. I should've been screaming at him to stop. I should've run away the moment he told me to meet him after class. But I couldn't deny that hungry urge I'd had inside my stomach every single time he looked over at me today.

"Fuck, babe, scream louder for me."

As I clenched around him, my pussy pulsed, and my screams slowly turned to moans. I grasped his muscular shoulders and eased myself the rest of the way down onto him until he was nestled inside my hole. After a few moments, he wrapped an arm around my waist to pull me closer to him until my tits pressed against the sides of his face. He drove himself up into me hard and ruthlessly, slipping his other hand between my legs and rubbing my clit.

"Harder," I moaned, my voice becoming louder.

He pounded into me, picking up his pace, and sucked on the soft spot on my neck.

"I-I'm gonna come, Blaise! I'm—" I cried out, my legs trembling. "I'm coming!"

"Fuuuuck," he grunted against me, slowing his thrusts. "Get out of the car and onto your knees. I wanna come all over your face and those nerdy little glasses of yours, and make you a pretty slut."

I paused, my breath hitching. "B-but we're in public. We're still at school. We—"

"Nobody will see, Vera." He blew a ragged breath out of his nose. "Do it. Now."

"Blaise, I—"

"Fuck," he groaned, grabbing my hips and fucking me as hard as he could. "Forget it." He pounded into me, nearly sending me up against the ceiling. Then, suddenly, he stopped. "I already came inside you."

My eyes widened, and I tried to climb out of his lap. But he held me still and pushed himself deeper.

"Blaise! You came inside of me?!"

He sat back and offered me an exhausted smirk. "You don't have to worry about anyone seeing you now, babe. All my cum is buried deep in this soppy pussy of yours."

After scrambling out of his hold, I sat in the driver's seat and pulled my pants back up, needing to get to the pharmacy as soon as possible. I wasn't on birth control yet. Mom didn't deem it necessary.

"Can you not tell anyone about my writing or, honestly, that any of this happened?" I asked hurriedly, looking in his direction, but not at him. I couldn't believe that I had just let Blaise Harleen take my virginity in the middle of the school parking lot after vowing that I hated every ounce of his being.

What the fuck was wrong with me?!

"I'm not going to make promises that I can't keep."

"Please, Blaise. You can't tell anyone. Please," I pleaded.

"I like it when you beg."

I breathed out, frustrated. "Blaise, I'm being serious. You can't tell anyone!"

He crossed his arms over his chest, his forearms flexing through his shirt, and leaned against the seat. "I won't tell anyone."

"Thank y—"

"As long as you let me fuck you whenever and wherever I want."

"What?! Are you crazy?! No!"

"Do you want the whole school to know?" he asked, smirking at me.

My heart dropped, my chest tight. I didn't want *anyone* in Redwood to know what I had done. I didn't want anyone in Redwood to judge me. I wanted to be invisible. If Blaise told even one person, my life and reputation would be ruined.

So, I shook my head. "I don't."

"Well," Blaise started, "I guess you're going to be the bad boy's good girl for now then—until I want something else from you."

Chapter Four

VERA

"I'm so dumb," I muttered to myself, hurrying down the aisle in CVS to find the day-after pill or something so I wouldn't get pregnant.

I didn't know what the hell had been going through my mind when I let Blaise come inside me—hell, when I let him push me into his car! *What was I thinking?!*

"Can I help you with something, sweetheart?" a young guy with a name tag fastened to his shirt asked. He smiled at me a bit *too* sweetly and moved closer. "Are you looking for condoms?"

I nearly choked on my own spit and gave him a tense smile. "No."

"Well"—he stuck out his hand for me to shake—"my name is Jim if you need any help."

After glancing down at his hand, I awkwardly shook it, so he'd go away and stop talking to me. I probably looked like a whole mess—my hair crazy as hell, my cheeks flushed, and my eyes wide as saucers.

Once he finally left—but really, he kept staring at me from the register, like I might steal something—I searched through the boxes of Plan B and read through every single label on the back of each box, wanting to find the absolute best one. There was no way in hell that I would get pregnant with Blaise Harleen's baby.

No. Freaking. Way.

I crouched down to read the boxes on the bottom shelf and rubbed the wrinkles I was giving myself on my forehead. "Jesus Christ, Mom is going to kill me if she finds out that I'm in the middle of CVS, looking for some damn pills because I had unprotected s—"

"Are you sure I can't help you find anything?" Jim asked, giving me a fake smile.

At first, I'd thought he was being nice and had a thing for me with that handshake, but now, I could tell that he wanted me out of his store, that he thought I was planning on stealing something somehow.

"I'm fine," I snapped, wanting to be left alone.

"If you're not going to buy anything, then you'll have to leave."

Sighing through my nose, I picked up a box and hoped that I had enough money in my wallet to pay for it. Jim guided me up to the counter to check me out and get a poor girl like me out of his store as soon as possible.

"Did you find everything you were looking for today?"

I gritted my teeth. If someone had let me look in peace ...

"Yes."

After pressing some buttons on the register, he gave me that annoying smile. "Do you have a CVS card?"

"No."

"Would you like to donate to children in need?"

Damn, this guy was annoying as hell.

"No," I said, pulling out my wallet as he gave me a disappointed expression. But I didn't have any money to spare. Plan B was more expensive than I had thought, and I didn't even know if I had enough for it.

Once he clicked a couple more buttons on his register, he smiled at me. "Would you like a paper bag with that? It'll be ten cents extra."

"Oh my freaking God," I snapped, opening my wallet and pulling out the sixty dollars that I'd earned, working at the library this past Saturday. "Put it in a damn bag and let me pay already. I want to get out of here."

Jim placed the box into a small brown bag. "That'll be fifty-one dollars and twenty-three cents."

Reluctantly, I handed over the money and felt my heart drop. I had been working so many hours at the library and had even been thinking about picking up a second job to help Mom and to save up for a laptop. But things kept breaking around the house, and now, shit like this had happened because of my senseless decisions.

After Jim opened the register, he gave me my change. I counted it twice to make sure he hadn't gypped me and then shoved it into my wallet and hurried out of the store with my pills. I felt so stupid for what I had done. So much for being invisible for the rest of the school year.

Now, one of Redwood's baddest boys knew my secret.

"What's in the bag?" someone said as soon as I stepped out of CVS.

I glanced over to see João leaning against the building, smoking a cigarette.

He took one last puff on it, then tossed it onto the sidewalk and stomped it out. "Fuck it. I don't care." He nodded toward his black Mercedes with tinted windows that he'd bought with Poison's dirty money. "My mom's working, and I need you to watch Ana."

"João," I said, glancing down at the bag and chewing on the inside of my cheek. I might've agreed to watch her this morning, but I really needed to get home and think about everything I had done today. "I don't know if I can tonight. I ... I need to ..."

João walked toward the driver's door. "Get in the car, Vera."

Part of me debated on refusing and just walking home in the cold, but I now needed the money, and Ana wasn't *that* bad. Usually, she wanted to bake and watch princess cartoons. She was the total opposite of João, thankfully.

"You'd better pay me," I said, sliding into the passenger seat.

"You'll be paid when I get back."

"Hi, Vera!" Ana said from her car seat in the back. "Wanna make brigadeiros with me?"

"Sure," I said.

As João drove from the good part of town toward his house in the slums, I glanced down into the paper bag and chewed on the inside of my cheek. I hadn't thought that I would ever have to do something like this. The only women I knew who did shit this reckless were the girls that I wrote about in my stories.

When João pulled up to the side of the road, I grasped the paper bag tightly.

João took his house key off his key ring and handed it to me. "Take this. Don't let anyone inside the house who doesn't have a key. You know where the ingredients for brigadeiros are in the cabinets. I'll be back."

Once I grabbed the key from him, I helped Ana out of the backseat and walked with her to the front door to the small, dark house. Ana took the key from me and shoved it into the lock, opening the door.

After we walked in, I locked the door, turned the lights on, and made a beeline to the kitchen to grab a glass of water. I needed to take that pill now. I couldn't wait, nor could I forget. I didn't want to be pregnant.

"I'll get the cocoa powder out," Ana said, pushing a chair to the counter. "You get the sprinkles and milk."

Inside the bag, I ripped apart the box and pulled out the pill. After cursing to myself that I even had to do this, I popped that pill in my mouth while Ana was preoccupied and swallowed it whole. I didn't care how much money Blaise Harleen had, how attractive he was, or how he resembled *all* of my dirty-mouthed love interests.

I still hated him.

Chapter Five

BLAISE

An hour after Vera Rodriguez had scurried out of my car in a hurry, I parked it in my garage and sat in the fucking driver's seat. My dick was still covered in her juices and some blood, my mind numb from how fucking good she'd felt.

God, her pussy had squeezed my dick so fucking tightly that I couldn't stop myself from spilling my cum deep into her cunt. With a mind as dirty as hers, she fucking deserved it, and I hadn't missed the way she loved it too.

After taking a deep breath, I tossed my backpack over my shoulder and headed into the quiet mansion. Ten cars might've been parked in the driveway and garage, but nobody was ever fucking home here anymore. I always had this place to myself.

I grabbed some beer from the fridge and walked through the living room to the stairs to go to my room. Mom sat on the plush white sofa, dyed blonde hair in her face as she bent over to pull on some heels.

Wow, she was fucking home for once.

"What're you doing here?" I asked.

"I need you to accompany me to dinner next week," she said, fastening her black Versace heels and not looking up at me once.

No *hi* or *how was your day* or *oh, honey, you're home.*

But I didn't expect it anymore. I didn't know if I ever had.

Once she finally stood, she walked over to the mirror and applied some red lipstick. "Your father will be away on vacation, and I need to impress some important people at work."

I gritted my teeth and stared emptily past her, my chest tightening. Of course... It wasn't like she ever fucking cared about anything other than her image in this town.

"No," I said, throwing my skateboard right on her precious marble floor and heading upstairs toward my bedroom.

She fucking loved this floor, and I did everything in my power to ruin it whatever chance I got.

Mom stormed down the hallway toward me. "Get off that skateboard now, Blaise. You can't even comprehend how much this floor cost your father and me."

Instead of turning around to talk to her, I continued to my bedroom and snapped the door open. "It's not like you don't have the money to get it repaired, *Caroline.* If you see a single speck of dirt, you have someone over the next morning to clean because you can't do it yourself."

I slammed the door closed on her fucking face, but she opened it a moment later.

"What did I tell you about calling me that? I'm your mother, and I deserve your respect. I do everything for you, Blaise."

"Respect?" I chuckled lowly. "You're a fucking joke."

"You need to—" she started but was interrupted by her phone ringing. She clenched her jaw, gave me another heartless glare, and walked back down the hallway, away from me. "Yes, sweetheart, I'll be there soon."

She wanted respect but couldn't even look at me when I saw her for the first time all fucking month. She was a petty bitch, and I didn't give a fuck what I did in her house anymore. It wasn't like she really cared once her phone rang.

Downstairs, the front door closed, and I had this whole empty mansion to myself for the next few days, weeks, or maybe even months. Who knew when they'd decide to show back up? I didn't give a fuck.

I tore off my clothes from school, lay back on my bed, and pulled out my phone, scrolling through the notifications from the guys and from Skylar, who wanted to come over to fuck me later tonight.

She might've given the best head in all of Redwood, but she came and went as she pleased, just like my fucking parents. And I was getting tired of her bitchy *I don't give a fuck about anything* attitude too.

Another message came through my phone.

Skylar: So? When will you be home?

After deciding to ignore her, I grabbed Vera's notebook, which I had managed to steal while she was all flustered in my driver's seat, and opened to the first page of what seemed like a fleshed-out novel.

The two-hundred-paged college-ruled notebook had been completely filled, not a single page or line unused. I flipped through it, glossing over the boring parts of the story until I got to the nasty sex scenes that spanned almost ten pages each.

"Crawl, Evelyn. Be a good girl. Don't make me punish you in front of everyone."

Getting down on all fours, I crawled to him, swaying my hips from side to side, loving the attention that all my father's coworkers were giving me. Some held their drinks over their groins, while others let me see just how hard they were because of me already.

I knelt by Daddy's side and stared up at him through my lashes. He was hard through his suit pants, just waiting to be pleased. I pressed my thighs together to ease the ache between my legs as Aiden placed two fingers on my chin.

"Sit on my lap. Show everyone how quickly you can come by grinding your dripping little cunt against my thigh."

After climbing on top of him, I sat, facing him.

He placed a lingering kiss on my lips. "Turn around, sweetheart. I get to see your face as you come every night. Don't you think they deserve to see it too? I don't want to be selfish with you."

Hell, I didn't give a fuck about literature, but the pages that I'd read were straight-up porn.

"Come here, sweetheart," Aiden ordered. "Let me see that pretty face of yours."

With my face covered with cum, I crawled out from under the table. Aiden took my hands and helped me to my feet, then placed me on the conference table in front of all the men I'd just sucked off and made come.

Aiden maneuvered his way between my legs, unzipping his pants and pulling my ass to the edge. He positioned himself at my entrance and pushed himself into me. "God, sweetheart, you look so"—another thrust—"fucking"—another thrust—"beautiful."

I'd never thought that anything that dirty could come from a good girl like Vera. For as long as I had known her—when her mother used to bring her over while she cleaned our house, before my parents fucked that one up too—she was so soft-spoken and innocent.

But, fuck, from the way she'd stroked my cock with her pussy this afternoon, she was a horny little slut, aching for cock. My dick stiffened slightly as I remembered how nervous, shocked, and scared she'd looked when I told her that I had read her writing.

She'd do anything to stop me from telling the entire school her secret, and I planned to use that against her. I planned to make the good girl into my own personal, hungry cumslut.

Chapter Six

VERA

Since Mom was working a double shift at the diner today, she wouldn't be home for dinner, which meant that I had to scavenge through the canned goods in the cupboard for some ramen or corn or something we'd bought a long time ago for my brother and me.

Tonight, I'd watched João's sister for three hours and made back what I had spent on that damn Plan B pill. But I could have put that toward saving for a computer even if it was a cheap one.

Someone knocked on the front door.

"Vera! Open the door. I have food!"

After hearing Maddie's voice drift into the front room, I hurried over and opened it up for her. She held two brown bags filled with Chinese takeout in one hand and a bottle of root beer soda—my favorite—in the other.

"Is your mom home?" she asked, walking in and setting the bags down on the table.

"No, she works until eleven tonight."

Maddie frowned. "Aw, I bought extra for her."

I stared at my best friend and smiled, so fucking thankful for her. She might've been from the rich side of town with parents who would give her anything under the sun, but she was *nothing* like that arrogant, smooth-talking boy from World History, named Blaise Harleen.

"I'll put it in the fridge for her," I said. "She'll love you."

My brother, Mateo, walking out from his bedroom in the hallway. "I smell food."

"I got some for you too," Maddie said, handing him a bag.

He scurried back into his room with his Chinese food and shut the door. That boy was three years younger than me, but ate as much food as a grown-ass man.

Once we sat at the coffee table, I pulled out some food and my homework.

"I'm dreading History tomorrow," Maddie said, scanning her online English textbook to complete her homework. "The Grinch partnered me with Alec, out of all people. It's going to be annoying as hell, working with him."

"At least you don't have to work with Blaise."

Maddie chuckled. "Yeah, I guess I don't have it as bad as you."

"Ha-ha," I said, not laughing once.

"What was that during History anyway? Blaise just walked right into the room, pulled up a chair next to you, and gave you that heartbreaker smirk. What'd he even want from you? Didn't he tell you to meet him after school?"

Instead of answering her—because I didn't even know if I would be able to say *anything* without being completely embarrassed—I continued my homework with my cheeks flushed and my heart racing. Maddie would freak out if she found out what had happened, and I didn't know if it would be in a good or bad way.

She lifted her head from her laptop and looked over at me. "Oh God. What happened?"

"Nothing," I whispered.

"Bro, don't do that to me," she said, slamming her laptop shut and narrowing her eyes. "You have that guilty look on your face, like you did that time in third grade when you stole my favorite pencil."

"How the heck do you still remember that?"

A grin stretched across her face. "Well, if you hadn't stolen it, we wouldn't be friends today. I wouldn't be able to forget something like that. That was my *favorite* pencil ever. I still have it. *Now*, stop avoiding the question. What happened with Blaise?"

I took a deep breath and peeked over at her. "He, uh, found out that I write smut."

"WHAT?!" Maddie said, straightening her back and leaning toward me. "How?"

"Sometimes, I write scenes on scrap pieces of paper and shove them into my notebook, and ..." My heart pounded inside my chest, my throat drying. Six hours had passed since my little thing with Blaise, and I couldn't stop thinking about how stupid I had been. "And he found them when we were racing to World History."

Maddie stared at me through wide green eyes. "You're shitting me."

"God, it was so embarrassing! I can't believe that he actually picked it up and read it. And it wasn't even a tame scene. He read one of the dirtiest scenes that I had written to date." I covered my face with my hands, still embarrassed. "I don't know what to do."

"What a lucky bastard," Maddie said, shaking her head. "You don't even let me read your stories."

"He is not lucky! He's blackmailing me with it now."

"Nice." Maddie chuckled, grinning wickedly at me. "You need some spice in your life."

"No! I do not!"

"God, I'm so excited to see how this plays out," Maddie said, opening her computer again and still grinning like a madwoman. "Piper is going to have a field day when she learns you're being black-mailed. What's he want from you anyway?" Maddie asked. "For you to do the entire World History project by yourself and the rest of his homework?"

Not wanting to answer again, I scribbled my answers on my AP Statistics homework. And obviously—because she picked up on everything—Maddie looked back over at me and raised her brows.

"That's it, right?"

"No," I whispered, cheeks in flames again. "He, uh ... wants me to be ... his ..." I wanted to throw up at the mere thought of it. "His plaything, I guess."

Maddie smacked her hand down on the coffee table. "No, he doesn't."

"Yes, he does. He ... he ... made it *very* clear after school in his car."

She stared at me in shock for the longest moment of my life. "Bitch, you did not fuck him." When I stayed quiet, Maddie shot to her feet and tugged me up to my feet as well, violently grabbing my face in her hands and letting her mouth hang open. "Tell me you did not lose your virginity today."

"I ..." I started, mouth dry, but the heat grew between my legs as I remembered every filthy word that Blaise had said to me in the passenger seat of his car, how his huge cock had felt, pushing into me for the first time, how he'd used me so ... well. "I can't tell you that."

There was absolute silence for a solid three minutes. A wave of emotions crossed Maddie's face and through her piercing green eyes. She pressed her lips together and opened her mouth so many times that I couldn't even count it anymore.

After another moment, she grabbed my hand and dragged me to the front door. "I'm calling Piper. We're bringing you out for milk-shakes. And *you're* going to tell us every single detail of what happened today because I'm literally in shock."

"Maddie, it's a school night! And Mateo's going to be here alone if I leave him."

"Mateo! We're leaving. You gonna be good here by yourself?" Maddie shouted into the hallway.

He grumbled something incoherent from his bedroom, which almost always meant that he'd be fine. One of his friends was supposed to come pick him up anyway to play video games later tonight.

"You're not getting out of this one, V," Maddie said with a wicked grin. "I want to know everything. Every. Last. Detail."

Chapter Seven

BLAISE

As I reached halfway through Vera's smutty book, someone knocked on my front door. I had turned my phone off hours ago and refused to even look at my mother when she returned for only a moment to tell me that I would be attending dinner with her next week. I wouldn't do shit with her, and she knew that. She just liked the thought of being in control.

The knock turned into a forceful bang, and Skylar's shrill voice echoed through the house. "What the hell is your problem, Blaise? I've been waiting outside in the freezing rain for the past fifteen minutes! Open up!"

After rolling my eyes, I snapped Vera's book closed and hid it underneath my pillow. I would return to that later to pick it apart and figure out who Vera Rodriguez really was and what kind of freaky shit she was into.

Skylar continued banging on the front door, throwing a hissy fit that I used to think was cute. Now, I found it plain annoying because it was the same thing every other rich girl at Redwood did when they didn't get their way.

"Blaise! Open—"

I yanked open the door, leaned against the frame, and crossed my arms over my chest, letting out a long and hollow sigh. While we had plans to hang tonight, I didn't really want to see her. "What do you want, Skylar?"

Hell, I never really wanted to see her, but she was always all over me, and I didn't even have to ask her to come over. She was willing and horny and so goddamn aggravating sometimes.

Instead of waiting until I let her into my home, she walked right into the foyer and dumped her purse on the marble floor. "It's about damn time you opened the door. It's not polite to make a woman wait for you. We had a date."

After shutting the door behind her so the freezing rain wouldn't come in, I turned around in time to catch her lunging at me. She threw her arms around my shoulders and pulled me down to her, smashing her red-stained lips onto mine.

"Fuck, Blaise," she murmured against me. "I've been so horny all day."

Seizing her hips in my hands, I curled my fingers against her small, scrawny ass and tensed. Compared to Vera's curvier body, Skylar was nothing but a bony stick that really didn't do much for me. But she wanted to be around me.

Skylar moved her hands down the front of my body, sinking them into my gray sweatpants and grasping my cock through my briefs. She stroked me up and down through the thin material, moaning into my mouth.

"I've been waiting all day for this," she murmured, dropping to her knees and wrapping her fingers around the waistband of my sweatpants and underwear. Inch by inch, she pulled them down my thighs until my cock sprang out. "Fuck my mouth?"

After gripping my cock in her hand, she stuck out her tongue and slapped the head of my cock against it. My dick twitched. When she wrapped her tight, hot throat around my shaft, I closed my eyes and could think of nothing else other than that Evelyn's character who had sucked off all her father's coworkers in Vera's smutty book.

"You like that?" she asked.

I squeezed my eyes closed, grunting as she slipped my cock into her throat and began face-fucking herself with it.

"Come inside me," Skylar begged, grinding her ass against the floor. "Please."

I gripped her hair tighter and wished she would shut the fuck up. She knew that I never came inside anyone I used from Redwood. It had never happened with her before, and I wasn't about to let it happen now.

"Please, Blaise," she continued.

"No, Skylar, shut the fuck up," I gritted out.

She bobbed her head twice more on my cock, driving me higher, then pulled away. "Please."

The high that had suddenly come was gone within a mere moment, and I knew that even if I used her mouth for the rest of the night, I wouldn't be able to come when she was begging and complaining like this. I didn't know why she thought tonight would be different.

When she went to put me back into her mouth, I stepped back and pulled up my sweats. My dick was still hard, creating an imprint under the gray material, but I didn't give a fuck anymore. She'd ruined tonight.

"Are you fucking serious?" Skylar said, reaching toward me to grab at me again.

"I'm fucking serious," I growled, stepping back so she couldn't touch me anymore tonight. "I told you fucking no, more than once, and you still beg, like the cheap fucking slut you are. I'm not coming inside you. Ever."

She wiped some spit off the corner of her mouth and rolled her eyes. "Come on. I won't complain anymore, just let me finish you off. I know you want it. You've been stressed all day long without me."

But she didn't know that I had been completely fine without her. "No."

After shooting up, she narrowed her eyes at me. "What the fuck has gotten into you today? You're usually moody, but not like this. You didn't even sit next to me in World History and instead had to make a whole show out of sitting next to that nerd."

"Vera?"

"Whatever the fuck her name is," Skylar growled, crossing her arms. "What, are you fucking her now?"

"No," I lied between gritted teeth, stepping closer to her and towering over her because I didn't want anyone else to know what I knew about Vera.

If Skylar found out, then she would use that information to blackmail Vera too. And while I didn't give a fuck about Vera, *I* wanted to be the person who did it.

"Then, what the fuck is this sudden interest in her?"

I crossed my arms. "So, she's the reason why you're here tonight?"

"That didn't answer my question."

"I don't give a fuck if it answers your question or not." I swallowed hard and stepped away from her, staring at the ground and slowly pacing around the room. "You fucking stood out in the freezing fucking rain and sucked me off because you wanted to, what? Prove yourself to me? To show me that you are the fucking best at this shit? You don't really want to be here with me."

Nobody fucking did.

Skylar pressed her fake lips together and flared her nostrils. "Blaise, you know—"

"I'm not going to fucking listen to you," I growled, grabbing her by the upper arm and dragging her to the door. "Get the fuck out of my house. I don't want to see or hear from you for the rest of the fucking night."

Chapter Eight

BLAISE

Five minutes before the first bell rang at Redwood, I sat in my Ferrari F8 with my hand around my cock as I read the last page of Vera's notebook. After spitting on it, I stroked it faster and faster, grunting.

After Skylar had left, I'd pulled an all-nighter and read every page of this notebook. Every fucking page. And I still couldn't wrap my fucking head around how *Vera Rodriguez*—the nerdy, unpopular, innocent girl from World History—had this much of a filthy mind.

How could I corrupt a mind like hers? She'd probably get off on me blackmailing her.

"Fuuuuck," I groaned, wrapping my hand around the head of my dick.

Everyone around me was already rushing into the buildings to get to class. I could sit here all fucking day and jerk off like a fucking idiot, and nobody would notice. But I couldn't seem to fucking stop.

Glancing out the windshield, I spotted a flash of yellow rain boots hurrying across the street. With her ripped coat zipped all the way up to her chin and a pile of books in her arms, Vera cut through the student parking lot from the street and hurried toward the entrance to Redwood Academy's main building.

I closed my eyes for a brief moment, stroking my cock faster and faster.

God, I was a fucking loser for sitting in this car and fucking jerking off to this story when I could be fucking Skylar—or even Vera now—in the school restroom. I wanted to be inside Vera again, wanted her whimpering and crying into my ear.

All night, I hadn't been able to stop reading, stop thinking about the way she'd felt, the sounds she'd made, how her pussy had tightened around me when I came deep inside her cunt. It was the first fucking time I'd lost control like that, the first time I had come inside anyone after promising myself that I wouldn't—at least, not without a condom.

Chocolate-brown hair blowing in the breeze, Vera clutched her books tight to her chest and took two stairs at a time up the main staircase to the front door. I threw my head back and grunted, my warm cum spilling out into my fist.

I'd never thought *she* would be the one I lost control with. Since I had known her, she had been quiet and reserved and innocent—someone that I would never ever think about touching or blackmailing.

After sighing softly, I relaxed against my seat, wiped the cum off with a spare sweatshirt that I never wore anymore, and tucked myself back away in my pants. Two minutes before first class started, and I would actually be on time for once.

Spotting Vera one last time, I turned off my car. Before she could enter the building, João Rocha—leader of Poison—grabbed her wrist and pulled her back. I tightened my hand around the steering wheel and watched him move closer to her as he handed her something.

She stared at him for a few moments, exchanging a couple words with him and giving him her full attention. Unlike when other people talked to Poison, Vera wasn't shaking in fear of João. Instead, she talked to him like she knew him ... a bit too well.

"What the fuck?" I growled, throwing on my backpack and opening the door.

As I hopped up onto the curb, Vera disappeared through the front doors with João. I picked up my pace and stepped into the school, pushing and shoving whoever the fuck got in my way until I made it to the main hallway. I stared around, hoping to find her, but she was gone in the hundreds of students.

I rushed down the maze of hallways, trying to find either Vera or João but coming up empty. Skylar stood at my locker with her arms crossed over her chest. She must've been waiting for me. But I didn't have time for her shit right now.

When she saw me, she pushed herself off the metal lockers and hurried after me. "Listen, I'm sorry about last night. I wanted to come over and help you feel good. You've been more stressed than normal lately, Blaise. I can see it."

"You wanted to feel good about your-fucking-self," I said, pushing through a group of students to see if I could find them. I didn't know what the fuck I was doing or why I was doing it, but I couldn't stop. "Leave me alone."

"Blaise." Skylar pouted, grabbing my elbow and stopping me completely.

This bitch was going to ruin everything.

The bell rang throughout the halls, and I ripped myself away from her. "Get to fucking class. I have shit to do. We'll fucking talk later."

After giving me another eye roll, Skylar walked down the hall to whatever class that she had. I decided that I wouldn't find Vera like this, so I did the one thing that I knew how to do—flirt with the lady in the office to get Vera's schedule.

I strolled to the main office, passing Principal Vaughn on my way there and throwing my skateboard on the ground in front of him to piss him off. Then, I found my way into the main office and leaned against the counter, flashing a smile at the older woman.

"I'm looking for Vera Rodriguez's schedule," I said to the woman in the main office.

"And why is that, Mr. Harleen?"

My lips curled into an even wider grin, and I waved a few hundred-dollar bills of my parents' money at her. Eyes widening in greed, she tapped a couple buttons on her keyboard and printed out Vera's schedule for me. After exchanging my money for the schedule, I walked out of the office and found that Vera should now be on the third floor in AP Biology—a class that João Rocha wouldn't even be able to get into.

Though my first class was on the first floor, I walked up two flights of stairs to floor three and into the science wing, toward AP Biology. Instead of checking through the door window to make sure that Vera was there alone and not with João—I would have to talk to him later—I opened the AP Biology door and stepped right into the class.

From Allie Hall to Imani Abara to some nerdy kid named Akio, everyone stared at me with wide eyes and began to whisper. I scanned the room until they landed on Vera, who sat with her best friend, Maddie something, in the middle row.

Vera sucked in a sharp breath, cheeks flushing as she looked at me. She shifted around uncomfortably, tucking some brown hair behind her ear and shuffling her squeaky yellow rain boots on the tiled floor.

The graying science teacher cleared his throat. "Who are—"

"Wrong class," I said, keeping eye contact with Vera and backing out of the room.

While she might've been in class alone—without João—I wasn't going to let it go that easily. I wanted to know what they had been talking about, why she was so comfortable with João, and what the fuck he wanted with her.

Because Vera Rodriguez wasn't going to give her attention to anyone but me.

Chapter Nine

VERA

Ignore Blaise Harleen. That was my goal for today.

I closed my locker and glanced down at the tiled floor to ensure I hadn't dropped another scene from one of my smutty stories. I didn't need anyone else deciding to blackmail me, like Blaise was.

Piper pushed some pink hair over her shoulder and smirked at me. "I still can't believe you dropped one of your stories yesterday and that Blaise picked it up. That's some real romance-novel shit, Vera."

"Okay, okay," I said, glancing around the halls nervously. "Can you lower your voice?!"

Maddie looped her arm around mine. "We're just excited for you, V."

"How are you guys excited that I'm being blackmailed?!"

They looked at each other and grinned like psychopaths. Sure, my life wasn't *that* exciting, but I didn't need a distraction. We had only six more months in Redwood Academy, and then we'd all be out of this shitty town. A few months I needed to survive and *not* be blackmailed.

When the first bell rang, signaling that we only had a couple more minutes to get to class, Piper waved us off and walked toward the science wing for Chemistry. I shuffled closer to Maddie and kept my gaze focused on the ground as we walked.

As we approached World History, I spotted Blaise talking to the school slut, Skylar. There wasn't anything wrong with being a slut—hell, sex was what I wrote about in my stories all the time—but there was something about the way she touched Blaise that really ticked me off.

But I didn't care. Not today.

Because, in my world, Blaise didn't exist. Not until he threatened to tell all of Redwood about my word porn that I had been writing for what seemed like years now. Then, I'd entertain him for a few moments, and that was it.

When I walked past him, Blaise caught my eye and pushed himself off the red metal lockers, following me into the class and toward the back, where we both apparently sat now. And my *best friend* took her seat and grinned at me, as if she wanted all the details later.

Blaise pulled something out of his backpack and waved it at me. "Thought I'd make some edits to one of your stories. No need to thank me."

Furrowing my brows at the object, I realized that it wasn't one of the smutty stories that had fallen out of my notebook, but instead, it was the entire damn notebook. My eyes widened. "Where did you find this?"

"In your stack of books yesterday afternoon."

Blaise set the notebook on my desk, cracked half a smirk, and sat down in the seat beside me, completely pissing off Skylar, who glared at me from across the classroom. She must've thought that I actually wanted him. I didn't—let's get that straight—and I definitely hadn't touched myself last night either, thinking about what he had done to me.

Stomach tightening in knots, I looked down at the notebook to see my first-draft manuscript marked up with red pen, words crossed out and replaced with even filthier ones that I couldn't read without blushing.

"You actually read more of my story?" I asked, cheeks flushing at the thought of Blaise sitting down to read about two dirty-mouthed characters going at it. Wanting to divert the attention from me, I let out a laugh. "I didn't think you had the attention span."

"And I didn't pin you as a brat," Blaise said, sitting back in his seat and letting out a laugh, muscles flexing against his black T-shirt that seemed to hug him in all the right places. "But then again, I didn't think anything dirty could come out of that virgin mind of yours either."

"Can you not scream that to everyone?" I whisper-yelled at him, pursing my lips and glaring. I leaned closer to him and poked him in his hard, taut chest. "And I'm not a virgin anymore, thanks to you. You can stop calling me that."

"You're welcome."

This man had the damn audacity.

I flared my nostrils and turned back to my books, fuming. "It wasn't even that good."

He wiped his heartbreaker smirk off his face in less than a millisecond and looked in my direction. "What did you say? I thought I'd heard the girl who had begged for my cum tell me that it wasn't even that good. Does her little back-talking mouth need a reminder of who is in control of our situation? Because I can let everyone know how much of a slut you really are, Vera."

Pressing my lips together, I turned away from him and looked up at The Grinch, who started her lesson for the day, mentioning that, today, we would start our project.

"Is that what you want?" he asked me.

I cut my eyes to him. "No."

"Prove it," Blaise murmured into my ear, drawing a finger up my thigh. "Suck my dick."

"We're in class!" I whisper-yelled.

"Come on, Vera. We're in the back. That bitch barely looks at the class, and"—he gestured down to the huge bulge in his jeans—"look how hard I am for you."

Deciding that I'd only take a peek, I glanced down at his pants and gulped, the warmth pooling between my legs. I didn't know how he hid it in the hallways, not that I was looking, but his cock was pressed against his jeans, leaving a noticeable imprint down his leg.

He grabbed my hand and placed it on his cock, stroking it up and down and not letting me pull away—not that I wanted to, either. Since yesterday, my fucked-up body had been aching for him to push himself back inside me.

"All you gotta do is lean down behind the desk."

"You're not going to push my head down there?"

He chuckled. "I'm not a head-pusher, but you won't be able to resist it."

"I will."

Instead of arguing more with me, he unbuttoned and unzipped his pants, then pulled himself out, his thick, veiny, and hard cock throbbing in his hand. He leaned over, pushed two fingers into my pants, then my pussy, and curled them inside of me, hitting my G-spot.

"Thanks," he said, pulling out his now-wet fingers and moving the wetness around the head of his cock.

I cursed under my breath and leaned back in my seat, so I could see him stroke himself better, my pussy pulsing with excitement. My nipples hardened against my bra, my heart racing. Though I continued to remind myself that I *really* wasn't supposed to be enjoying this, I couldn't help it.

After muttering, "Fuck it," to myself, I wrapped my hand around the base of his cock and stroked it up and down, hungry to take him into my mouth.

But I wouldn't. Not here.

Brows furrowed and dark brown eyes fixed on me, he grunted so softly that I didn't think I'd heard him. I stroked him faster under the table, staring up at the teacher and rubbing my thighs together to relieve some tension.

Blaise pushed my legs apart and thrust a finger into me, his palm hitting my sensitive clit. I clenched around him and bit my lip to hold back a whimper, hand tightening around his shaft and making the head of his cock pink.

With his biceps flexing, Blaise took control and rammed his fingers into me harder and harder until I had to slap a hand over my mouth to hold back a moan while I tipped over the edge, an unruly orgasm ripping through my entire body.

The Grinch looked right back at us, right at me, and tensed. "Get with your partners and head to the library for research." She clenched her jaw, crossing her bony arms over her chest. "Blaise and Vera, stay behind."

And that was when I knew that Blaise had gotten us into a shit-load of trouble.

Chapter Ten

VERA

When The Grinch said our names, I pulled myself away from Blaise, let his cock smack hard against his muscular thigh, and pushed him away from me. My cheeks flushed red, my heart racing about a million miles a freaking second. I hoped that no other student had seen what we were doing back here because The Grinch definitely had.

It had only been a day—a single freaking *day*—since Blaise had begun to blackmail me, and *this* was the point we had gotten to. He had all the things he needed to ruin my life, and this man had forced me to give him a hand job in the back of class.

Definitely forced.

A couple students—*Skylar* and her crew—glanced over at Blaise, who didn't even look in her direction.

Blaise had that smug-as-fuck smirk on his face as he leaned closer to me. "Don't make it obvious. Your cheeks are as red as your ass will be tonight."

I gritted my teeth and glared down at my desk, ignoring the quizzical look that I knew Maddie was giving me right this very

44

second. God, she might've wanted me to finally let loose and have some fun, but this was *not* it. I couldn't control myself around Blaise.

Once the class departed and Blaise shoved himself back into his jeans, The Grinch crossed her arms and gave us a pointed stare. "I'm not blind. I could see what you were doing in the back of my class. I'd expect something as low from Blaise, but you, Vera?" She shook her head in disbelief, as if she ever really liked me. "I need to call the office."

"What?" I asked breathily, standing up and shaking my head.

She couldn't call the office. If Mom found out, she'd be so disappointed in me, and my whole life would be ruined. I had been working so freaking hard to get into a good college, so I could get my family out of the Redwood slums. I couldn't blow it.

"Do it," Blaise said to her, buckling his pants and standing to his full height, posturing over her and giving her the most menacing glare he could muster, which even terrified me. "I dare you."

My eyes widened, my throat closing. "Blaise ..."

Blaise stalked closer to her and picked up the class phone that rang to the office. "Here."

Mrs. Greenwich looked between us, gripped the phone in her hand until her knuckles whitened, and swallowed hard. "Don't do it ever again in my classroom or else I will have to call the office and get you both suspended."

I stood up and hurried over to him, wanting to get out of here now before she really did call the office. I didn't know how the fuck that Blaise Harleen had done it, but he terrified even the teachers. Maybe it was his money or that malicious look in his eyes. Either way, I didn't want to wait any longer here.

Blaise let out a laugh and grabbed my hand. "Come on, Vera. Let's go work on our project." He looked over his shoulder as we stepped out of the room. "Oh, and I wouldn't come looking for us if I were you."

"Is that a threat?" The Grinch asked, suddenly with a smidge more confidence.

"Yes."

Instead of walking toward the library, where the rest of the class had headed to, Blaise took my hand and led me all through the school to the secluded stairwell by the science wing. He shut the door to the stairs behind us, the sound echoing through the small, brightly lit hall. Blaise wasn't one to hide things, apparently.

As soon as the door closed, he had me pushed up against it. "Fuck, Vera," Blaise said on the back of my neck, nose trailing up it and breath warming my ear. "I have been fucking dreaming about coming in your pussy again. You felt so good yesterday. I'm not waiting any longer to fill you again." He undid his pants and pulled out his cock.

"What?! No!" I said, throwing my hands up in the air. "We just got caught by our teacher. We can't fuck in the hallway. I ... I can't ... I can't fucking let anything happen to my reputation here. I've been trying so hard to get out of this place."

"I won't let anything happen to your good-girl reputation as long as you do as I say."

"You don't control Redwood. If one more person sees, then—"

Blaise moved even closer to me, his lips curled into a smirk against my skin. "I might not control Redwood, but money does. And my family has tons of it. You don't know what a couple million dollars can do around here. It can take care of *anyone* in any way that I want." His voice was low and friendly, but there was more than malicious intent behind it.

Blaise sounded like he could ... like he could have someone killed —or worse ... ruin my entire life if I didn't do as he said.

Redwood was nothing compared to what he'd be able to do to me if I got on his bad side.

I glanced around. "But there are cameras, Blaise. We can't."

"Fuck the cameras," he said, pushing my pants to my ankles and bending me over.

Before I could stop him, he thrust himself into me and made me cry out in pleasure. After a few deep strokes, he leaned down, wrapped his muscular arms around the backs of my thighs, and picked me up right off the ground and into the air. My back against his chest, my legs folded against my torso, I sat helplessly in his arms with my legs spread in a classic full nelson position—my favorite position by far to write about.

"Vera, baby, didn't you write a scene like this? Isn't this what your dirty mind loves? The thought of the good girl being caught with the bad boy with his cock buried so deep inside, so much of his cum just dripping out?"

"God, it feels so good," I murmured to myself.

Locking his hands behind the back of my head, Blaise walked to the top of the stairs and faced the door at the bottom. If anyone —*anyone*—walked through it, they'd get a full show of my pussy getting fucked raw by Blaise's cock.

"Don't worry about it," Blaise said, kissing my neck. "I can make anyone disappear, if I need them to."

My pussy tightened around him at both the thought of being caught and the thought of a violent, dangerous, threatening man fucking me senseless from behind. If this wasn't every girl's horny dream, I didn't know what was.

Knowing I was on the brink of another orgasm, I whimpered out to him, "Fill my mouth."

At least then, I wouldn't have to worry about going to get Plan B again.

"I will, Vera," he said, still thrusting deep inside of my pussy, somehow getting deeper and deeper each time, each stroke pushing me closer to the edge of another leg-trembling orgasm. He gently sucked on my neck, definitely leaving a huge, blotchy hickey. "I can't fucking wait to see my cum drip out of your slutty little mouth and your eyes fill with tears after I ruin you."

My pussy tightened around him, clenching harder and harder. I dug my fingernails into his abdomen. God, if he kept this up, he was going to come inside of me, and I was going to fucking ... enjoy it more than I should.

"But I'm saving your mouth for another day. We're on school property. Someone might see," he said, throwing my words from the other day right back at me. "Isn't that what you told me? But I don't care who sees me using you. All I care about is how much you beg for it and how much cum I can fill your sopping cunt with."

Toes curling, I found myself tensing suddenly and screaming out his name, my voice echoing through the small stairwell. Blaise stilled and came inside of me, grunting into my ear and eventually pulling out. When he set me on the ground, I grasped the railing to stop myself from toppling over. His cum ran down my thighs and into my underwear, and I knew that I would have no choice but to pull them up and ruin another good pair.

"My house. Tonight. I'll pick you up, Vera. We'll reenact another one of your stories."

Chapter Eleven

BLAISE

After leaving Vera in the middle of the stairwell with those flushed red cheeks and her wild sex hair, I glided on my skateboard down the first-floor hallways. Vera wouldn't have liked it if I'd stayed any longer. At least, that was what I told myself.

Besides, if I had stayed, I'd probably have forced her to tell me what the fuck João had wanted this morning. But that would make me sound like a jealous, possessive motherfucker, and I didn't simp for any girl at Redwood, especially one who made smutty sex stories in her free time.

When I reached the end of the hallway, I spotted João standing outside the double doors, talking with his gang of friends—Kai and Landon. With my jaw clenched, I threw the skateboard over my shoulder and walked out of the building.

The guys stopped talking and looked over at me as I leaned against the stair railing. Rain droplets fell from the sky every now and then, splattering on my shirt, but I didn't move. Nor did I move when they all turned to me like they were about to get on my shit about something.

"The fuck you want?" João asked with a slight Brazilian accent.

"We need to talk."

"Then, fucking talk."

I nodded to Kai and Landon. "Alone."

João pulled a box of cigarettes from his back pocket, stuck one in his mouth, and lit it. "You want to talk to Poison about a job? You talk to all of us. Don't be a fucking pussy, Harleen. Your daddy might have money, but we don't do shit for rich bitches like you unless you fucking beg for it."

Getting pissed the fuck off, I placed one hand on his chest and shoved him back to Landon. "I'm not here to hire Poison. I'm here to tell you to stay the fuck away from Vera Rodriguez."

When Kai reached behind him, João straightened himself out and shook his head at him, as if to tell him he didn't need his help. João tossed the cigarette between my feet and stepped forward, meeting me eye to eye.

He curled his lips into a smirk. "And why's that, pretty boy?"

I gritted my teeth. "I don't need a fucking reason."

"Sure you do."

But what the fuck would I say to him? I didn't like the girl, not even a little bit. I just didn't want her paying attention to anyone else, nor did I want anyone else to have shit to blackmail her with. I was a greedy asshole who wanted all of her attention.

"Huh?" João said with a shit-eating grin. "You like her?"

After I shoved him back again, I clenched my jaw. "Get out of my fucking face, Rocha."

João chuckled at the guys and hiked his thumb back to me. "Blaise over here has a little crush on nerdy Vera Rodriguez. Who would've thought?"

Tired of his shit, I grabbed his fucking thumb and pulled it back, so fucking close to snapping it if he hadn't reacted. He yanked himself out of my hold, his laughter turning to fury. He shoved me back against the front entrance and hurled a fist at me, but I side-stepped it.

Once I tossed my backpack on the ground beside us, I pushed up my sleeves. I hadn't been in a fucking fight since last week, and my knuckles had been aching to slam into João's arrogant fucking face for a long time now.

I threw a fist and collided with the side of his face. João stumbled back a few feet, spit up some blood, then faked a left and hit me in the gut with a right uppercut. It hurt like a motherfucker, but I wasn't backing the fuck down. I wanted him to know that I was fucking serious.

After I landed another punch on his jaw, he lunged forward and grabbed me by the collar. I hit him again, and he used his grip on me to pull me down Redwood's front stairs. My foot slipped down the first step. Before I completely lost my balance, I snatched his jacket and yanked him with me.

We tumbled down the concrete steps until we landed on the side-walk. Blinded with rage and the need to feel fucking something, I slammed my fist into his face over and over as he hurled fist after fist at me too.

His knuckles collided, but I couldn't feel anything.

"Hey!" someone shouted from across the quad, running toward us. Probably fucking Principal Vaughn, wanting to get on our shit.

Suddenly, someone grabbed my shoulders and yanked me back as Jace Harbor, Redwood football star, grabbed João's shoulders and pulled him back.

"The fuck are you doing, João?" Jace asked. "We had a fucking de—"

"Get your fucking hands off me, Harbor," João said, ripping himself out of Jace's grip and wiping the blood off his chin on his hand. "We have a fucking deal, but that doesn't mean you can get into my other shit."

"Stay the fuck away from her," I growled at João, not giving a fuck about whatever business that football star had with Poison.

"You think Vera Rodriguez would ever like you?" João asked, spitting up some more blood and chuckling at me. "You're nothing but a rich, arrogant brat who leeches off his daddy's money. She'll see right through you."

I lunged at him again, but Jamal, Jace's best friend, stopped me.

"I don't give a fuck about how she sees me. She doesn't need to be in your fucking business."

"You sound jealous as fuck, Harleen. Does Vera know how much you like her?" João continued, pulling another cigarette out and shoving it between his lips. "No, she doesn't because she's been too into me lately."

Landon and Kai shot him a glare that I couldn't quite understand fully, but I could tell that they didn't like the last bit of what he had said. Which meant that he was either lying or had a different girl he was into ... or maybe both.

He was trying to get under my skin, and it was fucking working.

"Just leave her the fuck alone," I growled, tossing my backpack over my shoulder and grabbing my skateboard. Glaring at the ground, I stormed down the sidewalk, away from them and toward the student parking lot.

"Where the fuck are you going?" someone said to my left.

I expected it to be Jace Harbor, trying to get me to go back to school, or João Rocha, wanting to pick another fight with me, but it was Mr. Avery—teacher of some shit subject here and my fucking uncle, who had ties to Redwood's mob.

"Home."

Before I could slip past, he grabbed me by the shoulder. "Get your ass back to class."

"I should say the same thing to you. Why the hell are you in the student parking lot?"

Avery guiltily slid his tongue across his front teeth, then released me. "If you don't get out of my sight in two minutes, I'm calling your father."

I ripped myself away from him, wondering why he was really in the student parking lot, and grumbled under my breath, "It's not like he'd actually do anything about me skipping anyway."

Chapter Twelve

VERA

Despite needing to go buy another stupid freaking pill because Blaise couldn't keep his dick in his pants today, I had to work at the library at two thirty p.m., and I didn't have time to head to CVS after school. I needed the money, especially if this was going to keep happening.

I slipped into the old three-story building that housed thousands of books and pulled down my hood. Droplets of water dripped onto the thin black carpet, and the usually relaxing scent of paperbacks drifted through my nose. Except today ... I couldn't relax.

So, I pulled out my phone and texted the group chat between Maddie, Piper, and me.

Me: Please, can someone pick up Plan B from CVS? I'll pay you back.

Maddie: OMG, tell me you didn't whore it out with Blaise again!!!

Maddie: I fckn love you. <3

After slapping my hand across my forehead, I grunted and walked through the main hallway and to the library's counter. Sue, an elderly woman who had worked here for almost fifty years, waved at me with a wrinkled hand.

My phone buzzed again.

Piper: I can pick some up. I'll swing by the library in a couple hours. When do you get off?

Maddie: She gets off at five, and I'm coming with. I need the deets.

Halfway through my shift, the rude CVS employee from yesterday sauntered up to the counter with a pile of books in his arms. "Look what we have here," he said, voice teasing as he placed down the books about machinery. "I remember you."

Giving him my best customer-service smile, I didn't say anything to him and started scanning his collection of nonfiction books that looked boring as hell. Of course this guy would read some dry material and nothing spicy.

"You work at the pharmacy, don't you?" Sue said, smiling at Jim or James or whatever his name was. She tapped my arm and leaned toward me. "I go get my medication there all the time, and this boy is the sweetest."

"The sweetest, huh?" I asked, glancing at the CVS employee and hoping Sue didn't hear the distasteful sarcasm laced heavily in every one of my words. Because this asshole had been anything but sweet to me yesterday.

He leaned against the counter and grinned. "How are you doing, Sue?"

"Oh good, my dear," she said, nudging me. "Just trying to find a nice boy for my Vera."

God, between Maddie, Piper, and Sue, it seemed like everyone in this town was trying to find me a man.

"Vera," Jim repeated, turning his gaze on me and smirking. "We've met before."

After quickly scanning his final book, I pushed them across the counter toward him and gave him another fake smile to make my manager happy. I needed this job and the money way more than I cared about faking it with him. "Your books are due back in two weeks."

Once he stuffed them into his backpack, he swung it over his shoulder. "I'm sure I'll be seeing you before then. See you soon, Vera."

I gritted my teeth the entire time he walked down the main hallway and out the double doors that led to downtown Redwood. Sue began chatting about how lovely Jim was to her and how she thought we'd make a cute couple as I aimlessly scanned books in and out.

Even if Jim had been nice to me, I wouldn't even consider going on a date with him. He wasn't my type, and I kinda, sorta had gotten caught up with another bad boy who had a thing for fucking me in public. And, like the girls in some of my stories, I had self-diagnosed myself with body-betraying syndrome—or BBS, as I liked to call it.

Body-betraying bullshit.

Because I had stupidly gone along with it both times!

Five minutes before my shift ended, Maddie and Piper strolled into the library and immediately made a beeline for me. Piper shoved a brown paper bag across the counter as Maddie wiggled her brows.

"So, deets."

I grabbed the bag. "Thanks, *Piper*," I said, emphasizing her name because I really didn't want to give any sort of details out about fucking Blaise in the middle of Redwood Academy in front of Sue.

She thought I was an angel, and I planned to keep it that way.

After swallowing the pill in the restroom, I grabbed my coat from the back room and left for the day. Because Blaise still had my notebook, I hadn't been able to write any sort of stories today during work, and I was getting antsy to get back home.

Once I slipped into the backseat of Maddie's car, she drove us through Redwood. But instead of taking the turn to head into the slums, where I lived, she continued driving until we reached the hospital.

"Okay, okay," Maddie said, turning the car off and stepping out.

"You don't have to spill the details—though I *know* that you want to. But I pulled a couple of strings this afternoon and got you into my gynecologist's office. We're getting you on birth control tonight."

"Maddie," I said, chewing on the inside of my lip. "You know I can't afford—"

"Don't worry about it," she said, yanking me out of the car and starting toward the front entrance. "She owes my family a favor. Your mom won't even know about it. And besides, if anyone asks why we're here, we got you covered, don't we, Piper?"

Piper grinned. "Anytime."

"Thank you," I whispered, wrapping my arms around them and pulling them close. A small giggle escaped my lips, and I threw them a wink. "But that doesn't mean that I'm going to tell you girls shit about what happened today in World History, then again in the stairwell."

"Oh, bitch," Maddie said, grinning. "You bet it does."

Chapter Thirteen

BLAISE

I spent three hours trying to find Vera's address. She hadn't given it to me, and I was getting pissed the fuck off. After World History, I couldn't get her out of my fucking mind.

But after pulling some strings and bribing the right people with money, I had her address in the Google Maps app and her number in my phone and was about to head over to her house now. It wasn't that I was fucking obsessed with her, because I wasn't.

But she was mine.

Not fucking João's.

That fucker didn't know what was coming to him, if he kept that shitty fucking attitude up.

As I closed the front door, Skylar pulled up my driveway and cut her lights. I rolled my eyes and sighed under my breath, heading directly for my car and hoping to avoid her at all costs. I hadn't even invited her over tonight.

She hopped out of her car and hurried toward me, looping her arm around mine. "Where are you going, Blaise? We always have plans on Tuesday night."

"Not tonight," I said, ripping my arm out of hers and opening my car door. "Move your car, so I can get out. You parked right fucking behind me. There is a whole fucking driveway where you could've parked your shitty-ass car."

Skylar stood by my car and crossed her arms as I slammed the door. "I'm not moving my car anywhere," she shouted, her voice muffled. "We need to talk. You've been so fucking off lately, and you won't even tell me why. Did I do something wrong?"

Deciding to ignore the bitch—because I didn't really care for her anyway—I started the car and let the heat warm my face. The time on my phone read five thirty p.m., and I didn't want to waste another fucking second here.

"So, you're going to ignore me?!" Skylar said. "First, you ignore me. Then flirt with me in front of anyone during school. It doesn't make sense, Blaise. What the hell do you want from me?"

"Nothing," I said, staring emptily at her through the window.

"Is it because of that bitch from History? What were you even doing to her today?"

I wrapped my hand tightly around the steering wheel. "That's none of your fucking business, Skylar. Now, move your fucking car before I back into it."

"You wouldn't do that," she said, giving me those bratty eyes that I'd once thought were the sexiest damn things in the world. "You care about your pretty ass car too—"

Sliding the gear into reverse, I started backing up.

Skylar's eyes widened, and she hurried over to her car. "Fucking fine! You win."

After she backed out of my driveway, I waited for her to leave the neighborhood. I didn't want her following me to find out that I was actually going to Vera's home to pick her up, that I planned to bring her back to my place tonight. Skylar would use that against her.

Don't get me wrong; I didn't care about Vera. I just wanted to be the one to blackmail her. It was a fun pastime in this shitty place.

And it wasn't like I was about to head to the skatepark in the pouring rain tonight, so this would have to do.

When I was sure that Skylar was gone, I started the directions to Vera's house and took off. Fifteen minutes later, I pulled into the Redwood slums. Run-down houses and broken-down cars. Bars on some windows and ugly chain-link fences that did nothing to keep dogs from chewing through them and wreaking havoc on unsuspecting people. Garbage littered across yards and sidewalk-less streets. This place was filthy.

After glancing once more at Google Maps to make sure I had actually typed in the right address, I pulled up to the side of the road in front of a small one-story house that barely had a front yard and had blinds that were ripped.

I pulled up my hood, stepped out of the car, and walked up to the front door, and then I knocked twice. Moments later, the door creaked open, and a kid with chubby cheeks and brown hair appeared behind it with an Xbox controller in one hand and a box of off-brand Cheez-Its in the other.

"Is, uh, Vera here?" I asked.

"No," he said, looking behind me at my car. "Who are you? Her boyfriend?"

I scoffed. "No."

The kid snorted. "Didn't think so. Vera's too nerdy to date anyone."

"You her brother?"

"What's it to you?"

Knowing that I wasn't going to get anywhere with this kid like this, I nodded to the controller in his hand. Vera would be back sooner or later, and I didn't want to go back home to wait. "What game are you playing?"

"Raid of Durnbone."

"You got an extra controller?"

Chapter Fourteen

VERA

I waited impatiently in the gynecologist's lobby, my knees bouncing. While I really wanted to get on birth control, my stomach was turning at the thought of actually being sexually active. With Blaise.

The characters in my stories could have sex with every male in sight every single day and never had to worry about getting pregnant. Stupid fictional world and that insane body-betrayal syndrome.

"So, let me get this straight," Maddie whispered, leaning forward toward Piper and me. "He was touching you in the back of History, The Grinch caught you guys and threatened to suspend you, and then he told her to shove it." Maddie clutched her heart and grinned like a maniac. "Gah! Then, he fucked you in the stairwell. Girl, I-I don't even have any words."

"You apparently have a lot of them!" I whisper-yelled at her. "Please, be quiet."

"I bet you say that to Blaise too, huh?" Piper chimed.

After playfully narrowing my eyes at these girls who were supposed to be my best friends, I pulled out my phone and texted

Mateo. He usually expected me home right after work. I never took a detour anywhere without telling him. Mom was working late again, and he'd be home by himself.

Me: I'll be home soon. Please tell me you're okay.

As I waited for his reply, a nurse walked out from the back room. "Vera Rodriguez."

Maddie pushed me toward the door. "Tell Dr. Patel that I said thank you."

Once I made it into the back room, I sat alone for another five minutes before a young woman with tan skin and huge brown eyes walked in with a blue clipboard.

"Vera Rodriguez, I'm Dr. Patel. What brings you in today?"

"I was hoping to get on birth control," I said, my voice barely above a whisper.

"Are you sexually active?" she asked.

My cheeks flushed. "Yes."

She sat across from me and smiled. "No need to be embarrassed, sweetheart. We can find a plan that works for you, depending on your needs, desires, and schedule. We have a few options to choose from—the most popular being the pill, an IUD, or a shot."

For the next thirty minutes, she explained each and every option in detail. I stared at the pamphlet that she had given me and nervously scratched the back of my neck. Blaise was supposed to pick me up later, and I didn't know if I could convince him not to fuck me again tonight. Actually, screw that. With this BBS, I didn't know if I would be able to control myself.

"Is there anything that works immediately?" I asked, swallowing my nerves.

"Not immediately. Each will take about seven days to go into effect."

Seven days.

Seven days felt like an eternity. Hell, *last night* had felt like the longest damn night of my life to me.

"Okay, I'll, um ..." I rubbed my sweaty palms together. "I'll take the pills because we'll have to schedule another appointment for the IUD and shot, right?"

"Usually, yes. If I prescribe the pills, they'll be ready at your pharmacy in an hour or sooner."

"Let's do that," I said, standing. "Please."

Once Dr. Patel nodded, I walked back into the lobby to meet Maddie and Piper, who were talking sneakily to each other about me getting with Redwood's bad boy. When I approached, Maddie stood and looped her arm around mine, guiding me back to the car.

"So," she asked, "what happened?"

"I have some pills being prepared for me at CVS."

She grinned and nudged me toward the car. "CVS, here we come."

Five minutes later, we walked into CVS. Jim was behind the counter, reading one of the machinery books he'd checked out from the library, and I did everything in my power to ignore his curious stares. I bounced on my toes, waiting in line with Maddie and Piper to get my prescription.

"Back again?" Jim asked, standing a bit too close behind me.

I leaped into the air, clutched my chest, and turned around. "Don't worry about it."

"Who's this?" Maddie asked, brow arched.

I gave her that *don't ask; he's annoying as hell* look with my eyes, and she immediately snapped her lips closed. Thankfully, the pharmacist called me to the counter next, giving me an easy excuse to get away from him.

After taking my medication from the counter, I grabbed both Maddie's and Piper's hands and pulled them out of the shop without even looking at Jim again. I didn't know what his problem was, and I didn't plan on sticking around to figure it out.

"Please, just drive me far, far away from here," I said to Maddie once we made it to the car. I looked back at the doors to make sure he wasn't following us and sighed when we made it onto the main street alone.

I pulled the package of pills out of the white paper bag and stared at them, unable to believe that I was really doing this. After popping out the first one, I took a deep breath and swallowed it. These next seven days were going to be hell for me.

Because I couldn't have sex, *and* Blaise was going to blackmail the shit out of me.

"I'm taking you home, right?" Maddie said, turning into the slums.

"Yeah, I gotta make sure Mateo's okay."

The moment that Maddie pulled onto my road in the slums, I spotted Blaise's expensive car parked on the side of the road—in front of *my* house. My heart raced in my chest, and I jumped out of the car the second Maddie pulled up to the curb.

"See you tomorrow, I guess." Piper laughed. "Have fun with your boy."

But I wasn't going to have fun.

All I could think about was that Mateo had been home alone and Blaise wasn't in his car, which meant that he was either ... talking to João, who lived across the street, or he was inside my house with Mateo, doing God knew what.

I didn't care what Blaise did to me, but nobody touched my brother.

Chapter Fifteen

VERA

If Blaise had laid a single hand on Mateo, I would—

I shoved the front door open to see Mateo and Blaise sitting on the couch in the middle of a heated game of Raid of Durnbone with fantasy creatures. They were both leaning forward, forearms on their thighs and controllers in their hands, staring and shouting at the TV.

Furrowing my brows, I stared at them with wide eyes. Mateo was one of the least social people ever, had one or maybe two friends at school, and ... didn't really interact with anyone. And now, he was ... playing video games with Blaise?!

What the fuck was happening in my life?

They continued playing the game, so focused that I didn't even think they had seen me. I couldn't comprehend what the hell was going on right now, but one thing was for certain: I didn't want Blaise influencing Mateo in any sort of negative way.

Blaise was a bully, a blackmailer, and a bad boy. He didn't need to focus on school, didn't need to get into a good college. He probably had a job in his family's business lined up for him as soon as he got out of high school.

Mateo and I didn't have shit. We had to work for it. We couldn't get in trouble.

"Mateo," I scolded as I slammed the front door.

Mateo and Blaise both glanced at me for a quick moment but then returned to their game, controlling characters and making attacks on other players and doing whatever the hell they did in video games.

"Can't talk," Mateo said. "Playing."

"You look angry, V," Blaise said, trying out another nickname for me. He took another look at me, full lips curled into a smirk, as he continued to skillfully press buttons on the controller. "I told you that I'd be over later to pick you up."

"You said you'd be over to pick me up, not play video games with my brother," I said through gritted teeth.

Blaise's gaze flickered back to the TV screen for a moment as Mateo jumped into the air and threw his hand up in victory.

"Yes! I've been trying to defeat this boss for weeks now. Thanks, Blaise."

I arched a brow, snatched the controller from Blaise, and grabbed his wrist to pull him to the front door. "*Thanks, Blaise.* Now, it's time to go."

"I'm taking your sister out," Blaise said over his shoulder to Mateo. "Be good, kid."

As soon as we got out the front door, I stopped and crossed my arms. Thankfully, the rain had let up slightly, and it wasn't pouring anymore. I didn't want to go anywhere with him right now. I needed to make sure he hadn't corrupted Mateo with his filthy freaking mouth.

"You can't barge into my house," I said.

Blaise curled his lips into a dangerous smirk. "Mateo invited me to play with him."

"No, he didn't."

"You can ask him, Sunshine." He chuckled slowly, then waggled his finger at me and stepped closer. "That's it."

"That's what?"

"You're always a ray of sunshine."

"Very sarcastic," I said between my teeth. I twirled him around, placed my hands on his muscular back, and pushed him all the way back to his nice-as-hell car that looked so out of place in the slums. "Now, leave."

As I pushed him, Blaise opened the passenger door, turned us around smoothly, and gently nudged me down into the seat. "Good thing you're coming with me, Sunshine, isn't it? I have plans for us tonight."

Before I could try to get out of this mess, he slipped into the driver's seat and locked the car doors. "I don't care if you want to come with me or not. I know your secret, Vera, so you're going to do whatever I say, willing or not."

"So, your plan is to kidnap me?!"

He started the car and pulled off the curb, heading toward the main streets that led away from the slums and toward the rich sector of Redwood. "If you didn't want to be here, you would've hopped out of the car the moment that I shoved you into it."

I crossed my arms and stared ahead through the windshield. *Damn BBS.*

Fifteen minutes later, we pulled into the driveway of a white mansion with a beautiful yard with statues and blooming flowers— even though it was fall. I hesitantly stepped out of the car and followed him into the house.

While I had been to Blaise's place when I was a kid, I didn't remember it being so... *grand.* It might've been almost the same size as Maddie's, but everything here looked so much more *expensive.*

Hand-sculpted ancient statues. Marble floor. Artwork that must've cost millions of dollars each. This place was worth more than every single person in the slums combined—times freaking a hundred.

I walked through the mansion, careful not to touch anything because I'd never be able to pay for it. It was so much grander than I remembered it when Mom used to clean their home when I was a child.

"This is ... your house," I whispered.

Of course it was his house. I just couldn't wrap my head around how some people had so much money and others had to scramble for scraps, like my family. We worked our asses off to make ends meet, and Blaise ... he was handed money. Probably had more than a million in a savings fund and stocks somewhere—wherever rich people kept their money.

Blaise threw his keys down on the entry table, as if he didn't care if it scratched the marble. His family had enough money to have it replaced by tomorrow. Of course he didn't care what he did in his house.

"Yeah," he said, like it didn't matter to him. "Come on. I got your journal in my bedroom."

Lingering by the stairs, I arched a brow at him. "It *would* be in your bedroom."

"Gotta jerk off to it somewhere, Sunshine."

Chapter Sixteen

VERA

When we reached Blaise's room, I stopped at the door and swallowed hard. I hadn't been inside here since I had been a child, and now ... we were alone in this big house, and my body-betraying syndrome was acting up again.

"You coming?" he asked, standing inside his room with his brow arched.

After taking a deep breath, I stepped into the room and looked around. His room wasn't anything like I remembered it. In place of his toy cars and action figures were a shit-ton of posters and black furniture that reminded me of a cross between angsty teen skater-boy and a billion dollars. He had two skateboards thrown onto a black leather couch with red and white stickers on the bottom of the boards.

I left the door open a few inches behind me and walked farther into the room, spotting my notebook on his desk and hurrying over to it. "For once in your freaking life, can you stop stealing my journal?" I asked, snatching the notebook and opening the pages to make sure he hadn't torn any out. When I was certain, I placed it on his desk. "Why didn't you give it back during History?"

"Because I wanted to stroke one out between classes today."

While a small giggle bubbled in the pit of my stomach, I scrunched my nose and forced myself to groan. "Ew." But honestly, the thought of Blaise Harleen, Redwood's certified bad boy, getting off to my writing made me feel some type of way.

Blaise sat on the bed, leaning back on his arms posted on the mattress behind him, his muscles flexing against his black hoodie I tore my gaze away from him, the heat rising in my core.

Don't even think about fucking him. Don't even think about fucking him.

He gently brushed his knuckles against mine, then grabbed my hand and pulled me onto the bed with him. I nearly toppled over into his lap, but he skillfully maneuvered my body so I straddled his waist, as if he had done that with other women countless times.

And I'd bet he had too.

When he dipped his head to kiss my neck, I moaned softly and curled my fingers against his chest. "Blaise, we can't," I whispered, but my words were barely audible, and my panties were already soaked at the thought of him being inside me again.

Blaise answered me by moving his hands up and down my body, touching and groping and kneading every curve on me. He latched his mouth on to my neck and sucked gently, his slight hum making me clench even harder.

"I mean it, Blaise. No sex tonight."

"Oh, come on, Sunshine," he murmured against the crook of my neck. He slipped his fingers under the waistband of my pants and cupped my pussy through my underwear. "These panties are already ruined for me."

"Blaise," I whispered, closing my eyes for a moment and enjoying the way he touched me. I had never been touched by anyone before him, and I was quickly becoming addicted to the way his fingers moved skillfully around my body. "We can't have sex tonight, okay?"

"And why's that? Hmm?"

God, it took everything inside of me to move off him.

But I gathered up all the strength I had left and moved off the bed. He tilted his head up at me, as if he actually wasn't going to push me any further, unlike the way he had during school both times.

I gnawed on the inside of my cheek and shifted uncomfortably from foot to foot. "Because, Blaise, why can't you drop it? It's none of your business anyway. It's a private matter and—"

"Did you just start your period or something?"

"No!"

He moved closer. "Because I don't give a shit. I'll still fuck you."

"Ew, gross," I started, scrunching my nose and staring up at him.

"It's not that gross. It's natural."

Crossing my arms, I hummed to myself and hoped that he would drop it. But of course, that annoying asshole had to keep stepping closer and closer to me, and my BBS was about to kick in.

After taking one final breath, I stepped back and squeezed my eyes closed. "I have to wait a week before we can do anything together. I just got on birth control because of you, okay?"

Chapter Seventeen

BLAISE

"You're on the pill?"

Birth control.

I made Vera Rodriguez get on birth control?

"Yeah, dickhead," she said, crossing her arms and turning away from me. "I'm not risking getting pregnant, especially by a guy like you. I'm better off forcing myself to take a pill every single day for the rest of my life because *you* can't keep it in your pants."

"Oh, come on. I'd be a good father." I laughed. "I'd provide a shit-ton in child support."

While I tried to brush it off as if it were nothing, something stirred inside me. I didn't know why, but nerves bubbled up in the pit of my stomach, and I found myself remembering the last time that Vera had been in my room.

We had been kids at the time when her mother brought her over every Saturday, so she could clean our home. Back in those days, Vera would spend hours here, talking about how big our house was. That was when Mom and Dad started to fucking despise their own son, enough to fire Vera's mom and make me a miserable fucking mess here, alone on the weekends. They had taken away the only few hours of happiness I had every week.

"I don't care about your money," Vera said.

At some point during my little daydream, Vera had crossed the room and put a shit-ton of space between us. She now stood near my window, staring out into the backyard as the moonlight glimmered off her tan face.

"What's the problem then?" I asked, wanting her to continue talking.

When we had been kids, she used to talk for hours and hours and hours while I listened. Now, she barely spoke at all, especially in school.

She pressed her lips together. "You're the problem."

"*I'm the problem*?" I asked, brow raised. "How am I the problem?"

"Because of your attitude."

I held out my arms. "What's wrong with my rock-star attitude?"

She snorted, the corner of her lips curling into the slightest of smiles. She tried to hide it, but I caught the smile.

"Rock star, huh? That's a bit of a stretch. You're more of an arrogant, annoying asshole who feeds off his parents' money. I don't want my son to grow up like that."

And while what she'd said was true and it hurt, I covered up the pain with another lousy joke and hoped that she would drop any talk about my family. I didn't like talking about my parents. "So, you want me to give you a son?"

Vera cut her eyes to me and narrowed her gaze. "Did you not hear a word I said?!"

Oh, I had heard everything she said, but I liked getting her riled up.

"Anyway," she said, turning away from me again and hiding her face behind her brown hair, "don't feel special. I only got on birth control because I don't have the money to keep buying Plan B. It's getting out of hand."

"Isn't it only, like, fifty bucks?"

"Only?!" she said. "It takes me, like, five hours to make that much."

"Shit, really?"

"Yes!"

"I'd pay you that much if you just sat on my dick without complaining."

Vera snapped her head to me again, stormed over with that huffy, puffy attitude that looked sexy as fuck on her, and poked me hard on the chest. "I'm tired of all these little jokes you have tonight. They're not funny."

"They're not meant to be. I'm not kidding."

We stared at each other for a few long moments until Vera's lips curled into another small smile. She turned away to hide it, but I grabbed her arm and forced her to look back at me. When I saw her face, she was grinning from ear to ear and biting her lip to hold back a laugh.

I chuckled softly, not really seeing what was funny, but, fuck, I couldn't stop myself.

After clutching her stomach, she nearly doubled over with laughter. Her body trembled back and forth, the way it had years ago, as tears pricked the corners of her eyes. For the first time in years, she looked genuinely happy.

At least for me, it was the first time that I felt happy. Somewhat.

"I hate you," she said, giggles subsiding. She wiped the tears from the corners of her eyes and walked over to the bed, where she sat down and pulled off her dirty, off-brand Vans. "I hate you so much that it's not even funny."

"You're laughing, aren't you?"

"I'm only laughing because I feel like I'm going insane," she said, but I knew she was lying. She set her shoes neatly beside the bed and wiggled her toes in her pair of turtle socks. "I've been working nonstop lately."

"Mmhmm," I said. "Sure. We'll call it that. It's not because you're insanely attracted to me."

"No." She said the word with so much seriousness that I almost believed her. She looked up at me through huge brown eyes and arched a brow. "You have way too much arrogance for me to be attracted to you."

"What about my dick?"

"What about it?"

"You seemed to be very attracted to it during History today."

"Because you are literally blackmailing me!"

I smiled and shook my head. "Excuses, excuses."

I might've been blackmailing her, but that didn't erase the fact that she had jerked me off under the desk like she had been thinking about me all night. It didn't erase how tight her pussy had clenched on my cock when I told her that I'd come inside her again.

She shifted on my bed uncomfortably and looked back at the notebook on my desk. "Anyway, now that we've established I can't have sex with you for an entire week, I think you should bring me home. We have nothing to do here anyway."

But she had just taken her shoes off. She didn't want to leave now.

"I'm not bringing you home."

"Then, what are we going to do?" she asked.

I pulled out the chair at my desk and nodded to it. "Pull out your computer. We're going to write a scene for your book together."

Chapter Eighteen

VERA

"I don't have a computer," I said quickly, sitting down at the large black marble desk.

I was ashamed that I didn't have more money. Blaise seemed to ... get everything he ever wanted. He didn't even have to ask.

We were lucky that one of Mateo's friends had given him an old Xbox that they weren't using anymore. The most Mom could afford was a nice meal at the local Applebee's for our birthdays, and that counted as our gift.

Instead of pushing it, Blaise stood behind me with one veiny, large hand on the desk and the other on the back of the seat. "Do you really write all your stories by hand and hope that you don't lose them?"

"Yeah." I shrugged. "I mean, the only person who's meant to read them is me."

"You're fucking kidding me, right?" he said.

My cheeks flushed, and all I could seem to think about was how my family couldn't afford a nice laptop to write, because if I could, I would one hundred percent use it so I didn't lose my stories. "No, we can't affor—"

"You don't plan on sharing your stories with anyone ever? Oh, Sunshine ..." He shook his head and flipped through the pages of my notebook. "Have you fucking read this shit? It's hot as fuck. So many women—and men—would thank you for this."

Oh, he was talking about me sharing it. Not me ... not being able to afford shit.

"My dad knows some people in the publishing field. I could send it to them—"

"No."

"Vera, come on. This shit is gold."

"No, Blaise," I said, shaking my head.

The stories I wrote were my own fantasies. Nobody would read them and enjoy them. Blaise only did because he wanted to get into my pants. I'd be so embarrassed if someone actually ... took the time to read each and every smutty scene. How would I explain that to Mom?

"You can publish them under a penname."

"No."

"Why not?"

"Because!" I said in a breath. "They're too embarrassing."

"One chapter."

"No."

"Release one chapter on a free writing website, like Wattpig or Wittpad or whatever the hell that shit is called. If nobody reads it, then nobody reads it. If people like it, then ... you can decide to do whatever the hell you want with it."

After crossing my arms, I stared up at Blaise. "No."

"Then, I'll tell Redwood."

I sucked in a sharp breath and stood from my chair. "You wouldn't."

Blaise chuckled. "Oh, baby, you know that I would." He placed his hands on my shoulders and shoved me down onto the seat, then turned on his desktop computer and opened Google Docs. "You either release a chapter to the world under a pen name or I tell everyone in Redwood that you're a horny little slut who likes to write porn."

Once I wisely made my decision to release my writing under a pen name and *not* risk Redwood finding out what I did in my spare time, I stared at the blank Google document and sucked in a sharp breath.

Blaise opened my notebook to the first page and stepped back. "Why don't you read it aloud as you type? You know, so you don't make any mistakes on your first draft."

I cut my gaze to him and narrowed my eyes. "That's not the reason, is it?"

"I just want to hear how flustered you get." He pointed to the page. "Go ahead."

After swallowing all my embarrassment, I began reading my writing aloud as I typed the page on Blaise's computer. "'*Where do you want my cum?' Aiden asked. 'All over your face with the rest of daddy's friends loads, down your hot little throat...' He dipped his head, mouth against my ear. '...or buried in your cunt?'*" I started, my voice quiet.

"Louder," Blaise ordered from behind me, gently squeezing my shoulders.

"'*Inside me, please,'*" I continued, clenching my sopping cunt harder.

"Come on, Sunshine. I know how loud you can be," he murmured into my ear, moving one of his hands around the front of my throat and the other to my pussy. "You screamed for me in the stairwell today. I want you louder."

When I shuffled my thighs together to ease the tension between them, Blaise pushed them apart and sank his hand between them and into my pants, his fingers immediately finding my clit. I whimpered out and tried hard to focus on the screen.

"We can't ... we can't have sex, Blaise," I whispered.

"We're not going to. All I'm doing is making you feel good," Blaise said. "Now, continue."

"Aiden thrust into me twice more, his hands grasping my waist tightly and his mouth on mine. 'Oh, fuck,'" I continued reading, the heat warming my core and making my brain so numb. *"'Evelyn, you're such a good girl,' Aiden praised. 'Such a good fucking...' He slammed his cock into me and stilled. '...girl.'"*

Blaise sucked on my neck from behind, his fingers moving in circles around my clit. With his other hand, he strummed his fingers across my throat and chuckled darkly. "Fuck, Vera, your voice ..." he growled, sucking on my skin harder. "I'm so fucking hard, listening to you."

A small moan escaped my lips as he smacked my clit with his palm. I furrowed my brows and spread my legs a couple inches wider, aching for him to slip his fingers into me now. I needed it more than ever.

"After a couple moments, Aiden filled my pussy with his warm cum. 'You've done so good,' Aiden whispered into my ear, pushing some cum off my chin," I said in a breath, my nipples hardening under my shirt and sticking right through it. "Oh God, Blaise ... please, more."

Blaise slid his fingers from my clit to my entrance and thrust them into me. I threw my head back again and moaned louder this time, my cunt tightening around him, just the way it'd tightened around his cock this morning.

"More," I breathed. "Give me more."

After he seized my nipple between his other fingers, he tugged on it hard. I tilted my head to the side to give him better access and moaned again, the pressure rising quickly inside me. Heat rushed through my body.

"Don't stop," he murmured into my ear.

"While it was forbidden—wrong even—to be with Aiden Stark, I had known him for months now, slept with him several nights a week, and loved the way he handled me like no other man could, nobody

could find out about us, especially my father," I continued, on the brink of an orgasm.

"Just like you don't want anyone to find out about us, huh?" Blaise mumbled, the stubble on his face tickling my sensitive skin.

My legs trembled uncontrollably, listening to his deep, soothing voice in my ear. I shifted and pushed on his fingers buried inside me. The pressure was almost too much. If he didn't stop, then I was going to come so hard.

"Is that what you want, Vera?" he whispered, pounding his fingers into me. "You want to be treated like a slut? You want me to put a collar around this pretty little throat of yours and call you mine? Shoot my load deep in your pussy?"

Unable to stop myself, I screamed out as my legs jerked up into the air. Wave after wave of pleasure rushed through me at the mere thought of Blaise using me, of me being his little toy.

I might've hated the fact that he was blackmailing me, but I loved it too.

God, I fucking loved it too.

"Sunshine," he said darkly, drawing the word out, "you don't know what you do to me."

Chapter Nineteen

BLAISE

The next morning, I walked down Redwood hallways toward the main hall, where Vera's locker was.

Vera had started birth control for me. *For me.*

Fuck, if that wasn't the hottest fucking thing. I hadn't been able to stop thinking about it—*about her*. She had been so shy to tell me, but the thought of it got me so hard. I wanted to fuck her right then and there. But I couldn't. So, I'd teased her swollen clit all night with my fingers, then jerked the fuck off in my bed three times after I brought her home.

One of the dumb, spoiled brats who lived down the street from me shoved Mateo, Vera's brother, up against the red lockers, his hand curling around Mateo's collar. I picked up my skateboard and stormed over to him, ripping him off Mateo and shoving him back into the lockers.

"What the—" he started, but when he looked up and caught me towering over him, he snapped his pathetic freshman mouth closed. Fear flashed through his wide eyes, and that punk shut the fuck up real quick.

"What the fuck are you doing?" I growled.

A small group of freshmen gathered around us, but I didn't give a fuck. They could call the teachers, the principal, the dean, whoever they fucking wanted, but nobody was going to do shit about me bullying this kid the same way he had been bullying Mateo.

"Teaching this nerd a lesson."

I chuckled coldly. "What a fucking cliché you are."

The kid puffed out his chest and pushed his hands against mine, as if he thought he'd be all tough in front of his friends and try to fight me here. I had bruised his sorry-ass ego, and I didn't give a fuck. This kid would have to learn one day.

"You lay one fucking hand on me *or* on Mateo again," I said, gripping his collar and yanking him closer to me, "and I'll break every one of your bones, you punk-ass bitch. Don't even think about running back to your mommy and daddy either. They don't give a shit about you. You understand me?"

He pulled his hands away from me and gritted his teeth, but he didn't say a word.

So, I pulled him closer. "Do you fucking understand me? You don't fucking touch him."

"Fuck, I understand."

After glaring at him for another moment, I shoved him into the lockers and looked back to Mateo, who was straightening himself out and was now surrounded by a couple of popular sophomore girls.

As the punk stormed down the hallway, I nodded toward Mateo. "You good?"

"I'm fine."

"You're bleeding," one of the girls said, eyeing Mateo's nose.

"Go get him cleaned up," I said to her, throwing a wink back at Mateo and hoping he got my drift.

That kid barely had any friends and was awkward as fuck around girls, it seemed. He smiled slightly, then disappeared into another hallway with the girls and another geeky kid who looked to be like his friend.

Walking into the main hallway, I caught sight of Vera. Chocolate-brown hair cascading down her back, brown eyes wide, lips curled into a soft smile as she looked into her locker. I stopped and swallowed hard, then shook my head.

The fuck is happening to me?

Last night hadn't meant shit. Last night, I had only wanted to use her to feel good. That was why I had driven all the way down into the slums, spent hours playing video games with Mateo, then brought her back to my place.

No other fucking reason.

With my skateboard clutched to my side, I walked down the hallway and tried hard not to stare at her. She hadn't even noticed me, wasn't even looking for me, didn't even give a shit about me. All she cared about was me not ruining her reputation.

Before I could make it another step, someone grabbed my wrist and yanked me into a janitor's closet. A moment later, the single dim overhead light bulb turned on. Skylar stood in front of me with her arms crossed over her chest in the most unflattering light ever.

"What the fuck are you doing?" I asked.

"Sorry, I didn't think you wanted the entire school to know you're hanging with Vera Rodriguez, Redwood scum." She cackled and smirked at me, like I fucking cared. "You are trying to keep it a secret, aren't you?"

"Of course I'm hanging with her," I said, trying to brush it off quickly. "She's my fucking partner for the History project. What the fuck do you expect me to do? Let her do it all by herself?"

"Yes," Skylar said, strumming her manicured nails on her elbow and stepping closer to me in this already-cramped space. "I do because I know you, Blaise. I know that you don't give a fuck about school or your grades or anyone but yourself because your mommy and daddy don't give a shit about you."

Her words fucking hurt. She knew exactly what to say to get to me.

I stepped back against the trash bin. "What the fuck do you want, Skylar?"

She moved even closer to me, and I had nowhere to fucking go unless I wanted my ass to be covered with garbage for the rest of the day.

She placed one of her hands on my abdomen. "I want you to be honest with me."

"I fucking a—" I started. When she moved her hand down my abdomen to my belt, I shoved her back into the shelves with cleaning supplies and paper towels. "Get the fuck off me, you bitch."

"Or what?" she asked, stepping between me and the door. "Are you going to hit me?"

"I'm not fucking playing, Skylar. Move."

"No."

After gritting my teeth, I ran a hand through my hair. "You want to know what my fucking problem is? I never said that I fucking liked you, and you're acting like we're dating. I don't gotta explain shit to you. What's *your* fucking problem lately?"

Skylar crossed her arms. "That bitch is my problem. She's scum."

"You're the fucking scum!" I shouted, wanting to get it through that empty head of hers.

"You're the one who has been leading me on for months now."

"Bro, I'm not fucking having this conversation with you right now," I said, stepping toward her, about to shove her out of the way again.

But this fucking bitch knew what I was going to do, and she moved right in front of me, actually stepped closer, and kissed me.

Chapter Twenty

VERA

After Blaise had forced me to release a chapter of my super-smutty book online, I had been anxiously visiting the website on my phone all morning to see if anyone had read it. It was currently sitting at thirty-two views on the first chapter and had one comment that read, *More, please!!!*

I stared at my screen and grinned, heart racing. Never in a million years had I thought anyone would want to actually read my writing or want more of it. It was only one chapter, but ... it had taken so much courage to put it out there. I hadn't even let Maddie read any yet.

Once I forced myself to shove my phone into my pocket and vow not to check it until lunch—otherwise, I'd become obsessive—I did the combination for my locker and opened it up to grab books for my classes.

One by one, I aimlessly pulled out the books and held them against my hip. Honestly, I hadn't been able to stop thinking about last night at all. Blaise had brought me home only minutes before

Mom got home from her double shift, and I'd kinda, sorta actually had a good time with him.

Only problem was, now, I had to keep Blaise away from Mateo. I didn't need him to influence my brother in any way, shape, or form. Mateo had goals and needed to stay focused on getting out of this shitty town for good. Neither of us could stand it.

Some rowdy freshmen and sophomores walked down the hallway. I glanced over my shoulder to see Mateo and his friend right along with them. My eyes nearly popped out of my fucking head at the sight. Mateo rarely talked to *anyone*.

"Mateo?" I called down the hallway toward my brother.

He stood in the middle of a small group of freshmen and sophomores. My stomach tightened because, well, Mateo didn't have many friends to start with, and I didn't want him to get bullied. Redwood was filled with roaches dressed as people.

"Mateo!"

After I shouted for him a second time, he looked over his shoulder at me and grinned. Grinned! Mateo was socializing with people who I'd consider to be the popular crowd, and he looked as if he was enjoying it. I didn't know how to feel.

"What?" he asked.

"Are you okay?"

"Yeah, I'm good."

And with that, the first bell rang, and he disappeared in the sea of Redwood students. I waited for a few moments, then turned back toward my locker to gather the rest of my books for the first few periods.

Ever since last night, I couldn't get my mind off Blaise. I hadn't liked the way he was looking at me, or the way he reacted when I told him I got on birth control for him, or the way he touched me like he owned me, the way he ... made me come over and over and over last night.

Gah, I was fucking losing it.

Nerves zipped through my body. I glanced down the hallway

toward the main doors, where he always sauntered in, and bit the inside of my cheek when I didn't see him. He was late, as usual, but I ... I thought I had seen his car parked in the student lot when I came in.

Was I disappointed that he wasn't here? No. Definitely not. At least, this way, he wouldn't bother me and draw attention to us before first period. Hell, I could barely get through yesterday after he took me into the stairwell.

Once more and more people started to clear the hallways, I found myself lingering at my locker. Waiting. Just freaking waiting for him to show up. I knew that if I stood here long enough, until right before the second bell rang and I was supposed to be in Biology, he'd show. He always did, didn't he?

As the second bell rang, I cursed under my breath for how stupid I had been. What the hell was I doing here, waiting for Blaise Harleen? Why'd I feel something last night? It wasn't like it'd meant anything to him. He had only been looking for a quick fuck.

I quickly closed my locker and hurried down the hallway toward Biology. This would be the first time I was late for that class, and the teacher was *beyond* terrifying sometimes. I just hoped that—

Before I could turn the corner to head toward the science wing, a janitor's closet door swung open. Skylar, the fucking slut, sauntered out of the small, dimly lit room with her blonde hair wild, wiping off some spit from the corner of her red-stained lips.

She looked me up and down, her lips curling into a smirk. "Hey, Vera."

When my name left her lips, my stomach dropped. I found myself turning my gaze from Skylar to the janitor's closet, where Blaise fucking Harleen walked out with red lipstick on the corner of his mouth.

My fingers felt numb, weak. The books slipped from my hands and smacked hard against the tiled floor, the sound echoing through Redwood's empty halls. Blaise looked over at me, his hard eyes widening.

"Vera," he breathed out, looking between Skylar and me.

Stupid, innocent Vera had thought that there was something between them. Stupid, innocent Vera had gotten played like the many, many, many characters she had written about these past few years. Stupid, innocent Vera had fallen for the bad boy and was now suffering the consequences.

I didn't know if I was even breathing.

Blaise shook his head. "It's not what it looks like, I swear. I fucking swear to you."

Head spinning, I pressed my lips together so they wouldn't tremble, and then I scrambled to pick up my books and sprinted down the hallway toward Biology. Why had I been so stupid, creating a fucking fantasy in my head, thinking that I meant something more to him than a lousy hookup?

Blaise Harleen didn't date and wasn't faithful. Blaise Harleen fucked any girl he wanted, whenever he wanted, however he wanted. I probably wasn't even the only girl in this fucking school that he was blackmailing.

Blaise Harleen was nothing to me. At least, he couldn't be anymore.

Chapter Twenty-One

BLAISE

"Vera, wait up!" I shouted, jogging after her down the hallway.

Holding her books to her chest, Vera moved her short legs faster, her chocolate-brown hair flowing behind her shoulders. When I caught up to her, she had her gaze focused on the ground and pushed some hair into her face.

"Let me explain."

"No," she said sharply. "There's nothing to explain, Blaise."

"I didn't do anything. I swear."

Suddenly, she stopped and snapped her head up toward me. Tears had welled in her big eyes, and a heap of guilt rushed through me. I never felt guilt or shame or any-fucking-thing anymore, but ... she was upset. *I* had made her upset.

Skylar appeared at the end of the hallway, where we had come from, with her arms crossed over her chest and a menacing smirk on her ugly face. "He's lying to you, Vera. He always lies. He wanted a quickie before school."

"Shut the fuck up!" I shouted.

That bitch loved fucking up my life for no fucking reason at all lately. I didn't know what the hell her problem was because I had made it crystal fucking clear that I didn't want her anymore. Multiple times.

Could she not take the fucking obvious hints?

Vera didn't move an inch as Skylar strutted down the hallway toward us. When she passed us, she went to brush her fingers across my shoulder, but I pulled myself far away from her, so she couldn't touch me again.

"Don't cry about it," Skylar called over her shoulder to Vera. "He's always been this way."

I balled my hands into fists and gritted my teeth, wanting to follow that bitch down the hallway and take her out. Like all the other rich, bratty kids from Redwood, she didn't understand the words *no* or *stop* or *I don't fucking want you.*

They didn't exist in our vocabulary.

But, fuck, I wanted to finally show her what they meant.

Once she disappeared into a classroom, I turned back to Vera, who was quiet.

"You have lipstick on the corner of your lips," she said, voice so fragile that one little thing would make it shatter. "Don't try to gaslight me. I'm not like the other girls you fool around with in Redwood. I'm not going to take that shit."

When she turned away, I grabbed her wrist and twirled her back around until she faced me. I was desperate for her to believe me, for her to forgive me for what Skylar had done. I didn't want Vera to hate me.

"*She* kissed *me*," I said desperately, clarifying what I had meant and moving closer to her, only for her to step back even farther. I didn't mean to make it seem like nothing had happened. I just wanted her to know that … "I didn't kiss her back."

Vera pressed her full lips together and furrowed her brows, yanking her wrist out of my hold. Instead of walking away, like I thought she would again, she tugged her books closer to her chest. "I'm a fool for letting you use me. A fucking fool."

"You're not a fool. Please," I pleaded, never having sounded so desperate before. I didn't want anything so badly that it hurt me, that I had to beg for it and try not to be a fucking asshole. "I didn't do anything back."

Vera pursed her lips.

"You don't believe me."

"Why should I?" she shouted, fury raging in her eyes now. She looked around and stepped closer, poking me hard right in the center of my chest and lowering her voice to a loud whisper. "All you've done these past few days is blackmail me and fuck me."

"That's not true. We didn't do that shit last night."

"If I hadn't told you no, then you would've."

"Because you're hot as fuck, Sunshine."

"No," Vera said, cutting me off and gritting her teeth. "First of all, don't call me that anymore. I don't like it and don't want someone like *you* giving me a nickname. Second, don't fucking lie to me anymore. You could have anyone in this freaking hellhole of a school. I'm not hot as fuck. I'm not cute as fuck. Go fuck Skylar."

And with that, she twirled around and hurried down the hallway again.

I rushed behind her. "You don't get to say whether I think you're attractive or not, Vera."

"Yes, I do because guys like *you* don't ever think girls like me are attractive!" she said, loud enough this time that I bet everyone in the nearest classrooms had heard it. "That's not how this life works. It only happens that way in books and movies. And even then ..." She paused, her chin quivering. "Even then, it's all fake, fiction, and make-believe."

While I wanted to grab her hands and tell her that ... that it wasn't fake to me—because Vera was undeniably the sexiest girl here at Redwood—I knew that she wouldn't believe me, nor would she let me touch her again.

"You have lipstick on your fucking mouth," she said, her voice softer again. She stared up at me, at the lipstick that must've been smeared all over my lips because Skylar couldn't take no for an answer. The tears in Vera's eyes wavered. "All over you." Her voice was barely above a whisper.

Every word that came out of her mouth hurt more and more. I didn't know what to say or how to make her believe me. I didn't want ... I didn't want to lose her. She was the only person who paid attention to me and the only girl who I ...

Who I actually kinda, sorta fucking liked.

Even though I hadn't done anything, all I could feel was shame and guilt, emotions that I'd thought I didn't have anymore, not since Mom and Dad had stopped caring about me and I'd stopped caring about the fucking world.

One last time, she turned on her heel and walked down the hallway.

I should've done more to stop Skylar. I should've pushed her away the moment that she dragged me into the janitor's closet.

"Please," I whispered as she disappeared into her Biology classroom.

But it was too late.

I needed to do more. I needed her to see that, no matter how hard I tried to hide my emotions and feelings behind this blackmail shit, I fucking couldn't. I hadn't been able to stop thinking about Vera since the day my parents had fired her mother.

Chapter Twenty-Two

VERA

Rain poured outside. I stood behind the counter at the library and aimlessly checked out books for people while Sue talked my ear off about her sister in the nursing home. Usually, I loved chatting with her, but I couldn't focus today.

Not when Blaise sat on the black couch across from me, waiting for my shift to finish. He had already tried to talk to me twice today while I worked hard for my money, and I had done my best to ignore him. So, now, he sat there, doing nothing.

Nothing.

I didn't want to see him anymore.

All day, I hadn't been able to stop feeling like a complete loser for believing that there had been something more between us. Last night, I had ... thought I felt something more, something happy. But it was all a fucking lie. No matter how hard I tried, I couldn't get the image of Skylar's red lipstick smeared all over his lips out of my head.

"Next!" I called, staring at the monitor and clicking through a few screens.

"Busy today?" João Rocha said.

"What are you doing here?" I asked him, raising a brow. "I can't babysit now."

João placed a couple of princess books in front of me. "Checking out books for my sister." He placed a tattooed forearm on the counter, leaned against it, and looked over my shoulder at Blaise, who looked pissed off now. "I heard what happened."

"What do you mean?" I asked, scanning the books.

"You and Blaise."

I gritted my teeth. "How the fuck did you hear about what happened?"

But in all seriousness, I couldn't believe that everyone knew now. I didn't want anyone to know that I had gotten tangled with Redwood's bad boy. That wasn't how shit worked in my stories. There was always more buildup before the big blowout. I should've had more time.

"Word gets around," he said, looking back at me and flashing me a smirk that nobody should ever trust. Smirks from bad boys *never* got good girls anywhere. "But I can make the rumor die down, if you babysit tomorrow night."

After rolling my eyes, I pushed the books toward him. "There is no rumor, is there?"

João chuckled. "Not yet, but you know that Skylar is about to let it rip."

While I might've been safe for now, João wasn't wrong. I'd have maybe until tomorrow morning before the entire school knew that I had been fucking Blaise Harleen. Then, everyone would wonder why the fuck he wanted me.

Hell, I wondered about it too.

Compared to some of these Redwood girls, I looked like a stick of deodorant. I wasn't stick thin like them, didn't have the perfect body or smile or the clearest skin. And, God, I could barely have a normal conversation with someone without getting flustered.

"Fine," I said between gritted teeth and glanced over at Blaise, who now had his hands balled into tight fists and looked like he wanted to rip João's head off his body. "I'll babysit, but you have to promise me that you'll do more than shut her up."

João's smirk widened. "What're we talking?"

"I don't know," I said, not wanting to know what he'd do. "And I don't want to know what you plan to do with her or how you plan to shut her up. I hate her and want her to stop fucking with me."

"Will do. She tried to fuck with Landon last year anyway. She deserves what's coming to her." João smacked the counter, grabbed his books, and walked toward the doors. "Good talk," he shouted over his shoulder, then looked directly at Blaise, as if they had some kind of beef with each other. "See you tomorrow night, V."

I blew out a frustrated breath, knowing that he was going to get me in a shit-ton of trouble one day, and called for the next person in line. And lo and behold, CVS man stood in front of me with a wide grin.

"Getting around, are we?"

"I'm not in the mood for you," I said, snatching his engineering books from him.

"Of course you're not." He nodded in João's and Blaise's direction. "You got two bad boys fawning over you."

Scrunching my nose, I scanned his books. "First of all, gross. Second, I'm almost a hundred percent certain that they both have girlfriends." Or whores, in Blaise's case. Skylar wasn't the type of girl to be chained down, even to Redwood's bad boy.

"Does that mean you're single?" he asked.

After cutting my gaze to him, I clenched my jaw. From the corner of my eye, I saw Blaise looking over at us now that João had disappeared through the exit. And as bad of an idea as this was, I wanted to get back at him.

So, I swallowed the bile that had risen in my throat at the thought of flirting with Jim and nodded. "Yeah, I'm single. Why?" I asked loud enough for Blaise to hear without seeming too suspicious.

It wasn't like it actually mattered though, because Blaise didn't like me like that. He only wanted to get into my pants. I just hoped flirting with this annoying bastard would make me feel better about myself.

Jim rested both his forearms against the counter. "Because I want to take you out."

I slid his books across the counter and leaned toward him. "Yeah?"

Jim smiled—and not one of those fake smirks, but an actual, genuine smile. "Yeah."

Blaise still stared at us. I didn't know what had come over me, but I wanted to take it up another notch. I wanted to hurt him, like the way I felt so fucking hurt right now. It wasn't fair to me that he'd used me.

"I close up at nine tonight," I said, brushing my finger against his forearm and trying not to cringe at how awkward I felt. This was how the girls flirted in my stories. It had to be somehow hot, right? After convincing myself that I wasn't being totally gross, I smiled. "But I do have a break in fifteen minutes, if you want to wait."

"How long is your break?"

"Long enough."

Chapter Twenty-Three

VERA

When Jim actually decided to wait for my break, I anxiously tapped the counter. What the fuck had I done? Why was he actually waiting? I'd just wanted to flirt with him a little. I hadn't thought he would actually take something like that seriously.

What would happen when I took my break? Would he actually want to go into a back room and fuck me? That was what I had insinuated, but I ... I didn't know what the hell had been going through my head. I just wanted Blaise to feel like shit.

Jim walked around the library with his books for a couple minutes, then took a seat on the couch next to Blaise. With his jaw clenched and eyes narrowed at the kid, Blaise looked more furious than ever.

He said something to Jim that I couldn't quite hear. Jim looked over at him, at me, then said a few words back. All of a sudden, Blaise grabbed Jim by the upper arm, yanked him into the air, and dragged him, stumbling, to the doors.

They stepped out for a few moments, and I secretly hoped that

Jim wouldn't come back inside for the rest of the night. I didn't want Blaise to hurt him, but I definitely didn't want to feel obligated to have sex with him today.

I stared at the front doors, hoping to catch a glimpse of them outside on the sidewalk. But rain poured down so hard and so loud that I couldn't even see or hear any talking or yelling, which made my stomach turn.

"Sweetheart," Sue said, nudging my arm. "You can have your break now. When you come back, I have to leave to see my sister. Will you be okay with closing alone tonight? I know you always do it, but I like to try to stay behind as much as I can for you."

"I'll be okay," I said to Sue, smiling at her. "Thanks."

After grabbing my phone, I disappeared into the break room and locked the door behind me. Outside, rain pounded down on the roof even harder. Because I could barely see outside anyway, I pulled down the blinds and grabbed a cookie from a tray that Sue had brought earlier.

It was the only thing that I had to eat for dinner. I had emotionally eaten the snack I'd packed during lunch because I needed to get my mind off Blaise. I hadn't been able to think clearly all day because of him.

Collapsing at the back table, I checked my phone to see twenty new notifications since three o'clock about the chapter I had released online last night. More people had commented, asking when the next chapter would be released, and I ... felt so giddy.

For the first time today, I let myself smile.

Quite a few people had actually enjoyed my story, something that I'd *never* thought would happen. Maybe tomorrow, I'd have to type a couple chapters up on my phone while I watched João's little sister.

Once I finished my break, I took a deep breath and walked behind the counter. With his hair wet, Blaise sat on the couch alone, like nothing had even happened outside. When he saw me, he tapped his shoe on the ground impatiently.

I tore my gaze away from him, hoping he was pissed and hurt, and walked behind the counter.

Sue pulled on her raincoat and placed a shaky hand on my shoulder. "You can have the rest of those cookies. Be careful tonight. There's supposed to be a big storm. You should close a bit earlier than usual."

"I'll be fine," I said, smiling. "Have a good time with your sister."

Sue held her purse tightly in her hands as she walked past Blaise. When she reached the door, she looked back at me and waved. "Bye, sweetheart. Be safe tonight. I'll see you on Monday."

When Sue left, Blaise stood and made a beeline for me. I slid behind the counter and busied myself with checking in hundreds of books and pretending like I didn't see anyone at the counter. Nobody else was here now anyway.

"Who the fuck was that kid?"

I glanced up at him. "What kid?"

"Don't fuck around with me," he growled. "The guy you were fucking flirting with."

"Who, Jim?" I said, unsure of what the hell was happening to me because I'd never had the type of confidence to piss off someone like Blaise like this. "Oh, I've just been talking to him for a few days now."

"You're fucking bullshitting me."

"I'm not lying," I said, pushing back my shoulders and staring him right in the eye. "I met him at the store while I was buying Plan B because *you'd* had to be an asshole. He helped me find the best one and told me he wanted to take me out."

Jealousy mixed with ... hurt crossed Blaise's face. He shook his head. "You're lying."

"Why do you think he was waiting for my break?"

"You're fucking lying," he ground out, balling his hands into tight fists.

"He's studying to be an engineer," I said, coming up with the most ridiculous excuse for those library books. "He's so smart, witty, and he's actually going to make himself someone someday. He doesn't have to rely on his daddy's money."

As soon as the words came out of my mouth, guilt washed through me. I hated hurting people intentionally, but I couldn't stop. I shouldn't have said what I had said to him. I was jealous that he had all the money in the world and I had to work at a lousy library instead of doing what I loved every day.

He stared down at the counter, eyes shifting back and forth, and didn't say anything for a while. The more time that went by, the worse I felt. His jaw twitched.

"Tell me that you're lying," he said, voice quieter.

While I had wanted to hurt him, I now felt really freaking bad. Blaise usually always had something harsh to say to me. He wasn't this quiet with his words ever, and I didn't like it.

Not wanting to hurt him more—because I didn't like the way I felt when people hurt me—I stared down at the counter and pressed my lips together. If I kept talking or if I answered him, I knew I'd say something that I didn't really mean.

But he had kissed another girl today. He had let her touch him after he was with me last night, after ... spending time with me and encouraging me to release a chapter of my story online. I'd thought for a second he actually cared.

"You should go," I finally found the courage to say.

"I'm not leaving." Blaise shook his head, turned around, and walked back to the couch. He pulled on a pair of Apple AirPods Max, the kind that all the rich kids wore in the halls, and took out his laptop. "I don't have shit to go home to anyway."

Chapter Twenty-Four

BLAISE

Thunder rumbled through the library, a flash of lightning igniting the darkness outside the windows. I sat on a cheap-as-fuck black couch and edited a skateboarding video that I had taken at the skatepark last weekend on my laptop.

No matter how much Vera wanted me to leave, I refused to go anywhere. It wasn't like anyone was waiting for me back home. Here, Vera was actively ignoring me, which meant that she ... cared. At least, a little, right?

I glanced up from my computer toward the front counter. Vera scribbled on a scrap piece of paper, biting her lip and grinning softly. Fuck if she cared about me—probably not—because she was happy now while she wrote.

Tabbing over from my editing software to the bookmarked website where she had posted her story last night, I scrolled through the comments. She'd better have been checking this out, too, today because people wanted more.

I wanted more too. But ... not only of her stories.

I wanted to plead with her so badly because ... I didn't want her to hate me. I didn't want her to think that I was useless and that I wasn't going anywhere, that I would rely on my father's money for the rest of my life.

My parents already thought that I wasn't going anywhere in life because I loved skateboarding and rejoiced in royally pissing them off. Dad had even told me that I would never see a penny of his money when I finished high school if I didn't follow in his footsteps and take over the family business. But he didn't know that I planned on getting out of this freaking town as soon as I could.

His money made my life easier, but I didn't want to look at numbers and talk with clients all fucking day long. Hell, I didn't even know what he did all the time with all these solo vacations he took without my mother.

I tabbed back to my video editing software to rewatch the video I had taken, making sure that it didn't show my face. If Dad knew that I uploaded these stupid fucking videos on YouTube—because it was what I loved doing—he'd try to shut it down immediately.

When a young kid walked up to the counter with his mother, Vera quickly hid her smutty story and tossed some brown hair over her shoulder. She scanned the three books and waved them out of the library. With the storm outside, those were the last few people here, but Vera still had about two hours until she closed.

Suddenly, thunder crashed through the night, and the library went dark. I pulled off my headphones and heard Vera gasp softly. When I went to stand, Vera turned on her phone's flashlight and disappeared into a back room, mumbling something about candles.

I followed behind her, maneuvering between carts of books and counters. She rummaged through a closet, trying to hold her phone steady while searching for the candles and a lighter.

"I know she keeps these back here."

"Let me bring you home," I said behind her.

She jumped into the air, flashing the light at me and holding a hand over her heart. "You scared me half to death. You shouldn't be back here, and I can't leave. I have work to finish before my shift ends tonight."

I shielded my face from the blinding light. "Your coworkers can finish it in the morning."

"No."

"Vera, the lights are out, and I doubt this place has a generator."

"It doesn't."

"Let me bring you home."

"No," she said, moving toward a window. "I can barely see three feet in front of me while standing inside, Blaise. You're not going to be able to drive in this. And besides, you're not driving me home tonight. I'll call Maddie."

"The fuck you mean, you'll call Maddie?" I snapped, trying so fucking hard not to get pissed at her. "I'm here with you now. You're really going to call Maddie to take you home in this kind of weather?"

Truthfully, I just wanted to be the one who brought her home. I hadn't ever felt like I had last night with anyone else. We hadn't even had sex. The only time I felt anything anymore was when I fucked, and even then ... it was becoming mindless and meaningless.

Another crack of thunder rumbled through the library. Vera moved closer to me, her brows furrowing. The corner of my lips curled up. "You're not still afraid of thunder and lightning, are you?"

Vera began rummaging through the closet again. "Don't be ridiculous."

"You used to be."

She paused. "How do you know that?"

"Because we used to be friends."

"Friends?" She seemed to linger on the word, or maybe it was all in my head. "We were never friends, Blaise. Maybe acquaintances. But that was until your parents fired my mom for no reason at all and left us with no source of income."

But my parents had had a reason—me.

They didn't want me to be friendly with kids poorer than us.

They thought Vera and her family were dirty and disgusting people for me to play with. They wanted me to loathe my fucking life so much, like their sorry asses did.

And it'd worked.

Still, I didn't want to tell her that it was all my fault.

"Not friends?" I asked, spotting the candles on the top shelf. In the cramped space, I moved closer to her and reached over her short frame to grab as many candles as I could. Hearing her say that stung like a motherfucker.

With her back still turned, she tensed and glanced up at me. The dim light of her phone's flashlight slightly illuminated her face. She puckered her lips and swallowed hard, staring up at me. I placed the candles down behind her, our bodies still close. Fuck, I didn't want to move.

"No," she whispered, not moving either. "Not friends."

I clenched my jaw and stared down at her, wanting nothing more than for her to take it back. How could she fucking think of us as *maybe acquaintances*? What the fuck did that even mean? She'd loved visiting, fucking loved it.

"You're lying," I growled.

Vera didn't say anything.

Instead, she shifted her body, so she faced away from me and grabbed the candles. Still, she didn't move away and back into the library. I stepped closer to her and placed my hands on the table on either side of her body, trapping her.

"You're lying," I murmured, dipping my head to her ear. "Tell me you're lying."

She sucked in a breath and tensed, crossing her arms and trying to make herself smaller, as if that would stop me. Thunder cracked again, and she jumped back against my chest, a soft whine coming from her mouth.

I inhaled the scent of strawberry shampoo lingering in her hair. "Tell me."

"No," she whispered.

"Tell me," I said, moving my lips closer to her neck. They were millimeters away now.

I wanted to kiss her. God, I wanted to kiss her so fucking badly.

She didn't move away from me, like I'd expected. Instead, she seemed to move closer to me, touching me more, making my heart race like a motherfucker. She clutched the candles and stared down at the small space between her and the table.

Unable to stop myself, I pressed my body against her from behind. I wanted to be even closer to her. I couldn't stop the feeling that I had last night, in my room, watching her type away on my keyboard. Fuck, she did something to me, and I didn't know if I should like it.

"No." She suddenly squeezed her eyes closed and tensed harder. "N-no, Blaise, I can't. I can't. I ... I can't stop thinking about what happened during school today." She pulled away from me and hurried toward the front again. "We're ... we're not friends. We can't be."

Chapter Twenty-Five

VERA

An hour of ignoring Blaise later, my phone began buzzing from text messages in my friends' group chat. For most of the night, my phone had been fairly quiet—except a single message from João, reminding me that I was watching his sister tomorrow.

Piper: I know that Blaise is being an idiot ...

I pressed my lips together, waiting for Maddie to chime in about how this was excitement and how I was living life and collecting experiences. But I didn't want to hear that right now. If they were going to *try* to make me not be annoyed with him, their excuse was going to have to be good.

Piper: But Mateo was getting bullied during school today, and Blaise stopped it.

No way. No freaking way that happened.

Maddie: I heard that too.

Quickly, I peeked a glance at a pissed-off Blaise, then returned to my phone.

Piper: And I saw Mateo hanging with some sophomore girls too.

And while I wanted to believe that she was lying—that they were both lying to convince me not to be angry with the biggest Redwood asshole—I had seen Mateo hanging out with more friends than usual today.

Maddie: He's way more awk than you, V.

Maddie: Do you think he really scored those girls himself??

I stared at our group chat, then glanced up at Blaise. He still stared at his laptop and was blasting angsty pop punk music through his headphones so loudly that I could hear it from here. While I felt bad, I didn't want to believe that he had stopped someone from bullying Mateo.

Blaise did the bullying. He didn't stop it.

When Blaise looked up at me, I tore my gaze away and slipped my phone into my back pocket. I didn't want to waste my battery in case Mateo called and needed me to come home as soon as possible.

Deciding to busy myself, I wheeled a cart of books through the library and continued putting them back onto their designated shelves with the help of a couple candles and a flashlight I'd found in the back room.

It took me fifteen minutes longer than usual tonight, but I had put away all the books in this empty library and could finally go home early. From the window, the rain looked like it was letting up slightly. I could at least see outside now.

After wheeling the cart back to the front, I nodded to Blaise. "I'm going home," I said, though I doubted he could hear me over his music.

He pulled off his headphones and closed his laptop. "I'm driving you."

"Skylar's probably waiting for you," I said emotionlessly, like the mere thought of her didn't irk me.

"I don't have plans with anyone, except you."

I didn't want to blindly believe him. I didn't want to get hurt.

"I'm bringing you home, Vera," he said, using my real name and not the nickname that he had given me.

In a fit of anger, I had told him not to use it earlier, but I hadn't meant it.

While I wanted to refuse, I didn't want to walk home in this storm. It might've cleared up a bit, but it was still pouring down outside. All my textbooks in my backpack would get soaked and ruined. And I didn't have money to replace them.

"Okay."

Immediately, he shoved his laptop in his backpack and stood up, helping me blow out the candles. I hurried around the library to make sure we had gotten every single one of them, then returned to the front, where Blaise stood at the doors, holding my backpack in one hand and an umbrella in his other.

Neither of us said a word during the car ride to my place. I shifted uncomfortably in my seat, glancing over at how tightly his hand gripped the steering wheel, the veins bulging against his skin.

I hate him. I hate him. I hate him. I repeated the mantra to myself, forcing myself to look away and to *not* feel anything at the mere thought of those hands running all over my body again. But every time I closed my eyes, I couldn't forget the way he'd touched me.

When he pulled up to the curb, I let out a long breath and opened my door.

Holding an umbrella over our heads, Blaise walked me to the front door and handed me my backpack.

As soon as we stepped onto the doormat, Mateo flung the front door open and grinned. "Hey, Blaise."

"What's up, kid?" Blaise said.

Mateo awkwardly rubbed his shoulder. "I wanted to thank you for earlier at school."

Blaise tensed and nodded. "It's cool."

I glanced up at Blaise, heart racing. "What happened?" I asked, even though Piper and Maddie had told me what they thought had happened. But I wanted to see what Blaise would say because I expected him to boast and brag about helping out my brother, in order to get closer to me.

"Nothing," Blaise said, shrugging and staying quieter than usual. "Just some kids."

Mateo looked between us. "Well, I gotta finish my homework. I'll leave you guys alone."

But that kid usually had his homework done as soon as he got home, so he could play video games all night and not worry about stopping because Mom and *I* were on his ass about getting his work done.

When Mateo left, I turned toward Blaise. "Someone was bullying my brother today, and you stopped it, didn't you?"

Blaise shifted uncomfortably. "It's nothing, Vera."

"Stop calling me that," I snapped.

Blaise widened his eyes. "What do you want me to call you?"

I threw my hands up into the air. "I don't know, but not that."

"Not your name?"

God, he was getting on my nerves.

"Can you be normal for once?! Where has the unapologetic, arrogant-as-fuck, dirty-talking Blaise gone?" I asked, staring up at him, unsure of anything that I wanted anymore.

He had been on me all day, apologizing, and now … this? *This?!*

"What do you want me to say to you?" he asked, his voice almost desperate.

Truthfully, I didn't know what I wanted anymore. Did I want him or not? Did I like him or not? Was it attention from a boy that was making me all excited, or was it *his* attention that really drew me to him?

Suddenly, Mom appeared behind him, holding her hand over her head to stop the rain, though that did nothing. She was already soaked from head to toe, her black hair clinging to her face and neck. "Vera, who's this?"

Blaise stepped aside, moving the umbrella over her as well. I looked at him as he looked at me, his dark brown eyes softer than usual. I didn't know what he wanted to say to me, but his voice sounded so fragile again.

"Nobody," Blaise said, stepping back when Mom walked into the house to get out of the rain. His word cut like a knife in my broken heart. He looked over at me and moved back another step toward his car. "Not even a friend."

Chapter Twenty-Six

VERA

Blaise slipped into his sports car and turned on the car. A wall of rain might've separated us, but I could fucking feel how hurt he was by those last few words he had said to me. I gripped the door, wanting nothing more than to run over to him.

"Vera," Mom called behind me.

I stood at the door and frowned as Blaise pulled away from the curb and sped down the roads in the Redwood slums. He had come all the way down here not because he wanted to, not because he had to, but because of *me*.

"Who was that?" Mom asked, glancing over my shoulder. "He looked familiar."

"Who?" Mateo asked, walking out of his bedroom and grabbing some food that Mom had brought back for us from the diner that she'd worked a double at yet again tonight. He stole a handful of fries and stuck one in his mouth.

"The boy who just left."

I stood at the front door and looked back at Mateo, hoping he wouldn't say anything. I didn't want to hear Blaise's name again tonight. I ... I'd thought I wanted to hurt him, but I had gotten it so wrong. I hated making people feel bad.

And his last few words to me ...

They hurt like a motherfucker.

"Blaise Harleen," Mateo said. "Vera's boyfriend."

Mom looked over her shoulder at me with surprised brown eyes. "Your boyfriend?"

"Blaise isn't my boyfriend," I said, pressing my lips together so I didn't seem both suspicious and hurt that Blaise had left. "Mateo's just being a brat. Don't listen to him. I would never date him."

Lie.

"That's a lie." Mateo chuckled, stuffing another fry into his bratty mouth. "You always get so flustered whenever he comes around, and your cheeks get all red and blotchy, like they are now. I thought you were going to pass out at the sight of him the other night."

I balled my hands into fists, my cheeks flaming. "Shut up. I don't like him."

Lie.

"She totally does," Mateo said to Mom, heading back to his room. "She has a cru—"

Picking up a pillow from the couch, I hurled it at him and hit him square in the head. He snickered again and shut his door, leaving me alone to deal with Mom's silent judgment about Blaise and his family.

She unfastened her name tag and carefully placed it on the counter, next to the brown bag of food, and didn't look up at me. Not once. "Vera, you know what happened with the Harleens, don't you?"

"Yes, Mom," I said quietly, staring down at my feet. "Don't listen to Mateo."

"I want you to be happy," she whispered, looking back up at me and giving me a trying smile. Her eyes were creased, the tired lines growing deeper by the day. She did everything to make us happy, sacrificed her damn life for us. "And you have guilt written all over your face."

The tears that I'd wanted to cry all day wavered in my eyes. I crossed my arms and stared at her for what seemed like forever. I never talked to Mom about boys, mainly because I had desperately tried to avoid them—or as Mateo would say, they avoided me, which was mostly the truth—but today ... I needed someone.

Suddenly, I burst out in tears. Mom hurried over and wrapped her arms around my shoulders, brushing her fingers through my hair. I grasped on to her and held her as tight as I could. All this time, I had been trying to avoid Blaise Harleen because of what his parents had done to Mom, but ... I couldn't anymore.

I had lied to him today.

I had told him that our friendship meant nothing to me when I had the drawing he'd made me for my fifth birthday buried in my bedside drawer. For years, I'd kept it and wondered why his parents hated me so much. Was I the reason Mom had gotten fired?

"I don't know what to do." I sniffled, not even sure if Mom could comprehend anything.

After last night, I had begun to think that all this time, Blaise hadn't forgotten about me either. Then, I caught him with Skylar and couldn't even function. Why would he want me—*me?!*—when he could have her? I wasn't like the girls he normally hung out with.

No boys—not even the losers in Calculus—even looked in my direction.

But tonight, Blaise had stayed with me the whole night, asked if I thought of him as a friend back then, and looked completely devastated when I said no to not feel hurt, to hurt him, which was so freaking wrong of me.

"Do what makes you happy," Mom said. "Don't worry about me, but be careful."

"I know," I whispered.

After hugging me for a couple moments longer, she walked back into her room to get ready for bed. She had an early shift tomorrow, so I wouldn't have let her stay up much later with me anyway.

Deep down, I knew the only thing that I could do right now.

And that wasn't crying into Mom's shoulder.

I plugged my phone into the socket, sat on the couch, and pulled up a Google Doc because I didn't have any more notebooks to spare. And then I wrote and I wrote and I wrote our story so far until tears raced down my cheeks.

Mom peeked her head out of her room before she went to bed and furrowed her brows at my sobbing mess on the couch. "Are you going to be okay, sweetheart?" she asked, running her fingers through her wet black hair.

"I'll be fine, Mom," I sobbed, moving my fingers faster along the screen. With all the tears clouding my eyes, I could barely see my tiny-ass phone screen, but I continued writing because I had to get it out.

Before the night ended, I must've reread my writing five times. I wanted to put it out in the world, wanted someone to read it and to understand me, understand how I feared that I'd be another one of Blaise's girls that he dumped ruthlessly, how I feared that I'd never be good enough for anyone—relationship-wise and writing-wise, how I … wrote about love all the time, but never believed I'd ever find someone to love me completely.

My blood was soaked into every one of these words. My worst fears. My insecurities.

Everything.

I hoped that someone could relate.

As my finger hovered over the Publish button, I shook my head and erased almost everything. Everything, except one rough, hard sex scene that I had written tonight to get out my anger and annoyance.

I wasn't ready for people to read about the deepest part of me.

I wasn't sure if I'd ever be ready for something like that.

Chapter Twenty-Seven

BLAISE

When I pulled up to the skatepark at fucking midnight, a handful of kids from the slums were there. The rain had cleared about an hour ago while I rode around Redwood aimlessly, waiting for Vera to call me, to tell me she hadn't meant what she said.

But she never called, and I didn't want to go back home. If I went home, I would do nothing but think about her in my parents' big, empty house that they'd paid millions of dollars to not even fucking use.

I stepped out of the car and snatched my board out of the backseat, wanting to hurl my fucking fist into someone's jaw tonight. I didn't care who these motherfuckers were here. I wanted someone to hurt as bad as I was.

And I didn't want that to be Vera. At least, not right now.

Because ... I didn't want to fuck up more than I already had. I didn't want to lose her.

She was the only person who I fucking talked to, who I thought about, whose opinion I cared about anymore. My parents were assholes. All the other girls before her, like Skylar, had only wanted my dick, and then they dipped.

Vera … she … I hadn't given her a chance to leave me. I had black-mailed her and hoped that she wouldn't go anywhere. And for a couple days, she didn't. Then, Skylar had fucked that all up.

I couldn't lose Vera. I fucking couldn't.

I balled my hands into fists.

And what the fuck did she mean when she blew up at me about not being myself at school? She didn't fucking know shit about me. I was quiet all the fucking time—unless I wanted her attention. Did she want me to be an asshole to her? Was that what she liked?

Just as I tossed my board down, my phone buzzed in my pocket. I slipped my hand into my jeans and grasped it, hoping to the fucking Redwood gods that it was her. I didn't even care if it was an emoji or a GIF or even the fucking words *good night*. Something.

Instead of Vera's name on my screen, Skylar popped up with about a hundred useless-as-fuck questions about when I wanted to see her. I hurled my skateboard at the concrete. "What the fuck does she not get?!"

She wasn't the only one pissing me off either. That fucker João had purposely come into the library today, leaned closer to Vera, and told her that he'd see her tomorrow night.

What the hell did he want with her anyway?

Had she cut a deal with him or something?

João wasn't someone a girl like Vera should associate herself with. It was bad fucking enough that she had gotten tangled with me. João and his gang were fucking worse.

In the skatepark, I spotted someone from the slums who João had been doing *business* with lately. Whether that business be selling him drugs or doing something *more* for him, I didn't give a fuck. All I knew was that I wanted to fucking hurt him.

So, I did whatever the fuck I had to do to get on his every last nerve. And when he had enough of me, he kicked his board up and glared in my direction.

"Watch where you're fucking going, Harleen. Your daddy doesn't own the skatepark."

I skated up next to him and hopped off my board, shoving my hands against his chest. "Why don't *you* get out of *my* fucking way?"

He pushed me back. "Don't be a prick."

I straight-up fucking laughed in this kid's face. "Or what? You gonna hit me?"

The asshole hurled his fist right into my left eye. I rejoiced in the fucking pain, stumbled back to regain my balance, then lunged at him, letting my fist fly into his jaw and sending him down onto the concrete.

He scraped the skin of his palms and knees against the ground. Then, he spit up some blood and struggled to stand, grabbing his board and stepping away from me. "This is why everyone fucking hates you," he growled, storming away and disappearing through the trees that surrounded the park.

After he left, I grumbled to myself and touched my eye, which would be swollen by tomorrow. I walked over to an empty bench and sat down, grabbing my board and smashing it against the ground. I fucking hated myself.

What the fuck was wrong with me?

I glanced around the park, looking for someone else to fuck with. Gunther Zurn—a kid from Redwood who frequented the skatepark with his buddies—stood near a bench with one foot on his skateboard as he talked to ... Callan Avery, a professor at Redwood.

Mr. Avery stepped closer to Gunther and pulled something out of his pocket, sticking it against Gunther's abdomen. He spoke a few tense words with Gunther and shoved him back.

Yes, a fucking teacher at Redwood pushed one of his students, and nobody would ever give a shit about it either if they found out, especially with Callan's ties to the Redwood mob.

Gunther kicked up his skateboard, tossed it over his shoulder, then stormed out of the park, disappearing through the thick brush of trees surrounding this place. Callan tucked a gun back into his waistband and looked around, his gaze landing on me. Then, he walked over.

While he might've scared off everyone else, he didn't scare me. Callan—my uncle—was more of a father than my own dad. Hell, he had probably even slept with my mother a handful of times too. Who the fuck knew shit anymore?

"What're you doing with Gunther?" I asked him.

He wouldn't be threatening a teenager for nothing. Gunther had to have done something to Avery, either during school or with his *business* outside of the classroom. Avery didn't threaten people for the hell of it.

He cocked a brow up at me. "None of your business."

After rolling my eyes, I hopped on my board and skated down the halfpipe ramp. "Fine."

"You don't tell anyone what you saw," he said to me, stalking closer and stepping under the dim overhead light that ignited the skatepark after dark. "And what the fuck happened to your eye? You get into a fight?"

I stopped my board inches from his feet and kicked it up, staring him right in the eye and looking for another fight. I knew that he wouldn't give me one, but, fuck, I wanted it so fucking badly. "None of your business," I said through gritted teeth.

"You should be at home."

"*You* should be at home with your *lovely wife*," I said, spitting his words back at him.

We both knew that his wife—my dad's sister—was anything other than lovely. She was a spitting image of my father—absent from everyone's life, except her own, and didn't give a shit about anything other than how she could flaunt her money. She was an annoying fucking bitch.

"What happened to Vera Rodriguez?" he asked back, testing my patience apparently. Usually, he didn't stoop so low, but something must've really pissed him off. "I heard from a certain gang that you've been seeing her."

"Shut your fucking mouth," I growled, storming away from him before I punched him square in the jaw.

He might've been older than me and armed with a weapon, but I would knock his ass out cold right here.

Chapter Twenty-Eight

BLAISE

The next day, I stared into my empty locker and clenched my jaw, fingers tightening around my skateboard. World History had started twenty minutes ago. I hadn't wanted to fucking come to school today, but I couldn't stop myself from driving here this morning.

With Skylar knowing Vera's and my secret, I expected everyone to be buzzing with excitement over the newfound drama of me fucking *Vera*, the senior class's nerdy good girl. But I hadn't heard anything this morning, not even on social media.

If Skylar had opened her big fat mouth about Vera and me, word would've already spread through Redwood. So, it seemed like she hadn't, and part of me was fucking thankful, because while I didn't give a fuck who knew about us, Vera did.

After grabbing my computer from my locker, I dragged my feet all the way toward History. I opened the door to The Grinch glaring at me and walked into the class toward the back, where Vera was working on our project alone. One of Skylar's friends waved me over, but I ignored that bitch, like I had been ignoring Skylar for the past week. She seemed to be absent today.

Once I took my seat next to Vera, I pulled out my phone and scrolled through all the needy thirst-traps that these Redwood bitches flooded social media with, not even taking the time to look at any of them. My thumb continuously swiped vertically across the screen, not slowing down once until I came to some skateboard shit that an influencer had posted.

I needed a distraction because the scent of Vera's strawberry shampoo was lingering in the air heavier than usual today. And I couldn't fucking think straight. Fuck, I hadn't been able to think straight all night.

"I, um ..." Vera said, leaning an inch closer to me.

When I looked up at Vera, she opened her mouth and then snapped it shut.

"What?"

"What happened to your eye?" she asked, voice small.

"What do you care?"

She pressed her lips together and glanced back down at the project she'd been working on all morning without me. Gnawing on the inside of her cheek, she looked back at me and shrugged. "I just ... I ..."

"You what?"

After the hopeful expression on her face fell, she looked away from me. It looked like she felt the way I had last night—completely and utterly fucking shattered. And I was all for hurting people like this.

My chest tightened.

Everyone was in this world for themselves, apparently.

"Nothing," she whispered.

As much as it fucking hurt me, I turned my gaze away from her and back toward my phone. I tapped out of my social media and scrolled through the hundreds of notifications that I had gotten between last night and now. I had forced myself to turn off my phone completely last night, or I would've called her.

New story by an author you're following: Steamy One-Shots

I stared at the notification, then at Vera, then back, my finger hovering over the screen. Before I clicked on it, I lowered the brightness on my phone, so even if Vera looked over at my phone, she wouldn't know that I fucking cared.

She didn't deserve to know. We weren't friends anyway.

After I tapped on the notification, one of Vera's stories appeared on the screen. It wasn't the one that she had been working on lately, but an erotic scene that looked to be taken out of a longer story.

As I scrolled down the page, I found myself getting harder and harder. I didn't want to give her the satisfaction of knowing how fucking horny she'd made me, but, fuck, this was hot. Everything she fucking wrote was.

Vera pulled out her phone and searched something for our project on her tiny screen while I read her filthy fucking smut. All this sex in here was rough as hell—with biting and choking and hair pulling.

Was that what she wanted from me? A good, rough time because nobody else would give it to her? At least, that was what she had thought. She didn't know that these past few years, I had threatened anyone who showed even the smallest of interest in her.

She didn't know that she had been mine since we were four.

"For those of you who need a laptop to do research"—The Grinch gave Vera an annoyed and pointed look, which ticked me off —"you can head to the library."

Vera must've noticed the way that fucking bitch had called her out because her cheeks flushed and she quietly turned off her phone. "I'm going to the library. You can, uh ... stay here if you want or leave. I'll finish our project by myself."

After she quickly scurried out of the classroom, I threw my backpack over my shoulder and stalked up to the front, glaring down at The Grinch sitting at her desk.

She looked up at me through green-framed glasses. "Can I help you, Mr. Harleen?"

I leaned down and lowered my voice, so nobody else would hear. "You're fucking lucky we're in the middle of the school day. If you call Vera out like that again, you'd better watch your fucking back. I don't give a fuck who you are."

Not caring to listen to her response, I stormed out of the classroom and followed Vera's awkward-as-fuck figure hurrying toward the library through the desolate hallways. She wasn't getting away from my shitty-ass attitude today.

When I caught up to her, I grabbed her by the back of her neck, stopped her completely, and shoved her into the nearest empty classroom. Vera Rodriguez wasn't getting a pass from how she had made me feel last night at the library or from that new chapter she'd posted online.

If she wanted a rough, unforgiving asshole, then that was what I'd give her.

Chapter Twenty-Nine

VERA

I yelped in surprise, but Blaise slapped his hand over my mouth, locked the door behind us, and pressed me up against the nearest whiteboard. As he pressed his body against mine from behind, I tensed and placed my nervous hands on the board, fingers turning white.

He released his hand over my mouth and slipped it around my throat, pulling my body against his as much as he could. I sucked in a sharp breath and pressed my thighs together because I hadn't been able to stop thinking about every time he had taken me during school.

"Wh-what are you doing?" I asked, voice trembling.

My birth control hadn't taken full effect yet. I still had about four or five days until it did.

"This is what your horny, slutty cunt wanted, isn't it?" Blaise growled, sinking his free hand between my thighs and cupping my pussy. "For me to be the same asshole that I'd always been," he said, tracing his nose up the column of my neck, making me shiver. "So here the fuck I am."

Pleasure raced to my core. "Wh-what are you talking about?"

"I read what you posted online last night," he said into my ear, grinding himself against my ass. He grabbed a fistful of my hair and pressed me against the whiteboard even harder. "Every last fucking word of it, Vera."

"You read my story?" I whispered, throat drying.

Blaise answered me by pushing my jeans and panties down to my knees. "Spread your fucking legs."

And like the horny fucking slut I was, I spread my legs and arched my back, desperate for him to be inside me again, aching to be close again—because for the life of me, I couldn't seem to tell him how I really felt about him.

"Fuck," he grunted, sprawling a hand over my bare ass. He spanked, then groped a handful of it. He pressed himself harder against my ass, his dick bulging against the rough material. "Fucking buck your hips up and down, V."

I gripped on to the whiteboard and nervously glanced toward the door. "I don't know if—"

Instead of waiting for me, he forcefully gripped my hips and moved them up and down against his jeans, ruining them with my wetness. He pressed himself harder against me, letting me feel every inch of him through his pants.

Heat gushed between my legs. God, this couldn't be happening right now.

"I'm going to fuck you."

No *please*. No *can I?* No condom.

He undid the zipper on his jeans and pulled out his huge cock, slapping it against my wet pussy and teasing my clit with it. He pushed the head of it inside me, cursed under his breath, then slammed all of himself into me.

I placed a hand over my mouth and cried out into it as pleasure shot through my body.

"Tell me you're a filthy whore," he demanded, pounding into my pussy.

My pussy tightened around him, and I whimpered out, the mere thought of saying it aloud in the middle of an empty Redwood classroom making me actually feel like one.

He pulled back on my throat, his mouth against my ear. "Fucking say it."

"I'm a filthy whore," I whispered.

He sank himself deeper and deeper inside of me with every thrust. "Louder."

"I'm a filthy whore," I said, only a bit louder.

A low growl escaped his mouth. "I want you to fucking scream it, so everyone in this fucking school can hear you. That's what a good whore would do, isn't it? Scream so loud while her cunt gets filled?"

"I'm a ..." The pressure rose in my core. "I'm a"—higher and higher. I was about to tip over the edge—"filthy ..."

Blaise was shoving himself into me so hard that my mind became mush.

"I'm a filthy whore!"

"Good fucking girl," he cooed, grabbing a dry erase marker from a metal tray and handing it to me. "Now, write it on your bare thigh, so you don't forget it." He pulled back on my throat and buried his face into the crook of my neck. "If we were alone, I'd write it on this pretty fucking face of yours and force you to look in the mirror at yourself while I fucked you, so you knew what you were."

Whimpering from how much I enjoyed this, I took the cap off the marker and pressed it against my inner thigh, beginning to write *Filthy Whore* on my skin. He pounded into me so hard that I couldn't write neatly, no matter how hard I tried. My pussy tightened around him as I made the final marker stroke.

"You're not fucking done," Blaise grunted before I could set the marker back in the tray.

He sucked harshly on my throat, his stubble tickling my skin. Heat rushed to my pussy, and I tightened on his huge cock, about to come undone again. I curled my hand around the open marker and sucked in a sharp breath.

When he pulled his mouth away from my throat, my skin ached dully. There wasn't a doubt in my mind that he had left a huge hickey on my neck, one that I didn't know if I could hide with my hair.

"What do you want me to write now?" I whispered, voice trembling.

"Draw an arrow from your stomach to your cunt," he ordered, picking another fresh spot on my neck to ruin. He placed his hot mouth on the skin, sucked harshly on it, and watched over my shoulder with hooded eyes.

With a shaky hand, I did as he'd instructed.

Leaving another hickey, he tugged up on my skin slightly, then released it. "Above it, you're going to write *Dump cum here*, and then you're going to fucking beg for me to dump my cum inside you, like a good little slut."

I tightened around him, clamping down on his huge cock. "But ... I-I ..."

"Don't fucking tell me that you don't want that. Your drooling pussy is fastened on my dick so hard right now." He sucked harder on another area of my throat and placed the tip of the marker against my stomach. "Write it."

My hands trembled from the sheer ecstasy, but I wrote the words on my stomach. Pressure rose in my core, and we both knew that I was so fucking close to coming all over him.

"You don't get to come again until I come inside you."

"But m-my birth control i-isn't ready y-yet."

At this point, I didn't really fucking care. All I wanted was for him to fill up my aching cunt and grunt in my ear as he did. I wanted the sound of his orgasm to push me over the edge, so I could come with him. It'd felt so good last time.

"Then, tell me to fucking stop, and I'll stop."

But he showed no sign of slowing down, nor stopping.

I gripped the whiteboard so hard that my fingers turned white and whimpered. "Blaise ..."

"Tell me to stop."

I didn't want him to stop. I wanted him to keep going. I wanted to come with him. Badly.

"Tell me to fucking stop right now," he grunted, his voice becoming more and more taut. He gripped my hips and slowed his thrusts a bit in order to push himself deeper and deeper inside me. " ... or my cum will fill your cunt up past your fucking cervix."

Moaning loudly, I threw my head back. "Please, come inside me! Please!"

"Fuuuuck," Blaise grunted and stilled deep inside me.

Wave after wave surged through my body. My legs trembled uncontrollably. And I couldn't stop the moans that escaped my lips. The pleasure wouldn't stop pumping through my body as Blaise left another hickey on my neck.

When he pulled away, I gripped on to the whiteboard harder, so I wouldn't fall over.

"Skylar hasn't said shit to anyone in Redwood about us, but after today, everyone is going to know how fucking slutty you are, Sunshine," he growled. "Because you're going to walk around Redwood with my cum dripping down your thighs, with your panties ruined, and with hickeys that I left you, decorating this pretty throat of yours."

Chapter Thirty

BLAISE

After I fucked her senseless inside an empty classroom, Vera collapsed into the teacher's maroon-cushioned swivel chair and curled her knees to her chest. She rested her head back against the seat and blew out a deep breath, dark brows furrowed.

I wanted to stay, to talk to her, to ask her what the fuck I could do about Skylar.

But that wasn't what she wanted from me. All she cared about was getting her pussy pounded, and that was fucking it. She didn't give a fuck that I'd stayed with her all last night at the library, that I had driven her home in the pouring rain, that I had taken care of that fucking prick who wanted to fuck her on her break.

Tearing my gaze away from her, I pulled up my pants and snapped on the button. Once I grabbed my laptop, I walked toward the door without so much as a *goodbye* or a *see you later* or even a *thanks for letting me use you*.

"You're going?" she whispered.

No fucking response from me.

"Wait!" she said.

When I turned around, she shuffled to button up her jeans. Then, she furrowed her brows harder and stared at me, her cheeks blotchy and red. After clasping her hands together, she played with her fingers and gave me a nervous smile.

"What the fuck do you want?" I asked her, trying to sound like I didn't give a fuck. But really, I was glad that she had called me back to stay with her for a little longer. I didn't want to go to class, and I really didn't want to leave her after that.

After every time that we had sex, I left right away because that was what I'd always done, but ... I didn't want to keep being that asshole to her. I didn't want her to think that I didn't care, though somehow, at the same time, I wanted her to think exactly that.

"I, um ..." she stuttered and crouched down next to her textbooks, opening one up and pulling out a piece of white cardstock sheet. "I was going through my stuff last night, and I ..." She shuffled from foot to foot and couldn't look me in the eye. "I found this hanging around."

"The fuck is this?" I asked, snatching and staring at the drawing that a four-year-old must've done.

Vera stepped toward me, nervously staring at the drawing and chewing on the inside of her cheek. She shuffled her dirty, off-brand Vans on the tiled classroom floor. "You don't remember?"

"Remember what?"

After scratching the back of her head and giving me a whiff of her strawberry shampoo, she took the drawing from me and folded it back up. "Oh, it's just, uh ... you gave it to me for my fifth birthday. I found it last night."

I let out an empty chuckle. "I made this shit for you?"

She was lying. She had to fucking be. I hadn't made that for her. And if I had, why the hell did she still have it lying around her house anyway? I thought she fucking hated me for everything that I was, like everyone else did.

"Yeah," she said, voice softer this time. She peeked up at me and gave me a half-smile, her nervous eyes searching mine. "You did. You don't remember?"

"No." The word came out cruel, hopefully jarring, just like she wanted from me. "Why would I remember a stupid drawing that I did fucking thirteen years ago? Come on. Think with your fucking head."

The more I said, the harsher I became. I felt nothing but hurt from last night, and part of me wanted her to hurt worse. I wanted her to understand the pain of feeling like nobody gave a shit about her.

She thought I had everything because my parents had money. But I didn't have shit.

"Oh," she whispered, looking down.

Because I wanted to be an asshole—that was what she asked for, right?—I snatched the paper back from her and walked to the classroom door. This drawing was *meaningless* to me. "I don't give a fuck about this."

"If you don't want it, then give it back," she said, grabbing my elbow.

I tore myself out of her hold. "No."

"Please," she said, voice filled with desperation. "You gave it to me. It's mine. I want to keep it."

With my back turned toward her, I stopped in my tracks and clutched the drawing in my fist. I stared down at it, and ... and I fucking smiled. This wasn't much, but she wouldn't have kept this shit—and she really wouldn't have brought it to show me—if she didn't care.

If Vera really didn't think we had been friends at any point, if she wanted to fuck me and leave, if she didn't give a shit about what I thought, then she wouldn't have kept this all these years. Vera cared.

Vera fucking cared.

"Please," she whispered, placing a hand on my shoulder. "I want to keep it."

After wiping the smile off my face, I turned back around and thrust my hand toward her. "Take it then."

She stared down at it for a couple moments, her eyes lighting back up, and she grasped the drawing. Our fingers grazed against each other's, and I hoped that she didn't notice the way I tensed when they did.

"Thank you," she whispered, not moving away from me.

My heart raced faster and faster, my breath hitching. I swallowed hard.

Neither of us stepped back. Neither of us looked away. We fucking stood there.

And I couldn't stop myself from taking her face in my hands and kissing her passionately on the mouth. I couldn't stop myself from drawing her closer to me and wondering if she fucking cared about me as much as I cared about her.

"Blaise," she whispered breathlessly between kisses, curling her fingers against my shoulders.

I had just fucked her against the whiteboard, but I wanted her again. I wanted her differently this time.

"God ..."

Suddenly, the doorknob jiggled. Vera breathily pulled away, her eyes wide and her cheeks flaming red.

When the door swung open, Mr. Avery walked into the room with a grocery bag that smelled like cooked food and arched a brow at me. "What the fuck are you doing here?"

Vera scooted behind me and stared at Callan in fear.

"Just leaving," I said, though I had wanted to fucking stay here with her all day.

After nudging Vera toward the door, I followed after her and passed him. Callan Avery let Vera shuffle down the hallway toward the library, but he caught me by my shoulder and yanked me back.

"We need to have a fucking talk."

132

Chapter Thirty-One

BLAISE

"What do you want?" I asked, tossing my backpack over my shoulder and grabbing my skateboard. Instead of waiting for Callan Avery to scold me, I walked to the door. "I don't have time. I gotta get to class."

Avery seized my shoulder again. "Tell me you didn't fuck that girl in my class."

I stopped walking and rolled my eyes. "Come on, Avery. It's not like you haven't fucked anyone in here before. I know Aunt Georgina isn't sucking your dick. She's out with her girlfriends every night, isn't she?"

While it was meant to be a harmless joke, Callan shoved me away. "You could've used any other fucking classroom, Blaise. Don't use mine next time, or I'll write you up and get you suspended."

My eyes widened. Not at his empty threat, but by how defensive he had gotten.

"No shit. You have fucked someone in here, haven't you?" I ambled around the room and shook my head, chuckling. "But who could it be? Definitely not any of the cheerleaders. I mean, not that you couldn't score them, but they're not really your type, just like Georgina isn't."

He gritted his teeth. "Get out of my fucking classroom."

"But I thought you wanted to talk." Another chuckle left my lips. "It's not Nicole or Jasmine or Aiza. Couldn't be Juana. She's probably your type, but way too loud. And her voice"—I scrunched my nose—"too fucking annoying."

"Out. Now."

Suddenly, someone knocked on the door. Callan tensed and glanced over, his jaw clenched. A moment later, Sakura Sato—one of the girls in the running to be valedictorian of the senior class—peeked into the classroom.

"Callan—" she started, but then she spotted me in the back of the classroom. Her cheeks flushed red, and she quickly looked away. "I-I mean, Mr. Avery, you said that you wanted me to meet with you during lunch about an assignment."

After eyeing Callan, I curled my lips into a smirk and sauntered to the door. "Would've never guessed, Avery. Is that why you were at the skatepark last night? Needed to take care of"—I glanced at Sakura, who quickly averted her gaze—"someone."

Mr. Avery drew his tongue across his teeth. "Sakura, give us a minute."

Sakura quickly scurried out of the classroom, keeping her head down the entire time.

When the door closed, Callan grabbed me by my collar and shoved me against the wall. "If you speak a fucking word about this to anyone, I will fucking kill you. You understand?"

Still, his threats were empty.

At least, to me they were. I didn't doubt that he would kill anyone else. He had ties to the Redwood mob, who had done far worse things than kill a couple people. But good ole Uncle Callan wouldn't hurt me.

"You don't mention anything about Vera to Redwood, then your secret is safe with me."

He growled, but shoved me toward the door and straightened out his suit. Apparently, Aunt Georgina had done more to piss him off than anything I'd expected.

"Get the fuck out of my classroom and send Sakura in."

Finding my way out of his class, I held the door for Sakura to enter. "Have fun."

She murmured something so quiet that I couldn't hear and disappeared into his classroom. The bell rang through the building, and suddenly, students spilled out into the hallways. A group of freshmen and sophomores walked in my direction, and I spotted Mateo surrounded by a couple of girls.

"Hey, Blaise," Mateo called.

"You wanna play Raid of Durnbone tonight?" I asked, needing to find an excuse to show up at Vera's front door tonight. As far as I knew, she had plans with João, and I wanted to get there before he did.

I needed to see what the fuck that was all about.

Not only that, but Mateo was also a pretty cool kid to hang with. He didn't have drama like the rest of these fuckers did at Redwood. I'd order a couple pizzas, and maybe it'd repair some of the damage that Skylar had done.

Chapter Thirty-Two

VERA

Blaise must've gotten in trouble with Mr. Avery because he didn't meet me in the library to work on the project. Or maybe he'd decided to skip because of what had happened in that empty classroom when he ... kissed me.

I walked down the hallway toward the cafeteria at lunchtime and brushed my fingers over my lips. We had kissed before whenever we had sex, but this time, it was different. And by the look on his face, I knew he'd thought so too.

Once I collapsed onto one of the red stools connected to the table, Piper plopped down in front of me. "I know we always mess with you about Blaise, but Maddie supposedly has herself a guy too."

"Her best friend's brother?" From our table, I spotted her in the hallway and smirked. "She thinks she's being sly, but they are so obvious. Oh God. Like, *waaaay* too obvious. Her brother is going to find out sooner or later."

"And you know how possessive he is of her," Piper said. "Especially with one of his hockey buddies. That'll be a screaming match and a half at their house when the day finally comes."

I scrunched my nose and took a sip of water from my bottle. "You know it."

When Maddie was finished swapping spit with the captain of the hockey team, she bounced into the cafeteria and sat next to Piper. "So, did things finally work out with Redwood's steamy—"

Before she could finish asking me anything, João walked over to our table.

"The deal's done," João said, tapping the table. "I'll drive you to my place after school."

When João sauntered to Poison's designated table in the back of the cafeteria, Maddie snapped her head to me and smirked. "Okay, Ms. I Don't Want Any Drama, My Senior Year Is Going to Be Boy-Free, what was that?"

Piper nudged Maddie and winked. "And he's going to drive her home too!"

I snatched some cheese-and-chive crackers from her and tore open the packaging. "Oh my God. You guys are so annoying. He just wants me to watch his sister tonight. Nothing is going to happen. He's not even going to be home."

Maddie and Piper side-eyed each other and grinned. "Suuuure."

After rolling my eyes, I shoved a cracker into my mouth and looked up as Blaise stepped into the cafeteria. I sat up taller, spotting his swollen eye that had turned purple, and forced my thighs together.

With his backpack thrown over one shoulder, he sauntered toward a table in the back, opposite of Poison, where other rich kids sat. I guessed he hovered between the skateboard punks and the *too rich for their own good* kids.

As he sat, he made eye contact with me. I stared back at him and pressed my lips together, my stomach still fluttering from our kiss. I didn't know what was wrong with me because one second, I hated him, and the next, I wanted more of him.

"Whew," Maddie said, wiggling her brows. "You guys back on?"

Reluctantly, I pulled my gaze away from Blaise and turned back to the table, though I could still feel the intensity of his stare on me. It was burning into my side, begging me to look back over at him. And while I wanted to, I didn't want anyone to suspect anything.

João had already taken care of Skylar for that particular reason.

"No, we're not back on," I said, tucking some hair behind my ear and hoping that they would drop it. But knowing their annoying asses, they definitely wouldn't. I had all the drama that my friend group could ever want.

Hell, I was still being blackmailed for writing smut by Redwood's bad boy! For crying out loud, it didn't get better than that in those sleazy, drama-crazed romance books either.

"Hmm, really?" Piper said, grinning from ear to ear and leaving closer to me. "Is that why he's coming this way?"

My cheeks flamed red, and I sat up taller. "What do you mean, he's coming this way?!" I whisper-yelled, shielding my face from his direction and hoping to the Redwood gods that she was kidding.

She *had* to be kidding, right?

"Vera," Blaise said to my left, his deep voice sending shivers down my spine.

All I could remember was how he had touched me inside Mr. Avery's classroom, how he'd degraded me like I had wanted, and how he'd kissed me so passionately afterward.

Maddie giggled and playfully kicked me under the table. "Oh, Vera!"

I cut my glare to her, then reluctantly glanced up at Blaise. Even though he had come into the cafeteria moments ago, he had on his backpack and his skateboard in his hand, like he was already about to head out.

"Y-yes?" I asked, looking around at everyone staring.

And when I said everyone, I meant *everyone,* because nobody could have *any* privacy at Redwood Academy. Everyone knew every-one's business. I was surprised João was able to keep my little sexca-pades with Blaise under wraps so well so far.

Blaise pulled a notebook—my notebook that he'd kept stealing

—out of his backpack and placed it on the cafeteria table in front of me. "You dropped this on your way to the library during History. Thought I'd return it to you."

I narrowed my eyes at the notebook, then raised my gaze once more to meet his. "Thank you, Blaise. How *kind* of you," I said with sarcasm.

He gave me his infamous smirk and walked away. "No need to thank me. I left a surprise inside for you."

Somehow, my cheeks warmed even more. I clutched the notebook hard in my hands and stared down at it, hoping that nobody else had heard what he said, outside my friend group. When he left the cafeteria and everyone turned away, I pulled the notebook to the edge of the table and peeked.

On the first page, a single Plan B pill lay in a plastic baggie along with a sticky note that read, *I would apologize for coming inside you, but I'm not sorry. You feel too good. I'd do it again.*

Taking three Plan B pills within the span of two weeks probably wasn't healthy for me, but neither was getting pregnant right now. So, I sneakily tossed it into my mouth and swallowed it with a gulp of water.

Still, I couldn't help but read his little note again. And again. And again. Looking way too into it even though I shouldn't, finding little things that he probably hadn't really meant. Blaise Harleen thought I felt good.

Not my pussy.

Me.

What a charmer that boy is. Not.

Chapter Thirty-Three

VERA

"Yay! João's home!" Ana, João's little sister, shouted, hurrying to the door and standing on her tiptoes to open it up later that night. When she yanked it open, she sprinted out into the front yard all by her lonesome. "Landon and Kai are here too!"

Instead of running to João like I expected, she ran right into the arms of Kai, the quiet kid in Poison's. He picked her up and spun her around, making her giggle. I grabbed my belongings from the living room and stood in the kitchen, waiting to go home.

"Thanks," João said, cigarette in his mouth. He pulled out his wallet. "We had to take care of someone."

"Speaking of taking care of people ..." I said, lowering my voice so Ana wouldn't hear. I inched closer to him and zipped up my coat. "What'd you do to Skylar? She wasn't in school today." Not that I was really complaining about that.

João pulled the cigarette out of his mouth and blew out a puff of smoke. "So what? She didn't show for school today. Not unusual of her," he started, taking another long drag of the cigarette. "Don't worry about it and don't ask."

While I'd wanted her to pay for *intentionally* hurting me—because if Blaise had been serious, then that was exactly what she had done—I didn't know if I wanted to push the subject with João and Poison. They did some pretty fucked up things.

Shit that I didn't even want to say aloud.

"Here," João said, slapping a few hundred-dollar bills in my hand.

My eyes widened. "This is way more than usual."

"Shut up and don't complain about it," João said, nodding to the door, where Landon and Kai stood tensely, like something had just happened. "Thanks for watching my sister. Get out of my fucking house."

Not wanting to spend another minute here and *definitely* not wanting him to take back the money he had given me, I zipped my mouth closed, grabbed my backpack, and hurried out the door to walk back home.

For a fall night in New England, it wasn't *that* cold, surprisingly. Usually, the weather here was either snowing and below freezing or *pulling off my clothes* type of heat because it was so freaking hot. But tonight ... it was comfy.

When I crossed the street, I spotted Blaise's car parked on the side of the road. I picked up the pace and walked a bit faster, hurrying toward the house to kick him out before Mom got home. While he hadn't been disrespectful to Mom last night, his parents were the ones had fired her. Mom might've sacrificed her personal life to keep a roof over our heads, but I wanted to protect her from her past.

Which included Blaise ... even though it was kinda a shitty thought.

I hurried up the sidewalk and yanked open the front door. Blaise sat on the couch with Mateo, playing another game of Raid of Durnbone with him. After spotting three large pizza boxes on the small coffee table, I raised a brow.

We never ordered out. And if we happened to, then it definitely wasn't from an overpriced place like Vancello's Pizza. It was, like, twenty bucks for one small pizza that probably wasn't even that good.

"Did you bring those over?" I asked.

Blaise glanced over his shoulder at me, eyes widening when he saw me. "Finally."

Mom stepped out of the bathroom in a pair of sweatpants—she must've gotten home early from work—and grabbed a plate, already filled with pizza, from the kitchen counter. I stared between her and Blaise and Mateo, not sure of what was going on.

"He did, sweetheart," Mom said, giving Blaise a small smile.

I narrowed my eyes at him, not sure where this nice guy persona had come from, and dumped my backpack beside the couch. After taking a cautious seat in a chair opposite of Blaise, I chewed on the inside of my lips and glanced over at Mom.

"Did you get off early tonight?" I asked.

"Only one shift today," she said, biting into the pizza.

"You're not going to have any?" Blaise asked me, his fingers moving along the controller, but his eyes flickering from the monitor to me. "I didn't know what kind you liked, but there's cheese and pepperoni."

After Mom handed me a plastic plate that must've been five years old now, I grabbed a piece and realized that Blaise—the rich, arrogant kid—was eating off a plate that must've been even older. A rich kid like him eating in the slums with a bunch of nobodies? It stunned me.

"Shouldn't you be eating steak on a golden platter or something?" I asked, my voice snippy because I still didn't get what he was up to tonight. Sure, we might've shared a moment—*a kiss*—at Redwood today, but ...

He hadn't said anything all day after lunch. And I had begun to think that it was all the heat of the moment again, but ...

God, what am I doing? Why am I acting this way, pushing him away from me again?

I bit into my pizza and glanced over at the small TV screen. Maybe it was because if he did like me—and that was a big *if*—we wouldn't work out. He would get tired of me and move on to someone prettier, like Skylar.

What could I possibly offer him that he didn't have already? He could score any girl in Redwood without even trying, he could buy whatever he wanted, and he would have a job without having to work endlessly for it as soon as he left high school.

Tears built in my eyes, but I held them back and took another bite of the pizza.

"What's wrong?" Blaise asked, his gaze on me now instead of the screen.

"No!" Mateo shouted, sitting back on the couch and blowing out a breath. "We almost had him, but he killed me!"

"Sorry, kid," Blaise said, setting the controller down on the coffee table next to the pizza boxes and barely paying him much attention now. He furrowed his brows and leaned his elbows onto his thighs. "V?"

I pressed my lips together, wallowing in my own insecurities. "Nothing."

After rolling his eyes, he grabbed an extra pizza box that nobody had touched, stood, and grabbed my hand. "See you later, Mateo and Ms. Rodriguez," he called, tugging on my hand to the doorway. "I want to bring you somewhere."

Chapter Thirty-Four

BLAISE

"Where are we?" Vera asked, staring out the window at the brightly lit skatepark. A couple of kids that I didn't recognize walked to their beat-up '99 Nissan next to us with their boards, and Vera's eyes widened. "You brought me to the skatepark?"

"Yeah."

"I thought we were going back to your house," she said, staring in awe at a guy riding, doing flip tricks on the concrete.

I pulled the key out of the ignition and tapped the pizza box in her lap so she'd know to pull it out of the car with her. "Yeah, well, it's boring there," I said, wanting to avoid the conversation.

Truthfully, I didn't want to bring her back to my place right now.

It wasn't anything like her house. Sure, her place was smaller, but at least it was homier, instead of dark and sleek and uninviting. At least her family lived there with her, and she had people to talk to, instead of talking to four bland-ass walls. Hell, I'd barely fucking spoken a word to any housekeeper that my parents had after Vera's mother got fired.

"Am I going to watch you skateboard?" she asked, following me out of the car.

"Maybe."

I opened the trunk to retrieve my skateboard, a helmet, and kneepads.

Vera giggled over my shoulder, the sound making my chest light. "Wow, I didn't pin you as the type of guy who uses a helmet or kneepads while skateboarding."

"These aren't for me."

Clutching the pizza box, she furrowed her brows and looked around the nearly empty skatepark. "There's nobody else here. Who are they ..." she started. When my lips curled into a smirk, she backed a foot away and shook her head. "Oh, no. I don't think so."

I snatched the pizza box from her hand and tossed her the helmet and kneepads. "Put them on. You're going to need them. You can barely walk on your own two feet without stumbling."

She grasped the protection gear in her smaller hands. "Which is exactly why I'm not getting on a skateboard! You think I'll be able to glide on that thing?!"

"I'll help you. Put them on."

"Blaise!" she cried, shaking her head and staring at the black helmet. "I can't do this. I'm going to fall over and get hurt."

Because I knew she wouldn't put the helmet on willingly, I set the pizza box down on top of my car, grabbed the helmet from her, and fastened it on her head. As I buckled the strap under her chin, she frowned up at me.

"You're not going to get hurt. I'm going to teach you."

"Knowing you, you'll let me fall and laugh."

I roughly clutched her chin in my hand and pulled it up, so she looked directly at me. "Do you really think that I would let you get hurt, Sunshine?" I asked, taking the kneepads from her hands and staring down at her.

She didn't really think I would intentionally hurt her, did she?

She crossed her arms over her chest and mumbled, "Well, maybe emotionally."

After I playfully rolled my eyes at her, I crouched down and strapped the kneepads on her. I didn't know if I had fucked up or if Vera was speaking from insecurity or if it was both. But I loathed the fact that she thought I would hurt her.

All I wanted to tell her was how I really felt.

"I don't know how I feel about this," she whispered, nervously playing with her fingers.

I opened the trunk back up and scrambled through the shit in there for the elbow pads because I knew that I had them somewhere in here. If Vera hurt herself, she wouldn't ever let me take her back here.

Once I found them, I strapped them onto her, too, and handed her the skateboard. To my surprise, she actually grabbed it from me without whining or complaining too much more.

I nodded to an empty space, where beginners usually hung out. "We'll start there."

Vera scrunched her nose and walked with the board to the small declines. "Here?"

Leaning my phone against a metal bench with the back camera facing the beginner area, I hurried over to her and placed the skateboard on the ground.

She stood in front of it and stared at the concrete. "I'm scared."

I held out my hands for her to take. "There's nothing to worry about."

"Um, how about dying?" she said, like it was the most obvious thing in the world. "What if I fall and break my neck?"

"Shit." I chuckled. "That would be terrible, huh?"

After teasingly shoving my shoulder, she let out a small laugh and glanced down at my hands while chewing on the inside of her cheek. "If I get hurt, I'm never coming back here again. Do you understand me?"

"I wouldn't expect anything less."

She glanced back up at me and placed her hands in mine. I tugged on them lightly, helping her stand up on the board. Now on four wheels instead of two legs, Vera trembled slightly, her legs unsteady.

"B-Blaise," she said, clutching my hands tighter.

"I got you, Vera. Relax and try to steady your legs."

"I can't."

The board wiggled back and forth under her feet, her knees almost buckling. I placed one foot between her two trembling legs and steadied the board enough so she wouldn't shake.

After a moment, I slowly eased my weight off the board until she gained her balance herself. She looked down at the board, then at me, a small smile crossing her face, but she still didn't let go of my hands.

"Now what?" she asked.

Without asking for her permission because I knew she'd say no immediately, I gently tugged her down the small ramp. She shouted in terror as the board began gliding slow as fuck and squeezed her eyes closed.

"Blaise, it's going so fast! I'm going to fall over."

"Open your eyes, V."

She squeezed her eyes closed even harder, her balance slipping. "Blaise!"

"Stand still."

But she had already put too much of her weight on the back of the board to try to stop herself from gliding down the decline. The skateboard went flying down the decline, and her body flew in the opposite direction.

She shouted as she fell, her eyes still closed. I curled my arm under her body before she could even get close to the ground and picked her up.

With her chest rising and falling quickly, she slowly opened her eyes. "You stopped me."

"Like I said I would," I said.

After standing back up on her own two feet, she pushed some dark hair out of her face. "I don't know if I can do this," she whispered, curling her fingers into my chest. "I'm so bad and so scared to fall."

Little did she know that I had been scared to fall too, but I had fallen the moment she showed up to my car that afternoon in Redwood.

Chapter Thirty-Five

BLAISE

"Don't let go!" Vera shouted two hours later.

When the board glided with ease down the beginner's slope, I released her hands. She widened her eyes as big as saucers and rode down the slope, her speed increasing with every moment that passed.

"Blaise! I said not to let go!"

"But you're doing it, V! Keep going."

Vera steadied herself as much as she could but didn't show any sign of stopping when she came to the end of the skatepark. Unlike how I had shown her to stop—to place her weight on the tail of the board—she jumped off the board and tumbled onto the concrete, arms first.

Oomph.

The skateboard slammed into the park bench and nearly knocked over my phone. I jogged over to Vera, who turned onto her ass and leaned back on her hands. I expected for her to frown at me, but she was actually … smiling.

"I did it."

I grabbed her hands and tugged her to her feet. "You did."

Once she wiped the sweat off her forehead with the back of her hand, Vera glanced over at the pizza box that must've been cold by now. "Gah, that was a lot of work. I'm hungry," she said, skipping over to it and collapsing on the concrete beside it.

After grabbing a slice of pizza, I lay back in the skatepark bowl and stared up at the dark sky. Vera sat crisscross next to me with the helmet and kneepads still on. It must've been around ten p.m., but we had this place all to ourselves tonight.

Leaning onto one of my forearms, I unstrapped her helmet and placed it down on the opposite side of my body, so she could lie down beside me. Vera took a bite of the pizza, slumped her shoulders forward, and lay back, staring up at the sky.

"That was ... fun."

My lips curled into a soft smile. "Good."

She didn't know how much her coming here with me meant to me. Nobody hung out with me at the skatepark or pretty much anywhere else. It ... fucking meant more to me than anything else ever had.

But because I ruined everything that I ever fucking had, I found myself asking the one question that I'd told myself I wouldn't. "You have a good time with João tonight?" I asked, the words acid on my tongue. As soon as the question left my mouth, I knew I had destroyed fucking everything.

But I couldn't take it back now.

With the pizza halfway to her mouth, Vera froze. She turned her head to the side to stare at me, but I didn't look at her. I couldn't. She might've cared about me a little, but not the same way that I wanted her. She only wanted me for sex, just like ... everyone else did.

"What do you mean?" she asked.

"You know what I mean."

I balled my hand into a tight fist by my side, feeling so fucking useless. While I could intimidate any other kid at Redwood, Poison was different. The only way I'd be able to keep someone like João away from Vera was if I kicked his ass so badly that he wouldn't be able to walk for weeks. Even then, he'd get his buddies after me.

Again, Vera became silent and took a bite of her pizza. "I'll tell you, if you tell me about your black eye."

"I got into a fight. Nothing more than that."

"Why'd you get into a fight?"

Pressing my lips together, I stared up at the stars, like we used to do in my backyard as kids. Except way back then, I hadn't cared about losing Vera because I never thought I would. I'd thought she would be in my life forever. Now, I knew differently.

"I already answered one of your questions. You have to answer my question first."

"No."

"Vera," I said through gritted teeth, "come on. Don't be a bitch."

"I'm not being a bitch. Why can't you just tell me why you got into a fight?"

"Because you don't need to know."

"Well, you don't need to know about João then, and if that makes me a bitch, then—"

"I got into a fucking fight because I like you, all right?!" I shouted, unable to stop because, fuck, I needed to know what she was doing with João. I needed to know how much fucking money I had to spend to get rid of his ass, to get him off my girl. "I fucking like you, Vera."

Chapter Thirty-Six

VERA

"Wh-what?" I whispered, turning my head to face Blaise.

I must have heard him wrong. He couldn't have actually said that. There was no way.

With a slice of pizza halfway to his mouth, he stopped and turned toward me with a soft expression on his face. He didn't make a move to take back what he had said, but he didn't seem to want to say anything more.

"No," I said, suddenly sitting up and looking down upon him. "Tell me you're lying."

For years, I had waited for someone to show even the slightest bit of interest in me. I wanted to feel like the girls did in the books I wrote, but all I felt now was fear. I dropped my pizza, wrapped my arms around myself, and shook my head, unable to believe it. Not *wanting* to believe it.

"Blaise," I whispered, scrambling to my feet and turning away from him, "you're lying to me, right? You have to be lying to me. It was a joke. A funny joke that I ... that has to be it, right? You've always made bad jokes like that."

Hell, Blaise *never* made jokes like that.

I'd dreamed that the day a boy told me that he liked me, I would feel butterflies in my stomach, warmth would burst through my chest, and I'd be the happiest damn girl alive.

Right now though, none of this made sense.

Blaise Harleen didn't like me. He couldn't.

Blaise Harleen could like anyone else. Literally *anyone*.

Even though he had a slice of pizza in his hand, he sat up, opened the pizza box, and stared into it emptily. At some point when I had asked him if this was all a joke, his soft expression had fallen.

"Yeah." He tossed his slice of pizza into the box and chuckled. "It's a joke. Chill out."

"Blaise," I whispered.

So many thoughts and emotions were rushing through me. While I had practically begged him to admit to me that it was a joke, when he'd actually said it ... I wanted him to take the words back. I wanted them to be both the truth and a lie at the same time.

"You think I would actually fall for you, V?" He laughed coldly, standing and grabbing his skateboard. "Don't kid yourself. I'm the guy holding your little smutty stories over your head and black-mailing you with them."

But something about the way he'd said it, about the sudden coldness in his voice ...

He towered over my smaller frame and showed no remorse on his face, no sadness or pity. I stared up at him, wanting to push him away from me, wanting to pull him closer, wanting to kiss his face and then run away from him.

Fourteen years ago, I'd liked Blaise, too, but his parents had to ruin my life. And then I had gone on hating him for as long as I could. Only bad things came whenever I liked him, whenever we got too close.

My stomach twisted, and I fought the urge to hurl up the pizza.

If I told him how I felt back—how I really felt deep down—then he would hurt me.

Blaise was a playboy, a bad boy, a player who had probably slept with half of Redwood Academy by now, including the teachers. And I was just a nerdy good girl who wanted to be unseen.

He wouldn't change for me. That only happened in my books.

Chapter Thirty-Seven

BLAISE

A half hour later, I gritted my teeth and walked down an aisle at Walmart, trotting behind Vera. Her straight dark brown hair bounced slightly around her shoulders, the scent of her strawberry shampoo drifting behind her.

Why had I said that my feelings were a fucking joke tonight?

"You know that you don't have to stay," Vera said, gaze averted. "I can walk home."

But I refused to leave her here alone. For one, her walk home would be close to an hour as the temperature dropped. This late at night? Fuck no. And no fucking way I'd leave her at Walmart by herself. Creeps hung around the exits, waiting to grab girls like V.

Plus, Mom had texted me about her being home tonight. I didn't want to see that bitch.

"Get what you need. And then let's get out of here," I snapped.

After I'd royally fucked up at the skatepark—I didn't know if she'd ever want to go there with me again—she had asked me to drop her off at Walmart because she needed a few things. I'd thought she actually wanted some space from me because it was awkward as fuck in the car.

Vera marched right toward the office supplies and grabbed herself two college-ruled notebooks and a box of cheap black pens. After hugging them to her chest, she glanced up at me and smiled. "Okay."

"You gonna write your smut in those?" I asked, desperate to keep this thing up.

And by thing, I meant this *blackmail* that really wasn't so much blackmail anymore. If it were, then I wouldn't have caught feelings. I would be using Vera's pussy without giving a fuck if her birth control was active yet or not.

She nodded. "Yeah, I filled my others."

I nodded, not knowing what the fuck to say anymore. I should've never fucking told her how I felt today. I shouldn't have even brought her to the skatepark. I should've played video games with Mateo, eaten pizza, and watched her nervously watch me in her living room.

Vera walked to the self-checkout and scanned her items, tapping on the Pay With Cash button on the screen. After pulling out a worn wallet that looked like it had been used for years, she took a couple hundreds from it.

My eyes widened slightly at the sheer amount of money she couldn't have gotten from the library alone. She'd told me she made barely minimum wage, shelving books.

How the hell did she have that *much?*

"Where'd you get all that money from?"

Once Vera stuffed a hundred-dollar bill for a ten-dollar purchase into the machine, she placed the excess cash into her wallet and bagged the items. "Um ... I got it from ..." She paused and dared to glance up at me. "João."

"João?" I asked through gritted teeth, tensing at the sound of his name. "What kind of shit did he get you into? Why is he giving you this much money, V? You know it's probably all illegal and—"

She grabbed her bag. "I'm babysitting his sister."

"You're what?"

"I'm babysitting his younger sister," she said, looking up at me. "Okay?"

"You mean, you're not"—I stopped short and sucked in a quiet breath—"dating him?"

"Dating him?!" Vera exclaimed, walking to the exit. A cold gust of air rushed in through the open doors, and she pulled her thin jacket closed. "Of course I'm not dating him. He's almost as annoying as *you* are."

While I wanted to give her a playful response back, I found myself letting out a breath and slumping my shoulders forward. A weight lifted off my shoulders, and I finally felt like I could breathe easily again.

All this time, I'd thought he was trying to get with her. But maybe he was? At least he wasn't blackmailing her too. At least she didn't like him or was doing his dirty work behind my back to earn some cash.

"Besides, I think João is dating someone anyway," Vera continued.

But I hadn't been listening. I had stopped after she said she wasn't dating him—where, in the mere tone of her voice, I heard that she *wouldn't ever* date him. Maybe she'd do it to piss me off, like she had with that Jim guy at the library at some point. But not for real.

"Blaise?" Vera said, placing one hand on her hip and standing on the passenger side of my car. "Earth to Blaise. Can you open the door? It's freezing out here. I think my fingers are going to fall off."

After unlocking the car, I slipped into the driver's seat and drove her to the slums. Every now and then, I clutched the steering wheel tightly and glanced over at her, still wishing that I hadn't told her that this was all a joke.

Now that I knew João meant nothing to her ...

Fuck, would that change anything? She had been frightened as fuck when I told her that I liked her, even more scared than when I'd held up her smutty notebook that afternoon a few days ago and told her that I knew all her secrets.

"Thanks for driving me back," she said once I pulled to the curb.

She unbuckled her seat belt, and I unbuckled mine, following her to the front door. I didn't want to go back home. I wished that I hadn't made things fucking awkward. We had been having a good time at the skatepark. What the fuck was wrong with me?

When we reached the door, Vera said a quick goodbye to me and walked into the house, bumping into her mother.

"Go ahead, sweetheart," Ms. Rodriguez said, nudging Vera into the house. "I want to talk to Blaise about something."

Vera eyed her mother for a moment, and then she gave me a small smile and disappeared into the hallway. I stuffed my hands into my jeans pockets and nodded.

"Is something wrong?" I asked, nervous because I didn't want her to stop me from seeing Vera.

That was what my parents had done years ago. And I wouldn't blame Ms. Rodriguez if that was what she wanted to do now—hurt me in order to get back at my parents after all these years. Little did she know that they didn't give a fuck about me. They wouldn't care.

"We're having a small get-together with some of Mateo's friends for his birthday on Sunday," she said, smiling softly at me, accentuating the wrinkles by her eyes. "It's nothing huge, but I wanted to invite you to stop by."

My eyes widened. "Me?"

Mom and Dad might've forced me to attend some prestigious birthday parties for their friends and coworkers, but I hadn't ever really known the people enough to want to go. Hell, nobody I knew ever really invited me anywhere.

Now, this family—Vera's family—was inviting me to a birthday party?

"It's nothing big," she reassured. "And only if you have time. If you're busy, don't worry—"

"I'll be there," I said breathily and with a smile. "I'll definitely be there."

Chapter Thirty-Eight

BLAISE

After I dropped off Vera, I drove back home. Mom's car was parked in the garage.

"You've been out all night," Mom said, crossing her skinny-ass arms and pursing her fake lips at me when I entered the house. After journeying across the room, she stood in those slutty heels of hers at the door. "What did I say about coming home late, Blaise?"

"Yeah, whatever," I grunted.

Usually, I'd tell her off or curse her out. Throw a temper tantrum to get her attention—whether that be the good or the bad—and make her scream at me for ruining her house. But tonight, I couldn't seem to give a damn about her attention anymore.

All I wanted was Vera's. And all I had gotten from her today was fear, disgust.

"Are you even listening to me?" she asked, unfastening her diamond earrings.

After kicking off my shoes, I walked up the stairs without so much as a response. It wasn't like she actually cared for one. She tried to mother me to feel better about herself for her and Dad spending ninety percent of their lives away.

"I'm speaking to you, Blaise Harleen," she shouted.

I continued up the stairs with my skateboard and phone, staring at the marble floor and feeling so empty. I wished that I hadn't told Vera anything in the first fucking place. It was too soon, and I didn't know if I *liked*, liked her like that.

Fuck, I couldn't know after only a few days. But maybe I could after fourteen years of wishing something would happen with her, of pushing away any guy who showed interest in her, of flirting with the women in Redwood's front office so they'd switch me into any classes that I could get with her.

It wasn't fucking fair. I'd had one fucking chance, and I'd ruined it.

"Blaise!" Mom shouted.

"What?!" I snapped, twirling around from the top of the stairs and glaring down at her. "What the fuck do you want? You want me to get out of your hair, and I fucking do that. And now, you're fucking screaming at me for it. Shut the fuck up."

Mom stared at me with wide eyes and placed a hand over her chest, as if she was stunned, as if I'd never screamed at her before, as if she fucking cared about me at all. All she gave a fuck about was herself.

A moment passed, and she cleared her throat. "Don't speak to me like that."

"Don't speak to me at all," I growled. "It's not like you've made an effort all these years."

"That's not true," she said, rushing up the stairs after me.

I turned on my heel and walked down the hallway toward my bedroom, where I wanted to barricade myself in for some peace and quiet so I could deal with all this shit running through my head.

"I've tried."

"When it was convenient for you!" I said, anger rushing through me, making my chest tight and my eyes hot. "The only time you care about me—the only time *anyone* cares about me—is when it's convenient for you."

Everything inside me hurt so fucking badly. Nobody gave a shit. Ever.

"Blaise Harleen."

When I reached my door, I spun around to face her again. "What's convenient for you this time, Mom? Hmm? You want me to attend another fancy dinner with you to impress your colleagues? Flirt with some girl, so you can secure a deal with her father?"

Mom straightened herself out and pursed her lips again. Her face had been injected with shit so many times that she didn't even look the same as when she'd fired Vera's mother, when my whole world turned upside down. I could barely even recognize her anymore.

"I've heard a rumor," she said softly. "About you hanging out in the slums."

Before she could say another word, I slammed the door in her face and locked it. The only person she fucking cared about was her reputation and herself. Me hanging around Vera made Mom look bad. And me hanging around Vera made Vera look bad.

I couldn't fucking win.

Nobody cared about me.

After pulling on my headphones, I blasted pop punk music into my ears and sat down on my bed with my laptop. I downloaded all the skateboarding videos I had taken since last time and pulled up my video editing software. I was supposed to have a video out tonight for my YouTube channel.

But while I wanted to edit more content for my social media, I found myself watching the video I had taken of Vera learning to skateboard at the park tonight. We were standing close, my hands on her hips.

I cursed under my breath and balled my hand into a fist. In the video, she looked up at me like nobody had fucking looked at me before. I'd thought she—my throat tightened—felt the same way as me. I was wrong.

Vera fell over so many times but continued to stand up, adjusting her kneepads and helmet every time. Still, I couldn't believe that she'd actually tried. Nobody tried shit like this with me. All the girls who I'd *thought* were interested in me just wanted to come over to fuck.

Not Vera.

But then again, Vera didn't like me.

As I replayed the video of Vera on my computer, my phone buzzed. I paused the video and turned toward my phone, deep down hoping that Vera was on the other end, asking me to come over so we could talk.

Skylar: I'm sorry.

Skylar: I shouldn't have gotten in the middle of you and Vera.

I growled. I shouldn't have even looked.

This bitch wasn't sorry. She probably needed something.

Skylar: I want to talk.

Skylar: Please, Blaise. It's important.

I ran my hand through my hair, then gripped it, tugging on the ends because I didn't know what to do. I fucking hated Skylar with all my heart, especially after what had happened in the janitor's closet. But I wasn't sure if Vera would ever come around.

She hadn't even told me about who João was to her until I asked her about it *again*. It was clear that she didn't trust me, that she wanted to get me jealous as fuck, that she didn't want to date me like that. Fucking mixed signals.

Skylar: Can you come pick me up? Something has happened.

Skylar: Please. I can't talk about it over the phone.

After cursing under my breath, I closed my eyes and rested my head against the headboard. All I wanted was for someone to fucking love me. Someone. Fucking anyone at this point.

Chapter Thirty-Nine

VERA

Maddie looped her arm around mine as we strolled through the mall on Friday night, her vanilla perfume wafting around us. Piper was sick, and Blaise hadn't showed up to school today, so I hadn't seen him since he'd brought me home last night.

Thank the Redwood gods that João had been extra nice with the money he gave me for watching his sister because Mateo's birthday party was on Sunday, and I needed to get that twerp something other than a pack of gum, which had been my present to him last year.

"You think he'd like something from GameStop? Like a T-shirt or something?" I asked, gazing into the small store filled with video games and anime T-shirts.

The games were far too expensive for me right now—unless I could find one for, like, twenty bucks.

"Hmm, maybe." Maddie tugged me into the shop and smiled at the nerdy guy behind the counter. She marched right up to him without a care in the world and looked over her shoulder at me. "What kind of anime does he watch?"

"Um ..." I nervously glanced around. "Something about giants?"

"*Attack on Titan*?" the employee said, his nametag reading Viraj. "Maybe?"

He led us to a section of anime T-shirts and pulled out about fifteen shirts, holding them out to me. I grabbed the shirts and shuffled through them, not sure which one he'd like or even wear.

"What do you suggest?" Maddie asked Viraj.

"Personally, my favorite character is ..." He took the shirts from me and pulled one out with a male character who had a hard gaze and a pissed off expression on his pointed face. "This one. His name's Levi. He's pretty cool, but people also like this guy too." He pulled out a shirt that read *Eren*.

I chewed on the inside of my cheek and picked this guy's favorite character shirt because I didn't know what the hell I was doing. If Mateo liked it, he liked it. If he didn't, then oh well. I'd keep the receipt.

After I checked out, I followed Maddie to the food court. She ordered milkshakes for us.

"So, how are you and Blaise?" Maddie asked as we waited.

Fuck, I had really hoped that she wouldn't ask. I had made it all day without questions.

"He, um ..." I tucked some hair behind my ear. "Uh ... he told me that he liked me."

"WHAT?!" she shouted so half the mall could hear her. "WHAT?! Why didn't you say that from the beginning? Vera Rodriguez, why the hell did you wait until now?! You should've called me the minute it happened! When did he say that?"

"Yesterday."

"YESTERDAY?!"

"Yeah," I said, brushing it off like it was nothing. But truthfully, I hadn't stopped thinking about it at all. It had been on my mind all night, all day, every single freaking moment since the skatepark. "But it was a joke."

Maddie rolled her eyes. "I know you think that but—"

"He said it."

"That's a lie," Maddie said as an employee placed our milkshakes on the counter. Maddie grabbed two red straws and shoved them into the shakes. "What did he say exactly? Because I know that he likes you. It's obvious."

"He was being serious about it being a joke," I said, not wanting to believe her.

"What'd he say?"

"He asked me if I really thought someone like him would like me," I whispered, my chest tightening. My throat dried, and I found myself tensing at the memory of last night. "That he was the one blackmailing me so we could have sex."

Maddie furrowed her brows and drew her cheeks in as she sucked up some milkshake through her straw. "That's weird. How'd he say that he liked you?"

The cup chilled my palm, but I gripped it and took a long sip of my shake, walking through the food court with Maddie. "He asked me how I knew João, and I ... I didn't want to tell him because I—"

Why hadn't I wanted to tell him again?

"Because you're a nervous, anxious mess," Maddie finished. "Now, continue."

"Anyway, I told him that I'd tell him if he told me how he got his black eye."

"And?"

"And we argued for a few moments."

"And?"

"And then he told me that it was because he liked me," I whispered, the words warm on my tongue. They sounded so laughable now. "It came out of nowhere. Like, how does him saying something like that give him a black eye?! It—"

"Mmhmm ..." Maddie hummed.

"What?"

"What were you guys doing before that?"

My cheeks flushed. "Skateboarding."

She grinned wickedly. "So, you're telling me that *Blaise Harleen* brought you skateboarding and then told you that he liked you, and then out of nowhere and without *you* freaking out about it, he said it was all a joke?"

Worriedly, I rubbed my arm. "Maybe I freaked out a little bit."

"Of course you did," Maddie continued, sliding onto a wooden bench. "What'd you say?"

"I asked him if he was kidding."

Maddie rolled her eyes. "Oh my God, Vera, you're hopeless sometimes."

"What?" I exclaimed. "He had to be kidding. Why would he like me when he could choose from literally every other girl at Redwood? He has everything he could ever want, and if he doesn't have it, then he could get it easily. Why me?"

"Because you're smart and funny, you have more of a personality compared to all these other bitches in Redwood, you are hot as fuck and hardworking, you can—"

"Stop it," I hushed her. "Please."

"No," Maddie said, sipping on her milkshake. "Because it's true and you don't believe it."

I sat on the bench and stared at the ground, my lips threatening to tremble. My entire body tensed again, and I found myself holding my breath. "You're right," I whispered. "I don't believe it. I've never believed it."

"Well, you'd better start," Maddie said. "Because I'm about to smack some sense into you if you don't. Blaise likes you for real, and I know that you like him too. You've always liked him, ever since we were in, like, middle school."

"I have not!"

"Liar." Maddie smirked. "You've wanted his dick, even then."

"Can you not scream that?!" I whisper-yelled at her, noticing people staring.

"It's true," she said. "And I'm going to help you snag him."

"How are you going to do that?" I asked.

She grabbed my phone. "We're going to text Blaise."

Chapter Forty

VERA

Maddie might've gotten into my head. Just a bit.

I paced around my living room on Saturday morning and gnawed on the inside of my cheek. Nerves zipped up and down my arms, my stomach in tight knots. She had convinced me to message Blaise last night, but I still hadn't gotten a response.

At the skatepark the other night, I had freaked out more than I should've. But I didn't want to get hurt, especially not after I'd found Blaise and Skylar in the janitor's closet again. I didn't want to be stupid and blind, like some of the girls in books were when they let the hero take advantage of them every step of the way.

I wanted to be strong. I wanted to ... to not be so insecure all the time.

"I'll be back later," I shouted to Mateo, who fumbled through his closet, looking for something to impress the girls he had invited over to his party tomorrow afternoon. "If you need me, call me!"

Mateo looked out of his bedroom and wiggled his brows. "Gonna go see your boyfriend?"

"He's not my boyfriend," I said, pulling on a scarf and zippering my jacket.

After smirking wickedly at me, Mateo disappeared back into his bedroom. I rolled my eyes and stuffed my hands into my coat, knowing that I would have a long walk for maybe even nothing. Blaise might not actually be skateboarding today.

So, I retraced my steps to the skatepark in hopes that he'd be there. Maybe he'd be at a fancy brunch with his mother and father and their snotty, rich friends. But maybe ... I'd get to see him on his board today. Though I didn't know the first thing that I'd say to him if he was there.

Once I trekked for thirty minutes through the cold, the skatepark came into view. To shield my cheeks from the searing wind, I put my head down and power-walked to the entrance of the busy place.

At least ten percent of Redwood Academy must've been at the skatepark today. I walked on the edge of the park, dodging groups of people skateboarding inches from me. They did tricks on bars and rode down steep slopes, riding a lot faster than I had.

I stared in awe, secretly hoping that Blaise was here. I didn't want to have walked down here for nothing, and I had nobody else to hang out with. No way would I stay home all day as Mateo asked for my advice on the hundreds of bad outfits he'd put together for tomorrow.

When I found a bench, I sat my ass down and hoped that nobody would crash into me. From my seat, I scanned the parking lot and spotted Blaise's blue Ferrari F8 among the shittier cars from the slums.

I inhaled excitedly, my chest warm and light. *He's here.*

Glancing around at the people zooming by, I spotted Blaise sitting on a bench across the park. With a pair of headphones on, he had his board in his lap and another longer board propped up on the bench next to him.

My stomach turned, my insecurities rushing through me. Who did that board belong to? Was he here with someone else? Was that why he wasn't answering any of my messages? Maybe he really had been joking about liking me. Maybe he was with Skylar.

A girl with dyed red and black hair—someone who must've been a sophomore at Redwood—walked over to him. She had the typical E-girl look with a perfect nose, freckles that lightly decorated her face, and flawless mascara.

Mouth drying, I stared at them and couldn't seem to look away. I clutched my purse to my body and wondered why I had come here again.

What the fuck was I thinking? What the fuck possessed me to walk thirty minutes in the cold for this?

Blaise had made it clear that the feelings he'd admitted for me were a joke.

Nothing more.

Why'd I think coming here, seeing him and talking to him, would make a difference to either of us?

He wanted to get into my pants. Hell, he was blackmailing me —*blackmailing me!*—and somehow, I'd thought he felt differently.

Just when I was about to stand, Blaise nodded to the girl and moved his longer board off the bench, so she could sit next to him. She retied her shoelaces and gazed out into what Blaise had called the bowl.

Another guy rode up to her and stopped, leaning down to kiss her. Blaise looked over at them once, then hopped up from the bench and set his phone down against his longboard, holding it upright, as if he was recording something.

The knots in my stomach uncoiled. I forced myself to take a steady breath and to stay, unlike the natural urge I'd had inside me to run far away from here and from Blaise. I didn't—I shouldn't —trust him.

But I didn't want to run away.

Not yet.

That was what girls in books did. They assumed. They overre-acted. They hurt the ones they loved to protect themselves. And while I wanted to be different—so badly—I knew how they felt. I knew how much it hurt to feel like shit and how much strength it took to find my confidence.

After dropping his board, Blaise hopped onto it and slid into the bowl, crouching and moving his body at angles to keep himself balanced with ease. When he came up on the other side, he grabbed the concrete edge with one hand and the board with the other, then propelled his body upward, using his momentum.

The board slipped from his hand and rolled down into the bowl. Thank the fucking Redwood gods that he caught himself from colliding headfirst into the ground, and instead, he slid down the edge.

Shaking his head, he grabbed the board and found his way back to the top. After a couple more tries, he nailed the flip he had done in the air and came up on the other side with a smile. Yes, *a fucking smile* on Redwood's bad boy.

Warmth spread throughout my chest, and I couldn't stop myself from smiling too.

Blaise continued to practice more and more dangerous flips and tricks on his board in the big bowl. I crossed one leg over the other and watched like a freaking creep as he did his thing and rode.

One trick, he fucked up as he skateboarded at full speed toward me. He crashed right into me, his board flying toward the walls of the park and his body hitting the concrete to my left.

"Shit." He hopped up quickly and dusted himself off. "Sorry, I —" When he looked up at me, he stopped and widened his eyes. "Vera," he said breathlessly. "What are you doing here?"

"I'm ..." Nerves shot through me, but I swallowed them. "I'm here for you."

Chapter Forty-One

BLAISE

"You're here for me?" I repeated because I didn't understand her.

Why would she come here for me? She had work this afternoon and could've been at home, writing her smutty little stories, cozied up on the couch and not in the freezing cold. Besides, she'd made it clear that she didn't like me.

"I tried texting you," she whispered. "You didn't answer."

"Shit," I said, looking over at my phone that I had leaned against my longboard across the skatepark. I had turned off all my notifications the other night after Skylar messaged me because I didn't want to be bothered. "Sorry. What'd you need?"

Her brown eyes widened, becoming almost doe-like. "Um ... nothing."

"Nothing?"

"No, I didn't need anything."

"Then, why'd you text me?" I asked, still confused.

I wasn't trying to be an asshole, but she was confusing as hell. She'd freaked out the other day when I said that I liked her annoying ass, and then she'd texted me for nothing. If she'd texted me at night, she'd probably wanted to hook up or some shit. Her birth control should be working now, right?

"Your birth control working now?" I snapped, working myself up. "Is that why?"

"What? No!" she said, nervously clasping her hands together and playing with her fingers. "I mean, yes, it's working now. It's been a week, but I didn't want to hook up with you, if that's what you're insinuating."

"Then, why'd you text me?" I repeated.

"God, Blaise, because," she said, rolling her eyes and averting her gaze, "why can't I?"

"Because we're not friends and you don't even like me. There's no point."

For the love of the Redwood gods, I wished I had shut my fucking mouth. Vera had shown up at the skatepark and had been watching me for who knew how long in the freezing cold. She was the only person that I had fucking talked to in the past thirty-six hours.

"I'm sorry," she whispered. "I shouldn't have come."

When she stood, my chest tightened.

No, she can't leave.

I grabbed her wrist and yanked her back toward me. I couldn't shut my fucking mouth and took my hurt out on everyone else, like my parents took it out on me.

She inhaled sharply and stared up at me worriedly. "I just wanted to see you."

"How long have you been here?"

"Maybe forty minutes now?"

"Forty fucking minutes?" I asked in fucking disbelief that this chick had been sitting here in the cold for nearly an hour for me. "Why didn't you stop me?"

She shrugged shyly and looked at the concrete. "I didn't want to bother you because you seemed to be having a good time. You always seem so pissed off that it was kinda nice, seeing you so ... I don't know ... happy?"

After a couple moments, I clutched Vera's wrist tighter and stepped closer to her. The heat from her skin was fucking contagious because my entire body warmed. "You're really here for me?"

She shifted from foot to foot and glanced down at my hand circled around her smaller wrist. Once she slipped herself out of my hold, she teetered from foot to foot, her cheeks flaming red. "I was just, um ..." She paused, then gulped. "Yeah, I'm here for you."

Warmth spread through my chest, my heart racing. Part of me couldn't believe that she was here, standing in front of me, because ... she'd wanted to see me. Nobody ever really wanted to see me for me.

Every second that I didn't respond to her, Vera blushed even harder. "Uh, are you here with someone else?" she said, glancing over my shoulder at my longboard and phone on the other side of the skatepark. "You have another board with you, and, uh, you were talking with a girl."

My lips curled into a smirk. *Is she jealous?*

"I'm here alone," I reassured, grabbing her hand again and walking around the bowl toward the bench with my board on the other side of the park. My stomach felt so light and fluttery—something I hadn't ever experienced. "If you wanna ride, that's a longboard. It's easier than a skateboard. You'd probably have fun with it."

When we reached my stuff, I turned off the recording on my phone and tucked it away into my jeans pocket. Then, I picked up the longer board and set it down in front of her. It must've been nearly twice the size of the skateboard that she had used the other night.

Staring down at it with wide eyes, she shook her head. "Maybe some other time. There are far too many people here. I'd probably run into someone."

I placed my foot on the board. "We don't have to ride it here. We can leave."

Still, she seemed hesitant. "I have to work in a little bit. I should probably be going soon."

But I didn't want her to leave. Not yet. Literally moments ago, I'd found out that she was here because of me because *she'd wanted to see me*. And while there was a small voice in my head that said she might've wanted something from me like everyone else did, I ignored it.

Vera tugged her jacket together and zipped it up as far as it could go. "It's getting cold."

"Let me drive you."

She shook her head. "No, no. You're having fun. Don't let me stop you."

"I was about to leave the park anyway." *Lie.* "I'm driving you to work."

"Are you sure?" she asked, stuffing her hands into her pockets.

Once I gathered my stuff, I grabbed her hand and led her to my car. She slipped into the passenger seat as I deposited my shit into the trunk. Vera rubbed her hands together when I started the car.

"So, were you recording your skateboarding tricks?" she asked on our drive toward the library. "You had your phone out."

"Yeah."

"For what?"

"I, uh"—I slid my palm across the wheel's leather curve—"have a YouTube channel."

"You run a YouTube channel for skateboarding?" she asked, eyes widening. She pulled out her phone and tapped on the YouTube app. "Really? What's it called?"

I drew my tongue across my teeth and gripped the steering wheel tighter. I hadn't shown anyone my YouTube channel. No family. No fake friends. Nobody at Redwood Academy. It was my thing that nobody knew about.

"Come on. Tell me," Vera teased. "Or is Redwood's bad boy embarrassed about it?"

When I pulled to a stop in front of the library, I grabbed her phone and typed in the name of my channel—because I didn't want to ruin what was slowly forming between us. She barely trusted me as it was.

She stared at the screen with wide eyes. "You really do have one," she whispered, scrolling through the hundred videos that I had posted. "And almost two hundred thousand followers. Jesus, Blaise."

"It's nothing," I said.

"Nothing?!" Vera asked, shutting off her phone and glancing up at me. "It's so cool!"

"You think?"

She grinned and unbuckled her seat belt. "Of course I do."

The lightness reappeared in my stomach, my chest warming. I didn't know what it was, but Vera Rodriguez was doing something to me—something that I didn't know I could stop, something I didn't know I *wanted* to stop.

Chapter Forty-Two

VERA

"Hey, sweetheart. How's your day going?" a middle-aged man asked, placing three books on the library's counter and looking for conversation with a girl half his age, who was still in high school. "I'm returning these."

Deciding to ignore him, I scanned the books into the library and sent that man on his way out of here. From the couches across from the main desk, Blaise gritted his teeth and glared at the man's departing figure.

I attempted to hide a smile as I placed the books on the cart behind me. Three hours ago, I had doubted that Blaise actually planned to leave the skatepark, but he continued to insist that he drive me to work. And then he stuck around and told me that he had work to do here anyway. But I'd bet that he just wanted to drive me home too.

Once the man left, Blaise glanced over at me and arched a brow. I slipped onto my stool and clicked through the library's computer screen aimlessly, acting like I didn't see how jealous and possessive he seemed right now.

It was kinda ... cute.

Wait, cute?! Did I just call Blaise Harleen cute?

After shaking my head in disbelief, I pulled my notebook out of my backpack to pass the time while I waited for the next customer. My stomach fluttered as I reread the last paragraph that I had written about a bad boy who attended a prestigious high school and fell for the good girl who had come from nothing.

Had I been working on a story about Blaise and me? Maybe.

It was a kind of therapy for me, the kind that might break me in the end. If things didn't work out with the bad boy, the heroine in my story would be heartbroken. The heroine being ... me.

Problems always seemed easier to deal with in fiction.

In real life, they left a never-healed scar over my heart.

"Writing about what you want me to do to you next?" Blaise asked, suddenly leaning over the front counter.

I widened my eyes and snapped my notebook shut, not wanting him to read even a sentence of this story. It wasn't for his eyes—and would *never* be for his eyes. I might've shown up at the skatepark for him today, but I didn't want him to know how much I liked him.

Hell, a couple of minutes ago, I was calling him cute, and this man was still holding my smutty stories over my head, promising to blackmail the fuck out of me. First, it had been my body-betraying syndrome that I had caught from the romance books I had written and read. Now, it was some sort of Stockholm syndrome.

Jesus Christ.

"Um, no," I said, keeping myself as calm as I could. I shoved the notebook away in my backpack, rested my arms against the counter, and looked up at him. "Now, can I help you? Do you have books to check out? Because if you don't, I need to work."

Blaise chuckled. "There's nobody here."

"Not true. I just checked in a guy's books."

"More like he checked *you* out. Fucking creep." Blaise gritted his teeth and stared back at the door, as if the guy would stroll back into the library to attempt to get my number. "It's not like you're doing much anyway, Sunshine. You're writing smut at work. Your panties are probably ruined."

"Blaise!" I scolded. "What is wrong with you?! This is a library. Keep your voice down."

He smirked and leaned forward, gaze falling to my thighs. "Tell me I'm wrong."

I pressed my legs together and pursed my lips, the warmth gathering inside me, making me hot in all the wrong places. But if I let on that I was horny enough, this man would jump the counter and fuck me at the main desk.

"Y-you're wrong," I finally stammered.

Peeling his gaze away from me, Blaise looked over his shoulder, then toward the back rooms, as if he was searching for something or someone else here. "Anyone else working with you tonight?"

"No," I said, releasing a breath once I figured he only wanted to tease me.

"Good." Blaise hopped over the counter, so he stood behind the main desk with me.

My eyes widened. "What are you—"

"Give me your panties."

"Wh-what?!" I whisper-yelled, sitting up straight. "Are you crazy?! I'm working."

Blaise hummed, crouched beneath the counter between my legs, and tugged on my thighs to pull me closer to him. I inhaled sharply, the heat growing in my core, and glared down at him.

In one swift movement, Blaise reached under my skirt and pulled my underwear down to my ankles, and then he shoved them into his pocket. I forced my thighs together, heart pounding.

"Blaise, what are you doing?" I yelled softly at him. "I'm working! You can't—"

He pulled my thighs apart and placed his hot mouth right over my cunt. I gasped and tensed as his tongue skillfully moved around my clit. Pleasure and warmth shot through my body, my nipples hardening against my bra.

"Blaise," I whispered.

"You're supposed to be working, baby," he mumbled to me. "Not moaning my name."

Desperate to hold back a whimper, I bit my lip and concentrated on the library's keyboard. Holy fuck. His tongue moved in torturous circles, faster and faster, his fingers slipping inside me. I tightened around them and attempted to hold back another whine.

"Blaise, you need to s-stop. W-we can't do this h-here."

He chuckled menacingly against me. "I'm not going to stop until you come all over my mouth, Sunshine. You can't tell me what I can and can't do with you. Your pussy is mine. Your body is mine. *You're mine.*"

When the last few words came out of his mouth, a rush of delight exploded through me. I curled my toes and tried to stop my legs from trembling. Who would've thought that the bad boy calling me his would make me feel so good?

"Hey, Vera," someone said from the counter.

I snapped my head up to see Jim from CVS standing in front of me. I sucked in a sharp breath. My heart thrashed inside my chest. Blaise seemed to tense for the briefest moment at the sound of a male's voice, but then he placed my thighs on his shoulders and buried his face between them.

"H-hi," I stuttered. "How can I h-help you?"

"I wanted to return these," he said, placing the books on the counter.

"Mine," Blaise mumbled against my clit, only loud enough for me to hear.

He pounded his fingers deeper and harder into me, his tongue moving faster. I clenched my pussy, desperately trying to hold off on the best orgasm of my entire life, and grabbed the books.

"O-okay."

"*Mine.*"

"How've you been?" Jim asked, leaning against the counter.

"*Mine*," Blaise murmured, his voice becoming more agitated by the second. "*Mine.*"

"I've been—"

"She's fine," Blaise growled louder this time. He pulled away from me and glared up from behind the desk at Jim, who stared at him with wide eyes. "She'd be doing even better if you shut your fucking mouth and left, so I can give her permission to come." Blaise still pumped his fingers in and out of me. "Because I'm not going to give you the satisfaction of watching my girl come."

My body jerked at his words.

My girl.

"If you come on my fingers right now, Vera"—Blaise glared at Jim still as he curled his fingers against my G-spot over and over, driving me freaking wild—"I'm going to fucking punish you, and even your filthy mind won't like it."

"L-leave, J-Jim."

Blaise snapped his head back to me, pumping his fingers as fast as he could. It was like he wanted me to tip over the edge right here and right now, so he could punish me. The pressure rose higher and higher in my core, my legs shaking.

"Don't ever say his name again while you're about to come."

"I-I'm sorry," I whispered, knitting my brows together and throwing my head back, desperately attempting to hold back my orgasm. "P-please leave right now. I-I don't know how much longer I can—"

"Fucking hell," Jim said, scurrying back. "Remind me never to come to the library again."

"Next time you flirt with my girl, I'll fucking kill you," Blaise snarled at him.

When the library doors closed, Blaise nestled back between my legs. He pulled my ass to the edge of my seat and posted my feet on the counter, spreading my legs wider. My pussy pulsed with pleasure, the pressure building higher and higher.

"Mine." He buried his face between my legs and found my clit with his tongue. "You're mine."

"Please," I whispered. "Can I ... can I come?"

"Tell me you're mine."

"Y-yours."

Blaise curled his fingers one last time against my G-spot and ordered that I come for him. I slapped a hand over my mouth and stared down at him as he continued to lick my clit, driving another wave of ecstasy through my body.

"I'm yours."

Chapter Forty-Three

BLAISE

After spending all day with Vera, I parked my car in the garage and smiled foolishly at the steering wheel. Still, I couldn't believe that she'd actually walked all the way to the skatepark today to find me because she'd wanted to see me.

I tucked my keys into my pocket and slipped out of the car, slinging my backpack over my shoulder and heading for the foyer.

Somehow, that woman had convinced me to actually show her my YouTube channel.

Nobody in Redwood knew about it, especially my parents. They wouldn't understand why I wanted to create videos and build my own brand instead of taking over Dad's stupid business that he spent more time with than his family.

"Blaise!" Mom screamed when I stepped into the house. "Where have you been?"

Not wanting to deal with her shit right now, I yanked my headphones out of my backpack, slipped them over my ears, and turned on some pop punk music to drown out her shrill voice. Then, I continued through the house to the stairs.

Mom stood in the living room, blocking the stairs, with fury written across her fake face. She screamed at me. Thank fuck that I had the noise-canceling function on my headphones, so I didn't have to hear her.

Before I could pass her, she ripped the headphones right off my ears and bent the headband with so much force that they physically snapped in half.

I tore them away from her, rage rushing through me. "What the fuck?!"

"You skipped the fucking dinner!" Mom shouted at me, shoving me back. "How many fucking times did I remind you about it? I fucking needed you there tonight. We're trying to secure a huge business deal. What the hell is wrong with you?"

"I told you that I wasn't going!"

"You have nothing in that head of yours." She seethed, picking up a wine bottle from the coffee table that she must've been drinking. She waved the bottle at me. "Fucking nothing. I bet you were at the skatepark today, weren't you? Ruining your fucking life with those no-good kids from the slums. If you don't get your act together, you'll never be able to run your father's business."

"I don't want to run Dad's business," I said between gritted teeth. I gripped my broken headphones in my hand. I'd be able to buy new ones, but that wasn't the point. These headphones were the only thing keeping me sane here. "I don't know how many times I have to tell you that. It's not like you listen to anything I tell you anyway, Caroline."

"You disgust me," she said, forgoing a wineglass and taking a sip right from the bottle. "You're grounded, Blaise. You're not allowed to go to the skatepark anymore or hang out with anyone from the slums. Do you understand me?"

I rolled my eyes. "I don't give a fuck."

She could ground me all she wanted. But she wouldn't enforce shit when one of her friends called her and wanted her to go out for the night. She'd be out there in a fucking heartbeat, and I'd be free to do whatever the fuck I wanted anyway.

"What the hell do you mean, you don't give a fuck?! You need to respect me."

"I haven't had respect for you since you fired Luciana Rodriguez for *nothing*!"

"Oh, don't start with her," Mom said, rolling her eyes and walking through the living room. "You always bring her back up. *Luciana this. Luciana that.* You should be thanking me that we don't have someone like *her* working for us. Her family is trash."

Balling my hands into fists by my sides, I growled and forced myself to turn around to head up the stairs. If I stayed down here with this bitch for another second, I might actually do something to get myself thrown into jail.

"We're not done with this conversation!" Mom screamed.

I pressed my lips together and walked toward my bedroom, where I'd fucking disappear into until she left for the week, for the month. Who the fuck knew how long it'd be after how much I'd *disappointed* poor mother tonight. Doubted I'd see Dad anytime this year either.

After slamming my door closed, I locked it and tossed my skate-board down in front of it. If Mom somehow got into my bedroom tonight, I hoped she tripped on it because fuck her. She didn't give a damn about me.

My headphones were fucking busted, so I turned on my speaker and decided to piss her off even more. If I made her angry enough, she'd leave for the night or lock herself away in the bathroom on the opposite side of the house.

I turned on some pop punk that I had been listening to at the skatepark as loudly as it would go, then crashed on my bed, pulling out my laptop and wishing that I had never come home tonight. This day had quickly gone to shit because of her.

At least I had a reason to get out of this shithole tomorrow— Mateo's birthday.

Chapter Forty-Four

BLAISE

Sunday morning, I walked out of the mall with two shopping bags for Mateo's birthday party. Mom had left sometime during the night, like I'd expected, so I didn't have to deal with her grounding bullshit. I slid into the car, tossed the bags onto the passenger seat, and pulled out the gift bag to slip a PS5 box into it.

I had preordered it nearly a fucking year ago for myself, but Mateo would probably get more use out of it than I would. Plus, I could buy another one from a scalper for double the original price if I really wanted it.

After wrapping my other gift in a black matte gift bag, I placed them both on the seat and headed for Vera's house. Most parties I attended with my parents were black-tie events, so it felt fucking weird to show up in my regular clothes, but Vera's mom had insisted.

To my surprise, cars were parked heavily on the side of the road in the slums. I found a space in front of a small, run-down house near the corner of the street, where a young girl who couldn't be older than five ran around the front yard.

As I stepped out of the car, I grabbed the PS5 gift bag and shut my door.

"The fuck you doing in the slums?" someone said from behind me.

I turned toward the small house and saw João Rocha sitting on the front steps, taking a long drag on his cigarette.

The little girl ran up to him and wrapped her small arms around his shoulders. "When's Mama coming home?"

"Soon, Ana," he said, still staring at me. "You here for Vera?"

While I wanted to say some shit to him, I wasn't going to make a scene in front of his sister. I still had a fucking problem with him flirting with Vera in front of me the other day at the library, and I would take care of him one of these days.

Ignoring him, I walked down the street and toward Vera's busy house. I knocked twice on the door, unsure if they would even hear me. It sounded loud inside, like Mateo had invited half of Redwood to the slums.

As I was about to walk right into the house, Vera opened the door.

"What are you doing here?" Vera asked in surprise. Dressed in a long-sleeved maroon dress that hugged her curves, she stared up at me with wide eyes. "I can't go out with you today. I have my brother's—"

"Birthday party," I finished, holding out a gift bag on my index finger. "I know."

She furrowed her brows and stepped to the side, letting me pass. "You know?"

"Not everything is about you, Sunshine."

Though I wouldn't be here if it wasn't for her. I would be bored as fuck in my house by myself, listening to some depressing and angsty music that wouldn't save me, no matter how many songs I blasted.

"Blaise!" Mateo called from the kitchen, leaving the two sopho-more girls at the counter.

"What up, kid?" I asked, grabbing his shoulder and squeezing. "Happy birthday." I nodded back toward the kitchen at the girls gossiping about something with Mateo's friends gathered in a circle. "You gonna leave those girls over there by themselves?"

"Nah," Mateo said, walking backward over to them. "I just wanted to say thanks for coming. Mom told me that she invited you, but I didn't think you'd actually show up."

"Come on," I said. "Of course I would."

Once Mateo mingled with his friends, Vera stepped closer and arched a brow up at me. "My mom invited you? Why didn't she tell me? How long have you known about Mateo's birthday party?"

My lips curled into a small smile. "None of your business."

She pressed her lips together tightly to try to hold back a smile. "Why didn't you tell me?"

"Because."

She rolled her brown eyes and opened her mouth to say something, but the front door burst open.

"I brought pizza!" Maddie, Vera's best friend, said, thrusting the front door open and entering with six pizza boxes in her hands. "Happy birthday, Mateo! I still remember when you were shitting in your diapers."

Ms. Rodriguez hurried out of a back room and over to Maddie to grab the boxes from her, shaking her head. "Maddie, I told you that you didn't need to bring anything," she said. "This is too much."

"Oh, don't worry about it," Maddie said.

After she helped Ms. Rodriguez lay out the pizzas on the kitchen counter, Maddie turned toward us and widened her eyes when they landed on me. She cut her gaze to Vera and grinned evilly. "It's about time that Vera brought you around."

"I didn't invite him," Vera said.

"You didn't?" Maddie asked, brows furrowed.

"No. My mom did." Vera tucked some dark hair behind her ear. "Is Piper coming?"

"No, she's still sick."

"So, you invited Maddie and Piper, but not me?" I asked Vera.

"Isn't she a terrible girlfriend?" Maddie asked, smirking at Vera and shaking her head.

"We are not dating, Maddie," Vera whisper-yelled to her best friend as if I wasn't standing right between the two of them. She averted her gaze from me, her dark hair shielding her eyes, and blushed hard as fuck. "Stop it."

While I didn't know what the fuck we were—Vera didn't like to be seen that much in public with me, but she kept coming back around—I found myself smirking at her. In all my player days at Redwood, I never had a girlfriend. But the thought of Vera being my first did something to me.

"The worst," I hummed, grabbing a Styrofoam cup from the kitchen counter.

Without sparing me a glance, Vera grabbed Maddie's wrist and dragged her to the other room, looking like she was about to scold her. But Maddie couldn't seem to care as she giggled all the way into the hallway.

"Thank you so much for coming, sweetheart," Ms. Rodriguez said, walking up to me, holding three twenty-dollar bills in her hands. "Mateo appreciates it. Now, do you know where I can find Maddie? I told her not to bring all those pizzas."

"She walked into the back bedroom with Vera," I said, nodding to her and glancing down at the bills in her hands.

My parents always told me that the poor fought like scavengers with each other for every last penny, that they wouldn't share, no matter what, that they didn't care about anyone but themselves as they tried to fucking survive.

But Ms. Rodriguez—the woman who my parents had fired and who worked double shifts almost every damn night—looked like she wanted to repay her daughter's rich friend for buying some pizzas. It was one of the most generous fucking things I had seen. Ever.

Once Ms. Rodriguez left, I poured myself a drink, sat back on the couch with a Styrofoam cup of root beer, and looked around at the party. Warmth spread through my tightening chest. Genuine smiles, conversation, people here.

It wasn't like Mom and Dad's parties, where there were nothing but fake smiles and even fake people, looking for ways to use everyone else to gain popularity or money. Sitting here almost didn't feel real. It seemed too good to be true.

Chapter Forty-Five

VERA

Before the party, I had made plans to hang out with Maddie for tonight. But at some point, she left the party without telling me and texted me ten minutes later with a winky-face emoji, demanding that I had a good night with Blaise tonight.

"Are you sure nobody else will be here?" I asked Blaise, gnawing on the inside of my cheek and eyeing the small milkshake bar centered in the middle of Redwood's ritzy section with a view of the ocean.

He had insisted I come out with him.

It wasn't that I didn't want to be seen with him—I had been to the skatepark without a problem. I just didn't like the rich Redwood families and students who attended Redwood Academy, and I wasn't ready for the drama that would surround my dating—*are we dating?*—Redwood's bad boy.

"Don't worry about it." He cut the headlights. "Maddie's brother is having a crazy, wild party while their parents are out of town. Nobody is going to be out tonight, especially not down here." When he still saw my hesitation, he continued, "If it makes you feel any better, we can grab the milkshakes to go and sit at the Overlook?"

"What're you trying to do, get into my pants again?" I asked, arching a brow and stepping out of the car. A gust of wind chilled my skin, forcing me to zip my jacket. "Kids only go to the Overlook if they want to fuck."

"I'm not going to deny that." Blaise chuckled, shutting his door and stuffing his hands into his pockets. He opened the door to the milkshake shack. "If I wanna fuck you, your horny ass isn't going to say no."

My cheeks reddened. I mean, he wasn't wrong.

After scanning the room to ensure that I didn't recognize anyone from school, I stepped into the shop and walked up to the counter, staring up at all the flavors of ice cream and types of shakes. I had only been here once with Maddie in the summer because this place was expensive as hell.

"Order anything," Blaise said, pulling out his wallet.

I glanced down at it and gnawed on the inside of my cheek, then turned back to the menu. I didn't want him to pay for me, but I doubted that he would even let me argue to pay for my own.

"Can I have a vanilla milkshake?" I asked the employee.

"Vanilla?" Blaise tsked, leaning against the counter to order an Oreo deluxe milkshake. He turned around to face me, crossing his big arms over his chest, his biceps bulging. "So boring, Sunshine. Thank fuck that's not how you like it in bed too."

"Blaise," I scolded quietly, looking around to make sure nobody had heard him. "Stop it."

"Or what? Hmm?"

"Or I'll ... I'll ..." I started, but then stopped short.

"Blackmail me?" Blaise offered, taunting me with the blackmail he still had on me.

But somehow, I didn't mind it so much anymore. Sure, he could hurt me and tell everyone, but part of me thought that he wouldn't do that. Not now. Not after the day we'd spent together yesterday.

Once he paid for our milkshakes, Blaise drove us to the Overlook. A couple of cars were parked near the rocks with kids from Redwood inside, probably swapping cum. Because it was dark, I didn't mind getting out of the car with Blaise and sitting with him on the rocks.

"You didn't have to get Mateo anything," I said after a while, feeling so … guilty.

Maybe that wasn't the right word, but I didn't know how else to explain it. Blaise and his family might've had all the money in the world, but that didn't mean he needed to spend it on a gift for a kid he had barely known for a couple weeks.

A few hundred bucks was pocket change to Blaise. To my family, it wasn't even enough to cover a quarter of rent. Mom saved every single penny for us to get by and to have a somewhat-decent life.

And it wasn't *any* present, but a PS5! Those things had supposedly been on preorder for a year, and people still didn't get them on time. When they had initially been released, bots had bought up all the stock, and now, scalpers sold them for, like, a thousand bucks each.

The PS5 surpassed my gift to Mateo, but at least he liked that *Attack on Titan* shirt that I'd bought him.

"Of course I had to get the kid something," Blaise said.

"No, you didn't," I argued. I sipped on my vanilla milkshake and stared out at the moonlight glimmering against the crashing waves in the ocean. "He would've appreciated you showing up."

"I wasn't going to show up to his birthday empty-handed." Blaise sipped his shake and suddenly became tense. "Besides I, uh …" He paused for a long moment, scratched the back of his head, and glanced away from me. "I got you something too."

A gush of warmth spread throughout my chest.

"You … what?"

"I got you something too," Blaise repeated, setting down his milkshake on the rock and leaping up from his seat. "Hold on." He jogged over to the car, opened the trunk, and rummaged through it for a moment.

When he returned, he held a single black matte gift bag. After hesitantly taking the bag from him, I stared down at it. My stomach twisted into knots, and I didn't know if they were the good kind or not. Nobody—other than my family and my close friends—had ever bought me anything.

"Why?" I asked, nervous to open it. "What is it?"

"Open it up. You'll see. It's just something for your writing."

I scrunched my nose and pulled the black tissue paper out of the bag, giggling softly to myself. "I swear, it'd better not be a dildo because—" I stopped and sucked in a sharp breath, my eyes widening. "Blaise ... wh-what's this?" I asked, looking over at him, my voice barely audible.

Blaise shrugged one shoulder—the way he did when he wanted to act like he didn't give a fuck—and barely gave me a smile. "I thought you'd get some use out of it. Do you, uh ... do you like it?"

I furrowed my brows, reached down into the bag, and pulled out his gift.

A brand-new MacBook Air.

Chapter Forty-Six

BLAISE

"You bought me a laptop," Vera whispered, gaze stuttering between one side of the box and the other. She glided her fingers against the matte box and frowned. "Why would you get me something like this?"

"Because I—"

She shoved the box into my hands. "I can't. No. I-I don't like it."

My chest tightened, my throat closing. "Why don't you like it? You can use it to write."

"Because, Blaise ..." She suddenly stood on the rocks, hopped onto the pavement near my car, and paced back and forth. "Why would you spend that much money on a gift for me? That's insane! You know what else you could've done with that?!"

So, this was about money, not because she didn't like it.

"It's okay, V," I said, leaning back on the rock.

"No, it's not." She ran a hand through her dark hair and shook her head for emphasis. "It's not okay. I can't accept something like that, especially for no reason at all! I hate feeling like I owe people something. And with you ..."

As she continued to pace around the Overlook, I set my milk-shake down on the rock, stood up, and stepped into her path. She attempted to walk around me, but I seized her waist and stopped her completely.

"Don't touch me in an attempt to convince me to keep it. It's not going to work," she argued. "It's way too expensive, and I don't have anything but sex to pay you back with. I can give you nothing that you already don't have."

God, she was so wrong.

My family might've had money, but to me, Vera had everything that I'd always wanted—family and friends who cared about each other and not because of the cash they had in the bank or their pres-tige. Vera's family and friends cared about her for her.

That must've been the greatest fucking thing in the world, and Vera didn't even realize it.

"You don't have to pay me back," I said softly.

She tore her gaze away from me and glared at the ocean. "Yes, I do. I have to."

"Why?"

"Because, Blaise."

"Tell me."

"Because that's how my mom raised me, okay? We might not have a lot, but you're not supposed to take things from people, espe-cially when it costs upward of a thousand dollars. Or more. People work hard for their money, and this is too much for me."

I handed her the laptop. "I'm not bringing it back."

She shoved it toward me. "Yes, you are."

"No, I'm not."

Nobody else would've questioned how much I'd paid for it or fight me to bring it back. Anyone else—Mom, Dad, Skylar, my family and *friends*, who I couldn't really call friends—would've gladly taken that laptop just because.

But Vera didn't want that, and she still stuck around with me. *With me!* The guy who nobody really gave a fuck about enough to ask to hang out, to show up at the skatepark for no reason other than to see me, to let me take them on a date and not expect something in return.

"If you force me to keep it, I'm going to be freaking furious at you."

"But you need it," I said. "How much easier would your life be with school and writing?"

"That—"

"Answer the question."

She crossed her arms and glared up, her hard brown eyes softening. "It would help."

"Then, you're keeping it."

"But that doesn't mean I wanted you to buy me a laptop with your father's dirty money."

I pressed my lips together and debated on whether I actually should tell her or not. If I told her the truth—that I hadn't bought this with my father's money, but the money I'd made off ads on my YouTube channel—then she really wouldn't let me convince her to keep this.

But I didn't want to lie to her.

Deep down, I was desperate to show her that not everything I had was because of my father's money. The majority of the stuff I used day-to-day—like those headphones Mom had broken in two pieces—I had bought myself.

"Your parents—"

"I bought it myself, Vera. I didn't use my parents' money."

After suddenly dropping her annoyed expression, she lowered her widening gaze to the laptop between us. She stretched her fingers across mine on the box and curled them around the digits. "You ... bought this with the money you made from ... YouTube?"

"I want you to keep it," I whispered. "Please."

This was the first purchase I had made for someone else with my earnings. This was proof that I ... I wasn't the guy she thought I was, no matter how much I tried to lead on that I was. I just didn't want anyone to hurt me more than this world already had.

"Blaise ..."

"Just shut up and take it, okay?" I said, desperate for her to keep it.

Even if we didn't end up together, even if Skylar decided to fuck things up again, even if Vera decided that I wasn't worth her time anymore, she had made me feel things that I'd never thought I'd feel for someone.

Shit, she made me feel like I wasn't some fuckup or just another fuck to someone.

Steadily, I pulled my hands from under hers on the box, so she held it herself. When I released it completely, she didn't shove it back at me or demand that I return the laptop I'd picked out for her.

Instead, she glanced up at me through glossy eyes and said, "You really bought this for me?" Her voice was softer than the first time she'd asked, and sounded like she really couldn't believe that it was possible.

"Yes, I bought it for you," I whispered, tucking some dark hair behind her ear.

Chin quivering, she swallowed hard and placed the laptop down on the hood of my car. Then, she curled her arms around my torso, pulled me into a hug, and rested her head on my chest. I tensed in surprise, not knowing how to respond.

Sure, I had hugged a girl before, but not like this.

This was more than a *catch you later, thanks for the fuck* kind of hug.

This fucking meant something.

"Thank you so much," she whispered, staring out at the ocean. "You don't know how much you mean to me."

Chapter Forty-Seven

VERA

The words had slipped out of my mouth before I could stop them.

I widened my eyes and tensed in Blaise's arms, unsure if he had even heard what I said. I sure hoped that he hadn't because I didn't even know where that had come from. Blaise was nicer to me than he had initially been, and I maybe kinda, sorta liked him.

But what did he really mean to me?

And what on earth had compelled me to accept his gift?

All my hopes were lost when Blaise cupped my chin and forced me to look up at him. Underneath the moonlight, his eyes were a mess of browns—hazel, chocolate, and even flecks of caramel swirling around his dark pupils.

"What do you mean?" he asked.

My eyes widened, and I tensed harder, then tugged away and looked down. "Hmm?"

"What did you mean when you said, 'You don't know how much you mean to me'?"

"I, um ..." I swallowed nervously. "You know ..."

Hell, how would Blaise know? I didn't even know what I meant. I had said whatever came naturally to me at that moment. I hadn't known that was how I actually felt about him, like he meant more to me than someone I liked.

"No," he said. "I don't."

"Blaise," I whispered, glancing around at a car behind us that had turned on their high beams. I squinted my eyes and pulled away from Blaise, deciding that it was too cold out here and too public to be having this conversation. "Can we ... talk in the car?"

After Blaise cursed at the assholes behind us, he opened the passenger seat. Before I could sit, he sat in my seat, pushed it back as far as it would go in his small sports car, and pulled me onto his lap. He took the laptop from my hands, set it in the driver's seat, and seized my hips. "Talk."

"I ... I didn't mean like this," I whispered.

"Tell me," he urged, pulling my hips down so I sat flush against the front of his pants.

When I felt the slight bulge inside his jeans, I curled my fingers around his shoulders and whimpered, warmth spreading throughout my core. He slipped his hand between my legs and gently rubbed my pussy through my pants.

"What did you mean?"

"B-Blaise ..."

He moved his fingers faster. "Come on, Vera."

Slowly, I ran my fingers from his shoulders, down his muscular chest and abdomen, and to the button on his jeans. I curled my fingers around the waistband and ground my pussy against his dick, hoping he'd forget about it.

Blaise pulled his hand from my clit, unbuckled his jeans, and pulled out his stiffening dick. I furrowed my brows and clenched, heat warming my core. As I stared down at it and imagined it stuffed inside me, he wrapped his arms under my legs and somehow—some-freaking-way—turned me around, so I sat on his lap with my back against his chest. He pulled my pants to my ankles and rested my feet against the dashboard.

Inhaling sharply, I leaned back against him and hoped that nobody saw us. At least the guy with the annoying headlights had left. But there were other cars behind and in front of us, with people probably inside them, doing exactly what we were.

"I'm not going to give it to you until you explain yourself," Blaise said, pressing the head of his cock against my entrance.

"Please," I whimpered. "Please ..."

I didn't know if I was pleading for him to give it to me or for him not to make me say it aloud—or maybe both. Saying how I felt out loud would make it real. It let him know exactly how to hurt me, if he wanted.

With his cock still pressing against my entrance, he curled his arm around my waist and sank his hand between my legs. He cupped the folds of my pussy, his fingers lightly pressing against my aching clit, and then he dipped four of his fingers into me.

Immediately, I tightened around him and squealed, the pressure rising in my core.

Knuckles deep, he curled all four fingers over and over inside me, massaging my G-spot. I pressed my body against his. More and more pressure built up inside me, my entire body tensing.

Just when I was about to come all over his thick fingers, he stopped. I whimpered and tried bucking my hips against his hand, but he held me in place and chuckled darkly in my ear.

"This is my pussy, Sunshine. And you don't get to come until you tell me what you meant."

"Blaise," I murmured, whining softly. "Please let me have it."

"Say it," he growled.

I pressed my lips together and furrowed my brows, my chest tightening as I merely thought about admitting all my feelings that I had for him. He began curling his fingers into me again, moving them faster than before and pushing me higher. I dug my nails into his thigh and attempted to hold back another moan.

He brought me moments away from coming again, then stopped.

"No," I pleaded. "Please don't."

"Tell me what I mean to you."

Again, I whimpered as he began massaging my G-spot again. He pressed the head of his cock against my entrance too, threatening to fill me up with both his fingers and his hard cock once I gave him what he wanted.

I didn't want to say it, but ...

But I didn't know how much longer I could take this torture.

"I'll stop again," he warned.

"No!" I begged. When he began to slow his fingers, I cried out, "I like you! Okay? I fucking like you, as more than a friend. So much more than a friend, Blaise. Now, please don't stop this—"

With his fingers still buried inside me, he shoved his cock into me. I jerked my legs into the air and off the dashboard, the pressure in my core shooting up. I moaned loudly, my entire body trembling everywhere.

He dipped his face into the crook of my neck, gliding his teeth against my sensitive skin. "Fuck, V," he growled, pumping into me hard and fast. "Say it again."

"I like you," I cried, tilting my head to grant him better access. "Oh God, I like you so much."

Blaise continued to pound his dick into me, and at the same time, he curled his fingers against my G-spot. The heel of his hand smacked against my clit over and over, pushing me over the edge.

Wave after wave of pleasure rushed through me, my body numb. And in that moment, I didn't say it aloud, but I knew that I liked Blaise more than I'd let on, more than I'd told him, maybe even more than I'd told myself.

I might've loved Blaise Harleen.

Chapter Forty-Eight

VERA

After I spilled my heart out to Blaise, he drove me home and walked me to the front door. I clasped the laptop to my chest. Still, I couldn't believe that he had bought me this. I felt like I didn't deserve it.

"All right, well ..." I said awkwardly, grabbing the door handle and turning the knob. We had spent the entire night together, but I didn't know the first thing about relationships. Hell, I didn't know if we were in an official relationship. "Thank you for this. And, um, have a good—"

Blaise stepped closer to me, cupped my chin, and kissed me.

I inhaled sharply, cheeks flushing at the thought of Mom or Mateo seeing us. But it seemed like Blaise didn't mind so much. He had never really cared about being seen with me, the poor, nerdy, and even a little bit weird girl.

It was me who had a problem with it because he wouldn't be the one hearing the whispers about a girl like me dating someone like him, the name-calling. He wouldn't see all the side-eyes from the popular girls.

Only I would.

Nerves piling up in my stomach, I pulled away and stared at the ground. *How is this even real? How is Blaise Harleen—the popular guy who can have anything he wants—kissing me at my front door?*

"Sorry," Blaise apologized.

Yes, the bad boy had *apologized*.

While I wanted to run and hide from the embarrassment, the look on Blaise's face dropped moments after I pulled away. My chest tightened, uneasiness sitting heavily in my stomach. I grabbed a fistful of his shirt, pulled him down, and kissed him again.

This time, when I pulled away, I quickly stepped into the house. "Good night, Blaise."

He stood outside with the goofiest grin on his face, his thumb wiping the excess saliva I had left on the corner of his mouth. "Night, V."

Butterflies fluttered in my stomach. I shut the door and pressed my back against it, my breath quickening. Things were good. Almost too good. And I wondered what the hell would fuck this up soon.

Nothing could ever be easy in Redwood.

Suddenly, the light turned on, blinding me.

"Oh my God! I almost just passed out," Maddie said from the couch.

Dressed in the shirt I'd bought him, Mateo sat next to her with a bowl of popcorn on his lap and fake gagged. "In disgust."

"No, you brat." Maddie shoved Mateo and jumped up. "You kissed Blaise!"

I held the laptop closer to my chest and arched a brow. "Were you guys spying on me?"

"I'd rather puke than willingly watch you swap spit with Blaise," Mateo said.

"If kissing makes you wanna puke, what'll happen when you find out that they've fuck—"

"Maddie!" I scolded, playfully narrowing my gaze at her. "Stop it!"

Mateo shot up from the couch and placed the popcorn down. "Vera, you're disgusting."

Once Mateo disappeared into his bedroom, looking like he was actually about to puke all over the shirt I'd bought him, Maddie rolled her eyes at his dramatics. "Now that he's gone ... it wasn't my *plan* to spy on you. I decided to come back about an hour ago to help your mom clean up a bit. Those sophomore kids had left this place a mess, like I'd thought they would. I stayed because I wanted to make sure you got in all right." Maddie stepped closer to me and dropped her gaze to the laptop. "Did lover boy get you a present too?"

My cheeks warmed. "That's not the only thing he gave me tonight."

Maddie smirked. "God, you're nasty, and I love it."

I burst out laughing, all the tension from tonight finally leaving my body. Maddie shrugged on her jacket and grabbed her purse along with a plastic bag filled with leftover pizza that Mom must've been forcing her to take home.

"I'd better get all the deets at school tomorrow."

Once Maddie finally left, I prayed that Mom hadn't been listening in on our conversation, and I hurried to my room. I sat on my bed and unboxed the MacBook, my eyes widening in awe at the sleek, costly piece of metal.

I couldn't believe my eyes. This was more than I ever could've imagined.

After plugging it into the charger, I logged in to Google and furiously typed the next chapter of my story. Inspiration hit me hard, and I didn't stop until it was nearly three in the morning.

Deciding that I needed to go to bed, I posted the chapter online, closed the laptop, and lay on my mattress, grinning to myself. This still didn't feel real. So much so that I could barely keep my eyes closed.

Instead, I logged in to my online writing platform and scrolled to the notifications

Almost immediately, someone liked the chapter. I smiled and stared at the screen, in awe at how fast someone had clicked on my story. Two weeks ago, I hadn't thought that anyone would even read it. Now, people were clicking on it the moment it was posted.

Sunbeam34: @holywater needs to get in here asap. Omg.

While I tried, I couldn't stop the grin from stretching across my face.

Holywater: I'm here and ready for smut.

More likes flooded into my notifications. Sunbeam34 and Holywater continued to tag each other back and forth, as if they knew each other in real life. I scrolled through the notifications to make sure I didn't miss any comments. And then ...

SkateboardingPunk: fuck.

Warmth spread through my chest, butterflies fluttering in my stomach. I almost couldn't believe my eyes. This wasn't just anyone. It was Blaise Harleen, my ... guy. He didn't need to tell me for me to know it was him.

Nobody else named SkateboardingPunk would've been reading this kind of smut.

More notifications popped up on the screen at the end of the chapter.

Sunbeam34: I need another chapter tonight.

Sunbeam34: That was so good.

Sunbeam34: brb, going to change my pants.

I pulled the blankets over my mouth and snickered into them to stifle my laugh, so I wouldn't wake Mom or Mateo. Just as I was about to shut off my phone for the night, another comment popped up.

SkateboardingPunk: @Sunbeam34 same.

Something about that boy ... God, he did something to me. Something only my characters had felt before. Something I never wanted to lose.

Chapter Forty-Nine

BLAISE

When the bell rang throughout Redwood's halls the next day, I stood up from my seat in English class and tossed my backpack over my shoulder. Usually at this time, Skylar, the school's most annoying slut, would be dragging me to the cafeteria.

But I walked out of class without her filthy hands all over me.

She must've been sick, or maybe she had begged one of the jocks on the football team to come inside her too often and accidentally gotten herself pregnant. I stifled a laugh. Shit, that actually sounded like something she'd do, then try to hide it from all of Redwood by faking being *sick*.

At least I didn't have to worry about her fucking up my life with Vera.

I walked down the hall, passed Callan Avery, who leaned against a locker outside his classroom, texting—probably his little toy—on his phone. He definitely didn't smile like that around my dad's sister.

"Blaise!" he called.

Not wanting to talk to him right now, I continued down the hallway.

"Blaise!" he shouted, louder this time.

Man, this guy didn't know when to fucking stop.

I gritted my teeth and turned around to face him. "What?"

After he glanced around for anyone lurking in the hallways, he nodded to his classroom. I rolled my eyes and followed him inside, slouching down at a desk. If I had it my way, I would be in the cafeteria right now with Vera, but I at least had some respect for Callan. *Some.*

More than any other shitty teacher here.

"What?" I asked with annoyance. "Aren't you having Sakura Sato for lunch? Don't want to miss getting in one of your student's pants, huh? Make this quick."

Avery locked the door—which meant that this was serious—and clenched his jaw. "I'm not going to entertain you with my love life, Blaise. I doubt you really care for it anyway, seeing as you hate your father's side of the family as much as I do."

Pissed, I rolled my eyes. "Then, what do you want me for?"

Callan walked to his desk, placed his hands on it, and leaned forward, staring me down. "Where the fuck were you last night?"

"Out."

"Where?"

"Why does it matter to you?"

"Where?" he repeated, voice dead fucking serious.

I stood up and growled. "The Overlook. What the fuck is wrong with you?"

"You were at the beach?"

"No, the Overlook."

He ran a hand over his tired face and paced the room. "Same fucking thing, Blaise."

"Why do you want to know all this shit anyway? What's it matter to you?"

"Shit's happening in Redwood," he said. "Who were you with?"

"Who the fuck do you think?"

"Vera?"

"Yeah, now, are you going to tell me any shit or not? I have lunch."

After glaring at me for a couple moments longer, he stormed to the door, unlocked it, and pulled it open. I tossed my backpack over my shoulder and walked toward him.

He snatched my arm before I could pass. "Stay out of trouble."

"You too, Cal. You fucking too."

Once I pulled myself out of his grasp, I walked into the hallway toward the cafeteria. *What the hell was that about?*

He had looked so serious, as if the shit that happened in Redwood involved *my* family.

As much as Avery hated his wife and my dad, he tried to protect us whenever he needed, whenever Dad's money wasn't enough. It was rare, but it happened at times. And it felt like one of those times.

Deciding to brush it off because Dad's problems weren't *my* problems, I stepped into the cafeteria and scanned the room. When I spotted Vera sitting with her friends, I stopped and gripped my back-pack strap harder until the veins in my hand swelled.

I wanted to sit with her, but I didn't even know what we were. And by the way that Vera tensed when I kissed her at her door last night, I wasn't sure if she wanted to be spotted with me or even merely close to me in public. She thought that everyone would talk shit behind her back, but they wouldn't. If they did, they'd have to deal with me.

She glanced up at me, cheeks flushing, and quickly looked back at her friends. I sighed softly and was about to turn away from her when I spotted her pulling her sweatshirt off the seat next to her and peeking a glance back up at me.

We stared at each other for a long time. Did she want me to go sit with her? When she nodded toward the seat with a very slight tilt to her head, I found myself moving toward her, emotions rushing through my body.

Before I could even get halfway to her table, João Rocha stole my seat and leaned closer to her. I growled, loud enough to garner the attention from the tables beside us, and stormed over to him, snatching him by the collar and lifting him from the seat.

"Cool your fucking temper," he said, shoving his hands into my chest and ripping himself away from me. "I'm here for Vera, not your pissy bitch attitude."

"Well, Vera's fucking mine," I said between clenched teeth, only loud enough for the girls at Vera's table and João to hear. "Get the fuck out of here and don't talk to her again."

Being the bitch that he was, he looked over at her. "I need you to watch Ana tonight."

Quickly, Vera stood up between us. "It's fine, Blaise. I can watch her tonight."

Hating that he was even talking to Vera, I gritted my teeth and glared at him as he turned away from her and headed back to Poison's table in the back of the cafeteria.

"Eight o'clock," he called over his shoulder. "Don't be late."

Chapter Fifty

BLAISE

After bringing Vera to the skatepark after school today to teach her how to ride a bit more, I dropped her off at home and eyed João Rocha's house as I headed back home. He stood outside with his friends—Landon and Kai and even Imani Abara, a girl from the rich side of town.

I gripped the steering wheel tighter, but I didn't have the damn negative energy to want to kick his ass tonight. I had just spent the past few hours with Vera. So, I reluctantly ignored his arrogant ass.

The moment I drove into the ritzy sector of Redwood, I sensed something was off.

Maybe I should've paid more attention to Avery earlier.

Two police cars sat in the driveway, almost blocking my entrance into the garage. After grumbling to myself, I pulled into my driveway. I rolled my eyes and drove around them, inches away from damaging public property—but it wasn't my fault that Dad must've gotten himself in trouble somehow.

Once I made it into the garage, I turned off the car and shut the door, attempting to figure out what the hell could've happened now.

The last time the police had shown up at our house, Dad had been caught dick deep in the police chief's wife. And the chief had wanted a shit-ton of money to cover it up and recoup the loss of his wife's pussy.

Annoying as fuck.

But I fucking hoped that he hadn't done some shit like that again. I didn't care about how it affected Mom or his stupid status. I didn't want to sit through dinner after dinner after fucking dinner to help him polish his reputation again.

I ran a hand over my face and groaned. They had to know I was home. Security must've told them. Sooner or later, they'd come to find me, if they wanted me to polish up their reputations again.

As expected, one of Dad's security guards walked into the garage in a black suit and that pissed off expression he always had. Without saying a word to me, he nodded toward the door he had just come through.

Grumbling, I rolled my eyes, grabbed my shit, and followed him into the house.

When I walked through the door from the garage to the foyer, I stopped and stared emptily at Dad standing beside two police officers and glaring at me. Fucking great. First time seeing him again in, what, three months now? Had it been that long?

"The fuck is this?"

Dad scowled. "Blaise, not now."

"What a fucking amazing time to be alive," I growled, tossing my backpack on the ground next to the door and picking up my skateboard. "Get a visit from my lovely father and the police, all wrapped into one."

While Dad's glare hardened, Mom acted like the innocent *could do no harm* mediator in front of the police. "Blaise, come here," Mom said, hurrying over to the door and wrapping her arm around my shoulders. She lowered her voice to whisper to me. "If you know something, don't say anything to them. Not until the lawyer gets here."

I furrowed my brows. "What do you mean? What's going on?"

Redwood's big, macho police chief and the head cheerleader's father crossed his arms and inspected me from head to toe. He stood next to another policeman, who had his thumb on his gun, as if he was preparing to pull it on me.

"Where have you been?" the chief asked.

"Ou—"

"He's not answering any questions until our lawyer arrives," Dad said.

"That makes him look like a suspect."

"I don't give a fuck what it looks like," Dad said, voice harsh.

"A suspect?" I asked, confused about what the fuck was happening. "For what?"

Mom glanced at Dad nervously, and Dad looked at the chief until the big man in uniform pressed his lips together.

"Late last night, we found Skylar Walker's body washed up on the town beach."

Chapter Fifty-One

BLAISE

"She's fucking dead?" I asked in disbelief.

Skylar had texted me, like, a few days ago, and now, she was dead? Someone had straight-up murdered that annoying bitch and tried to pin it all on me. For what? Not answering her texts?

"Yes," the nobody cop confirmed.

I pressed my lips together and stared at the ground. At least she was out of my hair.

"You don't seem too sad about that," the chief said, eyeing me carefully.

Truthfully, I wasn't fucking sad about that. She had been annoying as fuck and way too needy, messed with my relationship with Vera, and always wanted to come over to have a good time. I hadn't even liked her at all.

Dad cleared his throat. "We're not commenting until we have our lawyer."

"We're taking him in for questioning," the chief said, stepping toward me and snatching my right wrist. He yanked it behind my back so forcefully that my shoulder popped. "Your lawyer can meet him at the police station."

"Get your fucking hands off me," I growled, yanking myself away from him.

He snapped my wrists back, threw me onto the ground, and placed his knee on the back of my neck to keep me still. It wasn't like the other cop didn't have his gun already pointed straight at me. They could've fucking asked nicely.

After he forced my wrists behind my back, he snapped handcuffs around them. That fucker put all his weight on my spine for a couple seconds longer, like he wanted to break it, and then he finally shoved himself off me and grabbed my wrists.

They didn't even let me scramble to my feet before they pulled me up and forced me toward the front door. If anyone had seen the police pull up to the house or a police car even in the driveway, they'd be peeking out from behind their curtains and see me leaving the house in cuffs.

Personally, I didn't give a fuck. But my parents did.

"I didn't fucking do anything!" I said between clenched teeth.

Once they shoved me into the backseat, they slipped into the car and drove me all the way to the police station. I followed them into the back and sat in an interrogation room, glaring at the chief, who sat quietly across from me.

Something wasn't right.

Who the fuck is putting the blame on me?

A couple moments later, my father's lawyer stepped into the room. It might've been past midnight, but this man had on his finest suit and a leather briefcase. I sat back on the cold metal chair and let out a long breath, knowing that this night would go on forever. These fuckers still hadn't even undone my cuffs.

"I'd like to speak with my client alone," he said.

After huffing, the chief stood up and walked out of the room.

My father's lawyer sat in front of me and stared me down, as if he was trying to figure something out. Then, finally, he said, "You didn't do it."

"No shit, I didn't do it," I snapped. "How could you fucking tell?"

"Men who are guilty look nervous."

"That was sarcasm, you fucking prick. Now, get me out of here."

He blew out a deep breath and drew his tongue across his front teeth. "They suspect that the time of her death was mid-day Saturday. You were at the skatepark, then at the library. You have an alibi."

"How'd you know I was—"

"Doesn't matter. They're trying to pin this on you for a reason."

"Because my father can't keep his dick in his pants."

The lawyer hummed in agreement, and I fucking laughed because Dad must've given this man so many problems in the past. He'd probably suspected something like this would arise at one point or another.

When the door opened, we both shut the fuck up and looked over at the police chief.

"You had your time alone. Now, we have questions to ask you, Mr. Harleen. And we need you to be honest."

Chapter Fifty-Two

VERA

"**V**era!" Maddie shouted from outside my house, pounding on my window.

I slowly opened my eyes and pulled the blankets over my head, hoping that this was a dream. João hadn't come home to get Ana until, like, two in the morning last night, and I didn't know how much sleep I had actually gotten. *What time is it anyway?*

"Vera! It's freezing-ass cold out here. Open the freaking window!"

After grumbling to myself, I sat up against my headboard and glanced toward the window. My eyes widened when I really caught Maddie standing outside, banging on the glass, her eyes big in an urgent stare.

"Open up. It's important."

I leaped out of bed and hurried toward the window, then unlocked it and pulled it open.

Maddie jumped through it and into my bedroom, shaking the rain off her bright yellow rain jacket. "You need to answer your messages!"

Wiping my tired eyes, I sat back on the bed and pulled the blankets around myself. "Maddie, it's, like"—I glanced at the digital clock Mom had gotten me for my birthday last year and groaned—"four in the morning. We have school in three hours."

"Yeah, well, who cares? We have a problem."

"I didn't get to sleep until two thirty this morning."

"Did you see Piper's text message?" Maddie asked, ignoring my pleas to sleep.

I grabbed my phone from the charger. The screen lit up with at least a hundred messages from the group chat I had with Maddie and Piper, starting at three in the morning. I furrowed my brows and scrolled through them to make sense of what had happened.

"All you guys said was my name and, like, called me a bunch of times."

Maddie rolled her eyes and pulled my phone away. "It's about Blaise."

"What do you mean?" I asked, sitting up straight. "What happened?"

"You know, I would roll my eyes and poke fun at how much you fucking like him, but ..." Maddie paused for a long moment, tore off her jacket, and sat on the edge of my bed. "You know how Piper's dad works at the police station?"

"Yeah," I said, tugging the blankets closer to my chest. "Why? What about it?"

"Well, Piper overheard him telling her mother that Blaise Harleen had been brought in."

I slammed my hands against the mattress. "What the hell do you mean? For what?"

Hours ago, Blaise had dropped me off at home and told me that he was going to the skatepark for a little bit. Had he gotten into a fight with someone there? Had the police found something on him, pinned something on him? He was innocent, right?

Maddie stayed quiet, brows furrowing together.

"For what, Maddie?! What happened? Tell me."

"They brought him in for questioning about the murder of Skylar Walker."

"The ... murder of Skylar Walker?" I whispered, my mouth parched. "S-she's dead?"

"Apparently, they found her body washed up on the beach."

My heart dropped, my body going rigid.

Oh my fucking God. This couldn't be real. She had to be lying.

I scrolled to the very first message that Piper had sent in the group chat this morning, stating that she had overheard her father say Blaise really had been taken into custody for the murder of his ex-fling.

With my blankets pulled tightly around my body, I paced my small bedroom and stared at the ground. Fear and horror ran my blood cold.

There was no way that Blaise would kill someone, right?

Maybe if he had a reason, but I didn't know how dark he could get. He had threatened guys to stay away from me for so long. And Skylar had fucked up our relationship by bringing him into the janitor's closet. Would he kill her for me?

My throat dried. No. No, he couldn't have. He wouldn't have.

"You don't think he did it, do you?" Maddie asked.

"No," I whispered, shaking my head for emphasis.

Still though ... I barely knew the guy. He had blackmailed me. *Blackmailed!*

If he could blackmail someone he liked to get what he wanted, could he kill someone he hated to keep who he wanted? Would Blaise risk everything for me? Would he be messy about it, thinking that his father's money could get him out of it?

I mean, it probably could, but ...

I stopped in the middle of my room and shook my head to get rid of the thought. What was I even thinking anymore? Blaise wouldn't kill anyone. He couldn't. He might've acted all tough around everyone else, but I had seen how vulnerable he could be.

"He didn't do this," I repeated to convince myself. "No, he didn't."

In the midst of my panic attack, I glanced out my bedroom window into the rainy night and across the street at João's house.

Heart pounding against my rib cage, I stepped toward the window and pressed my fingers against the glass. "Fuck."

Fuck. Fuck. Fuck. Fuck. Fuck. Fuck. Fuck.

This was my fault.

I had asked João to take care of Skylar Walker because I was angry and furious and so fucking done with the way she had touched Blaise. A couple days ago, she had disappeared.

"João," I whispered. "What did you fucking do?"

Chapter Fifty-Three

VERA

Not wanting to wake Mom or Mateo, I crawled out the window and stormed across the street to João's house while Maddie followed behind me. I pulled up João's contact on my phone and texted him, needing him to get his ass out here now.

Me: Get outside right now!

He texted back almost immediately.

João: It's four in the fucking morning.

Me: I don't give a fuck, João.

Me: Now!

I crossed my arms and stood in front of his house, tapping my foot impatiently. His bedroom light turned on, and a moment later, the front door opened. Wearing a pair of sweats, João stepped out of the house and pulled a sweatshirt over his bare abdomen.

"What the hell do you want, Vera?" João asked, walking toward us and glancing over at Maddie and giving her a sour expression that he usually saved for Blaise during school. "And what the fuck is she doing—"

Before I could stop myself, I shoved my hands into his chest. "You fucking killed her?!" I whisper-yelled at João, forcing him to stumble back onto the wet grass. "What the hell is wrong with you?!"

"What are you talking about?"

"You killed her!"

João pulled up his hood, growled, and yanked me closer. "You can't fucking scream shit like that in the middle of the slums, Vera. You should know better than that. And what the hell do you care if I killed her or not? It's not any of your business."

"Not my business?!" I shouted.

João slapped a hand over my mouth and shoved me against his car. "The fuck did I just say about screaming?"

I pulled his hand away and glared up at him. "It is one hundred percent my business if you killed Skylar," I whispered to him. "That's not what I meant when I said that I wanted you to take care of her."

A confused expression crossed his face for a moment, and then he stepped away from me. "Oh, you're talking about Skylar."

I furrowed my brows. "Who did you think I was talking about? Who'd you kill?"

"Forget it," João said. "Look, as much as I would've *loved* to be the one to end that bitch's life, I didn't do it. I have better things to do than to entertain a rich whore like her who'd do anything to suck off someone's dad."

"Well, who was it then? Landon? Kai?" I asked, racking my brain for someone.

But the more I thought about it, the less and less I believed that Kai—the quiet computer whiz in Poison—could've killed someone. And Landon? He might've been scary, but to end someone's life? I had known these guys for so long. The only person that I knew who could kill someone and not give a fuck about it was João. So, he was either lying to me or ...

"It wasn't Poison. All we did was find some shit on her and bully her with it."

"That was it?" I asked, skeptical.

He shrugged half-heartedly. "Might've kicked her ass a bit."

"And what'd that entail?"

"Tying her to the back of my car and dragging her down the side of the road," João said, an amused expression on his face. I couldn't tell if he was serious and was rejoicing on the thought or if he was fucking with me.

"You didn't kill her?" I asked again for clarification.

He sprawled a hand across his chest. "Vera, you think so lowly of me. We don't kill unless we get paid or they've pissed us off enough," João said. "Skylar was annoying, but not enough for any one of us to end her."

I furrowed my brows and glanced back at Maddie, who held an umbrella over our heads. Still, none of this made any sense. If Blaise hadn't done it and Poison hadn't done it ... then who had killed her?

"What can you do about it?" I asked.

A lifeless chuckle escaped his mouth. "What'd you mean?"

"You need to find me information—find out who killed her, when they killed her, and why they're trying to pin this on Blaise," I said, poking him hard in the chest. "And I need it as soon as you can get it."

João laughed right in my face. "You're fucking kidding me. No."

"Yes." I crossed my arms. "Or I won't ever watch your sister again."

After grinding his teeth together, João stared at me blankly. "The fuck you think you can boss me around for? You're going to watch Ana because you need the money, Vera. I'm not getting you any—"

Done with taking his bullshit, I stepped forward. "You're going to get me that information *and* pay me when I watch Ana because *you're* doing more than just selling drugs while I'm babysitting your sister. You're fucking killing people, and if you don't want people to know—"

"Fine," he gritted out.

My eyes widened slightly.

Wait, all this time, I just had to put my foot down and João would do as I asked?

"Good," I said, straightening out my oversize Redwood Academy T-shirt and smoothing out the fluffy pajama bottoms I had gotten from Walmart, which were now soaked up to the ankles from the rain. I regained my composure and shoved my shoulders back. "I expect it soon."

And with that, I turned on my heel and headed for Maddie's car.

Was I bullying the bad boy now? Was that the monster Blaise had made? Shit, I should've cared, but I didn't at the moment.

Blaise was in trouble, and I needed to see him.

Chapter Fifty-Four

BLAISE

"You need to clean up your act!" Mom screamed, pacing around the foyer with her fur jacket still draped over her shoulders.

We'd finally gotten back from the police station ten minutes ago.

She shook her head, hair flipping in every direction, and glared at Dad, who chatted with his lawyer at the front door. "Talk some sense into your son."

Dad said a couple last words to him, then opened the door to let him out. He would be back in the morning when we had to go back to the police station to answer more questions about Skylar's disappearance and the last few texts she had sent me.

Mom cleared her throat, causing Dad to roll his eyes.

"Where were you the other night?" Dad asked half-heartedly to me.

"With a friend."

"There you go," Dad said to Mom.

"Which friend?" Mom asked.

"Someone."

"That girl from the slums?" she urged. "That no-good bitch?"

I gritted my teeth and stood up. "You don't even fucking know her, so stop fucking calling her that. She might not have any money, might live in a run-down house in the slums, but she's a better fucking person than you've ever been, especially to me!"

"Don't lie to yourself, Blaise," Mom said. "You deserve better."

"Vera is better than me in every fucking way."

But she couldn't see that. She would never be able to see that. All she saw was money.

Someone banged on the front door.

Mom rolled her eyes and stormed over. "Who the fuck is it now?"

When she pulled the door open, Vera and Maddie stood outside in the pouring rain. Vera stared up at Mom with wide eyes, then glanced past her at me. Without even being invited into the house, Vera pushed past Mom and hurried to me.

She threw her arms around my shoulders and buried her head into the crook of my neck, so I could feel the tears she cried on my skin. "I was so worried about you. A-after Maddie told me what happened, we went to the police station, but you weren't there."

"Get her out of my house this instant," Mom growled, turning on her heel to glare at us.

Because I didn't want Vera to deal with Mom putting her down, I grabbed her hand and brought her toward the front door, where Maddie stood. If we had stayed inside any longer, Mom would have fucking cursed Vera out and called her every name in the fucking book.

That wasn't happening to my girl.

I slammed the door behind me and stood on the porch with them. "You heard?"

"Skylar ... she's really dead?" Vera whispered.

"I guess so. They said they found her body washed up on the beach."

"Why are they blaming you?" she asked.

"Because of my dad," I said, rolling my eyes. "Long story that I don't want to get into." After glancing down at my watch, I frowned and ushered Vera toward Maddie. "It's late, and you have school tomorrow. We can talk more about this later. I promise."

Before she walked back to Maddie's car in the rain, Vera grabbed my shirt collar and pulled me closer to kiss me hard on the lips. "Don't say anything that will get you thrown into jail, please, Blaise."

I rested my forehead against hers. "I won't, Sunshine. I promise."

Though ... I wasn't sure that I'd be able to keep that promise. I hadn't done anything, but this was Redwood. If they wanted to throw me in jail, they would come up with the most outrageous evidence and blame me.

Once they left and drove down the road, I took another breath and walked into the house.

"You're ruining our entire reputation!" Mom screamed at me as soon as I shut the door behind me.

Dad rubbed a hand over his tired face. "Quit it, Caroline."

"Everything we've worked so hard for, and he wants to hang out with a girl from the slums."

"Please," Dad grunted. "All you do is yell at him."

Mom crossed her arms. "It's not like you do any parenting. You're never home."

"Neither are you," I said under my breath.

She acted like she was some sort of perfect parent or something. She disappeared for weeks, if not months, at a time without so much as a goodbye or an *I'm off to Paris; I'll see you whenever.*

When Dad ignored Mom, which pissed her off even more, I slumped down onto the couch and closed my eyes. Today had been so long for no good reason at all. I couldn't believe that they were trying to pin this on me.

Skylar had been a whore, had probably been out with half of Redwood these past few days. And they only had some texts between us, where I was kinda, sorta fucking angry with her. That was it. Nothing fucking else.

"Vera looks familiar," Dad hummed, sitting on the couch to untie his brown dress shoes that he must've worn every day and scrunching his eyebrows. "Almost like that house cleaner that we used to have. What was her name? Rodriguez?"

Mom glared at the back of his head and crossed her bony arms over her chest, seething hard as fuck. "Well, you would know, wouldn't you? You used to fuck her all the time when I was out with Blaise."

My mouth dropped open, and I stared at them with wide eyes.

Was that why Mom had fired her? Ms. Rodriguez had always been so nice and genuine. I doubted that she'd do something like that willingly. But I didn't put it past Dad to force himself on her, hold it over her head that he'd fire her if she didn't fuck him.

Dad was a fucking sleazeball either way.

After that, Mom had hired all the house cleaners herself, made sure they were old enough to be my grandmother, and hadn't let them be alone with her husband. Did I blame her? Truthfully, I didn't give a fuck.

She had only married him for his money. She had known what she was getting into.

Knowing that they'd fight for the rest of the night—Mom screaming at him that this wouldn't have happened if he hadn't fucked the police chief's wife and Dad yelling back that if she had been able to please him, he wouldn't have had to—I departed up the stairs to my bedroom.

It had been a long fucking night, and I didn't want to deal with it anymore.

Tomorrow, I'd be back at the police station with my lawyer to fight whatever kind of evidence that they thought they had on me. I hadn't done shit, but they needed someone to put away. And Mom was right. If Dad hadn't fucked with the police, then they wouldn't be pointing fingers at me. I'd be at school tomorrow with Vera.

God, I wished she had stayed with me tonight. I didn't know what would happen to us if they put me in prison.

Chapter Fifty-Five

VERA

After third period, I walked to my locker to deposit my books. Blaise hadn't shown up to school today, and I didn't blame him. Whether it was because of the rumors flying around Redwood or because he was being interrogated again, I was glad he'd stayed out of the messiness in Redwood Academy.

My stomach tightened into knots. All day, I had texted him, but he hadn't gotten back to me. I hoped that he was okay—and not just because of the whole murder thing. Granted, I had shown up at his house in the middle of the night. His mother had seemed angrier that I had come to visit him than the police trying to pin this on him. I could only imagine what she'd said about me once I left.

I stood at my locker and frowned, chest heavy. For the longest time, I'd thought that Blaise had everything, but I had never once seen his father within the past few weeks, and I had only heard that his mother was a bitch from him.

His family life seemed like shit. It made sense why he had spent so much time at my house, even before we admitted feelings for each other. Blaise's parents didn't give a fuck about what he did until it affected them.

"Is it true?" Mateo asked, walking up to my locker between fourth period and lunch.

"Is what true?" I asked, shoving my books in.

Mateo stepped forward and lowered his voice. "You know, about Blaise?"

"No, of course it's not true," I said, slamming my locker and following him toward the cafeteria. "You know that he would never do something like that. He has basically been hanging out with us all weekend anyway."

Mateo frowned and stared at the ground. "I know. It's just ... everyone's talking about it."

"Who?" I asked, stepping into the cafeteria. Fury raced through me.

Fuck that. I wasn't stupid. I had been hearing the rumors all day. Since the moment I'd stepped into school, all I'd heard were the whisperings about Blaise running through every single classroom.

I stopped at the doors and listened to *everyone* quietly chatting about Skylar and Blaise—some people thought he had done it and some people thought that there was no fucking way. Some people went as far as to say he had done it but would get out of it because of his money.

Maybe he could.

Rumors flew around Redwood Academy faster than anywhere. And I hated them so much. All I wanted to do was prove that he hadn't done it, convince everyone that this wasn't his fault. Blaise couldn't do something like that. It wasn't like him.

Once Mateo sat down with his friends, I found my way toward my table with Maddie and Piper, who still looked sick. Her cheeks were pale, and her eyes seemed so tired. I slumped down in the seat across from her.

"You okay?" she asked, trying to smile.

I pressed my lips together and stared down at the table. It was rude not to answer her, but I couldn't stop listening to the constant rumors rushing through my head. All these people believed one simple lie.

I wondered who the fuck had started the rumor that he had done it anyway.

Probably one of Skylar's friends.

"Vera?" Piper asked, leaning forward. "Are you—"

"Excuse me!" one of the rich, popular girls shouted, gathering the attention from every student in the cafeteria. She stood up next to some of Skylar's friends and pursed her lips. "We all know what happened. Skylar has passed on, and she is going to get justice. The police are interrogating Redwood's own Blaise Harleen."

I balled my hands into fists and glared harder at the table. The fuck was wrong with these girls? They didn't even know who had done it.

"He will be—"

"He didn't do it!" I shouted, slamming my hands onto the table and standing.

I didn't know what had come over me, but I couldn't shut myself up.

Everyone stared at me, including a couple of teachers overseeing the lunch period. I swallowed hard and stared at the student body, desperately wanting them to believe me. Blaise was innocent.

"How do you know?" one of Skylar's friends asked.

My heart pounded against my rib cage, the nerves building up higher inside me. All the curious eyes and prying ears were on me, waiting for me to say something, to admit the truth, to give Redwood more gossip.

To my surprise, Nicole—head cheerleader and police chief's daughter—placed a hand on Skylar's friend's shoulder and gently squeezed it. "We don't know the full story," she said quietly, very unlike her.

"Vera," Maddie whispered, nudging me from behind, "why don't you sit down?"

"No," I snapped.

I didn't want the school to judge me for being with Blaise, but that wasn't as important to me as making sure Redwood Academy didn't blame him for something he would never even be capable of doing.

Another of Skylar's friends stood up and crossed her arms. "How do you know he didn't do it? He had been pissed off at her for weeks now. He wouldn't talk to her in public, and he hasn't been out in Redwood lately."

"That's because he's been with me," I announced to the entire student body, spilling the one secret I had wanted to keep until at least the end of the school year. "He was at the library with me on Saturday night, and we went out for milkshakes with me on Sunday. Blaise Harleen is innocent."

Chapter Fifty-Six

VERA

"Y ou're lying," one of Skylar's friends snapped, pressing her lips together and glaring at me. "Blaise would never take you out on a date or hang out with someone like you. He was only around Skylar. They spent every night together."

Every night together? Maybe before me.

I winced at the thought. Hearing her say these things to me brought up the memory of catching them together in the janitor's closet. Skylar had orchestrated it all, and Blaise hadn't had anything to do with it—that I knew—but still, I couldn't push the night-marish feelings away.

No matter how many feelings that Blaise had admitted for me, I was still insecure, still didn't think someone like him could actually like me the way he said he did. But I liked him. I really truly liked him, and I wasn't going to let this bitch get in my way. I couldn't.

"I'm not lying. I have proof."

"Then, where is it?"

Swallowing hard, I pulled out my phone and scrolled through

our text messages from the other night when he had taken me out to milkshakes. Nothing to prove he was there with me. I scrolled through my pictures and apps for any sign that we were together.

But there wasn't anything. And it was my fault.

I hadn't wanted anyone to know that we were together. I hated that fact now. I wished I could take it all back, wished I had taken a picture, a memory of us together. But I didn't have anything from that night, except the laptop.

"So? Where is it?"

I stared down at my phone and shook my head. "I swear. I swear we were together. You saw us hanging out at lunch last week. Some of you have seen us in the hallways." I glanced over at Mateo and hoped he would say something. Both Maddie and he knew where I had gone.

As Maddie stood to come my defense, Mr. Avery—one of the Redwood teachers, who I believed was related to Blaise—walked through the cafeteria doors and cleared his throat, capturing the students' attention.

"You're right," he said. He draped his arm around my shoulders in the *nice as could be, caring teacher* kind of way. "Vera doesn't know what she's talking about. She's been under a lot of stress in my class lately."

"But—"

Maddie and Piper both gave me a quizzical stare. I wasn't in Mr. Avery's class.

"I know today has been hard on you all, so finish up your lunch," he said, grabbing my backpack and guiding me toward the exit of the cafeteria, his grip on my shoulder tightening, his fingers digging into my muscle. "I'll bring Vera to the nurse."

"Wh-what are you doing?" I asked, furrowing my brows once we stepped out of the cafeteria. I tried to stop because I wasn't going to the nurse's office, but he continued to push me along toward his classroom. "I'm not in your class."

When we reached it, he guided me in and closed the door behind us. "You can't say shit like that aloud to the entire school," he said, clenching his sharp jaw and staring over my shoulder at the door's window. "Bad people are trying to pin this on Blaise, and I doubt that he would want you to get involved."

"Bad people?" I whispered, heart racing. "Like ... like who?"

"I can't tell you," he said. "Let me figure this out. Stay under the radar."

"No, I'm already part of this. I don't want anything to happen to him."

"Nothing will."

"Nothing will?!" I asked, throwing my hands up into the air.

Usually, I didn't talk back to any teacher or authority figure, but this wasn't making any sense, and Blaise was in trouble. Even when they proved he hadn't done it, his reputation at Redwood would be ruined.

"They're trying to blame her death on him. The police want him in jail."

"I'll take care of it," he repeated.

"How?"

I had so many questions. How would a teacher do anything about this? He didn't have any power, especially not in Redwood Academy. The principal commanded everything here, and I didn't want Blaise to go to prison for murder.

He was eighteen. They wouldn't even send him to juvie.

"That's none of your business," Mr. Avery said.

"But what are you—"

Before I could say another word, someone opened the door behind us. I expected it to be Maddie or Piper or even Skylar's annoying-ass best friend, who wanted to confront me about what I'd said during lunch.

Instead, João Rocha stood at the door and stormed into the room. After eyeing Mr. Avery, João snatched my elbow and tugged me to his side.

"You're coming with me," he said through clenched teeth, dragging me out of the room.

"Wait, stop! What are you doing? I need to ask him questions. Mr. Avery—"

"No more questions," João growled, harsher than usual. "None for him."

I tried to pull away because I wanted more information from Mr. Avery, but he wouldn't release me from his grip until we stood two hallways down from Avery's room. When he finally let me go, I rubbed my elbow.

"What the hell was that all about?!" I whisper-yelled at him. "I needed to—"

"You shouldn't trust Avery," João said. "I don't."

"Why not?" I asked.

"Because he has ties to the Redwood mob."

My eyes widened. "The mob? Redwood has a mob? I thought that was all a rumor."

"Don't fucking scream it like that," he said between gritted teeth. "Some kids at Redwood work with them. If you fuck up and shout it all over Redwood, they will shut you the fuck up—and not in any way that you'd like."

I pressed my lips together and gulped. He was serious.

João cut his gaze down the hallway, where some freshman kids walked with their friends toward their next class. "Listen, we can't talk about this shit here and now. I have information for you. I'll pick you up after school."

"I have work."

"Well, too fucking bad," he said. "You tell me what's more important—work or Blaise?"

"Blaise," I said without a doubt.

A week ago, I wouldn't have even thought about choosing Blaise over work. But something about that boy drew me to him, and I couldn't let him go so easily. He had known that I wrote dirty smut and kept it to himself, bought me a laptop, spent time with my family, and taught me how to skateboard.

Things he hadn't had to do.

Things that proved I was just as important to him as he was to me.

"I'll meet you at your car," I said, clutching my backpack straps. "And you'll tell me everything."

Chapter Fifty-Seven

VERA

This whole mess had started when I stupidly decided to meet the bad boy by his car after school one afternoon. Now, I was meeting another bad boy in his car after school for a whole different reason.

I slipped into his tinted black Mercedes and nervously bounced my leg, staring at all the students leaving school and gossiping about Blaise being a fucking murderer. "Tell me what you know, João."

"Not here."

He started the car and drove us out of the lot, then through Redwood streets. My stomach twisted as I saw signs for leaving Redwood. He was bringing me down back alleys and into a dense wooden area.

"You're going to great lengths to keep this secret," I whispered, staring out the tinted window at the trees we whizzed by. Part of me was a bit nervous that João wasn't bringing me anywhere just to tell me what had happened, but to keep me quiet too.

Was this what he did to other people? Was this what he did to people he *killed*? Who had he killed? He'd said he had taken someone's life when I was talking about Skylar. Was he angry that I was kinda, sorta blackmailing him with his sister?

My stomach twisted into tighter knots. "João …"

"Shut up, Vera."

I sucked in a sharp breath and reached for the door handle, tugging on it. But it was locked. João glanced over at me, clenched his sharp jaw, and rolled his eyes without saying a single word.

"Let me out," I whispered. "Please."

"Relax," he said, turning into the driveway of an abandoned warehouse, which was decorated with vines, moss, and dirt. It seemed like this place hadn't been taken care of for decades. "I'm not going to hurt you."

"No, you're just going to kill me here."

Once he drove farther, I spotted a motorcycle in the back. Was that Kai's bike?

He parked the car next to it and nodded to the door. "Get out."

After weighing my options, I stepped out of the car. If he was going to kill me, I couldn't run. He'd chase me down and probably have fun doing it. I didn't want to give him the satisfaction of hearing me scream and watching me try to run. I sucked at it.

When I stepped inside the secluded warehouse, Landon and Kai stood on the opposite side. Nerves rushed through me. I had never been alone with all three of them like this. What were they planning on doing with me?

"What is this?" I asked.

João grabbed my shoulder and pushed me forward to them. "Move."

"But—"

"Move."

Landon and Kai met us halfway, and then João shoved his hands into his pockets and grimaced at me. I squeezed my eyes closed and waited for him to pull out a gun to shoot me dead. This was going to be my last—

"Honestly, we couldn't find much on Blaise and Skylar," João said. "At least, not in the fucking time that you gave us."

I opened my eyes and glanced between the three boys. "Wait, so you're not going to kill me? You have actually found information?"

"Kill you?" Landon asked, looking at João. "What the fuck did you tell her we were going to do?"

"I didn't tell her shit. She fucking came up with this idea by herself," he said, looking back over at me with hard brown eyes. "As I was fucking saying, if you'd listen to me, we don't have much information. But what I could get was that Blaise's father slept with the police chief's wife. So, the police chief is trying to put the blame on Blaise to get back at his father."

"Also, I think Skylar had some mental issues," Kai said. "At least, from what I have gathered through her text messages and phone, she'd been seeing a therapist every Tuesday and Thursday. They had spoken briefly about sexual assault and drug addiction over text."

"You were able to sneak into her phone?" I asked.

"Don't worry about it," João said, his voice final.

I might have wanted to see what she had written to Blaise, but I couldn't. It wasn't my place, and if anyone found out, they might become suspicious.

"So, what'd you find? Who do you think did it? Do you think it was Mr. Avery? You said that he was part of the mob?" I asked João, having so many more questions and not so many answers.

Landon and Kai cut their gazes to João.

"What're you fucking telling Vera everything we know about everyone in fucking Redwood?" Landon asked.

"I thought she knew. I was surprised that Blaise hadn't told her already. They're fucking related. And besides, she kept blabbing on and on to him. She wouldn't fucking stop. I needed something to shut her up today."

After glaring at João's profile, I crossed my arms. "So? Do you think he did it or not? You said you don't trust him."

"I don't fucking know. If Skylar's death really was a murder, I think that the mob had something to do with it. But I don't think it was him. He wouldn't try to put the blame on Blaise. They're related."

"That doesn't mean anything," I said.

From what I had seen, Blaise's family didn't care about him at all. All they cared about was their reputation. Everything they did was for their selfish reasons. Not because they cared about their son. They didn't give a fuck about him.

"That's all I fucking know and all I'm going to get you. You have to do the rest," João said, holding out a callous, scarred hand toward me. "Unless you're going to pay up."

I stared at him and gritted my teeth. I knew that I wouldn't be able to get much from him, but at least it was something. I wouldn't be able to blackmail him with his sister anymore or hang that over his head. Plus, I needed the money from him when I babysat. I didn't want to push my luck.

"Fine, thank you."

"I'm surprised you gave her that much for free," Kai joked.

"Shut the fuck up. She watches Ana for cheap," João said, and then he turned toward me and jingled his keys. "Let's go. I'm bringing you home."

Chapter Fifty-Eight

BLAISE

"That little friend of yours can't come over, Blaise," Mom said, pulling off her pearl earrings in the middle of my room. She stared at herself in my mirror, then looked at me on the bed through its reflection. "I'd better not find anyone over here. You're grounded, and this time, I mean it. Your father and I will be home for the next two weeks at least. And nobody—and I mean, fucking nobody—will be over here."

She had been in a pissy mood all day. This must've brought up bad memories of when she found out Dad was cheating on her for the fifteenth time. I didn't know why she hadn't left the first time. Probably still wanted his money.

I rolled onto my stomach and stared out my window, suppressing the urge to roll my eyes. Mom thought she had all the fucking control in the world, but really, she had none. She had none with Dad. She had none with me. She had no control over her actual life.

If she wasn't such a bitch to me, then maybe I would actually feel bad for her.

But I didn't.

"Okay," I said, texting Vera to come over. "Nobody is coming over."

Mom wasn't going to tell me shit about what I could and couldn't do. I had spent all fucking day sitting in the damn police station and answering question after question after fucking question about Skylar and my whereabouts on the day she had died. It was non-fucking-stop. The police came at me over and over, trying to do everything and anything that they could to pin this on me.

When she finally fucking left, Vera texted me back.

Vera: I'm already on my way. I need to see you. We need to talk.

Me: Meet me a couple houses down. My mom's a bitch.

I turned on the music on my iMac to pretend like I wasn't about to sneak out my window and glared at the broken headphones on my desk. Mom hadn't let me go back to the mall to get some new ones. Hell, they hadn't let me out of their own sight since this whole thing had started.

I'd been stuck in this shithole all day.

By myself.

Just waiting for Vera to get out of school. I wanted to see her so badly.

Over the light hum of the music, I could hear Dad and his lawyer speaking loudly with each other. They were talking about me or about Skylar's death. From the evidence that he'd gathered, Dad's lawyer thought that she had killed herself.

I didn't care what had happened to her, but I wanted this to be over.

After opening my window, I slipped out of it and jumped down to the first floor. My feet hit the ground hard, my knees almost buckling. I didn't know how the fuck I would get back in with Vera and with all the security Mom had ordered for around the house, but I would make it work.

Once I snuck around all the security outside, I walked toward the Stop sign at the end of the road. I pulled my hood up to stop the slight windchill and waited. A sleek black car—João's car—pulled up a few minutes later, and I gritted my teeth.

"What the fuck is she doing with him?"

She scurried out of the car and waved him off. He did a U-turn in the middle of the street and drove past us, glancing out his driver's window at me. I glared at him, hurried over to her, and grabbed her hand, snatching it up in mine and feeling its warmth.

"What are you doing with him?" I asked.

"He had information that I needed about Skylar and her death."

While I wanted to be angry with her for being with him, I knew that he was the only one who would be able to keep her safe at school. Who the fuck knew what kind of drama and rumors were spreading around Redwood about me right now? If she got caught up in this mess, I would never fucking forgive myself.

As much as I hated it, João could keep her safe.

And he would because she watched his little sister. He trusted her.

"It doesn't matter," I said, pulling her along back toward my house and praying that security would let me in without telling the bitch that I called Mom. After passing a security guard, I nodded in hopes that he wouldn't say shit. And he didn't, thankfully.

"Are you sure this is okay?" Vera asked, nervously looking at the guard.

It wasn't, but she didn't need to know that.

Once we made it all the way upstairs, I shut and locked the door. Then, I turned around, threw my arms around her, and hugged her. It had been too long of a fucking day, and nobody had really been on my side.

All my parents wanted was to keep their names out of this all.

Vera sighed softly and squeezed me tighter, the scent of her strawberry shampoo drifting around me. Not wanting to let her go, I picked her up and brought her to the bed, making her sit on top of me in my arms, bridal-style.

She rested her head on my shoulder and hummed. "Some girls were talking badly about you at lunch today, and I wanted them to know that ... you didn't do anything. Mr. Avery pulled me out of the cafeteria and told me not to say anything about you."

"What do you mean, he pulled you out of the cafeteria?" I asked. "What did he say?"

"He ... he said that there were some bad people who were trying to pin this on you. Is that true? Who's after you? What ... what did you do?" She furrowed her brows and stared up at me with wide eyes. "Please tell me."

"It's just my dad. He's fucking slept with half of the town," I said, hoping that she'd drop it.

I didn't want to bring up that I knew Dad had slept with her mom. Maybe forcefully. I didn't want to fucking get into *that*. Not now.

"Is that all that Avery said?"

"Yeah," she whispered. She chewed on the inside of her lip, her expression uncertain. "And I ... I kinda told the school that ..."

"You told the school about what?"

"I told them that ... I told them that, um ... you and I are kind of, um, hanging out."

"You told them that we were together?"

"Mmhmm," she said, not looking me in the eye.

My heart raced in my chest, warmth spreading throughout my body. I pressed my lips together to suppress the widest fucking grin that I wanted to plaster on my face. All this time, Vera hadn't wanted to be seen with me. She hadn't wanted to be associated with me. But now, she had told the entire school that we were together.

She really ... she really fucking cared about me.

She had been willing to risk everything to protect me. Everything.

"We don't have to hide anymore," she whispered, peeking a glance at me. "I'm sorry if you still wanted to—"

Before she could finish her sentence, I smashed my lips against hers. I'd been waiting for fucking years for this. I'd been waiting ever since my parents had fired her mother. I'd wanted her so bad. And now, I would have her.

Chapter Fifty-Nine

VERA

"You're mine," Blaise growled against my lips. "Mine."

I moaned softly into his mouth, curling my fingers into his chest and feeling the taut muscle. So many thoughts had been rushing through my mind today, but when he kissed me, everything seemed to disappear, as cliché as that was.

Blaise curled his arms around me and drew me closer to him, so our bodies were flush against each other. "Mine."

He sank his nose into my hair. I shifted in his arms, so I straddled his waist. He grasped my jaw in his rough, callous palm and forced me to really look at him.

"Blaise," I murmured breathlessly, "I'm yours."

With deep brown eyes, he stared at me and lightly tapped his lips against mine. Tingles ran up and down my arms as the warmth pooled between my thighs. He lifted his hips, letting me feel his hardness.

"I'd do anything for you. Fucking anything," he murmured, grasping my face and pulling me toward him.

For the second time tonight, he crashed his lips hard against mine.

Somehow, this time, I needed him even more than before. I grabbed his shoulders and tugged him closer, wanting to be wrapped up in his strong arms. Today had been so stressful with all the rumors floating around, but I'd do anything to protect Blaise.

Twirling us around so I lay on the bed, Blaise pressed his lips against my collarbone, then peppered kisses down the center of my chest. He slipped his hands under my sweatshirt, slowly moving up the sides of my body, his fingers curling around my breasts.

My breathing hitched. The feeling of his hard fingers on my soft skin making my core warm. I whimpered and clutched the bedsheets, tugging up on them, my legs beginning to shake already and he hadn't done much.

"Relax," he said against my neck, pulling off my sweatshirt. He kissed down my chest again, his lips finding the ends of my bra near my cleavage. He groped me through the thin material, drawing his fingers over my nipple poking against it.

My pussy clenched, and I tried to suppress another moan.

"The music's on. Moan as loud as you want, V."

I lay back on my bed, relaxing against the soft cotton under my body. He curled his fingers under my bra cups and took a shaky breath, his eyes darkening. We had slept together countless times before, but tonight was different.

It seemed like we could both feel that.

While Blaise had taken me hard and fast every other time, he slowly pulled down the cups of my bras and let my breasts fall out of them. His mouth found my nipple, and he sucked it between his lips. Tingles ran up and down my body again as he sucked harsher. He slipped his hand between my legs and rubbed my clit.

I arched my back, a moan escaping my lips. Heat rushed to my core, and I swallowed hard. "I'm yours, Blaise."

He slipped a finger inside of me, and I clenched around him.

Thrusting it in and out, he moved his fingers until my panties were soaked.

Then, he crawled down the bed, hooking his fingers under my pants, tugging them all the way down my body, throwing them to the side of the room. He sat between my legs and placed his hands on my knees, every muscle in his upper body flexing. My abdomen tensed, and I pulled my legs together, admiring all that thick muscle that was *mine*.

He pulled my legs apart and gazed down at my wet panties, a smirk stretching across his lips. "Fuck, I bet you taste even better than last time. You're soaking fucking wet for me, Sunshine." He lay down on the bed on his stomach, his head between my legs.

I ran my hands through his hair, tugging lightly right when his tongue hit my clit. He massaged it in circles, each time a little faster. I gazed up at the ceiling, trying to take deep breaths.

"Watch me please you," he murmured against my cunt, his tongue moving faster.

He slipped two fingers inside my tight pussy and curled them against my G-spot. I stared down at him, arched my back, and came. Hard.

Wave after wave of pleasure rushed through me. I pulled a pillow over my face and screamed into it, my cunt pulsing over and over on his large fingers.

When he pulled them out of me, he grabbed my hand and placed it right on the front of his sweatpants. "Feel how hard you fucking make me, V."

He made me stroke him through his gray pants. I clenched my pussy and grasped him through the material, desperate for him to be inside me now, plunging himself so deep, making me come over and over and over again.

"Take them off," I said. "God, take them off now."

Curling his fingers around his waistband, he knelt between my legs and slowly pulled his pants down, revealing his thick cock inch by inch. His dick sprang out, grazing against my entrance and clit.

I wrapped my hand around its base and stroked it against me, watching the pre-cum drip onto my glistening cunt.

He lightly grasped my throat and pulled me toward him, caressing my cheek with his other hand. "I've been waiting for you to be mine for years."

"Years?" I whispered. "Since we were kids?"

He pressed his lips to mine and pushed me back onto the bed. Then crawled between my legs, pressing his cock against my entrance. He grazed his teeth against the side of my neck, his breath warm.

"Tell me you'll always be mine."

I curled my hand into his soft hair. "I'll always be yours," I said, pulling him closer.

Blaise plunged himself into me, his thick cock filling up my pussy. I dug my nails into his back, the pressure almost too much to handle. He pumped in and out of me slowly, gently sucking on my neck. Pleasure surged through my body, and I curled my toes.

He had barely been inside me for a whole two minutes, but I was on the brink of exploding with pure ecstasy again. I curled my fingers into his shoulders as he slipped a hand between my legs, rubbing my swollen clit.

My chest heaved up and down. "Please come inside me," I begged, whimpering into his ear. "Please, I need it so badly. It'll make me—"

He slammed himself into me hard one last time and grunted deeply against my neck. I clamped down on his dick and moaned into his ear, my whole body trembling against the bed.

Chapter Sixty

VERA

Since Blaise's parents were home, we opted for a quiet night—at least, besides the steamy fuck we'd had. I sat on his bed next to him and pulled the laptop he'd gifted me out of my backpack. I needed to write. I didn't know what I wanted to write about, but after today, I really needed something.

So, I opened my Google Docs and found the story that I had been writing about Blaise and me. I didn't want him to see it, so I turned the brightness on the laptop all the way down until the screen was nearly black.

Angsty pop punk music played from a speaker on Blaise's desk as I wrote. He sat next to me with his back against a wall and his laptop in his lap. When I glanced over, he was scrolling through hundreds of skateboarding videos for his YouTube channel.

Today, while trying to distract myself from the rumors floating around Redwood about him, I had started snooping more on his channel and reading through the comments under his videos. While there were so many people who loved his content and commented about how it'd helped them, there were also some E-girls who ... *simped* over him.

Like hard-core.

Their profile pictures were picture-fucking-perfect. And I had felt so many insecurities that I had to completely log out of YouTube this morning. He would never really respond to any one of the desperate comments, but still, I might've been a little jealous.

Blaise was mine.

I glanced over at him again, insecurities still nipping at my insides, especially since Skylar's friend had brought them up today. When she'd told me that he and Skylar hung out all the time, it'd kinda fucked with me. But what could I do?

I couldn't believe her. I couldn't believe any of them. All Redwood did was lie.

While my stomach twisted and turned, I looked back at my laptop and continued to type where I had left off last time. So much had happened since the last chapter, so many bad fucking things. And I didn't even know where to start.

Somehow, someway, my fingers began gliding across the keyboard. Writing was cathartic for me, an easy way to blow off steam and deal with my problems while not actually dealing with them in real life.

"What's that?" Blaise asked twenty minutes later.

I snapped my gaze to him, my heart racing inside my chest. "What's what?"

"The story that you're working on."

Before he could read another word of it, I snapped the laptop shut and awkwardly scratched the back of my neck, laughing nervously. "Oh, this? It's nothing," I forced out of my mouth. *Way to act natural.*

"Come on. What is it?" Blaise teased, placing his laptop on the bed and leaning closer, his warmth breathing in my ear and his index finger curling around a strand of my dark hair. "You haven't stopped typing for, like, the past ten minutes."

Once I slapped his hand away because it made me nervous, I sat up taller and pretended like his proximity wasn't affecting me as much as it was. Blaise Harleen made me anxious in the best way possible.

"It's just ... something that I'm working on."

"I haven't seen it before. It's a new story?"

My cheeks flushed. "Um, yeah."

"What's it about? You're on, like, chapter sixty already."

"Um ..."

I chewed on the inside of my cheek and glanced away from him, unable to keep eye contact. I didn't want him to know that I was writing a story about us. I didn't know what would happen next, and I didn't want it to end. I hoped that our story would be as beautiful as the fictional ones that I wrote about, where the girl always got the guy, no matter the problems they faced. I wanted us to be as happy as those couples one day.

I wanted to be as happy as those girls because I had never been before.

I didn't want to jinx us.

"It's this cheesy, cliché high school romance," I said, waving at him. "You wouldn't like it."

"Try me."

Gripping the laptop harder, I stared down at the metal and hoped he dropped it. I didn't want him to think that I was obsessed with him. I might have been, but I didn't want to seem crazy. I wanted to keep us like this for as long as I could.

"Come on, Sunshine. Share it with me."

He reached for my laptop, but I pushed his hands away and scrambled off the bed.

"Not right now. I'll let you read it when I'm finished." Though ... that might've been a lie, depending on whether or not we were still together.

Maybe one day, he'd get bored of me. Rich kids did that a lot.

But as much as I tried to convince myself, that didn't seem like Blaise.

"You're going to make me wait?"

"Yes."

He playfully rolled his brown eyes. "But I'm your number one fan."

Butterflies fluttered in my stomach. Warmth spread throughout my chest. And a damn smile broke out on my face. I couldn't stop all those tiny little feelings erupting through me. Blaise loved reading my work. The bad boy—the guy who always got into fights, skateboarded around school, and didn't give a fuck about anyone or anything—was *my* number one fan.

And it wasn't a lie either.

I peeked over at his laptop to see my writing profile bookmarked on his computer.

A small giggle escaped my lips, and Blaise stared at me with a goofy smile of his own.

"What are you laughing about? I can't be my girl's number one fan?"

There it was again.

My girl.

"Hmm?" he asked, pulling me into his arms and onto the bed, his fingers gently digging into my sides to tickle me. "I can't be your biggest supporter?"

I laughed into a pillow so hard that tears formed in my eyes. "I'm not laughing about anything, I promise," I said between giggles. When I finally got him to stop with the tickling torture, I straddled his waist and wrapped my arms around his shoulders, my laughter dying. "I hope that you'll love my story as much as I do when I share it with you one day."

Chapter Sixty-One

BLAISE

Vera's shrill scream jerked me awake. I shot up in my bed, realizing that she wasn't next to me anymore even though we had fallen asleep together last night, and twisted my head toward the door.

Mom had a fistful of Vera's hair in her grasp, dragging her to the door. Mom's hand was wrapped so tightly around the locks of Vera's silky brown hair, and she was yanking her so forcefully and so quickly that Vera couldn't even scramble to her feet.

"Get the fuck off her!" I shouted, jumping to my feet, shoving myself between them, and forcing Mom back into the hallway. I glared at the pure spite and jealousy in her eyes, the way she sneered at Vera, who had been doing nothing but sleeping in my bed. "What the fuck is wrong with you?!"

Vera stood behind me, sobbing and grabbing her head. I wanted to comfort her, but if I moved from my spot, I didn't know if Mom would hurl herself back into my room and hurt Vera even more. Vera quickly pulled on her pants and gathered her things behind me.

"I told you, nobody comes over!" Mom screamed, nostrils flaring.

Once Vera gathered all her things in haste, she pushed by me and Mom, hurrying out into the hallway. She didn't look either of us in the eye, but continued to mutter, "Sorry," over and over, tears streaming down her cheeks.

"Get that girl out of my house," Mom said. "Now! I already told you that I don't want you associating with someone like her. You know what her mother has done to this family. They're no-good, money-hungry whores."

Before Vera could make a beeline out of the house, she froze and slowly turned back toward me, eyes wide. "Wh-what did she say?" she asked quietly, standing at the foot of the steps.

Dad padded out into the foyer from one of the guest bedrooms in a pair of sweatpants and his college sweatshirt, his hair disheveled, as if he had just woken up. He ran a hand over his face, line creasing. He must've not slept in their bedroom last night.

"I already told you that nothing happened between us," Dad grumbled to Mom.

"You're a liar!" Mom screamed, tears racing down her cheeks. She grabbed a sculpture on a side table that Dad had bought for several hundred thousand dollars and hurled it at him. "A fucking liar."

After Dad sidestepped the statue, it hit the wall, feet from Vera and crumbled to pieces. I hurried past them both and snatched up Vera's hand to get her out of here as soon as fucking possible. Of course, they had to be crazy when I had Vera over. They had been so fucking absent until I brought someone that I cared about over.

"What did your parents mean?" Vera asked, voice trembling. "Please tell me that m-my—"

I scooped her into my arms and carried her to my car, setting her in the passenger seat and shutting the door. I needed to get her out of here quickly. We didn't have time for questions that I didn't have the answers to right now. Mom would rush out any second now.

When I slipped into the driver's seat, I threw the car in reverse and backed out of the driveway. I gripped the steering wheel and hit the gas pedal, zooming forward and not saying a word until we were far enough away from my house.

I pulled over to the side of the road, parked the car, and gently rubbed Vera's head. "I'm so fucking sorry, Vera. I should've never asked you to come over. I should've taken you home. Are you okay?"

She sniffled, her teary eyes making my chest tighten. "Tell me what your mother meant."

After letting out a long sigh, I frowned. "I don't know if it's true. My dad has slept with half of this town, but my mom likes to start drama, if you haven't noticed. She's insecure because of him and pieces together the smallest things to make an assumption."

"My mom ..." Vera shook her head, more tears falling from her cheeks. "She wouldn't have done that. I know she wouldn't have risked her job to sleep with your father. Your parents were paying her well."

"I know she wouldn't have."

"Why does your mom hate me so much?" she asked, voice quiet.

"She hates herself, not you. She's insecure, and you intimidate her."

"Me?" she sobbed. "Intimidating?"

"You're the only woman who can make me happy. She can't even do that."

Vera wrapped her arms around herself and stared out the window, tears trembling in her eyes. "I want to go home." Vera sniffled again, her shoulders trembling. "Please. I just want to go home. School starts in two hours."

My chest tightened, and I cupped her face in my hands, swiping my thumbs across her cheeks to catch the tears. "I'm so fucking sorry, Vera."

This was all my fucking fault. I should've been more careful with her. I couldn't risk losing her over this.

"It's not your fault," she said after a long pause.

But it was, and we both knew it.

I drove her home in silence as she muffled her sobs in her hand. Once I dropped Vera off at home and promised her that I'd see her during school, I sped back home quicker than I ever had before and skirted into the driveway. My blood was boiling, my teeth grinding. *The fuck is wrong with Mom?*

When I stormed into the house, all the artwork lay on the floor in pieces, the pillows were thrown off the couches, and glass was shattered all over the marble floor. I followed their screaming voices through the house to Dad's home office.

"You're crazy!" he shouted at her, sitting at his desk.

"What the fuck is wrong with you?" I yelled at Mom, storming into the room. "If all he does is make you insecure and cheat on you, then fucking leave him, Mom. What don't you fucking get about him walking all over you? You're—"

"Blaise," Dad scolded, standing from his chair.

"Don't fucking interrupt me," I growled at him, clenching my jaw and nearly chipping my teeth at the sheer amount of pressure I used to grind them together. "I'm done with this family. I've done everything you've ever wanted, and you guys don't give a fuck until something happens to me, only because *your name* is associated with it."

Mom huffed. "If it wasn't for—"

"I'm done," I declared. "I'm fucking done for good this time. And I'm leaving."

I didn't know that was what I had planned to say before I said it. Somehow, as soon as the words jutted out of my mouth like spears, a weight that I had been carrying for years now lifted off my shoulders.

I didn't know where the hell I'd go, but leaving was my only choice. They'd treated me like shit for years, and I had dealt with it. But as soon as Mom had laid a fucking hand on my girl, that was the final straw.

"I'm leaving," I repeated more to myself. "For good."

Chapter Sixty-Two

VERA

Gently, I rubbed my head where Blaise's mother had yanked my hair this morning and sat at the lunch table. Blaise had apologized about it all morning, asking me if there was anything that he could do to make it up to me.

It wasn't his fault that his mom was a bitch. He wasn't to blame.

He'd seemed desperate to make it up to me somehow, so I had briefly told him to get me spaghetti and meatballs for lunch—something that'd be easy. Honestly, I didn't think he'd even remember. He had so much on his mind.

Whispers echoed through the cafeteria about Blaise, even after I'd stuck up for him yesterday. I pulled out my brown paper bag of food that I had thrown together before I left this morning and glanced over at Piper, sighing.

"Where's Maddie?" I asked, the thought of Mom being with Blaise's dad still haunting me.

Though I knew it wasn't true. It couldn't be true. Mom wouldn't do something like that, especially not to our family.

"With *you know who*," Piper said.

"Who?"

"Her brother's best friend. In the restroom. Probably doing the dirty."

I curled my lips into a small smile and opened my water bottle. "You know that—"

João Rocha slammed his palm onto the table, fingers sprawled out against my lunch bag. He took it and looked inside, scrunching his nose and handing it back to me. "You got no good food."

"Did you expect a five-star meal?" I snapped, hiding my lunch from him.

"No, but I expect you to watch my sister tonight."

"I'm busy."

"Don't fucking test me, Vera. We had a deal."

"Fine," I huffed, staring up at him. "I'll watch Ana."

"Good," he said, turning away from me. "I'll bring her over at four."

From across the cafeteria, I spotted Mateo sitting with his friends and staring back at me. Once he glanced around at them uncomfortably, he said something, then stood and walked over to me. He eyed João's departing figure and took his place at my side.

"Hey."

"Um, hey," I said. "I thought you didn't want me to talk to you today."

"Where's Blaise?"

"I don't know."

"Do you think he will want to come over tonight?" Mateo asked. "To game?"

"Don't you have plans with a couple of your friends tonight?"

After Blaise had driven me home this morning, Mateo had told me that he was hanging out with some sophomore girls after school today, so I wouldn't bother him about where he was or who he was hanging out with.

"Yeah, I do ... but Blaise has been through shit these past couple days. He probably has a lot going on with the police, but can you tell him that if he wants to come over, I'll be home to play with him?"

"Why don't you ask him?"

"You think he'd want to?"

"Sure. Why not?"

I didn't want to get into specifics about Blaise's home life or how Blaise didn't really have friends and skateboarded alone all the time. Mateo and Blaise were more similar than I'd thought—maybe than even *they* thought.

If Blaise didn't have to be at the police station or didn't want to spend time at the skatepark alone to think everything through, he would one hundred percent want to come over and play with Mateo. I'd bet he would be ecstatic that Mateo asked.

"I'll text him."

My eyes widened. "You have his number?!"

"Yeah, I ask him about ..." Mateo stopped, cheeks flushing.

"About what?"

"About girls all the time. Nothing weird."

Scrunching my nose, I stared at him. He didn't even say goodbye as he twirled around and walked back to his table, taking a seat next to a girl with pretty green eyes, long black hair, and mascara skills that I would kill for.

Not *really* kill for, though.

RIP, Skylar.

Just kidding. She was a bitch.

"So, any news on Skylar?" Piper asked, taking a bite of her ham sandwich.

I rested my elbows on the table and leaned forward, sighing and remembering what Mr. Avery had told me yesterday. Whether there was truth to it or not, I wasn't sure, but I didn't want to find out the hard way. Who knew who was listening? This was Redwood. There were always people looking for the latest gossip.

"Nothing," I said, not completely lying.

With this morning's happenings, I hadn't had much time to really look into it more.

"Did Blaise even come to school today?" Piper asked.

"Yeah, he did," I said, spotting him at the door.

When Blaise walked into the cafeteria, the whispering stopped. In one sudden movement, like something out of a horror movie, everyone watched him walk into the room and toward me.

While the rumors bothered me, Blaise didn't seem like he cared at all. He ignored everyone and hurried toward me with his rain jacket zipped all the way up to the neck and a brown paper bag of Italian food from a ritzy restaurant downtown that must've cost a hundred dollars a dish.

He set the food in front of me and sat to my left, blocking the stares from everyone else, including Skylar's annoying friends. "I didn't know what kind of meatballs you wanted, so I got you regular," he said, pulling out the bag's contents.

Bread. Olive oil. And a heaping container of spaghetti and meatballs.

"You didn't have to do this," I said, gently patting him on the forearm.

Blaise shrugged it off like it was nothing. "And my mom didn't have to do what she did to you this morning. You don't fucking deserve shit like that," he said. "Nobody does. I get that now. So, I left."

"What do you mean, you left?"

"Fuck my parents," Blaise growled. "I'm not staying there any longer."

"Where are you going to go?" Piper asked.

Again, Blaise shrugged. "I don't know. We'll see."

Chapter Sixty-Three

BLAISE

Halfway through lunch, my phone buzzed in my pocket. I rolled my eyes and pulled it out, expecting it to be Mom or Dad demanding that I come home tonight because they wanted me to chat with their lawyer about the Skylar situation.

Instead, it was my uncle.

Callan: Meet me in my class.

I stared at the text message and sighed through my nose, wanting this drama to be over already. It was bad enough that I'd had to deal with Mom's bullshit this morning. But Callan knew who was trying to pin this on me. I couldn't miss talking to him.

While Vera might've let me sit next to her during lunch, I highly doubted that she wanted me to kiss her goodbye before I met up with Callan. So, I gently patted her knee under the table and leaned forward.

"My car. After school, Sunshine."

She curled her lips into a small smile and tucked some strands of hair behind her ear, nodding at me. "I'll be there."

"You'd better."

Once I dumped my half-eaten lunch in the trash, I ignored the whispers around me and walked out of the room. Principal Vaughn stood right outside the cafeteria in the hallway, chatting with another teacher with his arms crossed.

"Mr. Harleen," he muttered. "What are you doing?"

"Shut the fuck up, Vaughn," I growled, walking past him and down the hallway toward Callan's class.

I expected Vaughn to say something back, but he was smart and decided to keep his mouth closed.

I was so sick of people talking shit about me. If he had said something, I would've probably socked him in the mouth. And I wouldn't have regretted it either. Principal Vaughn had more than that coming to him.

After walking up a flight of stairs, I found Callan's classroom and knocked twice on the door. He opened it after the second knock and tugged me into the room by the collar, locking the door behind me.

"What information do you have?" I asked him, not wanting to waste time.

Callan sighed through his nose and walked back to his desk. "You're in deep shit."

"I didn't fucking do anything."

"I know that."

"Well, who the fuck did it then?"

"It was a job," he said.

"You? You fucking killed her?!" I asked, eyes bugging out of my head. "You?!"

"No, not me," he said, clenching his jaw. "The mob. I don't take jobs involving students."

"Why is the Redwood mob in on it? What'd they want with her?"

Callan clenched his jaw and walked to his desk. "It's a long fucking story that I can't talk about in school. There are people here that're in on it too. I've been trying to stop it since I found out about it."

"Wow," I said sarcastically, walking back toward the door to leave. I could've been finishing lunch with Vera and relaxing for once. Not listening to this dickhead. "Great information. This was a really amazing use of my time."

Before I could make it to the door, he grabbed my elbow. "I'm not finished."

"Well, this shit isn't my fault!" I shouted, ripping myself out of his hold. "You're connected with the mob. Do something about it. Tell them not to blame me because they're not going to win against my father's lawyers."

"They'll eliminate your father's lawyers," Callan said in a hushed tone. "This shit is serious. I'm doing everything in my power to stop this."

"Well, try fucking harder."

Cry me a fucking river that some annoying asshole had died. All she did was ruin my fucking life and show up at my house, unannounced, because she was jealous that I gave another girl my attention. She'd tried to ruin my life when she was alive, and she was *still* doing it.

This wasn't fair. None of this was fucking fair.

"They made it seem like a suicide. Sent text messages from her phone beforehand to a *therapist*. Made her seem crazier than she was," Callan started, leaning against the whiteboard and crossing his arms. "Her parents suspected that it wasn't a suicide, so the mob is scrambling."

"So, they need someone to fucking blame it on," I clarified.

"And because you had to fuck her—"

"That's all that happened between us," I said through gritted teeth. "Nothing more."

"Yeah, but you were the only guy at this school that people saw her with."

"Well, tell them to blame it on my fucking father and mother. Not me. I didn't do shit."

"If I try to avert the blame away from you to your parents, your father is going to give me fucking hell," Callan said. "Not something I want to deal with right now. I have too many other people to keep safe and away from this."

"Like Sakura?"

He grimaced and looked over through hooded eyes. "Yes."

"What, you guys are actually a thing now?"

"That's not any of your business."

"Not my business until I tell everyone you're fucking a student."

After balling his hands into fists on top of the desk, he drew his tongue across his teeth, looking pissed the fuck off. And he should be because I didn't want to have to hang this over his head any more than he wanted me to do so.

"Take care of this, *Uncle*."

Chapter Sixty-Four

VERA

After school, I leaned against Blaise's car and edited a chapter of my new untitled book on my phone while I waited for him. I didn't want to pull out the MacBook that Blaise had gotten me here; I'd wait until I got home for that.

"Fucking finally get to see you," Blaise said, walking toward me and unlocking his car.

I quickly shoved my phone into my pocket, cheeks flushing, and opened the passenger door. Before I could slide into it, Blaise grabbed my wrist and pulled me back, slipping into the seat himself. He pulled me into his lap and shut the door behind me.

"You don't like PDA yet, but, God"—he grunted—"I've been thinking about you all day."

Warmth exploded in my core, and I gently ground my hips against his as I straddled his waist. He was already hard, his dick bulging against the front of his pants. I sank my hand between our bodies and stroked him.

At least Blaise had tinted windows.

Blaise slipped a hand up my skirt and plunged it into my panties, his rough, large fingers teasing my clit for a couple moments before he pushed them inside me.

"You were writing smut before I interrupted you," he said, smirking. "I can tell by how wet you are."

My cheeks grew hotter. "N-no, I-I wasn't."

"Sunshine," he purred, pumping his fingers in and out of me, "read it to me."

"I-I wasn't. I pr-promise."

His fingers stilled inside me, his gaze hardening. "Don't play with me, V. You're going to read me the new story that you're writing, and I'm going to finger this wet pussy until you're begging to come. Understand?"

Whining softly, I nodded and pulled out my phone. My core pulsed around his fingers, desperate for him to start moving them in and out of me again. I stared at my phone, trying to find a part that he wouldn't recognize.

This story was about us, and I didn't want him to figure it out.

Not yet.

"I'm waiting," he said.

"O-okay," I whispered, swallowing hard, my pussy clamping down on him. " *How long have you been waiting for someone's cock to slide all the way up into this pussy?' he asked me, drawing a finger up my leggings and cupping my pussy in his large, tattooed hand.*"

Blaise slowly pumped his two fingers into my pussy, his thumb moving in circles around my clit. I curled my fingers into his shoulder and gripped my phone in my opposite hand.

" '*He pressed his fingers against my core through the thin material and chuckled against me, rubbing me even harder and faster. 'A long time, it seems.' He slid his other hand up the side of my body, wrapped it around my throat, and pulled me closer, trailing his nose up the side of my neck and biting down softly on my jaw. My breath hitched, and my nipples hardened.'* "

Blaise dipped his head to my breast and drew his teeth along my nipple that now pressed quite obviously against the front of my shirt.

Pleasure shot through me as he took it right in his mouth over the fabric and nibbled on it.

"Nipples hardening, just like they are now, hmm?" he hummed, fingers moving faster.

I furrowed my brows, my cunt clamping down on his fingers, and moaned softly. "P-please ..."

"Continue reading," Blaise ordered.

" *'He grabbed a fistful of my dark hair and pulled it back roughly, forcing me to look up at him. I squealed at the sudden movement as he continued to rub my pussy roughly, his hand slipping into my pants and claiming what no man ever had before. 'Is this what you need?'"*

"This is what you need," Blaise answered himself, gripping my waist with his free hand and now pounding his fingers up into me.

I dug my nails into his shoulder muscle, the sloppy, wet sounds of my pussy filling the car.

"Please, don't stop," I pleaded, tilting my head back and closing my eyes. "I need it."

"I didn't say that you could stop."

I looked back down at my phone, the pressure rising higher and higher in my core, and desperately tried to find the place where I had last read. "I-I can't find where I left off," I murmured, my legs trembling.

Heat raged in my core as he added a third finger.

"Continue," he demanded. "Or I'll stop."

So, I found a random line and read from there. I didn't want him to stop. I needed this badly. We both needed this after the week we'd both had.

" *'Are you going to come already?' he asked me, curling his fingers into me. Gripping his shoulders, I threw my head back and let an earth-shattering orgasm rip through my body. I slapped a hand over my mouth to quiet my moans, so nobody else would hear, but he quickly pulled both hands behind my back. 'Enjoy the orgasm. It's the first one anyone has probably ever given you.' He continued to curl his fingers into me, making sure not to stop until I finished. 'I wanna hear you scream for m—'"*

Before I could finish the damn line, an orgasm surged through my body. I threw my head back, dropping my phone between the seats and coming hard on his fingers. My eyes rolled back in my head, my legs trembling.

Wave after wave of pleasure rushed through my body. I gripped on to his shoulders with both hands and bucked my hips like a madwoman on his fingers, desperately riding out my orgasm until my pussy stopped pulsing on him.

My wetness dribbled onto the front of his pants, right across his bulge. He leaned back against the passenger seat, sucked his fingers into his mouth, and rolled his eyes back. After grunting lowly, he finally slumped his shoulders back and relaxed.

Wanting to please him—because he'd had a long few days—I climbed to the driver's seat and shifted onto my knees, leaned over the center console, and undid his zipper. I didn't know how well I'd do, giving him a blow job. I'd never really given one to anyone before Blaise, but I wanted to help him out. I *needed* to help him out.

I wrapped my hand around the base of his cock and dipped my head, sucking as much of him as I could into my mouth. My eyes watered slightly, but I forced myself to take every last inch of him and began bobbing my head, hoping I could make him feel good.

He rested back against the seat and placed one hand on the back of my head, curling his fingers into my hair. "Fuck, Sunshine. You're fucking amazing," he murmured.

Gently, he began lifting his hips off the seat, thrusting himself in and out of my throat. I tightened around him and took more of him into my mouth, making myself gag. But instead of pulling him out, I flicked my tongue against his balls, like I'd seen girls do in porn.

So much spit and drool ran down the length of his cock, dripping onto his balls and then onto the seat. I gagged every time he hit the back of my throat as sloppy, wet sounds came from my mouth. But I was determined not to stop. I wouldn't stop until—

Suddenly, Blaise slammed himself into my mouth and down my throat, his cum shooting into it and filling me. I pressed my lips tighter around his cock, my cheeks puffing out to keep all his cum inside me.

When the last of his cum shot into my mouth, I slowly sat back up and stuck my tongue out for him to see it. He rolled his eyes back, groaning again, and watched me swallow him.

"So desperate for my cum," he said, gliding his finger across my bottom lip. "So desperate for me."

Chapter Sixty-Five

BLAISE

"Am I doing it?" Vera asked, glancing back at me as she glided on the skateboard in the middle of the slums. Just like I had taught her, she stopped the board before she hit a pothole and grabbed it from the ground, walking back to me. "I did it."

I leaned against my Ferrari and smirked. She had been skating up and down the street for the past half hour and hadn't fallen once. Every time she hopped back onto the board, she rode smoother and faster, actually getting the hang of it.

"Vera," João hummed, walking out of his front door while holding his sister's hand. He glanced over at me, surprisingly not making any backhanded comments for once, and continued toward us. "You promised you'd watch Ana."

Vera handed the board to me, walking to meet João on the sidewalk.

Ana squeezed João's hand and stared up at her brother. "Why can't I stay with Mama? Where is she? I miss her."

João crouched to her level, looked her in the eyes, and swallowed. "She's working."

"But it's not fair. She's always working."

After letting out a long sigh, João refastened Ana's light-up Velcro princess shoes, the Velcro so old and worn that they didn't even fasten closed completely. "I'll get you some new shoes while I'm out today, and we can show Mama later, okay?"

Ana frowned, but then she nodded and threw her small arms around João's shoulders. João was a dick, but even he had better fucking family relationships than I did. And I envied the fuck out of him for it.

"Don't fuck with my sister," João warned me once he stood.

Vera pulled Ana up and held her in her arms. "You want to make some brigadeiros tonight with me and Blaise?"

Ana looked over at me and grinned wickedly. "Yeah!"

"We gotta wait for Mateo, and then we can head in, okay?"

"Okay, where is—"

"Sorry I'm late," Mateo said, hurrying down the sidewalk with his hands clasped around his backpack straps and sweat rolling down his forehead. His hair was all disheveled and his shirt untucked. "I, uh, had to stay after school to finish something."

"We were at the school until, like, four thirty," Vera said. "What were you doing for that long that you—"

"I was busy, all right?" Mateo snapped, glancing at me for help.

I smirked, knowing exactly what he had been up to this afternoon just by the way he looked, and slung my arm over Vera's shoulders. "Don't worry about it, V. Stop being an overly possessive sister. Your brother is allowed to have some fun."

"You think I'm overly possessive?" she asked, arching a brow at me. Then, she must've actually registered what I had said because she scrunched her nose at Mateo, who walked into the house. "And ew."

After following Mateo into the house, I placed my skateboard against the wall and out of the way. Ana and Vera disappeared into the kitchen to make brigadeiros or whatever they were, and Mateo handed me a controller.

"You get any?" I asked, referring to the situation with a sophomore girl he had been telling me about.

He must've been with her after school.

Mateo tried to hide a grin. "We didn't go all the way."

My lips curled into a smirk as I clicked through the main menu screen for the Raid of Durnbone video game. We played for fifteen minutes before Vera's mother came home, immediately spotting me on the couch. Mateo paused the game.

"Oh, Blaise ... Vera told me what happened," Ms. Rodriguez said, brows knitted together. She dropped her ripping faux leather purse and hurried over to me. Before I knew what was happening, she wrapped her arms around me and pulled me into a hug. "I can't believe they're trying to pin Skylar's murder on you."

Gently, I patted her back in an attempt to not seem like a dick. I didn't know what to do.

Vera had hugged me many times before, but a parental figure? Nearly fucking never.

In all my life, Mom had only ever hugged me during photo shoots with her arm lightly draped around my shoulders and her grasp weak. When I was a boy, I'd thought she was just being gentle, but somehow, Ms. Rodriguez's hug was gentle, strong, and inviting.

I almost didn't ... I almost couldn't ... fathom how a mom could care for someone who wasn't their own child so much. Mom had fucking pushed me out of her vagina and still didn't give a shit about me.

"How are your parents taking it?" she asked.

Vera scowled from the kitchen doorway and turned away, muttering something under her breath. And I didn't blame her either. Mom had gone way fucking out of line this morning by screaming and yelling at Vera for no good reason at all. The least she could've done was not mention Dad and Vera's mother being together—if that even had any truth to it.

I hoped it didn't. I highly doubted it did.

"They're doing what they can to keep their names out of the news." I sighed and sat back on the couch, picking up the controller and staring emptily at the TV. Mateo was watching me now too. "Anything to keep us as Redwood's perfect family." I ground my teeth together, anger rushing through me. "It's fucking bullshit." As soon as the words left my mouth, I snapped my lips shut and widened my eyes, realizing I had sworn in front of them and Ana.

"Yeah, it is bullshit," Vera added, crossing her arms.

"Sorry, Ms. Rodriguez," I started. "I didn't mean to—"

"It's okay, sweetheart." She tapped my knee. "We get it."

"I'm going to get a hotel tonight. I can't stand them."

"Why don't you stay with us?" Ms. Rodriguez offered, looking around at Vera and Mateo. "We don't have much to offer but the couch. I'll make you breakfast tomorrow morning too. My shift doesn't start until eleven anyway."

My chest tightened as I stared at her blankly for a few moments. I didn't know if she was serious or not, if she'd take back everything she had just said because of what the public thought of me—that I was a murderer.

The more time that passed, the longer she waited without saying a word.

"You don't care about ... about what everyone thinks of me?" I asked, confused.

"Why would I care about that?" she asked. "You need a place to stay."

"B-but ..." I stuttered. I fucking stuttered.

She was ... she was serious.

They had barely known me for more than a month, and now, they wanted me to stay with them because I had nowhere else to go. My family would never do something like that. They would never even let it cross their minds.

I glanced from her to Vera, then back. "You serious?"

"As long as you're not sleeping in Vera's room, then—"

"Don't worry, Mom," Mateo started. "They're way past that poin—"

Vera stormed to Mateo and hit him hard on the back of his head. "Shut it."

Warmth shot throughout my tightening chest, heart hammering inside it. I never thought that I'd ever find people who'd do anything for me, who'd want to be around me, who didn't care what everyone else thought. I never thought that I'd find a family like this.

"You can stay with us," Ms. Rodriguez said, standing and walking into the hallway. "I'll get you some pillows and a blanket. I'm not taking no for an answer. You're not staying out on the streets or getting a hotel. Not when you have people who'll take you in."

And in that moment, I finally felt like I belonged, like I had people who cared about me for me. Not for my family's money. Not for my family's power. Not because they had to act like they cared. Vera and her family actually truly cared for me.

Chapter Sixty-Six

VERA

At seven a.m., I padded out into the living room in my school clothes and leaned against the kitchen counter, watching Blaise still sleep. Mom slaved away at the breakfast she'd promised him, the bacon sizzling on the skillet.

Blaise lay on the couch on his stomach, his eyes closed softly and his lips parted. When Mom laid out the food on a couple paper plates, I gently shook Blaise awake. He woke up with huge, confused brown eyes and messy bedhead.

"Morning," he mumbled.

"We have to eat quickly," I said. "School starts in thirty minutes."

He sat up and ran a hand through his hair to straighten it out, gazing toward the kitchen counter, where a plate of food sat for him. His lips curled into a smile, and he stood, grabbed the plate, then took a seat. "Thanks, Ms. Rodriguez."

"You're welcome, sweetheart," Mom said, disappearing into the hallway. "Now to get that boy up for school."

Blaise stuffed a piece of bacon in his mouth and moaned lowly in delight—but that sound did something to my dirty mind. "Your family loves you, Vera," he said, softening his voice and leaning closer to me. "My mom has never made me breakfast."

All this time, I'd thought Blaise had the life I wanted. But I hadn't realized until last night how much he wanted to have mine—with parents who cared about him, a brother who wanted to play video games with him all the time, and people who loved him, no matter what.

* * *

"Are you sure you're cool with this?" Blaise asked me ten minutes later, pulling into the Redwood Academy student parking lot in his sports car that garnered attention from all the people in the slums and even some of the rich students who came here. "I can drop you off around the corner."

"It's ..." I stared at all the students looking at us now. "It's fine."

Truthfully, I had already announced to the entire school that we were kinda, sorta seeing each other. And it was cold as hell outside. I didn't want to walk those extra few feet toward the building alone.

"Last chance," Blaise said, driving into his designated parking spot.

"It's fine," I repeated more to myself than to him.

When we stepped out of the car, the entire student body looked over at us. And it wasn't those interested, drama-filled stares, but ones with malice behind them. Some people snickered at us; others tried to hold back their laughter.

"Do they really think we're funny?" I asked myself.

Of course they did. Blaise Harleen had brought the nerd to school in his sports car. Never in a million years had they thought they'd ever see something like that, someone like *me* emerging from his passenger seat.

I wrapped my arms around myself, made sure to keep a few feet away from Blaise—*because PDA? Yuck!*—and walked toward the building. The coldness seared my cheeks as my stomach twisted even more. Even the teachers were staring at me.

Not Blaise. Me.

"What's wrong?" Blaise asked, looking down at me.

"Do you not see everyone staring?!" I whisper-yelled back, hurrying a few feet ahead.

He glanced around and clenched his sharp jaw. "Don't worry about them."

"How could I not worry? You know how I am."

Anxiously, I ran my hand through my hair and played with the ends of it to keep myself busy. It seemed like everyone at Redwood Academy had completely forgotten the rumors about Blaise supposedly murdering one of our classmates, and now, they were into the latest drama about the bad boy and good girl.

Why didn't they have anything better to do?

Letting out a soft sigh, I glanced at the ground and desperately tried to ignore the stares. I'd rather they talk about us than blame Blaise for Skylar's death though.

We walked up the front steps, and Blaise opened the main door for me. I hurried into the building, desperate to get out of the cold.

As we walked by, people glanced up from their phones and looked at me, snickering again. Jesus Christ, it was as if they had some dirt on *me* now. I hoped that they didn't think I had taken any part in Skylar's death.

Blaise had slept over last night and driven me to school, but it wasn't like we'd walked in together, hand in hand, swapping spit like some other couples did here. I didn't understand why everyone was staring at us.

Maddie and Piper stood by my locker, chatting tensely with each other, worried lines etched into their foreheads. I grasped my aching stomach, knowing that there was something off, and hurried toward them with Blaise hot on my heels.

"What's going on?" I asked Maddie.

She furrowed her brows and stared at me with worried eyes. "You haven't heard?"

"No," I whispered, glancing around at all the students staring at *not Blaise and me*, just me. My heart pounded as I raked through my mind, trying to figure out what I had done to make myself this much of an outcast today. "Do I want to know?"

"Show her," Piper said, frowning at Maddie. "There's no use in hiding it to protect her."

Maddie swallowed hard, pulled out her phone, and opened up Redwood Academy's social media app that shared information about news and happenings at the school, highlighted clubs that were in competitions, and spotlighted all things sports.

I took the phone from her. "Why are you showing me—"

My eyes widened, and I stepped back, hitting Blaise's hard chest. No, this couldn't be happening. This really couldn't be happening right now.

"What is it?" Blaise asked, looking over my shoulder and freezing too.

"My writing ..." I whispered, staring at the screenshots of my Google Drive blasted on the first page of the social app. Bile rose in my throat. "Someone found my writing and released it to all of Redwood Academy."

Chapter Sixty-Seven

BLAISE

When the phone began trembling in Vera's hand, I took it away from her and scrolled through Redwood's social media app. It was the entire story that she had been typing up from her notebook with the revisions that we'd made together back at my place.

Not only that, but the Google account it'd originated from was visible—*Vera Rodriguez.*

Vera took another step back against my chest and wrapped her arms around her body, shaking her head and mumbling, "What am I going to do? What am I going to do? I've tried so hard to keep this a secret."

"It's okay," Piper said, gently rubbing Vera's shoulder.

"Don't worry about it," Maddie reassured. "We'll take care of it."

"How are you guys going to take care of it?" Vera asked, tensing. "The entire school—even the teachers—has already seen it. They've been snickering at me all morning since I stepped out of Blaise's car."

"We'll get someone to take it down," Maddie said. "Hopefully."

"That won't do anything," Vera whispered, glancing up at me with fearful eyes. "Are you—"

"I didn't do it, Vera," I said. Even though I had blackmailed her with her stories, so much had happened between us since then. I hadn't even been serious about releasing them to everyone. "I fucking promise, I didn't do this."

"I know you didn't. I just ..." She glanced down at her feet and shrugged, a single tear falling down her cheek. "I don't even know what I was going to ask you. I don't know what I can do. I hate it here."

So did I.

"They're going to make fun of me," she whispered, resting her forehead against my chest. "I don't want them to make fun of me, Blaise. All I wanted was to be invisible this year. Redwood Academy is so cruel—so fucking cruel."

"They're not going to tease you, Vera," Maddie reassured.

But I knew Redwood better than anyone. I had seen it from the core, from the roots, from the rich parents who ran this town. Redwood feasted on drama, on forcing people to feel bad about themselves. They snorted that shit like a drug.

I couldn't stand seeing her look so helpless.

I didn't want kids to tease her. I didn't want Redwood to bully her.

Vera was my girl, and I would do anything to protect her.

"It's not Vera's," I declared, capturing everyone's attention, not sure if this would really fucking work, but I had to at least try. "It's mine. She's writing an amazing romance story in her free time, and she asked me to write a sex scene for her because she couldn't write it herself."

The murmurs slowly faded to complete quietness. I didn't know if they believed even a word of what I'd said, so I had to take it up another notch. I gritted my teeth and cursed myself for playing into Vera's good-girl persona for what I was about to say next.

"Come on. You guys think Vera could write something that fucking filthy?"

"*You* wrote that?" someone—who obviously wanted me to kick his ass—said through the silence. "I'd believe the good girl wrote that before *you*. You can barely pass English class without your parents' money."

I gritted my teeth and glared at this fucker.

"Blaise," Vera whispered, tugging on my shirt, "it's okay. Don't do this."

But I wasn't going to let these shitheads bully her. I didn't care what they thought of me.

"So fucking what if I can pass English or not? I wanted something to jerk off to," I said, rolling my eyes and picking up my skateboard, hoping that Vera would say something to convince everyone here. "The fuck do you guys care? Half of you think that I murdered one of our own classmates already anyway."

"Blaise," Vera whispered again, her voice even quieter.

"Isn't that right, Sunshine?" I asked. "You needed some help."

Vera softened her eyes, her entire persona suddenly shifting. Instead of standing tensely next to me, she parted her lips and stared up at me, eyes almost *smiling* at me. I watched her, waiting for her to confirm everything I had said to protect her.

"Isn't that right, Vera?" I asked again.

What is she doing? Why isn't she saying anything?

"Vera." Maddie nudged her.

"No." Vera grabbed my wrist and stepped forward. "Blaise didn't write that scene."

Quickly, I pulled my wrist out of her grasp and took her wrist in mine, yanking her back toward me. I clenched my jaw and lowered my voice. "What the fuck are you doing? Let me take the fall for you. It doesn't matter to me."

She pressed her lips together softly and shook her head, softening her voice so only we could hear her. "It's okay. I realize that ... it's not that big of a deal," she said, though I could tell by the tremble in her voice that it was.

"Vera ..."

"I'm being serious. It's ... it's fine."

"But—"

"I know how I reacted," she said, gulping and glancing around at the now-whispering students. "But you've ... helped me grow more than I could've ever imagined. A couple months ago, I would've died if anyone had found out about me writing romance. Now, I ... don't feel as bad as I thought I would. I'm still nervous about it, but ..." She softened her lips even more and looked down at mine.

For a moment, I thought she'd stand on her toes and kiss me in front of the entire school. But her cheeks flushed red, and she quickly looked away from me and tugged her wrist out of my hold.

"It's my book," Vera declared to the student body. "I wrote it."

Chapter Sixty-Eight

VERA

"I'm nervous," I whispered to Blaise, holding his hand as we walked into school on Monday. "I know that I admitted to the story being mine, and I'm not as insecure about my writing anymore. But ... I don't want anyone to bully me for it."

I honestly didn't know what had come over me the other day. I'd thought it was so ... heroic that Blaise wanted to take the fall for me that it kinda, sorta inspired me to tell everyone the truth. It would have come out sooner or later anyway once I started publishing.

"Nobody will bully you. I promise."

"You don't know that." My stomach twisted as we stepped out of the student parking lot and toward the school. I glanced around at the other students laughing with each other, probably about me. "People are ruthless."

"I'll kick their ass if they do. I don't give a fuck if it's one of Skylar's friends or a teacher."

I cut my eyes up to him. "Wow, that makes me feel so much better," I said sarcastically.

"Anything for you, Sunshine." Blaise chuckled.

When we stepped up onto the sidewalk, Blaise glanced down between us and paused. I looked down too, wondering what he was staring at. There wasn't anything there, so I gazed back up at him.

"What's wrong?"

"I didn't think you wanted to ..." He glanced down again and squeezed my hand in his.

"Oh," I whispered, not even realizing that we were about to walk into Redwood Academy hand in hand, in front of all those judgmental students who had snickered behind my back the other day.

As if he knew and understood that I didn't like the whole PDA thing yet, Blaise tugged his hand out of mine. My chest tightened at the loss of warmth, at the sudden emptiness inside me. And when he started toward the building, the loneliness festered.

While I might not want Redwood's attention, Blaise was the only person who I trusted to get me through this town's wrath. He had done so much more for me than anyone I had ever known.

So, I jogged to catch up with him and wrapped my hand around his.

"It's okay," he said, as if he was about to pull his hand away. "I don't mind."

"No." I squeezed his hand tighter and glanced up at him. "Please, don't let go again."

After glancing back down at our hands, he smiled. Yes, smiled—and not one of those infamous smirks either. He squeezed my hand tighter and turned toward the building, tugging me toward it.

Blaise Harleen, Redwood's bad boy, didn't hold anyone's hand in public.

Except mine now.

Butterflies erupted through my stomach, the nervousness of today disappearing almost completely. For the first time ever, especially after how he'd stood up for me the other day, I didn't mind the PDA.

When we stepped into Redwood Academy, there were even more whispers than the other day. People were staring at flyers on their lockers and laughing with each other. And I could only fucking imagine what the pictures were of.

Maybe Blaise and me? More of my writing?

I hurried over to a group of lockers, shoving my way through the crowd to stare in horror at pictures of two stepsiblings from Redwood—Jace Harbor and Allie Hall—standing at CVS's pharmacy, picking out Plan B with the words *whore, incest,* and *slut* written out everywhere.

Fuck.

What is it with people at this school?!

It was worse here than all those cheesy romance books.

Suddenly, the door Blaise and I had come through flew open. Allie Hall raced through the halls, plucking the flyers off the lockers as quickly as she could, her cheeks flushed as people stared and whispered in her direction until she reached her locker.

People were crowded around it, staring at something. She pushed her way through the crowd and collapsed suddenly. I swallowed hard, finding Maddie among the crowd, and grabbed her hand.

"What's going on?" she asked Blaise and me.

"I don't know."

When we reached Allie's locker too, I dropped both of their hands and clutched my stomach. There were pictures of Jace and Allie in the locker room, of him eating her out, of him fucking her, of his fingers in her mouth.

God, I wanted to puke. *What is wrong with people?!*

"Oh my God," Allie whispered, body heaving on Redwood's dirty hallway floor.

My chest tightened for her. I could only imagine how she was feeling—probably a thousand times worse than I had on Friday. Tears welled up in my eyes, and I snatched a couple of flyers off the lockers beside us, so nobody would see them.

Imani, Allie's best friend, shoved her way through the crowd and ripped the flyers off Allie's locker. "I'm sorry, Allie. I didn't see these ones. I would've taken them down. I'm so sorry." She continued to rip them all off until there weren't any more naked pictures of Allie in Redwood's locker room.

"You think this is fucking funny?" Jace shouted through the halls.

The chatting stopped. Students shuffled to the sides of the hallways and stared wide-eyed at Jace, who looked like he was on the verge of losing control.

Imani wrapped her arms around Allie's body and pulled Allie into her lap, stroking her hair. "I'm going to take you home," she whispered to Allie and wiped tears from Allie's cheeks. "Don't cry. People are mean, Allie. People are so mean. I'm so sorry."

"People are more than mean," I whispered to Maddie, grabbing her arm again. "They're fucking cruel."

"Who the fuck did this?" Jace shouted.

When nobody answered, Jace stormed through the halls toward Allie and Imani. "Allie is my stepsister. We're not related by blood, and all of you fucking know that already." Jace grabbed her hand and tugged her to her feet. "You can continue to talk shit about us, but I love Allie, and nothing you do is going to change my mind about it. Grow the fuck up and stop being childish about a relationship you know nothing about."

Everyone stayed quiet and glanced between them, then started whispering again.

"If you want to call Allie a fucking whore or slut or mention anything about incest, say it to my fucking face," Jace said, glaring from person to person. "Because you have to deal with *me* now. Nobody insults Allie ever fucking again."

The bell rang through the halls, yet nobody moved.

"Do you understand me?"

Nobody said a word.

"Do you. Fucking. Understand me?"

A flurry of yeses echoed through the hallway, and then everyone scurried to their classes. Jace wrapped an arm around Allie's waist and pushed the tears off her cheeks.

"Allie, I'm so sorry. If I had known someone was fucking watching us, I would've never done that. Fuck school. Let's go home."

"I can't miss another day," Allie whispered.

Imani scoffed. "If I can miss a day, you can too." She grabbed her hand. "Come on."

"Jace Harbor." Principal Vaughn stepped out of his office with arms crossed over his chest and hairy gray brows furrowed in a furious stare, as if this was their fault. "My office. Now."

Once they disappeared into the principal's office, Blaise seized my waist. "I'm glad that wasn't you. I would've fucking lost it and actually killed someone. Jace has some fucking self-control."

My lips trembled as I thought about how terrible Allie must be feeling right now.

"Guess you don't have to worry about people talking about your smut," Maddie said, leaning closer to me. "By the way, I totally read it last night, and, *whew*, girl, I had to fan myself *down there* more than once."

I smacked her hard on the arm. "Now is not the time for this. Is there something we can do for them?" I whispered to Maddie, tears welling up in my eyes *for* Allie and Jace. I barely knew them, but this was even crueler than what had happened to me on Friday. "Something? Anything?"

"Take down whatever flyers are left on the lockers," Maddie suggested. "That's all we can do right now."

Chapter Sixty-Nine

BLAISE

Vera hurried off after Maddie, like the good girl she was, tearing down pictures of Jace Harbor and Allie Hall that someone had posted all over Redwood Academy. Seemingly, she had forgotten all about what had happened the other day here.

My lips curled into a small smile as she disappeared into the crowd. I could still feel her hand in mine, the warmth that had exploded through my body after she grabbed my hand back and told me to never let go.

In the midst of students rushing around to get to class and chuckling at the naked pictures, Mr. Avery stood in the hall with his arms crossed, staring right at me. He must've wanted to talk about something. After nodding toward his classroom, he disappeared into the crowd too.

I followed behind him, sure to keep my distance. Last time, he'd told me that there were people at Redwood who were in the mob, watching and waiting and trying to pin this on me. Whatever information he was about to give me or whatever he wanted to say was supposed to be secret.

If anyone found out, they'd rat him out, and the mob would kill him.

While I didn't particularly like the guy, I didn't hate him as much as I hated my parents. He had looked out for me since I had just been some skateboarding punk who got in trouble to get my parents' attention. He had gotten me out of trouble almost as much as Dad's money had.

After waiting a couple minutes two doors down from his classroom, I walked toward it and looked around quickly to make sure nobody was watching, and then I slipped into the room and locked the door behind me.

"What do you have for me?"

He stood behind his desk and shuffled through some papers, as if he hadn't just beckoned me to come in and chat with him. "How's your father?" he asked me nonchalantly, scribbling something down on a blank sheet.

"Don't know. Don't give a fuck."

"He's home," Avery said, folding the paper and looking up. "You haven't seen him?"

"I left that shithole my parents call a home."

"How's he feeling about that?" Avery asked, sliding the paper across the desk. He wanted me to read it.

I stepped closer to him and glanced down at his messy handwriting. "Like I said, I don't care how that fucker feels. I hate them both."

The note read, *Don't say a word out loud. One of my students who works for the mob bugged the room, thinking I wouldn't notice.*

My eyes widened slightly, but I nodded and slipped the note back to him. While I didn't want any part of the Redwood mob drama, I was already knee fucking deep into this. They were trying to pin Skylar's murder on me.

Avery took the sheet, turned it over, and scribbled another

couple words down on it. "You should go see him. Your father doesn't stay in Redwood for a long time. Wasn't he supposed to be on vacation?"

"In Bali or Greece or some shit," I said, rolling my eyes. "I don't know."

When he slid the note back to me, I glanced down at it and gritted my teeth, wanting this to be over already.

I'm meeting with someone in The Family later this week to find information on who killed Skylar.

After snatching a pen out of my backpack, I took the sheet and wrote, *And to get me out of trouble*, on it because I didn't give a fuck who had killed her. I didn't want my name attached to it at all.

I didn't care about my reputation at Redwood, but if someone on my YouTube channel found out, my brand would be ruined. What would be worse, someone might target Vera and her family next, like some sort of payback.

Instead of writing a response, Avery nodded, which meant he had nothing else to tell me and wanted me out of here. I slung my backpack over my shoulder and walked out of his classroom without another word.

As I walked to my first period, I pulled some flyers off the lockers and crumpled them in my fist, still trying to figure out how the hell someone had gotten into her Google account to find Vera's story the other day. I hadn't been able to stop thinking about it all night; I had twisted and turned on the couch.

If someone had hacked either of us—because she had been writing on my computer—then why hadn't we gotten locked out of our accounts? Our computers? I had no failed password attempts or any recent text messages, asking me for double verification. Vera hadn't mentioned that anything seemed off about her laptop lately or her emails and online accounts.

I tossed the crumpled paper into the trash and rounded the corner toward my classroom.

A smart hacker would've changed our passwords or stolen a

bunch of my father's money, not screenshotted Vera's smutty romance novel that she had written at my house and blasted it all over Redwood Academy. What would that gain them?

From afar, I caught sight of Poison sauntering out of the principal's office and down the hallway. I eyed João for a moment, wondering if he could've asked Kai—the tech guy in their gang—to do something like this.

But ... I thought against it. João wouldn't do something like that to Vera because if Vera found out, then she wouldn't watch his sister, which, apparently, he needed her for. Don't ask me fucking why.

I shook my head. It couldn't be him.

This blackmail had been taken straight from Google Drive, which meant that it could've been taken from a computer or phone that we were already logged in to. We both always had our laptops and phones with us.

The only computer left was ... the desktop in my bedroom.

Chapter Seventy

VERA

After I finished up work at the library that afternoon, Blaise grabbed some pizza for dinner and brought me to the skatepark with him. Unlike last time I had come here, there wasn't anyone, except a few stragglers. But even they were packing up their gear and heading back to their cars.

I grabbed all my protective wear from Blaise's trunk and a board, then followed him to a bench. This whole skateboarding thing was growing on me, and I really wanted to learn *for him* because this man had almost taken the fall for me for writing smut.

Blaise had tried to convince everyone that it was *his*, so I wouldn't get bullied.

It might've been a few days since then, but I still couldn't get it out of my head. Never in a million years had I thought anyone would ever do something like that for me. Especially Blaise! It made me feel a type of way.

And after what had happened with Allie and Jace today, I was so thankful that I had someone like Blaise by my side. If anyone had blasted my writing all over Redwood before I started talking to Blaise, I would've actually died.

Like literally.

Once I pulled on my kneepads, elbow pads, shin pads, and helmet, I grabbed the skateboard and tugged Blaise toward a larger ramp than the beginner's that we'd practiced on last time.

When I hopped onto the board, Blaise seized my hips to keep me steady.

"Let go!" I shouted to him, wanting to do this on my own.

"Are you sure? This is a big—"

"Let go."

When his hand left my waist, I glided down the small slope and actually kept my balance; the board picking up speed. My eyes widened as I realized the board was quickly approaching the large bowl. And I couldn't decide whether to stop or keep going in time before the board turned almost ninety degrees downward and threw me off it.

I landed on my stomach with a thud in the middle of the bowl. The kneepads skidded against the concrete, easing the pain that would've shot through my body otherwise. I turned onto my back, heart pounding.

Blaise quickly jumped down into the bowl and knelt by my side. "Are you oka—"

A small giggle escaped my lips, my stomach bubbling with laughter. I clutched my belly to desperately try to stop myself from laughing in a serious situation like this, grinned up at Blaise, and said, "God, that was a rush."

I'd needed that after this week.

He didn't find any of it amusing at first as he scanned my body for any scrapes, cuts, or blood. When he didn't find anything, he pulled me to a seated position and cracked a smirk. "A rush, huh? You scared me to fucking death."

"What'd you think, that I'd died?" I asked, laughter dying down.

He chuckled like a doofus with a huge grin and leaned back on his hands. "No, I just ..." His laughter died down slowly, and he stared at me deeper than he ever had before, almost enough to make me insecure, like he was looking at every bit of me—the good and the bad.

"What?" I asked.

He tore his gaze away from me and shook his head. "Nothing. It's nothing."

I waited for him to continue, but he didn't say anything, so I stood. "I want to try it again."

"*You* want to try boarding into the bowl *again*?" Blaise asked.

I hopped up from the ground, grabbed the skateboard, and made it to the top. After setting the board at the edge of the slope, I gestured for Blaise to get out of the center before I slid into him.

He followed me up and stood by my side, hands on hips. "You sure?"

"It's a rush," I said, fixing my kneepads.

When he didn't respond right away, I glanced over my shoulder to see him trying to hide a grin. With amusement written across his face, he nodded to the bowl. "Go ahead then, Sunshine. Let me watch how much of a rush it is for you."

After swallowing hard, I stared down at the ninety-degree angle that I was about to glide down. When I had been on the skateboard and already moving, it hadn't seemed *this* bad. But maybe that was because I hadn't had much time to react.

My heart pounded against my rib cage, breath hitching. Before I could stop myself, I kicked the board up to catch it in my hands, shoved it into his arms, and hurried over to the pizza box sitting on the bench a few feet away.

"Just kidding," I said. "I'm hungry."

He smirked at me with amusement as I snatched the pizza and walked the long way down into the bowl—where I didn't have to drop at a ninety-degree freaking angle.

He slid down it and met me in the middle. "You sure you weren't just scared?"

"Me?" I asked, sitting down and grabbing a slice. I lay down and stared up at the dark sky. "Scared of falling through the air? Psh. No."

Blaise hummed, his smile ... making me feel things. It wasn't like I hadn't felt this way before now. It was just ... I couldn't explain it in words. My stomach was fluttering, my chest light.

"What happened to loving the rush?" he asked, lying down next to me.

"Did I say that?" I scratched my forehead, as if I didn't remember, scrunched my nose, and giggled. "I *really* don't remember saying that. Only psychopaths would love dropping, like, ten feet into concrete."

When he didn't respond for a long time, I glanced over at him to see him staring at me.

"God," he whispered, pushing strands of hair out of my face. While he had been smiling and laughing only a moment ago, his face was now relaxed, completely with no strain, only ... awe. He parted his lips and brushed the pad of his thumb across my cheek. "I fucking love you."

I sucked in a sharp breath. "Y-you what?" I whispered, taken aback.

Almost as if he hadn't realized he'd said it, Blaise widened his brown eyes. "I ... I didn't ..." he stuttered for a couple moments, stumbling aimlessly over his words until he finally pressed his lips together and stared at me even more seriously this time. "I love you, Vera."

Blaise Harleen loves me? Me?

"Are you ... serious?" I asked in a breathy whisper, placing the pizza down in the box.

After turning onto his side, he gazed into my eyes as he still stroked my cheek with his thumb. "I-I don't know what you've done to me, Sunshine, but I can't get enough of you. You've been the only person there for me, the only person who truly cares."

"Blaise, I ..."

"I know you want me to take it back and act like the same guy I was toward you that first day in World History, but I can't. I don't want to take it back. I fucking love you more than I've ever loved anyone. You're the best damn thing that's happened to me."

This wasn't a character saying this in one of my stories. This was real.

"You don't have to say it back right now." He took my hand in his and gently kissed my knuckles. "I promise I'll wait until whenever you're ready. I'm not going anywhere. So, if you want to run out of here, scared shitless, then you have another thing—"

My chest exploded with warmth. I turned onto my stomach, gently gripped his chin in my hand, and kissed him deeply, passion completely overtaking me. "I love you too."

Chapter Seventy-One

VERA

"I love you," I breathed out against his lips, gently tugging on the ends of his hair.

He took my face in his hands, moving his lips faster against mine and becoming filled with more and more needy passion by the second. I let my hands wander down his abdomen to his belt, needing him more than ever right now.

Never in a million freaking years had I thought someone would say those words to me. I had been alone for so long, throwing myself into love story after love story and wishing that I could find someone to love me as much as my characters loved each other.

Rain began to drizzle down from the sky around us, but neither of us seemed to care. Blaise flipped us over and knelt between my legs, dipping his head to deepen our kiss, then undid his pant button.

Placing wet kisses down my neck, he slipped his hands under my top and groped my breasts through my bra. Then, he trailed his lips lower down to my collarbone, his scruff tickling the skin bared to him.

"Fuck," he mumbled against me, biting down softly on my

shoulder. "You don't know how long I've been waiting for someone to say those words to me and actually mean it. You're all I fucking care about, Sunshine. All that I'll ever care about."

I threw my head back and spread my legs farther, giving him better access to rub his bulge against my covered pussy. "Please, give it to me," I begged, not caring that we were in a public space, that the park lights were blazing down upon us. I wrapped an arm around his neck and kissed him harder.

Thrusting a hand between us, I reached into his jeans and stroked him through his briefs. My pussy pulsed at how hard he was for me, at the thought of having him inside of me again. But this time ... this time, it would be different.

"These need to come off of you," Blaise said, seizing the waistband of my pants and pulling it down to my ankles. He repositioned himself between my legs, rubbed my bare pussy with two large fingers, and grunted. "God, V ..."

I moaned softly, tilted my head back, and fluttered my eyes closed. "Please ..." I whispered, stroking him faster.

The drizzle became heavier and heavier as thunder rumbled above us. Rain soaked through Blaise's jacket and shirt, making it cling to his muscular body. I tightened at the sight, running my fingers along his strong, flexed arms.

After pushing down his briefs, Blaise positioned himself at my entrance, rested his elbows on either side of my head, and kissed me softly as he slowly pushed himself into my desperate pussy. I dug my nails into his chest and shut my eyes, the pressure in my core rising with every inch.

"I love you," he murmured over and over and over. "I love you. I love you. I love you."

My pussy tightened around him the more he said it. I took his face in my hands once more and kissed him harder, slipping my tongue between his lips.

"I love you too," I whispered into his mouth between kisses.

He pumped in and out of me at first, taking his time with my body, unlike almost every other time he'd been inside me. Tongue in my mouth, hands in my hair, breath on my lips, Blaise grunted against me.

"More," I pleaded, lifting my hips to meet his. "Please."

At my plea, he wrapped his arms under mine, grasped on to my shoulders, and quickened his pace. My chest was flush against his. The rain poured down harder and harder now, drenching both of us.

Pressure rose higher inside my core. I clenched around him, squeezing him tighter by the second. Every thrust pushed me higher until I found myself holding my breath and digging my fingers into his back.

"Kiss me," I begged.

He rested his forehead against mine and pressed his lips to me. "Tell me that you love me again," he mumbled against my lips. "I want to hear you say it again and again and again, Sunshine."

"I love you," I whispered, tangling my fingers into his hair.

He thrust into me deeper.

"I love you."

Another deep thrust, nearly sending me over the edge.

"I love you so—"

One last thrust, and my body trembled uncontrollably. I opened my mouth to tell him again, but I couldn't moan out anything but his name. Over and over. I dug my fingers into his back, gripping his soaked shirt and crying out in pleasure.

Ecstasy surged through my body. My breathing became ragged.

After a few moments, Blaise pulled away and slowly took himself out of me. He pushed some wet hair off my forehead and smiled down at me, his hair dripping onto me. "I fucking love you, Vera Rodriguez. I always will."

Chapter Seventy-Two

VERA

Fresh out of the shower, Mom stood at her dresser with her hair wrapped in a towel and a plush robe that hadn't been replaced in years around her body. I wanted to get her a new one so badly. She needed it.

After our *make-out* session in the middle of the skatepark, Blaise had brought us home. I might feel like I was on top of the world, but worries still lingered in my mind. Not anything about Blaise and me. For once, I found myself comfortable and confident in our relationship.

I worried about Mom and what Blaise's mother had said about her.

"Yes?" she asked, not even looking over her shoulder to know I was there.

I swallowed hard, nerves nipping at my insides, and stepped into her bedroom that smelled like mango lotion. "Can I, um ... ask you something?"

After quickly placing down her lotion bottle on her dresser, she walked over to the door and shut it behind me. "Is this about birth control?" she whispered so the boys wouldn't hear us in the living room.

My eyes widened. "No."

God, I wished that it were. It'd be a whole lot easier to ask her about that.

She ushered me over to the bed and sat next to me. "You're being safe during sex with Blaise, right? Using condoms and everything?"

Cheeks flaming, I gently pushed her hand away from my shoulder and scrunched my nose. "Mom, please. I'd really prefer to not talk about this, especially while Blaise and Mateo are home. You know how Mateo likes to spread family gossip to just about everyone."

"I need to know that you're being safe, especially with Blaise now living here."

"Yes, Mom, we're being safe." I rubbed my sweaty palms together. "I'm on the pill."

This time, Mom's eyes widened. "Since when?"

"Since ..." *We started fucking so much that I was popping Plan B like it was gum.* "Since a couple weeks ago. Maddie brought me to her gynecologist. I didn't want to bother you because I know how busy you are."

And it was awkward as fuck.

"Sweetheart, if I had known you were seeing Blaise earlier, I would've brought you." She rubbed a hand over her forehead. "I should've brought you. I didn't know that you were dating. You never showed much interest in boys before Blaise."

"Yeah, well"—I scratched the back of my head—"that's sorta his fault."

Hell, he'd scared away Jim. I wouldn't doubt it if he had done that before with other guys.

"Anyway ..." I shook my head, trying to get off the topic of birth control. "That's not what I wanted to talk to you about." I played with the hem of my shirt and wished that we'd actually had privacy instead of Mateo and Blaise screaming at the video game in the other room. "This is more … serious."

"Oh God," Mom said dramatically. "Are you preg—"

"No! I told you that I'm on birth control."

Mom placed a hand over her heart and closed her eyes. "Good, but you know birth control isn't one hundred percent effective. There's always a chance that you can still get pregnant with it. And I'm not ready to be an *abuela*. I'm still raising you and Mateo."

"Don't worry," I said, mind wandering back to the night that I'd told Blaise I had started birth control.

He had begun talking about how he'd be a good father to our son and provide, and I'd bet he'd probably—

No.

I cannot think about that right now.

"Listen, Mom," I said to get us back on track. "I need to ask you about Blaise's parents."

"What about them?"

Again, I swallowed hard and averted my gaze to the ground. While I didn't want to bring this up at all, I couldn't get it out of my head. *What if Mom really slept with Blaise's father while working for him? What if she didn't want to and was forced? But what if she had wanted it?*

It wasn't any of my business, but … Blaise's mother had planted a seed.

What if her husband had been gaslighting her for years, making her out to seem crazy when maybe it really did happen? I didn't trust her, but that didn't mean I trusted Blaise's father either. They were both fucked up, proven by the way they treated their son.

"His mom said something to me the other day," I whispered, tears building in my eyes.

She had done more than only *say something*; she had nearly ripped fistfuls of my hair out while screaming at me. But Mom didn't need to know that.

Mom furrowed her brows, eyes widening. "What did she say? What's wrong?"

Before I could stop myself, I moved closer to her, wrapped my arms around her torso, and rested my head on her shoulder. Whatever happened, happened. It was in the past, but I wanted to know. Because if they'd had sex while I was a kid, then Mateo ...

I didn't want it to be true.

"What'd she say, Vera?" Mom said, gently rubbing my back. "You're scaring me."

"She said that ... you and Blaise's father ..."

I didn't have to say anything more for Mom to tense slightly. My stomach twisted and turned, bile rising in my throat.

I don't want it to be true. I don't want it to be true. I don't want it to be true.

"That we what?" Mom asked, as if she didn't know where I was going with this.

But I knew that she knew.

"That when you used to work for the Harleens, Blaise's father and you were ... *together.*"

"Vera!" Mom scolded harsher than she ever had and released her grip around me. Eyes wide with anger, hurt, and disappointment, she stared at me and shook her head. "Do you really think that I would do something like that to you, Mateo, and your father?"

I sat on her bed without her arms around me anymore and stared at the ground. Tears clouded my vision. She sounded so hurt that I would ask her such a thing, that I would think she'd do that to our family.

My chest tightened, and I grasped the blankets on her bed, pulling them to my chest. "I'm sorry," I whispered, trying to hold back a cry. I shouldn't have brought it up, but I couldn't have kept my mouth closed. "I just needed to know."

Before she could yell at me even more, I quickly stood up and hurried to the door. I didn't want her to see my tears because this was my fault. I'd turned a quiet night into one of stress and anger and sadness for her. She didn't get many nights off like this, and I'd ruined it for her.

"I'm sorry," I repeated again before slipping out the door. "I'm so sorry."

Chapter Seventy-Three

BLAISE

After Vera's talk with her mother—she hadn't told me what they'd chatted about, but I could tell that it hadn't gone well—Vera basically locked herself in her room and refused to let me in. Through the door, it sounded like she was sobbing into her pillow. So, I grabbed my board and headed outside to let her cool off.

I closed the door behind me and tossed the board onto the ground, vowing that I'd go buy myself some new headphones tomorrow. I hated riding without them. Everything was so quiet that I got lost in my loud thoughts.

Skating down the sidewalk, I spotted João sitting outside on his front step and taking a long pull from a cigarette.

"What're you out here so late for?" he called.

I flipped up the board and walked toward his house. "Could ask you the same thing."

"None of your fucking business, Harleen." He blew a puff of smoke from his nose and flicked the cigarette, some ash falling on the ground at his feet. "What's a pretty boy like you spending so much time in the slums for? Mommy and Daddy kick you out?"

Pressing my lips together, I leaned against the side of his house. "*None of your fucking business,* Rocha," I said, spitting his words back at him.

João gestured to Vera's house with his cigarette. "You living with Vera now?"

"Yeah, so keep your fucking hands off her."

"She's like a sister to me," he said, taking another long drag. "Plus, I got a girl."

"*You* got a girl?" I snorted. "Who is dumb enough to date you?"

"Why don't you ask your fucking mom? She'll tell you how good I give it."

"My mom wouldn't fuck you. You don't have any money."

João chuckled. "That's fucking depressing."

I shoved my hands into my pockets and laughed. "You're telling me."

An easy silence fell over us, and then João pulled out a pack of cigarettes from his pocket with a lighter for me.

I sat on the edge of his front step, one foot on my skateboard, sliding it back and forth. "Nah, I'm good."

"Suit yourself." He shoved them back into his jeans. "For real, you living in the slums?"

After leaning back on my hands and looking across the street at the blinds in Vera's room, I blew out a breath. "Yeah, I'm living with them now. My parents are annoying fucking pricks. And I don't want Vera around them."

Whistling, João shook his head. "Didn't pin you as the type of guy who'd actually leave the ritzy side of Redwood for some straight-A student who works at the library and doesn't have much of a social life."

"Didn't pin *you* as the guy who actually cares about family," I said, referring to the way he cared for and about his younger sister. "Plus, Vera is more than that. I've known her since we were kids."

"I know."

"How did you know that?"

"Kinda fucking figured." He took another puff on his cigarette. "You've literally forced Vera into having no social life, threatening any guy who has even shown interest in her since, like, middle school."

"Was it that fucking obvious?"

João chuckled and stood, opening the screen door to his house. "Listen ... if you hurt Vera, Poison will hurt you. And we don't play, especially not with former rich kids from Redwood. We think they all deserve to burn."

Chapter Seventy-Four

VERA

The next day after a relatively *quiet* day at school, I stepped out of Blaise's car and gazed at the house. I still couldn't stop thinking about how I'd ruined Mom's night because I had to ask her about the Harleens.

It was so stupid of me.

"Hey!" João called from across the street.

Blaise and I both looked over at him. João sank his hands into his pockets and glanced over at Blaise briefly. To my surprise, neither of them had said a hateful word to each other today. They were actually being ... civil, which was slightly off-putting.

"I need you to watch Ana tomorrow," João said.

"I have work until six at night, but I can watch her after that."

"Good. I'll drop her off at six."

"But I get off at six—"

Before I could utter another word, João shut his car door and walked to his house, where Ana stood at the door with a huge bowl of what was probably brigadeiro mix.

She dipped her finger into it and stuck it into her mouth. "Hi, Vera!"

"Are you having brigadeiros again, Miss Ana?" I asked playfully.

She smiled widely. "Yeah! Do you wanna make them with me tomorrow?"

"I'd love to!"

She erupted into a fit of giggles before João picked her up and brought her back into the house. She waved at me with her chocolate-covered hand as the door closed behind them, leaving me alone with Blaise.

When I turned back around to him, he was smiling softly at me. The last time Blaise had given me that look, we had been lying down in the middle of the skatepark with his fingers wrapped in my hair, and he had admitted to loving me.

My stomach fluttered at the memory. "What?" I asked. "What is it?"

He shook his head, looked away, and tried to wipe the grin off his face. "Nothing."

"Come on," I teased, playfully tapping his shoulder. "Tell me."

"It's nothing, Vera."

"Blaise ..."

"You're just good with kids."

I stared at him with wide eyes. "What?"

"You're good with kids," Blaise said. "And I was thinking about how you'd be with ..."

"With what?" I whispered, though I already knew what he was about to say. The memory of him joking around a few weeks ago at his place fluttered through my head again, my stomach becoming light.

Before, it might've been a joke. But now ...

"I'm not even going to finish it," he joked. "I don't want you freaking out on me again."

"No," I said, heart pounding in anticipation. "Say it."

While I wanted to be completely focused on him, I spotted Mom walking down the street toward the house from a bus stop. She stared at the ground and shook her head, her curly black hair covering her face.

I grabbed Blaise's hand to stop him and furrowed my brows. "What is she doing home?"

She was supposed to be working a double today.

"Mom?"

Snapping her head up, she stared at me through teary eyes. My eyes widened, and I hurried over to her, wrapping my arms around her shoulders. Worry erupted through my insides, the worst of the worst thoughts running through my head.

"What's going on?"

"I need to talk to you." She sniffled. "Please tell me that your brother isn't home."

"He's out with friends. What's wrong?"

After apologizing to Blaise for being a mess, she took my hand and pulled me into the house. Blaise lingered outside, riding his skateboard up and down the streets of the slums and out of our way for now.

"Mom, you're scaring me. What is it?"

She collapsed onto the couch and threw her head into her hands. "I'm sorry," she sobbed, voice cracking. "I'm so sorry, sweetheart. I lied to you, and I ... I haven't been able to stop thinking about it. But when you brought it up yesterday ..."

"Brought what up? What are you talking—"

Oh shit.

"About Blaise's father," she said between hiccups. "They sent me home because I couldn't hold it together at work. I had never meant anything to happen between us. I never flirted with him. I never made any advances on him. I barely even looked at him. But one day ..."

My breath caught in the back of my throat.

I sat down on the couch next to her and pulled her into my arms, gently rubbing her back. "Mom, you don't have to tell me. I was out of line for asking about it."

"I haven't told anyone," she cried. "Not even your father while he was alive."

"It's okay," I whispered, rocking her back and forth. "I'm sorry."

"All these years, I've pretended that it never happened. All these years, I've been lying to myself and to you both. I tried to be the perfect mother and wife while living with ... with the memory of ... of h-him."

Chest tightening, I pushed back my tears and held her tighter. "I'm so sorry."

Suddenly, she sat up, wiped her tears with the backs of her hands, and grabbed my forearms. "You can't tell anyone about this. Not Blaise. Not Mateo. Not anyone. It's dangerous to speak about and even more dangerous that Blaise is living with us. But I'm not going to let that sweet boy stay out on the streets or live in a hotel when we have a home for him."

"I won't say anything to him."

"Or Mateo," Mom said.

"Mateo ..." I trailed off.

If Blaise's father had taken advantage of Mom, right around the time that his mom fired her, then that would mean he could potentially be ...

"Is he ..."

"Would it make you love him any less if he was?" Mom asked, as if she knew what I was about to say, that I'd ask if Mateo was my half-brother.

"No, of course not. I would still love him the same," I admitted.

"Well then"—Mom wiped the last few tears from her cheeks—"that's that."

Chapter Seventy-Five

BLAISE

Saturday afternoon, I parked in the skatepark and pulled my board out of the back. Vera was at work today for another hour, so I had some time to myself here. Not that I didn't wish she were with me.

But I'd had so much on my mind lately, especially with Skylar's murder and Callan supposedly having a meeting to find out who had really killed her and what had happened. Not only that, but I still couldn't get the thought of Vera actually loving *me* out of my head.

After blasting music through my new headphones that I'd bought, I dropped my skateboard on the side of the skatepark's ramp and hopped onto it. All night and all day, I had thought about the way Vera had looked with Ana.

My own family was so fucked that, when Vera and I were ready, I wanted to be the best fucking father to our kids. I would love to start a family with Vera because she'd be so much of a better mother than my mom was.

"Harleen!" someone shouted a while later, so loud that I could hear it over my music.

I glanced up from my board and spotted Avery standing on the side of the park with his arms crossed over his chest and a pissed off expression on his face.

I kicked up the board and walked over to him. "Last time I saw Callan Avery at the skatepark, he was threatening a kid with a gun."

"Where's your girl?"

"Vera?" I asked. "Why do you want to know about her?"

Avery snatched my arm and dragged me to the parking lot. "I'm not here to play games and talk shit to you, Blaise. This is fucking serious. I talked to someone who had more insight on Skylar Walker's murder."

"What'd they say?"

"Get in the car," he said, shoving me into the passenger seat of his car. After slamming my door, he slipped into the driver's seat and locked the car, which meant that this was more fucking serious than he'd led it on to be. "Skylar was fucking your father."

My eyes bugged out of my head. "What?!"

"Don't fucking scream," Callan scolded, glancing around the park.

"You can't drop a fucking bomb on me like that and expect me to whisper-yell it to you," I said more quietly, though I couldn't believe this. "Dad is barely ever in Redwood, never home. How the hell was she fucking him?"

"He was never in Redwood to see you," Avery said. "Apparently, he met up with her a few times these past couple months before her death. They'd been seeing each other in secret for nearly a year, meeting at an upscale hotel."

I ran my hand through my hair. "What the fuck? So, are you saying my dad killed her?"

"That's not even close to everything," Callan continued, gripping the steering wheel. "There's a sex trafficking ring happening within the high school. Cheerleaders and many of the popular senior girls have been roped into it for a few years now. I've been trying to stop it, but—"

"What the fuck?!"

"Blaise, listen—"

I stared at him in shock with my mouth wide the fuck open, unable to believe another word that he said. This was all going on within our school, and nobody had said a word about it? How the hell had they all kept it a secret?

"Was Skylar in it? How didn't Principal Vaughn find out?"

Avery's grip on the steering wheel tightened. "Oh, he fucking knows."

No. Fuck no.

"He's taking part in it, isn't he?" I gritted my teeth and glared through the windshield. "I can't fucking believe this. I should've known because he's such a fucking pervert but ..." I ran my hand through my hair again. "Fuck. Skylar was really in the ring?"

"That's how she met your father, I believe."

Bile rose in my throat. "Bro, I'm about to fucking puke. The fuck is wrong with him?"

Avery rubbed the lines on his forehead. "As soon as I found out that the mob was involved, I tried to stop it because I knew something like this was bound to happen to one of my students."

"Can't we go to the police?"

"No."

I shook my head. "I know you can't because of your relations to the mob, but I can."

"You don't get it," Avery said. "The police chief is in on it too. This town has gone to shit."

So many emotions ran through my body—anger, confusion, hurt. I fucking hated Redwood with a passion and wanted to see it burn, just like the fucking rest of the students here, like João and Poison. How could people be so fucking terrible?

"What can we do?" I asked. "This isn't fair."

"It gets worse, Blaise," Callan Avery said, staring through the windshield emptily. He clenched his sharp jaw and shook his head, veins pressing against the backs of his hands from his harsh grip. "Where's Vera?"

"She's at work," I said, shaking my head and wondering why he was asking about her, especially after he told me all this. Couldn't he give me, like, five fucking minutes to process this all? "How can this get any worse?"

"Because your mother found out that your father was cheating again."

Fuck.

Avery let out a low breath. "And she hired the mob to kill Skylar."

"That fucking bitch has known the truth this entire fucking time?!"

"Your mother tried to hire the mob to kill Vera's mother years ago too, when she found your father and her mother together in their bed. But the boss refused because Vera's father did work for them every now and then."

So, it was true. Vera's mother and my father really had been together.

My brows furrowed. If they didn't kill Vera's mother because her husband was in the mob, then why would the mob kill Skylar, who was in the sex trafficking ring that the mob basically fucking conducted?

"It doesn't make sense," I whispered to myself.

"Where does Vera work?" Avery asked, turning on the car.

"Why do you keep asking about her, like you haven't been telling me all of Redwood's secrets? This doesn't make any sense. Why would the mob kill Skylar if they needed her to be part of their trafficking—"

"Because your mother promised them that Vera would take Skylar's place."

Chapter Seventy-Six

VERA

"Why don't you put away those last few books from the cart, and then you can head home for the night?" Sue offered, glancing around at the library, which had been much quieter than usual tonight. "I can close up."

I placed a couple more returned books on the cart. "Are you sure, Sue? I can—"

"Go home once you're finished, sweetheart. It's quiet tonight, and I'm sure you have much better things to do on a Saturday night than I do." She laughed softly to herself. "I remember when my sister and I were your age."

"I bet you both were rebels," I said, smiling back at her.

Sue blushed. "Oh, stop it."

"What'd you do?" I leaned against the cart. "Flirt with the boys?"

"Flirt with them? Oh, sweetheart, we were wilder than that. My father caught us both in the back of the quarterback's car and dragged us back to our house by the hair. Oh, the times. I remember it like it was yesterday."

A giggle escaped my throat. "Sue! In the back of the quarter-back's car—together?!"

"He was a hunk." She giggled. And if an old lady giggling wasn't the cutest fucking thing in the world, I didn't know what was. "Ahh, anyway, enough about me. More than once, I've seen you hanging out with that bad boy who comes around here."

Now, my cheeks flushed. "Yeah, we're kinda ... a thing."

Kinda a thing?! If Blaise had heard me say that, he'd have been pissed. We were definitely more than a thing. Hell, we had even said those three magical little words to each other that every girl ever dreamed of.

"Have you gotten caught in the back of his car yet?" Sue asked playfully.

"Surprisingly, no." I giggled, chest fluttering as I thought back to all those times that we should've definitely been caught in the middle of Redwood Academy. I was surprised that not even the cameras had seen us. We hadn't even ... hidden it at all.

After laughing again, Sue shook her head and waggled her finger at me. "Oh, I know it's more than that. Your smile is wider, and your eyes are brighter, more excited now than they've ever been."

My cheeks burned even hotter. "Maybe ..."

"Dear, I know—"

"Excuse me," someone said from the counter. Holding two books against his chest, Jim from CVS stood at the counter and stared at me. "Uh, I ... wanted to see if I could get these books scanned out and"—he looked down, then back up at me—"talk to you?"

Fuck.

Not that I didn't want to talk to the kid—scratch that. I definitely didn't want to talk to him—but I was at work and had a good-girl reputation to hold up with Sue. If I said something in front of her, her whole perception of me might change.

"I'm going to put some books away." I pushed the cart from

behind the counter and hurried through the library. "Sue can scan you out."

Hopefully, I could put many of these books away before he had the chance to walk through the library, find me, and begin chatting with me. I glanced behind me to see him chatting with Sue and thrust the books into their designated spots as quickly as I could.

I tucked some hair behind my ear and pushed the cart to the next aisle of books, searching through the romance books to put back a book with a hot, shirtless guy plastered across the cover.

Before I pushed it into the bookcase, I stared down at it for a few moments. When I published a book officially, I would have so much to think about. Who I wanted on the cover. What kind of cover I wanted—sexy man's chest or a pretty object cover. Who'd edit it.

Literally everything.

"Hey, can we talk?" Jim asked.

After shoving the book into the bookcase, I grumbled to myself and took the next book from the cart. "I'm busy," I mumbled, hoping that he'd go away and never find me ever, ever again. I hadn't liked him from the moment he was basically staring me down in the Plan B aisle.

"It'll be quick," he said, leaning against the bookcase where I needed to put the last book back. When he realized, he shuffled back to a standing position and shoved his hands into his pockets. "Sorry. I just wanted to see if you wanted to"—he scratched the back of his head—"go out with me tonight to get Italian ice."

"I have a boy—"

"As friends," he clarified.

"No."

"Come on, Vera."

"No."

"You're really not even going to give me a chance? Blaise Harleen could never—"

"You don't know the first thing about Blaise Harleen," I

snapped, glaring up at him. "I'm not going out with you. Not only do I have a boyfriend who would kick your ass for talking to me, but I don't want to go out with you. I never did."

"What about in the library, when you told me to stay so we could ... *you know* ... during your break?"

I gripped the book harder in my hand until my knuckles turned white. "I was trying to make Blaise jealous, and it worked. I never wanted to hook up with you. I'm sorry for leading you on, but I'm not interested. Please, leave."

Once he stared at me for a couple silent moments, Jim nodded and walked out of the aisle toward the exit of the library. I stared at him until he walked out those doors and disappeared into the darkness, and then I shoved the last book onto the shelf.

After wheeling the cart back to the counter, I grabbed my coat and my backpack and waved goodbye to Sue, and then I headed toward the door to leave for the night. Blaise was supposed to pick me up in about an hour, but he was at the skatepark, so I didn't even bother texting him to tell him to come get me now.

He was doing his own thing, which he needed after this past week. I'd make it home before the hour ended.

Plus, my phone was dead.

I stepped out into the chilly night and walked down the front steps to the sidewalk, heading in the direction of the slums. Within three strides of the building, I caught Jim pacing back and forth and running a hand through his hair.

"I thought I said to leave," I said, capturing his attention.

Jim snapped his head to me, showing me his teeth, and suddenly lunged toward me. Before I could stop him, he seized both my arms and pulled me toward him. I pushed away from him, wondering what the fuck had gotten into him, but he snatched my wrist and hurled me toward the ground with so much force that I tripped forward, my head bounced off the concrete, and stars danced in my vision.

I tried opening my eyes, tried to figure out what was happening, but the darkness was quickly taking control of my body. And I felt so limp, so weak, like I couldn't move any single part of me.

The last thing I remembered was Jim picking me up and saying, "I can't leave without you."

Chapter Seventy-Seven

BLAISE

When Avery pulled up to the library, I leaped out of the car and ran into the building. Fuck the *no running, no shouting, no nothing* rules here. Vera was in danger, and I needed to get her to safety as quickly as possible.

An older woman checked out a mother with her son at the front desk. I scanned the library for Vera, not catching sight of her, and rushed up to the front desk, placing my hands on the counter, heart pounding.

"Vera ..." I looked behind the desk to see none of Vera's belongings. "Where is she?"

"One moment, dear," the old woman said, sliding the books back to the family. "Let me—"

"Where's Vera?" I asked again, not giving a fuck whose books she scanned. "She was supposed to be working until six tonight, for another forty-five fucking minutes. You need to tell me where she is right now."

After the woman smiled at the family and waved them off, she turned toward me. "You're the boy that she's been talking to me about, aren't you? I recognize your face. Vera was telling me how much she—"

I slammed my palms down on the counter. "Where. The fuck. Is. Vera?"

She widened her eyes and shook her head. "S-she's gone. I gave her the rest of the night off. She left only a few minutes ago out"— the old woman pointed at the door I'd just walked through—"that door."

"Fuck," I growled. "Fuck!"

"What's wrong?" she asked, brows furrowed. "What happened?"

But I didn't even have the strength to answer her. I needed to find Vera on her walk home. She had to be on the way back to her house, but why hadn't she called me to pick her up? Why hadn't she fucking messaged me?

I stormed out of the library, bumping into Avery on the way out.

He followed after me toward his now-parked car on the side of the road. "Where is she?"

"She's gone. She's fucking gone."

My chest tightened. All I could think was the worst of the fucking worst. My mom had found Vera. My mom had captured Vera. My mom had thrust Vera into a sex trafficking ring that I would never be able to get her out of.

And if by a miracle that I did, if someone had touched her ... Vera would never be the same.

"Fuck," Avery cursed, running a hand through his thick hair and storming to the driver's seat. He started the car and sped down the road, heading toward the slums. "Where would she have gone? Home?"

Unable to stop myself, I hurled my fist into his dashboard. "Fuck!"

"Where's her house, Blaise?" Avery said, keeping so fucking calm that I hated him.

"Fuck!" I growled. "She's fucking gone!"

Something deep inside me knew. I fucking knew that Vera hadn't made it home. She should've ... she should've fucking told me where she was going, that she needed me to pick her up. I would've come in a fucking second.

"Where's her house?" Avery asked again.

"The slums," I said, looking out the window at every house, every person, every shadow to see if it was her.

She wouldn't take the long way home, not in this cold weather. She would be on the sidewalk, out in the open.

"We'll find her."

"No, we fucking won't."

"She'll be at home."

"She wouldn't have made it home in a few fucking minutes. She's gone."

Vera was fucking gone because of that bitch who wanted me to call her *mother*. Vera was gone, and I would—my throat closed up—never see her again. I'd tried so hard for her to be mine, to keep her safe. Now, I'd lost her.

I'd fucking lost her.

I banged my fist against the dashboard again. "No. No. No. No. No. No. No."

"Settle down, Blaise," Avery said, pulling into the slums. "Tell me where to go."

"Two streets down. One-story house."

Avery followed my directions and pulled up to the side of the road in front of João's house. I leaped out of the car again and sprinted toward Vera's house. None of the lights were on, but I smashed the front door open and searched every last inch of that house for her.

"No," I cried, voice fucking trembling. "Fucking no. You can't be gone. You can't."

She was the only person that I fucking cared about, the only woman to ever care about me. If she was gone, if Avery was wrong and they killed her instead of using her like they had with Skylar, then ... my life would be for nothing.

Every moment we'd ever had together would be gone.

After I tore her bedroom to shreds, I placed two hands on the bed and collapsed onto it. My legs were too weak to hold myself up any longer. My chest tightened more by the second. The tears that had welled up in my eyes now streamed down my face.

"Vera," I cried, head hanging low, "p-please, fight them."

Memories of her smile, of the way she had hopped onto my skateboard and ridden with me at the park, of having pizza, of ice cream at the Overlook, of every fucking moment we'd spent together drifted through my mind.

"Blaise," Avery said from the door, "she's not here. We must—"

"No fucking shit!" I growled, pushing the tears from my cheeks so I wouldn't seem like a bitch to him.

I stood up, pushed past him, and marched across the street to João's house.

I pounded my fist against the door. "Open the fuck up, João!"

A moment later, Landon—the muscle of Poison—opened the door. Kai, João, and Ana sat in the small living room, looking over at me. I stormed into the house with Avery hot on my heels and glared at João.

"Tell me you know where she is."

"Where who is?"

Anger rushed through me. This wasn't his fucking fault, but I couldn't stop myself. I snatched his collar and lifted him off the couch. "Vera, you fucking asshole. Tell me you know where she is."

"Get your hands off me," João said, shoving me away. "She said she had to work until six. She's supposed to watch Ana in fifteen minutes. I don't know where the fuck she is. I'm not on her ass twenty-four/seven." João eyed my uncle. "And the fuck is Avery doing here?"

Avery stepped forward and placed a hand on my shoulder. "The mob took Vera."

João's face dropped. "No, they fucking didn't."

As I heard the words come out of his mouth ... they made me

weak again. So fucking weak that if it wasn't for Avery holding me up by the fucking shoulder, I would've collapsed onto the floor yet again.

"You need to help us find her," I pleaded, knowing that Avery could only do so much.

One wrong move by Avery, and the mob would have no problem killing him, especially if he tried to stop this. He might've done work for them, but ... they weren't as forgiving as they had been years ago when they refused to kill Vera's father. They had started a fucking sex trafficking ring, for fuck's sake.

Poison took one long look at each other, and then João finally turned back to me. "What do you need?"

Chapter Seventy-Eight

VERA

Cold.

I was so cold.

Blindfolded and bound, I sat on what felt like a concrete floor in the middle of a silent room. I couldn't remember anything after Jim had thrown me to the ground and kidnapped me at the library. But from the goose bumps rising on my skin, I knew that all of my clothes, except for my bra and underwear, had been ripped off me.

Tears streamed down my cheeks. I stared at the darkness through the blindfold, trying to make out anything in the room, but I couldn't. I wanted to scream, to cry, to beg for my life, but I didn't even know if anyone was around.

I scrambled around on the floor, crawling around like a madwoman to find a wall or a door or something. I couldn't just sit around and wait for terror to happen to me. I needed to find Blaise.

He'd help me.

"Blaise," I murmured, knowing that he wasn't here but his name kept me sane. "Blaise."

Continuing to crawl on my knees alone, I bumped into a concrete wall. I twirled around, pressed my back against it as hard as I could, and tried to use it to help me stand. With my feet bound, I drove my weight through my heels and pushed myself a couple inches into the air.

Then, I fell.

Flat on my ass.

I tried again, getting what felt like a foot in the air before I fell shoulder-first into the ground once more. My body smacked against the concrete with a thud, and I whimpered softly, biting back a sob.

At this rate, I'd never make it out of here.

What is Jim planning on doing with me? Holding me here forever? Raping me?

All I had done was told him no. Why couldn't boys take no for an answer? Why did they think they were entitled to everything we were, to our bodies and our minds and our time? It ... it wasn't fair. I wanted to go home.

"Please," I cried. "Let me go home!"

When nobody answered, I scrambled to the wall again and desperately attempted to stand three more times—failing every single fucking one of them. I lay on my stomach with my cheek pressed against the concrete and my salty tears rolling onto my lips.

"Let me out!" I screamed, kicking my bare foot against the wall. "Please!"

No answer.

"Jim!"

Silence.

"Blaise will kill you if you touch me!" I shouted at the top of my lungs, wanting to intimidate him. Jim had never been one to fight or even seemed like he had a hard-core, bone-breaking bone in his body. "He'll kill you, like he killed Skylar!"

Suddenly, someone giggled.

Yes, giggled.

I sat up and turned my head toward the noise. Someone was in here with me.

"Let me out!" I pleaded, crawling over toward the sound, only to bump into a bunch of metal bars. I knelt against them and desperately tried to see through the blindfold once more. "Please, let me out! Please, I'll do anything."

A man chuckled to my left this time. "You can scream all you want, just like Skylar did."

My chest tightened, my throat closing.

"No," I whispered, shaking my head and pathetically scrambling back to the wall again. "No, you can't do this! You can't kill me. I have a family. Please, I ... I want to see them again."

Memories of Mateo and Mom drifted through my head. All I wanted was to hold them one last time, to draw them closer to me and breathe in their scent, to hear them laugh, to watch Mateo scream at his video game with Mom.

Those moments were everything to me. Fucking everything.

And Blaise ...

Another whimper escaped my throat.

"Blaise ..."

If this was the end of my life, if they really did plan to kill me right here and right now, then I would never see him again. I wouldn't get to publish my book or ride a skateboard alongside him. He'd be left alone in this world that he thought didn't love him.

I leaned against the wall and cried. "I need to see Blaise. Please."

There was so much that I wanted to tell him, so much that he *needed* to hear. I didn't just love that boy. Blaise Harleen was everything to me. Blaise Harleen had given me confidence and happiness and so much fucking love that my insides exploded with warmth every time I was with him.

I love him, I mouthed to myself, wishing he could hear me. "I fucking love him."

Suddenly, a door opened, letting in a gust of wind. I listened for any sign of life outside these concrete walls, of any way that I could get out or cry for help. I couldn't die like this. I fucking couldn't.

Waves crashing against the shore drifted through the room. The familiar scent of the beach—Mom had taken Mateo and me when we were younger—wandered into my nose. I sat up and swallowed hard.

Did they plan on killing me and throwing me into the ocean, never to be found?

"Please, let me go," I begged again.

I didn't know how many people were here with me because it certainly wasn't only Jim. That giggle from earlier and that man's deep voice. Whoever had just walked into the room. There were easily at least three or four people here.

Maybe even more.

Even if I tried to fight, I wouldn't survive this.

"Let me go," I cried, making one final plea. "I'll do anything."

"Of course you will," a woman said, her voice familiar. "The mob owns you now."

"W-what?" I whispered, heart pounding inside me. "What do you mean? Th-the mob?"

Another giggle drifted through the room, the same one from earlier.

"You can thank your mother for this, Vera Rodriguez. If she had kept her scummy hands off my husband and if you'd stayed away from my son, you wouldn't be here."

Oh my God.

Blaise's ... mother.

She spit on me. "Fucking Redwood scum. I wish they had killed you, like I asked, but I won't mind watching every rich man in Redwood take advantage of a piece of trash like you."

Chapter Seventy-Nine

BLAISE

I paced around Kai's home—which was like an underground damn bunker—and waited for him to hack into the security cameras around the library. What must've been twenty monitors were set up in Kai's main room, displaying different information on Redwood.

Avery had left to find any information that he could while Kai searched for any information on his variety of computer monitors in his home. Landon occupied Ana on the small couch, reading her a book about Barbies and princesses or some shit. And João had both hands placed on the back of a spare seat, watching the news on a screen.

"Can you hurry the fuck up?" I growled, becoming impatient.

After pulling out my phone, I checked for any messages from Vera. If her phone was turned on, then they might've been able to track her, but all the messages that I'd sent to her number failed to deliver.

"He can only hack into the footage so fast," João said. "Settle down."

I ran a hand through my hair. "I fucking can't. It's been almost an hour."

While João knew that the mob had taken Vera, he didn't know why. He didn't know that they were going to thrust her into the sex trafficking ring that they ran. If someone touched her, everything would change. It would be all my fault.

Vera would never forgive me for having such horrible parents.

Even if she did, I wouldn't let her. I should've walked away from my parents before I even started to pursue Vera. I'd just never thought that Vera would ever feel the same way as I did. I'd thought she'd only spend a couple days with me and be over with it, over me.

More tears welled up in my eyes. I never fucking cried, but I wanted to so badly—*again*.

"I'm in," Kai said.

On the screens, footage from the cameras posted around the library popped up. He skipped to five-ten p.m. and played the recording from inside the library. Vera stood behind the counter, talking to the older lady, when a kid walked up to the counter.

"Fuck," I growled. "Fuck!"

"You know him?" João asked.

"That's Jim," I said between gritted teeth. "He's been trying to get into her pants for fucking weeks now. What the fuck is he doing at the library? I've told him to stay away from her."

The recording continued to play, and Vera walked away from him and into an aisle. He appeared at her side a couple moments later, leaning against the bookshelf and talking to her. They exchanged a few tense words.

"Can you get the audio?" João asked.

Kai paused the recording, typed something into the computer, then replayed their interaction with the audio.

"Sorry. I just wanted to see if you wanted to," Jim said, "go out with me tonight to get Italian ice."

"I have a boy—"

"As friends."

"No."

"Come on, Vera."

"No."

"You're really not even going to give me a chance? Blaise Harleen could never—"

"You don't know the first thing about Blaise Harleen," Vera snapped. "I'm not going out with you. Not only do I have a boyfriend who would kick your ass for talking to me, but I don't want to go out with you. I never did."

"What about in the library last week, when you told me to stay so we could ... *you know* ... during your break?"

"I was trying to make Blaise jealous, and it worked," Vera said, becoming pissed off. "I never wanted to hook up with you. I'm sorry for leading you on, but I'm not interested. Please, leave."

After that exchange, Jim left the building.

João leaned forward. "Follow him. I want to see where he goes."

Kai flipped through the recording and followed Jim out of the library. He dumped the books into the back of a black van that didn't have any license plates and paced around the front of the library, shaking his head and glaring at the sidewalk.

A moment later, Vera walked out with her backpack. "I thought I said to leave."

He jerked her to him. When she yanked herself away, he threw her onto the ground so forcefully that her head bounced against the concrete. It seemed as if she had gone unconscious immediately.

I punched a hole straight through the wall. "Fuck!" My chest tightened at the sight of Vera on the ground, unmoving. "I'm going to kill that motherfucker for ever laying a fucking hand on her. He doesn't get another fucking breath."

"Find out where they went," João said, jaw clenched.

Kai followed the black van through Redwood with the security footage. Jim drove through the back streets of Redwood, away from the cameras, and we almost lost it a couple times, but then the van reappeared near the beachfront. When he drove into the back of a restaurant, the van disappeared from footage for good.

"Landon, stay here with Ana. Don't let anyone inside," João said, heading to a back room.

Kai stood up and followed after him, and I did too. They had driven me here, and my car was still at the skatepark.

"We don't have time," I said. "We have to go now."

"Call Avery. Tell him where to meet us," João said, opening a door.

"We need to go—" I started but then stepped into the room filled with guns and ammo.

What the fuck is this? I know Poison runs Redwood too, but ... this?!

Kai pulled open a drawer, picked up a gun, and loaded it with bullets, thrusting it into the waistband of his black cargo pants. Then, he did the same with another one and handed it to me. I widened my eyes and stared down at it.

"What is this for?" I asked.

"To protect your girl."

Chapter Eighty

BLAISE

Callan: I checked the van as well as the building we thought Vera was in. Nobody is there. Even the cellar has been cleared out.

I stared down at my phone in the passenger seat and growled, unable to believe that they had moved Vera so quickly. We had done one final scan of the tapes beforehand and hadn't seen one car leave that alleyway.

Me: What the fuck do you mean? Where the hell did they take her?

Callan: Meet me at Redwood Town Beach. That's the closest place they could've gone.

Me: How would they get her there without anyone noticing?

Callan: Just meet me there.

"New plan," I said to João. "Redwood Town Beach."

When we pulled into the town beach parking lot, I spotted four cars parked at the base of a stilted building, where tourists hung around during the summer months. Avery sat in his car about ten parking spaces away from the others.

Callan: The mob has a place here, but I need to figure out how to get in.

Callan: Let me go in first. I'll unlock it. Wait five minutes, then come in.

Callan: Understand?

Callan: I can't be seen with you or else the mob will know that I've betrayed them.

I gritted my teeth and stared through the windshield in João's car, glaring at the wooden fence and sand dunes in front of us. I wanted to go in there now to rescue Vera; I didn't think I'd be able to wait much longer.

Instead of waiting for my response, Avery got out of his car and walked up the stairs of the building to the platform up top that I used to hang at last summer. He padded around the top for a few moments, scanning the area.

Hell, I didn't even know if he knew what the fuck he was doing.

Balling my hands into fists, I glared out the window. "We need to go now."

"No," João said, one hand gripping the steering wheel. "Not yet."

"We have to go," I growled, knowing that they had trapped Vera somewhere here.

We needed to get her back as soon as we possibly could. I didn't want any filthy man touching her body. I would never fucking forgive myself if they did.

I was supposed to fucking protect her.

My phone buzzed in my lap, jolting me out of my thoughts.

Callan: Jim's here.

Callan: Heading toward the parking lot.

Callan: I'm walking down to where he left now.

When I spotted that fucking punk walking toward a car, I stormed out of João's Mercedes and toward the row of cars. Before he had a chance to even fucking unlock one of them, I seized his collar and hurled him to the ground.

"What the fu—"

I dropped on top of him, straddled his waist, and slammed my fists into his head over and over and fucking over again. Like Vera's head had, Jim's head bounced against the asphalt like a fucking basketball.

Blood spurted out of his nose and ran down his cheeks. That desperate kid tried to shield his face from me, but I crawled up to him, set my knees on his elbows, and pinned that fucker to the ground.

"You fucking piece of shit!" I screamed at him, raining down fists.

"G-get o-off of—"

I slammed my knuckles into his mouth, knocking out two of his teeth. "You want to kidnap my girl and trade her in a fucking sex ring?!" I shouted, tears clouding my vision.

My hands moved so fast and hit so hard that I was sure that I had missed and hit the pavement a couple times.

My knuckles ached, but I didn't stop.

I couldn't.

Adrenaline rushed through my body. He needed to fucking pay for what he had done, how he'd treated Vera like she was garbage, thrusting her to the ground, knocking her out, and shoving her into the back of his van.

Jim stopped resisting underneath me, instead spitting up some blood. I put all my weight on his elbows with my knees until his arms turned purple. I grabbed a fistful of his hair and banged his head against the asphalt until his eyes rolled back into his head and someone pulled me off him.

"He's dead," João said. "Let up."

When I ripped myself away from João—because I wasn't finished with Jim—João grabbed me again and shoved me back.

"He's fucking dead, Blaise. Forget about him and let's go get your girl."

My girl.

Vera.

I snapped my head toward the main building, where Kai stood at the foot of the stairs at the platform.

"Avery went this way," he said, nodding. "Come on."

Chapter Eighty-One

VERA

"She's ugly and pudgy," Blaise's mother said, her voice shrill. "Not your typical cheerleader from Redwood that you're all used to. But I'm sure one of you horny fuckers would love to be inside her anyway."

I whimpered and pressed my back against the concrete wall in the corner of the cell, as if I could disappear right through it. Tears streamed down my face, and I hiccupped.

"Let me out. Please, let me out," I pleaded, like I had been for the past fifteen minutes.

"Who wants to start?" she continued, something that sounded like her fingers drumming against the metal bars. "You know that they're the best when they're getting broken into this life. She'll cry, scream, and beg for you to stop the entire time you're inside her."

"No!" I sobbed, furiously shaking my head. "No, please, don't! Please!"

Her heels clacked against the concrete floor as she walked away from the cell and laughed menacingly. "Oh, look at you," she said to someone. "Getting hard, thinking about her already? I know you like those screamers."

My shoulders jerked back and forth uncontrollably. I didn't want anyone to touch me, never mind be inside me. This wasn't fair. This wasn't fucking fair. I hadn't done anything wrong. I wanted to go home. I wanted to just go home.

"Why don't you tell everyone what she feels like?" Blaise's mom urged. "I'll let you fuck her for free, just this once."

"No!" I screamed, voice cracking. Tears covered my cheeks. "Please!"

Suddenly, the cell bars scraped against the concrete floor, the door opening. I scrambled back against the wall even farther to put space between me and whoever the fuck was about to touch me.

Footsteps padded against the ground. I squeezed my eyes shut, even with the blindfold over me, and furiously shook my head, sobbing loudly.

This couldn't be happening. This really couldn't be happening.

I wanted to go home.

I wanted to see Mateo and Mom and Blaise one last time.

I-I just didn't want—

A cold hand grasped my ankle. I pulled my knee to my chest, tearing it out of the man's grasp, then thrust it into his chest as hard as I could. If they were going to touch me, then I refused to go down without a fight.

The man chuckled darkly, as if this was exactly what he wanted, and seized my ankle again—this time harder. "Fight all you want," he said. "The more of a fight you put up, the better it's going to feel for me."

He yanked me closer to him until my back was flat against the concrete. I didn't want to give him the satisfaction of fighting, but I didn't want his grimy hands all over me. So, I kicked him as hard as I could over and over, my feet cutting through the air.

"Let me out!" I screamed. "Let me out!"

Silence from everyone. Even Blaise's bitch-ass mother.

"Please, don't do this! Please!"

Ignoring my pleas, he grabbed my knees, thrust them apart, and crawled between them. I sobbed with everything that I had, my cries getting lost in the deafening silence of this cell.

What had I done wrong? Why couldn't things have been different?

If I'd never started dating Blaise—

No, I couldn't even think that.

If I'd never started dating Blaise, I wouldn't be happy. I wouldn't be—

The door opened, the scent of the beach drifting through my nostrils again. Someone else was here, and the man between my legs suddenly stopped. Loud footsteps padded down the stairs and into the room.

"I'll pay to take her first," a man said, his voice familiar. "Get the fuck off her, Peter."

"Callan Avery ..." Another woman chuckled. "Ah, I didn't think you'd want a taste of her."

"You thought wrong," Mr. Avery—Blaise's uncle and a teacher at our school—said.

I scrambled back from the man between my legs and shoved myself back against the wall again, curling up into a ball. I was fucked. *Mr. ... Mr. Avery?! He wants to pay for me? Pay to be inside me, even when he is so close to Blaise?*

Another sob escaped my lips, and I found myself unable to move, unable to fight back any longer. All four of my limbs lay so heavily on the ground. I didn't want to move. I didn't want to fight anymore. I loathed Redwood so much.

"How much?" the woman asked.

"How much do you want?" Avery asked.

"You know what our price is for a student from Redwood."

After grumbling, Avery walked toward the cell. "Take it out of my cut for this month," Avery said, the cell bars sliding against the concrete again. "Peter, I already said to get the fuck out of here. Vera Rodriguez is mine."

People shuffled around the room, and then Avery seemed to move closer to me. He seized my upper arm and pulled me to a standing position, but my legs gave out, and I dropped to my knees, ripping the skin as it collided with the ground.

"Let me fuck her alone," Avery said, wrapping his hand around my throat and lifting me.

"Only for double the price," the woman sneered.

"Fine," Avery growled.

My body felt too heavy to move. I had no more motivation to fight, no more to live.

"Please, make it quick," I whispered as I listened to more shuffling around the room and up the stairs. A couple stray tears fell down my cheeks as I thought about how Blaise would be crushed about this. "Please."

When the main building door reopened, gunfire echoed through the room. I jerked in Avery's hold and ducked my head, forgoing all the thoughts about wanting to die. Fuck that. I didn't want my life to end like this.

I didn't—

Suddenly, my blindfold came undone. The bright light that hung in the cell above blinded me for a couple seconds. I tilted my head down even further to shield my eyes. And within a moment, my restraints came off too.

Once my eyes readjusted to the light, I peered up and spotted Blaise hurrying down the stairs toward me. Avery crouched down and unraveled the rope around my ankles. Blaise wrapped his arms around my shoulders and pulled me toward him, holding me tight.

"My fucking God, I thought … I thought we were too late."

I tucked my face into his chest and sobbed my heart out. "I wanna go home, Blaise. Please, I wanna go home. I'm cold and …" I shivered as goose bumps rose on my bare skin. "And I …" I didn't even want to tell him what had started to happen. "I—"

"It's okay," Blaise reassured, peeling off his jacket and pulling it around my shoulders. "You don't have to tell me. Not now anyway."

Grasping on to his shoulders, I held myself up. "J-Jim ... he—"

"Don't worry about Jim," Blaise said.

"But he kidnapped—"

"He's dead," Avery said, pulling a gun from his waistband and glancing at Blaise. "And we have one last person to take care of, if you haven't already. Your mother."

Chapter Eighty-Two

BLAISE

"Can you take Vera home?" I asked Callan after zipping up my jacket around Vera.

She huddled next to me, shoulders shaking still, and buried her face into my chest. "No. Don't leave," she whimpered, shaking her head. "Please, don't go. I don't want to be alone with anyone, except you."

I cupped her face. "I have to finish this, Vera. My mom ... she doesn't deserve to live."

Eyes widening, Vera stared up at me. "Are you going to kill her?"

"If that's what it takes," I whispered, not daring to tell Vera that *I* had killed Jim with my own two hands. Not only that, but I'd found pleasure in doing it too. It was wrong to take a life, but not when that person had threatened everyone and everything you ever cared about.

"I can't take her home," Callan said. "Nobody can see me leaving here with you."

"They're going to know something is up if you walk out of here, unwounded, anyway."

Callan drew his tongue across his teeth, reached into his pocket, and pulled out a knife. Before I could stop his fucking psycho ass, he shoved the knife into his thigh and growled. Blood soaked through his pants.

"What the fuck are you—"

"Leave," Callan repeated, handing me the keys to his car. "I can't be seen with you. If anyone asks, say you stole my car."

After quickly seizing Vera's hands, I pulled her up the stairs and out of that underground chamber underneath the main building at the town beach. She clutched on to me as I hurried with her to the parking lot.

Some people from the Redwood mob lay dead on our path to the beach, others squealing out of the parking lot and away from Poison. We rushed down to João's car, and I tucked Vera inside the backseat.

"Where'd my mother go?" I asked.

"She escaped," João said, grinding his teeth together and glancing back at Vera. "Did they touch her?"

I pressed my lips together. "I don't know."

João growled and nodded to the others. "I'll take her back to Kai's place until you're finished with everything you need to do. She and her family will be safe. I never do shit like this, but I promise."

"Blaise," Vera said, glancing up at me from the backseat. Her eyes trembled with tears. "Please, be careful and come back to me. I need you so badly."

"I promise," I said, leaning down to kiss her one last time. "I promise I will."

Once João and Poison drove off with Vera, I headed to Callan's car and slid into the driver's seat. I didn't know if Mom was stupid enough to head back home, but that was where I needed to start.

Not giving a fuck anymore, I pushed the pedal to the floor and sped through Redwood toward our gated community. When I reached the house that I hadn't been back to in about a week now, I got out of the car and slammed the door.

I grasped the gun that Kai had given me and wondered if I'd actually be able to use it. Fury had taken control of me earlier with Jim, but I didn't know if I could hit Mom. I didn't want to torture her—she didn't deserve to be alive longer than only a few more moments. I wanted her dead.

After pushing open the front door, I heard Mom and Dad screaming at each other from somewhere inside the house. Glass was being thrown again, paintings torn off the walls and littering our foyer.

"You were trying to get *our* son arrested for a murder that *you* ordered?!" Dad shouted.

"I wouldn't let him take the fall for it," Mom yelled. "But she deserved death."

"All because, what? You think I fucked her?"

"Stop it!" Mom screamed. "Stop gaslighting me! Stop lying! I know you did! I've seen it."

"You haven't seen shit," he growled. "Because it never happened."

"Stop acting like I'm crazy!"

I hurried toward the back living room, following their voices as quickly as I could.

Mom sobbed, "You've been cheating on me since that bitch came to work for—"

When I turned the corner and walked into the living room, I watched Dad seize a gun from his briefcase, turn around, and pull the trigger. The bullet whizzed through the air and pierced through Mom's skull.

She dropped to her knees, taking one last breath, then fell onto the marble floor with a thud. I stared at Dad with wide eyes and gulped, my heart pounding inside my chest as he put the safety back on and tucked the gun away.

"You crazy fucking bitch."

Deafening silence fell over the room.

When I stepped into the living room, Dad cleared his throat.

"Don't ever say I never did anything for you, son," he said, as if he had known I was there the entire time. "Your mother is dead, the mob is paid off, and Vera is safe."

I dropped my gaze to Mom's corpse and set the gun Kai had given me on the coffee table, my hands trembling.

What the fuck did I just witness? When did Dad find out about her plans? Why has he paid off the mob? He didn't give two shits about me; he definitely didn't care about Vera.

"I expect you to come home," he said, straightening the cuffs on his shirtsleeves. "I need you to attend a couple work meetings with me. You will work for the company once you finish high school so—"

"I'm not coming home," I said, shaking my head. "And I'm not working for the company."

Dad gritted his teeth and turned back to face me. "What was that?"

"I'm not working for your company. I'm going to do my own thing."

After taking a deep breath, Dad turned back to his briefcase. "You'll change your mind."

I pressed my lips together and stepped toward him, not wanting to fight with him right now because who knew if he'd blow *my* brains out next?

"I, uh ... I wanted to ask you about Vera's mother."

Dad froze. "What about her?"

"Is Mateo your kid?"

Vera had mentioned it briefly, and with what Mom had said a while ago ... if this was the last time I saw him because I didn't plan on staying here, then I needed to know what had really happened.

Silence.

When his jaw finally twitched, he nodded. "Yes, but Vera is not mine."

Again, I dropped my stare and looked at my blood-soaked shoes. Mateo was my ... half-brother. I bit my lip to hold back a smile.

While I'd never say a word to him about it, unless Vera's mother did, I knew.

He was my flesh, my blood.

"Now," Dad said, clearing his throat and grabbing his briefcase, "I have work. If you ever need me, call me. I won't pick up, but I'll send you the money that you need for anything." He walked to the front door.

"Wait!" I shouted after him, and he stopped at the door. "You should do something for Mateo."

Dad chuckled and said, "I'll do what I please," and then he walked out of my life for good.

I stared at his departing figure and frowned.

Sometimes, the villain of our stories escaped alive.

Chapter Eighty-Three

VERA

Two weeks after the *incident*, I grabbed a box from Blaise's car and hauled it into his new apartment. Mom had told him that he didn't need to leave, but Blaise wanted some time to himself, and I didn't blame him.

He had been alone in that big mansion for nearly all his life. It might've been too much for him to be living in our small house when one of us was always home, or maybe he wanted to prove to himself that he could do things on his own with his own money.

I set my box down on the floor and sighed softly, sad that he wouldn't be stuck with me twenty-four hours a day. I wished that I could be with him all day, every day. Hell, I had barely left his side since he'd rescued me from the mob.

That was a whole other thing, but I was working through it with Blaise and a therapist that Blaise paid for.

"Stay with me," he said, catching me off guard. He walked into the apartment beside me, carrying another box as his biceps flexed. He set the box down on his granite countertop and smiled. "Please."

"You know my mom would never let me."

"She will if I ask."

Playfully, I rolled my eyes. "Yeah, but I don't want to leave them—"

"No way," Mateo—who had come with Mom to help Blaise move in—shouted, stepping into one of the spare bedrooms. He stuck his head out into the hallway, eyes bugging out of their sockets. "You have a gaming room with two computers and a large flat screen?! All those games too!"

Blaise chuckled. "You know Vera isn't going to be gaming with me anytime soon. I guess I have an extra computer. Hmm ... I wonder who'd be interested in—"

"No way," Mateo said, grinning like a maniac. "No fucking way you got that for me."

Smiling to myself, I watched Blaise and Mateo interact.

These past few weeks, they'd gotten even closer somehow. I had caught them way too many times, playing video games and talking until three in the morning.

Mom stepped out of Blaise's bathroom and smiled. "I finished setting you all up, honey." She moved closer to us and frowned up at Blaise. "You know that you don't have to leave us. You're welcome to stay."

"I know," Blaise said, glancing down at me and taking my hand. "I want to do this."

After Mom gave him a hug, she nodded to Mateo. "You have a doctor's appointment in an hour," she said. "We have to get going. Say goodbye to Blaise and Vera for now. We can come back later."

When Mom turned her back to head to the door, Mateo rolled his eyes, but he retrieved his coat from Blaise's couch. He stuffed his hands into his pockets and widened his eyes. "Oh, Blaise, I wanted to know if, uh ..." Mateo pulled out a white envelope from his pocket. "You left this for me?"

Blaise shook his head. "Nah, kid. I didn't. What's in it?"

Mateo reached inside the envelope and pulled out a check for twenty-thousand dollars from Harleen Inc. My eyes widened as I stared at the thin sheet of paper that was worth more money than I had ever seen before.

"Where the hell did you get that?" I asked.

"It came in the mail for me yesterday. I didn't tell Mom yet because I didn't think it was real." He peered over at Blaise. "I know it's your family's company, so I wanted to ask. What do you think it's for?"

Blaise looked at the check, then peered down at his feet and smiled softly, as if he knew exactly what it was for. "You should deposit the check into a bank account and use it for college or, uh ... something."

"You think it's real?" Mateo asked.

Blaise shrugged. "Not going to find out until you deposit it."

Mateo stuffed the check back into the envelope and grinned. "Okay, I'll do that today."

Once Mateo finally departed, Blaise shut and locked the door behind him. I lingered in the foyer and picked up my backpack from the barstool at the kitchen counter.

Blaise snatched it from me. "You're not leaving yet."

"No," I said, taking my backpack back and unzipping it. "I wanted to, um ..."

My cheeks flushed at the thought of what I was about to do. I thrust my hand into my backpack and gripped a stack of what must've been three hundred double-spaced and double-sided papers.

I pulled them out and handed them to him. "To give this to you, as a ... housewarming gift."

Blaise arched a brow and slid onto one of the stools beside me. "What is it?"

I glanced down at my feet, heart pounding inside my chest. "It's the story that I've been writing ... about us. It's our story. It's not finished yet. I still have to write the last chapter, but I wanted you to read it."

With brown eyes so big, Blaise peered over at me. "You wrote a story about us?"

Somehow, my cheeks burned even hotter. "Yeah, I did. And I plan on publishing it one day because I love us so fucking much." I moved closer to him, so I stood between his legs, and then I grabbed his face. "And I love you more than I ever thought I could. You're the best thing that's ever happened to me, Blaise Harleen."

After setting the manuscript on the counter, Blaise seized my hips and drew me closer to him. He kissed me softly, his mouth moving with mine, like it was meant to. I closed my eyes and enjoyed every moment with him.

When I broke our kiss, Blaise cupped my chin and gently glided his thumb across my lower lip. We stared at each other for a few moments, and then Blaise pulled his hand away to reach into my backpack. He pulled out a pen and slid the manuscript toward me.

"Title our story, Vera," he whispered.

I took the pen from his hand, stared down at the words that meant so much to me, and wrote, *The Bad Boy*.

Continue reading about Redwood Academy in Detention!

Read Detention Now!

Detention is the next book in the series, following Callan Avery (the sexy literature teacher) and Sakura Sato (valedictorian)! To get early access to this story, subscribe to my newsletter. I will be sending one to two chapters of this story for free per week, right to your inbox. <3

By signing up to my newsletter, you will also receive a FREE spicy chapter about Vera's mother and Blaise's father!

OR

Preorder Detention

Also By Emilia Rose

Scan the QR code with your phone to view all of Emilia's books!

Also By Emilia Rose

Contemporary Romance

Stepbrother

Poison

The Bad Boy

Detention

Excite Me

Paranormal Romance

Submitting to the Alpha

Come Here, Kitten

Alpha Maddox

My Werewolf Professor

The Twins

Four Masked Wolves

Monster Lover

Erotica

Climax: Erotic One-Shot Collection

About the Author

Emilia Rose is a USA Today best-selling author of steamy romance. Highly inspired by her study abroad trip to Greece in 2019, Emilia loves to include Greek and Roman mythology in her writing.

She graduated from the University of Pittsburgh with a degree in psychology and a minor in creative writing in 2020 and now writes novels as her day job.

With over 18 million combined book views online and a growing presence on reading apps, she hopes to inspire other young novelists with her tales of growth and imagination, so they go on to write the stories that need to be told.

Join Emilia's newsletter for exclusive giveaways, early chapter releases, and more!